Something about
Alexa

Something about Alexa

*The line between fantasy and truth,
a knifepoint of perception.*

LEANNE HOCKLEY

quill & chrome media
bringing stories and music to life

An Imprint of Quill and Chrome Media, Inc.
Victoria, BC

For more information:
Quill and Chrome Media, Inc. Rights Department
rights@quillandchrome.media
Victoria, BC

www.quillandchrome.media
Book and cover design by Quill and Chrome Media Inc.

Author photo credit: Duffield Photography

First Print: September 2023
ISBNs: 978-1-998030-01-9 (paperback), 978-1-998030-00-2 (ebook), 978-1-998030-02-6 (hardcover)

For my family

"The sweetest smiles hold the darkest secrets..."
— Sara Shepard, **Flawless**

*"We don't create a fantasy world to escape reality,
we create it to be able to stay."*
— Lynda Barry, **What It Is**

ONE

THE FIRST THING I feel is pain, broken skin razing the tips of my fingers. And warmth. Like blood.

My eyes flicker open.

It's dark. Very dark. Night air a cold, heavy shroud.

I push myself up onto my knees, leaves and bracken snapping beneath me, panic searing my chest. Overhead, branches claw at the sky, shards of moonlight slicing through.

Where am I? My first thought. My second: *Not again!*

Nocturnal wanderings. That's what the doctor had said when my mother, in a fit of sobriety, carted me the three and a half hours from Forks to Seattle to see a specialist. The first one happened last year, when I turned sixteen. Almost like a birthright. It was a mystery why it was happening. The bigger mystery—how Mom paid for that specialist appointment. Waiting tables at the local tavern and swilling most of her earnings away when shift ended hardly added up to enough savings. Either way, something worried her enough to find a way to make that appointment happen. I suppose I should be grateful she even noticed I was missing those nights.

A sharp crack breaks my reverie. Panting, hot and sinister, not far from where I'm hunkered. A howl pierces the night sky, too close. I jump to my feet, scan the sea of shadow.

They aren't real. Werewolves. Vampires. Just a slice of fiction that turned our little town upside down with tourism. But right now, in this moment...

They feel real.

My eyes have adjusted to the caliginous realm of forest. In the distance an opening looms, moonlight streaming between broken patches of trees. I graze the heel of my hand across my chin, checking for injury, sticky warmth catching in the faint graze of stubble. If I'm bleeding, whatever's out there will smell the blood.

Don't run. Don't become prey.

I run.

The forest is thick, choked with moss, ferns, and fallen boughs—a tangle of ancient deadfall. I know its landscape like the back of my hand. A fortress. Impregnable. But this is my backyard. By day, my haven when life gets too heavy. I may not know exactly where I am, but I know these woods, its hectares of seclusion.

My foot snags in a gnarled root, pitching me into the sludge of earth, grave cold. I force myself up, and stumble through the tangle of trees to where a clearing pools in the thread of moonlight. A tangle of overgrown lawn is shadowed by the looming shape of an abandoned mansion, turrets spiraling toward the star-torn sky.

Thank God! Relieved, I scramble up the embankment to the lawn, stopping by the hulking breadth of an outbuilding. Usually, when I need an escape, I go to my best friend Brody's house, meld within the warmth of his family. But sometimes I just need to be alone. This place, with its shattered windowpanes and mouse-worn floorboards, has been another escape—one where I take my favorite copy of classic fiction, find a room on the highest floor, and disappear into a world that is entirely my own.

Clouds slowly tamp the moonlight as I pause, try to still the erratic pulse of my heart and catch my breath. Whatever was in the woods hasn't followed. A distant howl suggests the animal has drifted away. Just a wolf. An ordinary wolf.

Distance brings perspective.

Raindrops, cool and light, start to sift from the sky, prickling my skin where they land. In what's left of the moonlight, I look at my torn fingertips. A film of blood stains my hands. I try to wipe them clean on the tangle of tall grass.

The creak of a door breaks the hushed patter of rain. I glance up, startled. A light wavers on, illuminating the back porch. *The mansion has working electricity? Since when?* I freeze.

"Dad?" A girl who looks to be my age steps onto the porch. A gust of wind lifts, gathering her long dark curls, tight as springs, into its airy fist. Sheltered from the rain beneath the porch cover, she raises a lean arm, the warm tone of café latte, to sweep her hair from her face before stepping off the porch into the mist of rain, eyeing the outbuilding, a questioning look on her face. She steps barefoot onto an overgrown trail that connects to the outbuilding, the rain weighting her nightgown, hugging the smooth curvature of her body. Mesmerized, I watch her, ignoring the raindrops streaming down my face, blinking into my eyes.

She stops, noticing me.

How it must look. Me. Standing on the edge of the wood, blood dripping from my hands, smeared across my face.

"Alexa!" A man emerges from the patio door, his complexion a shock of white amid the gloom. "What are you doing out here? It's 4am!"

"I heard something. I thought it was you...working in your lab." She gestures dazedly to the outbuilding. "I—I came out to see, but found..." She turns to point at me, but I have already morphed into the shadows. "I thought I saw..." she trails off, unsure.

"What is it?" The man casts a sharp eye to the wood's edge, scanning its deep, dark depths.

"Someone was standing there."

A distant howl strikes up, then another. A chorus of wolves claiming the night. The lone wolf reunited with its pack.

"Come inside," the father insists, placing a protective arm around his daughter's shoulders. "These woods aren't safe at night."

The girl hesitates before allowing herself to be led back inside. The porch light switches off.

I suck in the haunted air, adrenaline twitching from my limbs, and sag against the rough bark of a tree. *Who are they? Why are they here?* The mansion has been abandoned for as long as I can remember, its vacant wings gathering cobwebs. But now, squinting at it in the moonlight, I see the broken windowpanes have been replaced. The sagging stoop fixed. *When was the last time I was here?*

Summer had passed, a haze of work at the local Thriftway supermarket and surfing the waves at La Push, gathering around the fringe of beach fires at night. It had been a good summer. An almost normal one. The need to escape momentarily forgotten. And sometime during that summer haze, my derelict sanctuary had become occupied. Refurbished. Become not mine.

4am. Shit. The first day of school starts in just over four hours. I take a deep breath and skirt the overrun lawn, following the perimeter of trees toward the long strip of black drive out front. Worn stumps congealed with wax, nubby candles prickling the surface with limp and blackened wicks, dot the underbrush in mysterious intervals. *What the hell?*

I creep slowly past the covered front porch. More candles line its rails, melted wax trailing like tendrilled fingers. As I inch down the black granite, rivulets of rainwater furrow across the pavement, soaking my shoes—*shoes.* I'm relieved to see them on my feet, then distressed I'd had the presence of mind to don them before leaving.

As if my departure was premeditated.

I chance a glance back at the mansion. Curtains have been hung to soften the hollow emptiness of the mullioned windows. The drapery stirs in one of the top windows, a face appearing behind the cool glass of the window.

It's her. The girl. Alexa.

She watches me. Despite the swirl of rain between us and the muted silhouette of nightfall, I feel the intensity of her stare. The loneliness.

Something flares inside me, an inexplicable rush of emotion.

She raises her hand to the glass, touches it, as if reaching for me.

The bushes behind me rustle, and I whirl around, probing the darkness with my eyes, instincts on fire.

Just a deer. The animal bounds into the darkness.

I turn back to the window, heart hammering, but its empty, the curtain slid shut.

She's gone.

And once again, I am all alone.

TWO

"FIRST DAY OF our last year in this shithole!" Brody comes up behind me at my locker, claps a hand on my back. "Next year, we're free to go wherever we want."

"It's not a shithole, Brodes." The endless evergreens, rainforest, streams, and tides...a saving grace. Usually.

"And happy birthday, by the way," Brody drawls. "Sexy seventeen. Mom made your favorite cake. Dad's going to barbeque. Same ritual as always."

"Sounds great." First bell sounds as students surge through the halls. Jostled, I turn to face Brody.

"Hey...what the hell happened to you?" His face scrunches in concern. "You look like crap."

"Thanks."

"No, I mean it, man. What gives?" He jabs a finger at my chest where my shirt shifts to reveal a rake of scratches. "You look like a cat jumped you."

I yank my collar higher. "It's nothing." My skin still burns where I smeared antiseptic, the bathroom sink reddening as I scrubbed myself clean by the early light of dawn, a panic rising in my chest.

"And what happened to your fingers?" He eyes the clumsy bandages individually wrapped around my fingertips as I stuff a book into my bag.

"Not sure...just got a bit tangled in the woods out back." I slam my locker shut.

"Well, well, well," a voice from behind interrupts. A muscled shoulder clips me against the locker. "Ghost survived another summer."

"Nice, Kam," I shoot back, straightening. By now I should be able to scent his jock stench a mile away, note the migration of sheep-like adolescents forming around him. But I don't. "And where were you all summer? Juvie?"

"Ooooo...grew a backbone over summer, didja? For your information, I was out on my dad's fishing boat. Raking in lots of dough. Those are the perks of having a dad with a boat. Oh, I'm sorry...you wouldn't know anything about either of those things. A boat or a dad."

His groupies guffaw.

"This isn't middle grade anymore, Kam. It hasn't been for years." My body tenses. I'd grown. Almost to the same size as Kam, now. My lanky frame filling in, though I'd never be as big as him. But big enough to stop the back-lane beatings.

"And yet..." he taunts. "Still a vampire."

"Ghost...vampire...which is it, Kam?" a familiar voice cuts in. "Make up your mind."

"Miriam, stay out of it," I caution.

Brody grabs his sister's arm and pulls her closer to him. She shakes it off. "No. I don't need to stay out of it, Jayden. Kam's just jealous."

"Jealous?" Kam balks. "Of white-face here?"

"Leave the pallor of my skin out of it," I seethe.

"*Pallor?* Who talks like that?" Kam mocks.

"Cultured people." *You Neanderthal.* I focus on a spot on the wall past his shoulder, my muscles quivering with rage.

"Cul—" Kam breaks off with a laugh. "You live in a trailer park, vampire boy."

"Like I said: jealous," Miriam quips. "Forks, Washington, Kam. You calling Jayden a vampire means you just called him the hottest thing this town has to offer."

"Been a long time since *Twilight*, toots." Kam fixes an arrogant eye on her. "Pale's no longer in fashion."

"And yet, thanks to Netflix and streaming, it is. Cult classic, my friend. And with him?" She juts her jaw in my direction. "Team Edward has a run for its money."

A few of the girls in Kam's group scrutinize me closer, peering at me over lowered lashes, amused giggles caught in their throats. He glances around at their faces in irritation, then down the hall to where the principal is making the rounds. "This ain't over yet, Death," he hisses, receding into the flow of students as final bell sounds.

"Roid freak," I mutter.

"Roids got nothing on this," Miriam soothes, resting a hand upon my flexed arm. "Personally, I prefer this." She gives my bicep a squeeze and trails her fingers down my arm. "He's just jealous. Because you kinda do look like Edward Cullen. And we all know that's a good thing." She winks and saunters off.

"Ew, no, Miriam," Brody protests. "That's practically incest." He gives his head a shake and turns to me. "Ignore him, man. He's the same loser he always was. Come on, we're late for homeroom."

"Yeah...I'm coming." I take a deep breath, collecting myself as he starts to head down the hall. "Hey Brody, your mom say anything about that old mansion out in the woods? The one off that old logging road outside of town?"

Brody scratches his chin. "Uh...yeah. Someone bought it, believe it or not."

"I...I didn't know it was for sale. I thought it was abandoned."

"Yeah, I don't know. Guess someone owned it and put it up for sale. Though who'd want to fix it up after all these years sitting empty, beats me. It wasn't one of Mom's listings. One of her coworkers. Some neuroscientist or neurosurgeon and his family bought it and moved in. He's on a sabbatical year or something. Don't know. Why? You still go up there sometimes?"

"Haven't in a while. Just...heard something about it being occupied now, so thought I'd ask." A flutter whispers through my chest. The memory of the forest pressing in around me. Blood on my hands. Alexa. Her eyes...

He glances at his phone. "Dude, it's like twenty after. I'll catch up with you after class. And don't forget—birthday dinner at our place tonight, same as always. See ya!"

"Sure...yeah. See ya."

The halls are empty, the murmur of students behind closed class doors, a distant drone. I head into the boys' washroom, catching my reflection in the warped mirror above the sink. Dark crescents hang beneath my eyes. The pale skin that Kam with his deep tan loves to deride, looks sallow in the wan fluorescent lights. It looks like I didn't sleep at all. *Did I? Sleep?* Or when those nights happen, do I wander aimlessly, caught somewhere between conscious and unconscious. I look down at my hands, the bulk of the bandages, and pull the gauze off. The skin looks raw, peeled. As if scraped away. I close my eyes, try to remember. Nothing but the memory of pain and panic rises. The sound of the wolf's howl. The girl in the nightgown, rain molding her form...

I open my eyes, a riptide of anxiety coursing through my veins. It didn't happen all summer. Not one wandering. And never before have I come home bloody. Spent. As if I'd spent the entire night fighting for my life.

Taking a deep breath, I splash cool water on my face, trying to calm my fumbling heart. I shove the bathroom door open and find my homeroom. Students are cloistered around their desks in casual comfort. Everyone in this town knows each other. Everyone that lives here. Then there's the forty thousand plus surge in tourists that descend every year. Most still in search of eternal love with a vampire or werewolf.

"Jayden, welcome, find yourself a seat," Ms. Cash invites.

I nod at her in greeting and turn to scan the class for an empty seat, noticing some curious looks on the familiar faces. I know I look like shit, but still.

Then I see her. Three desks away. Long curls suspended over a coffee-rich shoulder. And her eyes. Blue as the deepest wildflowers in the Olympic forest meadows. Bluer. And clear. Like spun glass. Her eyes lift to meet mine when I enter, her expression softening in surprise.

"Over here, Jay," a voice calls. I look over and see Murphy Sullivan shove back a chair from an empty desk beside him. "There's space here."

I glance back to Alexa, but she's already dropped her eyes, pretending to study the books she has sitting on the desk in front of her. Closed books.

"Thanks..." I angle through the rows and settle into the vacant desk.

Time passes in a blur. School session introductions are missed, instructions unheard, as I stare at the back of Alexa's head, willing her to turn around. But why would she? The psycho in her backyard. The blood-soaked stranger, torn and tattered, wandering the night.

"Hey...Jay..." Murphy's hoarse whisper cuts through Ms. Cash's drone. "Yoohoo, anyone home?"

"Sorry...I'm just...distracted today."

"No kidding, you are. Hey, did you hear about Sophie?"

"What? No. What about her?"

"She's been missing since last night."

"What do you mean?"

"Missing. Her mom called mine this morning asking if we knew of any parties last night or something. She's been calling everyone trying to track her down."

"I didn't know."

"She was last seen with some friends driving out to that old logging road just outside of town."

I freeze.

"You know...the one near that street where that old, abandoned mansion is."

"It's not abandoned anymore."

"Oh. Well, anyway, yeah. It's got quite a few people freaking out. I don't know if she just got drunk and is hiding out somewhere, or what. Not like her to just disappear though."

"No, it's not." A tightness seizes my gut.

The bell sounds and everyone gathers up their belongings, heading to the door. A haze has come across my vision, the pulse of blood rushing through my ears. I can almost smell the tangy scent of iron on my skin, the cold raw air of night.

"If you hear anything, maybe get Mrs. Foster to call or something—Brody's mom. Neighborhood watch, kinda thing."

"Yeah, for sure."

"Or your mom if, you know...if she's—"

"It's fine, Murphy. I'll be seeing the Fosters tonight. I'll talk to Mrs. Foster if I hear anything."

"K...good. Happy birthday, by the way."

"Thanks." I watch Alexa stuff her books into her bag and slip a light pale pink cardigan over her spaghetti strap shirt. She glances up, her eyes meeting mine. My heart skips a beat, fumbles in my chest.

"Jayden, could I have a word with you a moment?" Ms. Cash calls above the din of the students leaving.

I hesitate. "Uh..." Alexa holds my gaze. And it's there, again. That sadness. A ghost amid the blue. I recognize it because I have a similar haunting. A million emotions tangle in my chest when she finally looks away and follows the crush of students out the door. "Yeah...sure."

I hang back until the class is empty.

"You're a senior this year," Ms. Cash begins.

"Yeah."

"This will be the year to really buckle down. And be sure to apply for as many scholarships as you can. You have a promising future, Jayden. As a scholar. Your mind...you have a lot of potential."

Embarrassed, I drop my eyes and shift my bag on my shoulder. "Thank you."

"No, I mean it. I still remember your comparative essay on the classics *Dracula* and *Frankenstein* last year. Your writing on that was incredible. And your insight into what constitutes a monster and what sympathies should be leant to a perceived monster, were well thought out. I see a future in Literature for you. A professor someday, perhaps?"

I shrug. "Maybe."

She strides around her desk, straightening some papers. "Well, you have shown tremendous promise with your writing and your ability to analyze and critically think. Whatever field you choose to pursue, I have no doubt you will excel." Her face softens, a line of sympathy crossing her brow. "There is a plethora of scholarship information at the school counselor's office. Take time this year to go over it and be sure to apply in time. I wouldn't want you missing out on college options because...because it's unattainable financially."

I look up, a lump in my throat. My home life isn't a secret. The town's small enough we all know each other's main business. The stuff you can see. Like the fact that I ride my bike home every night to a trailer park where veins of mildew line the exteriors, unkempt flower baskets overflowing with weeds. "I'll be sure to check that information out."

"How come you haven't joined any of the sports at Forks High? There are some decent athletics scholarships to be had. And you have the form for it. Why not try out for a team sport this year? To round out all scholarship potential."

Out the classroom door I see Kam with his cronies making noise and dominating the hallway, his Spartans jacket slung loosely over his shoulder. He sees me watching him and puts his fingers in front of his mouth like fangs.

"It's not really my scene," I reply.

She follows my gaze to Kam and his friends and sighs. "No, I suppose not," she concedes. "Just do your best this year with your studies. I'm sure you'll succeed. You have a promising future, Jayden."

"Thanks, Ms. Cash. I'll work hard."

"You do that."

*   *   *

It's a half day, students spilling out of the high school into a fine drizzle. I head outside to scan the throng of faces for Brody but instead find myself searching the crowd for someone else, my heart in my throat. Every flash of dark hair stops me. Every glimpse of pale pink—the shade of her cardigan.

Then I see her. Just a glimpse. Climbing into the cab of a red truck. I recognize her father at the wheel. He pulls out of the parking spot and heads toward the road, passing where I stand. She turns at the last minute, her eyes meeting mine. Those strange, beautiful blue eyes.

The world seems to stop. All I hear is my heartbeat until the truck pulls away in a cloud of exhaust and I'm left standing in the rain, staring after her.

I haven't talked to her. I don't even know who she is, for Christ's sake. I don't know what she thinks of me after last night. I don't know what *I* think of me. But there's one thing I do know: there's something about Alexa.

My heart lists strangely. Dangerously.

As if beating for the first time.

THREE

"THERE HE IS...the birthday boy!" Mrs. Foster pulls me into a warm embrace.

"Thank you for having me, Mrs. Foster."

"Dear God, Jayden," Brody complains. "When will you just call her Mom, for God's sake?"

"After we walk down the aisle," Miriam jokes. "Then it's official."

"Okay, ew, for the second time today." Brody makes a face.

"You don't want Jayden as a bonafide brother? Through marriage to your kick-ass twin sister?" She crosses her arms and leans back against the front hall wall, a smirk on her face. "You know he *did* propose when we were seven. So, it's kind of already arranged."

Brody pauses, contemplating. "Right, well, so long as you don't consummate." He shudders.

"Knock it off, you two." Mrs. Foster rolls her eyes and ushers me inside. "Come on out back. Kent has steaks on the grill."

A cloud of aromatic smoke balloons from the rear patio doors, confirming the fact. "Smells good," I say appreciatively.

"We don't call him King of the Grill for nothing, right?" We move through the house toward the back patio. "You feeling okay, hon?" Mrs. Foster asks, stopping to look me over. "You don't look so great."

I pull the collar of the shirt I'd changed into higher, concealing the scratches beneath. "Yeah. Just didn't sleep so well, is all."

"You sure?" A worried tone enters her voice. "Is it your mom?"

"No, no...everything's fine. I promise." I feign a smile. I don't mention that I haven't seen Mom since two days before. No birthday note. No phone call. Not that that's unusual. Everyone knows that. "She's had a good spell recently." It's true. Sort of.

"Okay." She doesn't have to say they're there for me, if not. It's a given. How it's been since grade school when I first met Brody, and by extension, Miriam.

Out back, the yard opens to tended gardens that rim the dark verdure of forest behind. An abandoned badminton net is set near the above ground pool, surface now marred by a few specks of bugs, indicating summertime usage is coming to an end. A tan, tough body rises from one of the Adirondack chairs on the patio. "Happy birthday, man."

"Sam, hey! This is a nice surprise," I say, clasping his hand and bumping shoulders. "Good to see you, buddy. Thanks for coming."

"Wouldn't miss it." Sam grins, taking a swig of a Coke.

"I didn't see you much at La Push this summer for the surfing."

"Yeah, I was doing some work with the elders. Learning stuff...you know." He runs a hand through his short black hair. "There is a lot happening on the reservation, young blood is needed to help."

"I bet."

"Jayden, get over here and let the old man give you a birthday handshake," Mr. Foster calls from the grill.

I smile at Sam— "'Scuse me a sec"—and head over to the barbeque.

"Happy birthday, son," Mr. Foster says, giving my hand a hearty shake, pulling me in for a quick hug.

"Smells amazing," I say.

"Damn straight, it does." Mr. Foster's grin fills his broad face. "Filet mignon. Only the best for the best, kid."

My heart hurts a little with all the spoiling. I wonder if Mom has remembered it's my birthday. I wonder if she'll be home later tonight.

As the evening progresses, I sit back and watch the closeness of the Fosters and Sam. Family. If only I'd had this in my life every day from day one. But I'm grateful to have found them. I can only imagine how my life might have gone without them.

The sun drifts deeper below the horizon. The sky bleeds indigo. Twilight.

"So how was your summer, Sam?" Mrs. Foster asks. "We didn't see you around much."

"Yeah, I was telling Jayden earlier that it's been busy on the reservation."

"Still tourists nosing around?" Miriam asks.

"Oh, yeah. Never ends."

Mrs. Foster stands to clear plates away from the patio table. "I know it once bothered the elders, all the attention."

"Some," Sam admits. "But some are grateful for it. It's a chance to share our true history. As for me...well, when a car full of girls come by, I just howl at them. Make them want me."

"Oh my God, Sam, you're hilarious!" Miriam snorts.

"I just wish it would end," Brody groans. "It's been how many years? I mean, when are we going to take all those embarrassing signs down. *No vampires beyond this point. Treaty line,*" he quotes. "*Entering the Twilight Zone,* or, *Entering Forks, population 3,175, vampires 8.5.* I mean, seriously? It's got to stop. That's why I can't wait to grad this year then good-bye, I'm outta here. Time to start living real life in a real town instead of some sappy story backdrop."

Mrs. Foster gets a sentimental look on her face. "It's not so bad, hon."

"Again, Brody...listen to me, man. Before *Twilight* there weren't half as many girls visiting this place, so lucky for us." Sam winks at me. "And you've certainly lucked out thanks to those books, Jay. Well, the movies to be exact, with your uncanny resemblance to the dude that played that vampire, Edward Cullen."

"Just stop." I roll my eyes.

"It's true, you do!" Sam laughs.

"Shouldn't Edward Cullen be graying at the temples by now?" I deflect.

"You know what they say...vampires stay forever young," Sam teases. "The next generation of *Twilight* fans only see Edward in the flesh when they come here and lay eyes on you. And the old biddies who fell in love with the character back in the day, you let them relive that precious moment—make them believe Edward is alive and well, and still forever seventeen. What was that actor's name again? The one who played the vampire?"

"Robert Pattinson," Miriam and Mrs. Foster chorus together at the same time.

Mrs. Foster flushes as her husband arches an eyebrow and gives her a wry look. "Well, that name rolled off your tongue pretty easily." He shakes his head. Mrs. Foster's flush deepens.

"Would have helped you if you'd looked more like him back in middle school too," Brody observes, twirling a fallen twig between his fingers. "Maybe would have kept King Kong Kam away."

"Yeah, well..." I clear my throat. "The vampire thing seems to have added more fuel to his fire now."

"Except now he can't lay a finger on you." Miriam smiles at me. "You grew up." She drops her eyes, fidgeting with the tab on her soda can.

"Changing the subject," Brody interjects. "Has anyone heard anything about Sophie Wilkinson?"

"Murphy told me about her." I set my drink on the table beside me, a chill fingering my gut. "Said she's been missing since last night. He asked me to have you call Sophie's mom if you've heard anything," I say to Mrs. Foster.

"I haven't heard anything more. Not yet," she replies.

"Probably had too much to drink at a party and is drying out somewhere," Miriam suggests. "It wouldn't be the first time."

"I don't think it's like her to just not show up, though. Or to not contact her mom," Brody hedges.

"You two were dating, right Jay?" Sam rises to grab another can of pop from a cooler filled with ice. "I heard you two were getting it on at La Push."

"Uh, yeah...no. We weren't."

"Jason said he saw you two mackin' out." Sam simulates smooching.

"That was...no..." I trail off.

"Wasn't she Kam's girlfriend last year?" Sam continues, scooping up a handful of pretzels from a bowl.

"For a bit, yeah." I shift, uncomfortable.

"Bet he blew up when he heard you two kissed then," Sam muses.

"He hasn't said a thing about it. To anyone." My knee starts to jiggle, tension filling my body.

"Maybe that's why he was being so jerky this morning—" Brody starts.

"Can we change the subject?" I insist.

"It wasn't Jayden's fault, anyway," Miriam states. "She just jumped on him at the beach one night during a party. She'd had too much. And she's had a thing for Jay for a while now." She glances up at me then away.

"Well, whose to complain about that?" Sam shrugs.

"I didn't appreciate it, actually," I protest. "I don't go for that. Especially since she's Kam's ex."

"Who cares? Why not go for it?" Sam laughs. "She's hot."

"Exactly what kind of parties are you kids involving yourselves with down there?" Mr. Foster asks lightly, though his voice has a serious edge.

"I hope you all aren't drinking too." Mrs. Foster crosses her arms.

"Mooom...of course we aren't," Brody complains. I glance up at him, but he slides his eyes away from mine.

I don't drink. I've seen what drink can do to a person. To the people you love. I shift in my chair.

The sound of a car crunching across the gravel of the front drive draws our attention. A sweep of headlights fills the inside house windows with light.

"I wonder who that could be." Mrs. Foster cranes her head trying to peer through the patio doors to the front. The doorbell sounds.

"I'll get it." Mr. Foster rises to his feet and disappears inside. Moments later he reappears with the town's police chief.

"Hey kids," Chief Hanson greets. "A birthday," he observes. "That's right, it's yours today, isn't it Jayden?"

"Yes, sir." I nod my head.

"What brings you here tonight, Trevor?" Mrs. Foster asks.

"Well...I'm sure you've heard about Sophie Wilkinson." He takes his hat off and perches on the edge of a chair. "It's getting darn close to twenty-four hours now, so the authorities are getting involved. We don't want to wait. Not when it's one of our own from town who's missing. It's out of character for Sophie to be gone this long without a word. Much of the town is coming together tonight to form search parties. Sarah is beside herself, as you can imagine. Not knowing where her daughter is."

"I can't even imagine," Mrs. Foster sympathizes. "What can we do? Where are people gathering to look?"

"Well, starting at the old logging road on the edge of town there. There's an old mansion on a road nearby, don't know if you're familiar with it."

"I am. Our agency just sold it this summer."

"Okay, well, she was last seen just down from that area with a group of friends. Apparently, they were attending some bush party with some kids from out of town. Somewhere along the line, Sophie disappeared. She hasn't been seen or heard from since."

"I'll get the flashlights." Mr. Foster's face is serious. "Brody, Miriam, get your hiking boots on. Sam and Jay, you coming?" We nod our heads. "Good. I want you all to stick together, you hear? Jill?" He turns to his wife.

"My Ozarks are in the hall closet; please grab them for me," Mrs. Foster responds. Mr. Foster reappears moments later with a pair of hiking boots in his hand for her.

The chief eyes me as I stand with the others, getting our stuff together. "Hey Jayden, mind if I talk with you for a moment?" He sidles over to me.

"Sure. No problem. I'm happy to help."

"It's not that," he says, his voice lowering.

Mrs. Foster glances over at us as she laces up her boots.

"What happened to your hands there?" he asks.

"Uh...I just..." My heart stumbles, gains speed, leaving me

lightheaded. "I hurt myself in the woods."

"Hm." His mouth purses. "Doing what?"

"I..." *What to say? What the hell do I say?*

The others have already moved into the front yard, Mr. Foster's car running along with Sam's beat-up old Chevy.

Wandering...I was wandering. I don't know what the hell happened!

A bead of perspiration forms at my temple. "Man, I don't know. I fell. Scraped it on...something. The ground. It was dark."

"Looks pretty bad," he says, taking my hand and twisting it toward the light.

Mrs. Foster is looking at me, worry lining her eyes.

The chief releases my hand. "You're a good kid, Jayden. I'm not worried about you. I only ask because you were seen in that area last night too. Were you at the same party?"

I can't breathe. Air lodged in my throat. "The same par—? No...no...I wasn't. I was just out...walking."

"Kind of late for a walk. You were seen at 1am."

1am? What the hell was I doing for the three hours between 1am and when I was standing on the edge of Alexa's yard at 4am? And how long had I been wandering before that?

"Yeah, it was late."

"Okay, well...if you remember anything about seeing her—seeing Sophie—you let me know, you hear?"

"Of course. Yeah. I will." My knees feel shaky, but I hold myself steady. I've lived my entire life in this town. Everybody knows me. They know I don't cause trouble. Evidently, the chief thinks so too as he places a reassuring hand on my shoulder before heading toward the front of the house. "All right, I'll probably see you guys there. Now don't any of your crew wind up missing, you hear?"

"Roger that, Trevor," Mrs. Foster calls as the chief disappears around the side gate to the front of the yard.

I swallow hard, my hands trembling as I pick up my light coat.

"Jayden." Mrs. Foster is standing by the rear patio doors. "Is everything okay?"

"Yes, yeah...he just...I guess someone saw me when I was out for a walk last night." I hesitate, not meeting her eye.

"At 1am?"

I give an uncomfortable laugh. "I sometimes need to get some air."

She's quiet for a moment. "Is it happening again?"

"Is what happening?" I chance a look up at her.

"The night wandering."

"You know about that?" A mix of fear and embarrassment wash through me.

"Your mom...she was...worried last year. She mentioned it. Listen..." She takes a step toward me. "The specialist...what did he say?"

"You know about him too?"

"I do, Jayden. What did he say about why it's happening? Your mom never filled me in afterward. Just said things were okay. Is that true? When's the last time it happened?"

"I don't know... May? Shortly after I saw the specialist. I guess that was the last time. He said it could just be stress related." Or night seizures. Or a form of somnambulism. Or they don't know why—*an anomaly.* There wasn't any money to continue with further investigation into the matter.

She takes my hands and turns them over, revealing the injured fingertips. "Brody mentioned you were covered in scratches."

"It's nothing—"

"Have you been injured during these episodes before?"

The torn flesh of my fingertips and scratches across my chest start to throb.

"No." I take a deep breath. "I just wake up...somewhere else." In the woods. Alone. *And scared. Scared as hell. Adrenaline pumping through my veins.* I pull my hands from hers.

Her voice lowers to a whisper. "I read that sometimes people who wander like that can hurt others. That they aren't in their right mind. They don't even know what's happening." Concern etches her face, her jaw tensing.

"I haven't hurt anyone." The words feel like a lie. But I'd never. *I'd never—*

"Were you dating Sophie?"

"No! That was one kiss at the beach. An uninvited kiss—"

"Okay. That's all you need to say." She exhales and presses her fingers to her temples wearily.

"I feel like I'm on trial for something I didn't do." My jackhammer heart drills a hole into my chest. The air suddenly smells like blood.

"Of course not, hon. Of course, not. I just wanted to check in on you. When I saw Chief Hanson talking to you…I knew you were lying to him. No, I know you, Jayden," she says when I start to protest. "Well enough to know when you're lying. You didn't want him to know about your night wandering, right? It's okay. I understand. I know you'd never hurt anyone. Not intentionally. Look, I love you like my own son. Just talk to me. If you need help, please…just tell me."

"I don't need any help."

Someone honks a horn out front. They're ready to go.

She takes a big breath. "Okay, then. Let's go find that girl." She gives my arm a squeeze and heads off to join the others.

Night has moved in, heavy and oppressive, the scent of rain thick in the air. A full moon skulks behind a skein of heavy cloud. I don't move, my heart still out of control. I touch my chest where the scratches lie beneath my shirt. In the wary light of the moon and patio lanterns, I look at my torn hands, the flesh-ripped fingertips. Worn raw. As if I'd been digging.

As if I'd been fighting for my life.

"Jayden, you coming?" Brody calls.

A foreboding breath of mist drifts from the forest, wraith-like. Alive.

"Yeah. I'm coming."

FOUR

LIGHT FLARES AMID the underbrush like ethereal fireflies. Rain presses down slick and heavy, the loamy scent of earth permeating the air, mixed with the woodsy sharpness of cedar and pine.

"Sophie! Sophie?" shouts echo. People move like ghostly apparitions through the night.

"She could be anywhere," Miriam says, rain streaming down her hood into her face.

We're on the street that leads to the mansion, groups spreading out in different directions, including up the old, abandoned logging road. As far as the eye can see, flashlights penetrate the darkness in roving intervals.

We move down the street, passing the iron gate of Alexa's home, the mansion towering like a monstrous specter against the low night cloud. Lights blaze on the bottom floor, the gates flung wide. I stop, seeing Alexa with her father and another woman, lanterns clutched in their hands, talking to some people in the front drive. Candles flicker under the cover of the porch along the railing.

Miriam walks right into me when I stop. "What is it?" She follows my gaze. "That's the new girl at school. Looks like her family is helping look."

Alexa glances our way, catching my eye.

"Mir...I'll be back in a second, okay?"

Miriam follows my gaze to Alexa. "We're supposed to stick together."

"I know. I'll just be a minute." I leave her standing there, following the black strip of drive toward Alexa. Alexa doesn't move, just watches me, her expression unreadable in the eerie lamplight. As I get closer, I see it's the chief talking with her father. A tall woman with deep, ebony skin and long, sleek jet hair, stands next to him, a crystal hanging from her neck down to her midriff.

"Jayden," the chief greets me. "Have you met Dr. Sven Johansson and his partner, Magenta Croy, yet? And this here is their daughter, Alexa. They're new to town here."

I can barely swallow, a lump of uncertainty swelling in my throat.

"We've already met," Alexa says. The soft cadence of her voice causes a quickening of my heart.

"Oh?" The chief casts a questioning look my way. "At school?"

"Unofficially," I manage.

"It's nice to meet you, Jayden," Magenta says, her dark eyes skimming over me. "If only under better circumstances."

"You didn't see anything last night, Jayden? Nothing you can remember?" I recognize the face of Mrs. Campton, a bed and breakfast owner, as one of the other townsfolk gathered around the chief.

"Sorry?" My voice catches. I force my eyes away from Alexa's to look at Mrs. Campton.

"Last night. I heard you were spotted out walking near here. Was there anything odd you remember?" she persists.

"I..." I feel Alexa's eyes on me. "I didn't see anything."

"If only someone could remember something," she frets. "Poor Sarah is inconsolable."

"I know, Judy." The chief wipes rain from his forehead with the back of his hand. "She's in good care right now while we're looking for her daughter. They're keeping her calm. Why don't you guys continue searching?"

The group moves off, their flashlights sweeping the woods in front of them.

"Dr. Johansson," the chief continues, fixing his eyes on Alexa's father.

"You said someone was out back of your place early this morning? Any details on what they looked like? Male? Female?"

"I didn't see the person, myself." Dr. Johansson turns to his daughter. "Alexa? Tell Chief Hanson what you saw." His voice holds the thick echo of a Nordic heritage.

I watch the candles flicker on the porch rail. The tiny flames burn and wobble like hula dancers, bending with the movement of air.

"I couldn't see," Alexa says. "It was dark. I just...I could have been mistaken."

The air seeps out of me. I can't breathe.

"There was blood on the grass," Dr. Johansson continues. "This morning."

"Can you show me where?" the chief asks. He follows Dr. Johansson and Alexa's mother to the rear of the property.

"Come?" Alexa inclines her head, indicating we follow.

I walk with her to where the chief stands with her parents.

"Somewhere around here." Dr. Johansson has stopped a short distance away from the mansion's outbuilding, light whispering across the exterior wall as they survey the back of the property line. "The rain seems to have washed it away now, though."

The chief crouches down, the beam of his flashlight scouring the wet, unkempt grasses.

"This was where you saw—or thought you saw—someone standing, correct, Alexa?" Dr. Johansson turns to face his daughter.

"Like I said...it was dark. I could have been mistaken."

Dr. Johansson holds his lantern up against the darkness, probing the deeper woods behind the property line. "Chief, something stirred up the wolves last night. It wouldn't have been a good night for a young woman to be out wandering alone."

"I don't think any night is a good night for that," the chief agrees.

Sweat pools in my armpits. A cold clamminess gnaws at my throat. I can't look at Alexa. Because I don't understand. She saw me. Our eyes met. And again, today in school... There was recognition on her face.

"Wolves..." the chief muses. "I'm not surprised. There's been an increase in animal activity this past year. A rogue pack has been spotted that's not from these parts." He straightens, running his flashlight one final time over the whorl of grass. "Best to keep cautious while on your property out here."

They wander back toward the house, leaving Alexa and I standing alone.

Words catch in my throat as I glance at her. Even in the ambient glow of our flashlights I can make out the intense blue of her eyes. "You didn't have to do that," I finally say.

"Do what?" Her voice is soft as a secret.

"You know."

"I guess I should ask then... *Do* you have anything to do with that girl who's missing?"

I shake my head. "I don't. Honestly."

"I didn't think so."

"I wouldn't blame you if you did think—"

"I don't." She's quiet a moment, studying me.

I swallow hard, my insides molten. A million thoughts pop into my head. Questions I want to ask. But words fail. I'm distracted by her eyes. Her presence.

She leans closer, suddenly. "I'm not afraid of you," she whispers.

After seeing me blood-soaked in the shadows of her backyard, staring up at her in her window... "Why not?"

Her eyes hold mine. I can't look away. Rain drifting between us, the cool forest air on my skin. "Because there's something about you," she says simply.

A strange feeling wends through my chest. "There's something about you too."

"Jayden!" Miriam comes running up to me. I become aware of a ripple of change in the woods around us. A murmur has risen among the searchers. The general atmosphere has shifted. "You didn't come back for me."

"Miriam, I'm sorry, I—"

She grabs my jacket. I see now that tears are brimming in her eyes.

"They found her, Jay. They found her."

"Oh, good—"

"No. You don't understand. They found her body, Jayden. She's dead!"

FIVE

"WHAT?" IT'S LIKE there's a ringing in my ears. As if I can't process the words.

"They found her buried in a ditch in the backwoods—" Miriam stops, sucking in a harsh breath.

I feel a hand touch mine. Alexa.

Miriam's eyes dart to where Alexa's hand has found mine then quickly looks away. "I'm going to go find Brody and Sam...and Mom and Dad."

"Okay. I'll find you guys in a minute."

Miriam hesitates a moment then turns to jog back around the house.

"Are you okay?" Alexa asks. "I know this town is small. Everyone knows everyone here, so..."

"Yeah. I'm okay, thanks." I feel her hand give mine a squeeze before releasing it. Conscious of the wounds on my fingertips, I stuff my hands in my pockets.

The murmurs start. I hear snatches of the details. *Dead. Found buried in a low ditch. Abandoned. Eviscerated. Signs of wolves...*

Something else.

"Do you want to come inside for a minute?" Alexa's voice draws me back. "Have some tea or something? To warm up..."

My heart skips a beat as I meet her eye. The rain shifts to a mist, a light breeze fanning the darkness. A strand of her dark hair catches in the current and drifts across her face. We both reach to move it.

"I—I'm sorry. I shouldn't have—" I stutter.

"It's okay." She tucks the strand behind her ear. "You were being sweet."

"Jayden?" It's Miriam, her arms hanging limply at her sides, hands lightly balled into fists. "Mom and Dad are ready to go. You coming?"

"Uh...yeah. I'll be right there." It's hard to know what to say to Alexa with Miriam standing there. "They're my ride home tonight," I say finally. "I have to—"

"No, I understand. You go. See you at school tomorrow."

I want to say something more, but several groups of searchers emerge from the forest to file despondently off the property, their voices in low murmurs, flashlights looming like eerie eyes lost in the night. I turn to say goodbye to Alexa, but she's gone.

* * *

"You sure we can't give you a lift all the way home, Jay? I can throw your bike in the back," Mr. Foster says when we return to their home.

"Thanks, but no. I could use the air."

"Just let us give you a ride," Miriam protests. "Some kind of monster is out there—a psychopath, maybe."

"You don't know that Miriam," Mrs. Foster soothes. "It sounds like there were signs that wolves were involved—"

"Yeah. And maybe not," Miriam shoots back. "When has there been an animal attack like that in recent, uh—ever? They said her insides were taken out, Mom! All her organs gone—"

"It's been a long night," Mr. Foster interjects, raising a hand to silence the conversation. "Miriam, wolves do that. Organ meat is most often the first that they consume."

"And bury their prey in a ditch?"

"Yes, Miriam, wolves do bury their—" Mr. Foster cuts himself off and bites his lip, his head hung low for a moment. "Please. Let's just all get some rest. Until the authorities get a chance to investigate further, we're not going to get any definitive answers."

Miriam crosses her arms tightly across her chest.

Brody gives me a half-hearted fist bump. "Later, Jay. Ride safe, okay?"

By the time I pedal away, the mist has deepened. The further I track from town the more nervous I feel. The dull beam of my bike light barely marks a path through the darkness ahead. Suddenly, the light glints off a hulk of steel. I veer sharply, nearly landing in the ditch, squeezing the brakes just in time. A truck, half-hidden in the mist, rests on the side of the road with the eerie look of abandonment. I scrabble to get my foot back onto the pedal to get the hell out of there when the driver side door swings open. "Jay?"

"Sam? What the hell, man! You scared the bejesus out of me!"

"Sorry."

"What are you doing here? I thought you went back to the reservation after the search."

"Yeah...I was going to."

An awkward silence stretches. Sam sits, staring vacantly out the front window of the truck.

"Sam?"

"Go home, Jayden."

"Not until you tell me what you're doing." I set my bike in the gravel alongside the road. "You okay?"

"I guess you heard they're saying wolves got at Sophie."

"I heard."

"Yeah, well, I also heard the police chief talking to the precinct. The nature of her injuries look like a wolf but...it doesn't look like just any old animal. Something more human—" He stops, his jaw set. His face takes on deep shadows in the milky hue of moonlight and drifting fog.

"I don't understand."

He gives a dry laugh. "I heard him myself. The wolves got to Sophie, but maybe they got there, after. They don't know. Because the way she was...taken apart..." He draws a deep breath. "It may or may not have been death just by primal animal jaws, Jayden."

The mist beads on my skin, enters my lungs, heavy and sinister.

"So now..." he gives another sharp laugh. "I hear some people start talking about werewolves."

"Seriously?"

"Yep." He punches a hand on his steering wheel. "Next thing you know, it'll be reason to bother us. And I don't mean the fun of flirtatious fans coming around. I mean people come sniffing around to see if we're to blame. As if maybe our tribe really does have some secret to our story."

"You're getting ahead of yourself, Sam. Besides, I thought you liked the attention. When the tourist girls came by—"

"Because of a story, Jayden! Something fake. Not real! This is serious. This is real life! But that's what people do, right? They don't know how to separate fantasy from fact, fact from fiction. They get an idea about something, and then when real shit hits the fan, they start making assumptions based on all the bullshit, made-up stuff." He turns an eye on me. "And what was with you? Hanging out with the pretty new girl instead of looking for Sophie."

"I was looking for Sophie!"

"Yeah? How hard did you look?"

"Wha—this is coming out of nowhere, man. What gives? And how do you even know about Alexa? You don't go to our school."

"Met her for the first time in class, did you?" His voice sounds suspicious. "First time you ever laid eyes on her then, is it? Sure, didn't look it."

My breath comes fast. I can't say how we first met. I won't.

"You're making this about a girl now?" I stride over to my bike and scoop it upright.

The wind suddenly goes out of Sam. "Sorry, man. I'm just—it's been a rough night. For all of us."

"Yeah, well…" I throw my leg over my bike, ready to leave.

"I said I was sorry, okay? I liked Sophie, Jay. Okay? It's out there. I liked her."

"Why? There's other girls. Why Kam's ex?"

"I just did, okay? And guess who she ends up kissing."

"That was one night, Sam. One moment! It meant nothing. Certainly, it meant nothing to me."

"Well, it meant something to her, no doubt. And that's just it, Jay. You glide through town unaware of the way the girls look at you. Talk about fiction and fact getting tangled, it's the fact that you look like some heartthrob vampire from a hit book and movie franchise and the rest of us are extras on your set."

"You're being ridiculous—"

"The girls don't even notice anyone else if you're around. Just because you're oblivious or don't care—" He runs his hands down the side of his face.

"They *don't* care about me, Sam. Not the way you think." Because it's a small town. Because they remember what I was: the skinny kid getting bullied. They know where I live. *They know anything more with me would be a disappointing, displaced fantasy.*

"Look, I saw Alexa when her family first moved here. I've been out a lot in the woods this summer…learning about our ancient practices and traditions. The elders are fearful our old ways are becoming lost with the younger generations—*my* generation. So, I've been out there a lot." He gestures to the shadow of forest. "And I've seen Alexa a few times. Out deep in the backwoods. I'd watch her. She's something, man." His voice catches. He shakes his head as if in awe, lapsing into silence.

"Out in the woods?"

He stares vacantly out the front windshield. "Yeah. I don't know what she was doing. Maybe just hiking, exploring, I don't know. Looking for stuff. I've seen her out there with her parents too. But I'm telling you, when I first saw her…her eyes…" He exhales a long breath.

"Did you talk to her?"

"Once. Yeah. She was out there in the bush one time alone. I just…went for it. Said hi."

My mouth goes dry. "And?"

"And…she was nice, man. We didn't say much, didn't talk long, but there was just something about her. She seemed different than the other girls. More aware…of all this." He gestures expansively to the rise of trees, the glitter of starlight poking through the swath of cloud. "It's like she has more substance. Depth. I thought maybe...maybe we'd connected, but then I saw the two of you tonight, and—" He stops, his jaw flexing.

I don't know what to say. I want to say it doesn't matter, that what he saw tonight was nothing. But I can't. Because it *was* something. I can't get her out of my mind.

He lets out a long breath. "I'm sorry, man. I didn't mean to light into you. It's not your fault. You didn't know." For a moment, his eyes look tear-damp, but it could just be a trick of the shadows. He wipes a hand hastily over his cheek and eyes, sniffing hard. "It's been a helluva couple days. I'm not thinking straight."

"You okay to get back to the res like this?" I ask gently.

"Shit, man, I'm fine." He twists the key in the ignition and slams the driver door shut, rolling down the window. "Just forget this whole conversation happened, okay? I'm not thinking right tonight. It's...been a weird twenty-four hours." With that, he accelerates away, leaving me in a cloud of thick exhaust.

SIX

I WHEEL MY bike down the lane into the trailer park, the midnight sky heavy above. My mind feels ready to explode with everything. I stop when I see my mother's old Ford sitting out front of our mobile home, drops of rain peppering its surface.

"She's inside, drying out." Across the lane a cigarette flares in the darkness.

"She drove?" My voice breaks, the pressure of the night conflagrating in my chest.

"No...no, bud. I drove her home. I'll walk into town in the morning and get my truck before work. Here's her keys." He jingles them softly.

"Dan, you can't keep being late for work because—"

"Better me late for work than your mom dead in a ditch somewhere. It's okay, Jay. She'll be needing her car when she sobers up so she can get to her own work. It's not a worry. Now, come on. Come get these keys." He takes another drag on his cigarette.

I set my bike down and cross the lane.

"They find that girl?" Dan asks handing me the keys.

I exhale a rattle of nervous air. "Yeah."

"Good or bad?"

"Not good."

"Damn," Dan sighs. "I was going to come out and look too, but..." He gestures to my trailer. "Other people needed some help." He runs a hand through his short, graying hair.

"That's okay, they had a lot of people out searching."

He nods his head and stubs out his cigarette. "Guess Sarah will be a wreck right about now."

"Yeah." A steel ball settles in my throat.

"How about you?" In the dim glow from a porch light a few homes down, I see his eyes fix on me. "You been doing okay? Didn't see you around here much this summer."

"Was busy living." The waves of First Beach enter my mind. The spark of the beach fire. A temporary taste of life as it should be. Carefree. Easy. Life how I want it to be.

My hand twitches.

"Have you been keeping up with the training I gave you? Martial arts moves must be practiced, to be remembered."

"Why don't you open a taekwondo place in town here, Dan?"

"And have the wrong people sign up?" He eyes me. "Kam been bothering you much this year?"

"No. Not since you taught me what you did."

"Defense." He pulls another cigarette from a damp carton in his pocket. "Truth is, this town is too small to make a run of a business like that. Which is too bad, as the logging here is dying down too."

"You could move, Dan. Start over. Open up a Dojang somewhere."

"I could." He nods toward my mobile. "But I'm needed here. So, I'll stay a while yet. Besides, when I came to Forks it was my start over then. I'm done with starting over."

A tight flutter of wings brushes nearby. Two tiny bodies tangle in the air above our heads.

"Blasted bats." Dan waves a hand above his head. "There's been so many of them this year. Especially lately. Even out in the rain like this. It's unusual." The shapes vanish in the murk and Dan lets out a sigh.

"Seems all the animals are out of sorts right now." I sag against the thin base of a maple sprouting from the tuft of grass in front of his trailer.

He rubs a hand across his chin, surveying the dark shapes of trees in the mist. "Animals sense stuff. Sense danger. Maybe they feel a shift in something around here."

A cold chill seeps down my spine. For I'd felt a shift too, this year. In me. And the night wandering—

"You better get on in and rest, bud," he says, clapping a big hand on my shoulder. "I imagine it's been a long night." He gathers his carton of cigarettes and opens the door to his trailer.

The bones in my body are suddenly the weight of bricks. Exhaustion, lead in my veins.

"Try and get some sleep," he advises. "I saw you head out last night, late. Better not do that tonight. Just stick to sleep."

My heart accelerates. "Dan...?"

"Yeah, bud?"

"What time did you see me leave?"

He hesitates. "Oh, I don't know. Eleven? Midnight, maybe? Where were you headed at that hour? It was a school night, wasn't it? First day? And I hear you have scholarship potential, so you better buckle down, bud. No girl is worth blowing your future for."

"There was no girl." My skin feels uncomfortable; too tight. I try to swallow. "Was just getting some air." It's hard to lie to him. He doesn't deserve lies. But I can't tell the truth: That I don't remember leaving. That I don't know where I went or what happened. *I don't remember anything.* Just cold air. Feral howls. Blood.

Then Alexa's face, angelic in the porchlight.

"I understand needing air. Hang in there, bud. Things will get better with your mom."

I'd lived with Mom long enough to know things weren't going to get better. But that wasn't it. Little did he know.

Dan's trailer door clicks shut, and I cross the short distance to my own place, slip the key in the door.

Inside, lamplight glows. I shed my wet coat and shoes. Mom is sitting in the overstuffed chair, her head lolled sideways, asleep. On the counter in the small kitchen area, a slice of apple pie sits on a plate, filling seeped onto the plate around it, congealed. A small birthday candle has been poked into the crust.

She remembered. My heart flickers.

I scoop up the worn afghan Mom kept from her youth, and gently lay it across her thin form, shut the light, and slip into my room, closing the door softly behind me.

I stare at my bed. How desperate I am to sleep.

How afraid.

I pace the short length of the room, once, twice, three times. Frustrated, I yank my shirt off over my head and undress to my boxers, and stand by my bed, hands clenched into fists, raw fingertips smarting at the pressure.

Get into the bed, Jayden—it's okay. It never happens twice in a row. There's always been more than a week or month between wanderings. Maybe you'll never wander again. Sleep. Sleep goddamnit!

I grit my teeth and yank the covers back and climb into bed, heart pounding. I pull the covers up around my face, trying to calm my breathing. I roll over. Roll over again. The clock on the nightstand glows 12:16am. In the narrow closet across from me, I spy my old corduroy bathrobe. Leaping up, I snag the tie from its loops and sit back on the bed, twisting the tie in my hands, the rough fabric chafing the broken skin of my fingers. Sniffing hard, I tie a knot tight around my wrist, looping the other end around the bed post and bind it firmly.

Just in case.

I lie my head back against the pillow. My chest rises and falls, as I try to relax. *You can't go anywhere, now. Don't worry.*

My eyes grow heavy. My body *needs* sleep.

Slowly, dreams saturate my mind. First Beach, evening waves riding high around the jutting rock, the curl of ocean frothing around me. The spark of beach fires making the sand glow. Sophie's face, close to mine. The fruitiness of coolers pungent on her breath. Then darkness. Trees. The brush of cedar in my face, rough bark. And earth—cold and covered with moss, bracken, fallen boughs—against my hands, my body. Howls in the distance…and another sound. The sound of flesh being broken. Tears running down my face. Or is it blood?

Alexa's face fills my mind. Blue eyes so bright, so clear. They are fathomless. My heart swells. I feel better. Safer. *There's something about you.*

A girl's voice: *Stop!*

My eyes fly open.

A weak trace of sunshine spills onto my sheets and comforter, now tangled and matted on the floor, the mattress bare beneath me. A sheen of cold sweat coats my skin. The loop around my wrist has left a deep, red welt. With trembling fingers, I loosen the tie and slide my other hand free.

Slipping into my robe, I open my door, the smell of strong coffee filling the cramped hall, and quickly dart into the bathroom, leaning against the door as I close it. My eyes in the smudged bathroom mirror are lined with crescent bruises. I grapple with the shower faucets, setting the temperature to scalding and step in, wincing where the water splashes over my exposed wounds.

The dreams spark and fade as I stand with my face to the spray. Sophie's long blonde hair swaying in the wind. It was one night. One night that ended as fast as it started. I'd barely seen her since. *What happened to her? What happened to me?* I strain my brain, trying to remember anything from the night before last. Trying to remember anything before I woke up in the forest's depths. *Did I see her? Did I—?*

A loud knock on the door startles me from my reverie.

"Honey? You okay in there?"

"Yeah, Mom! I'll be right out." I turn the shower off and, shivering, snag a towel from its rack, emerging moments later.

"There you are. I'm glad I get to see you before I head out. I'm picking up a morning shift today." She brandishes the sad looking plate of pie. "I brought your favorite home last night." Her face looks hopeful. Sorry.

"I saw. Thanks."

"Thought I'd forgotten, didn't you?" Her hand is shaking a little as she sets the pie back down when I don't take it.

All I can do is shrug. "It's okay."

"Did you have a good birthday?"

"The Fosters had me over."

A sadness ghosts her smile. "Oh, that's good. They're good to you."

"They are."

"Here, I have something I want to give you." She picks up her purse and starts rustling her hand through it.

"Mom, you heard about Sophie Wilkinson, right?"

She pauses. "I did. I'm sorry I couldn't help look for her. I got...busy." Guilt flushes her face, the whiff of alcohol still heavy from her pores.

"It's okay. There were lots of people."

"Did they find her?"

"She's dead, Mom."

"Oh God...I'm sorry to hear that. You had a thing for her, didn't you?"

"No. I didn't. Just friends, sort of. That's all."

She sets her purse down. "I better give Sarah a call and see if she needs anything."

"She'll have lots of people to help her."

"Right...right," her voice drifts off. We both know she won't call. And we both know Sarah wouldn't want Mom around anyway. They moved in different circles. Or rather, Mom was the one stuck in a circle. Going nowhere.

I swallow the wedge of bitter emotion catching in my throat.

"Well..." Mom drifts off in thought. "Oh—here I go again, almost forgetting." She reaches back into her purse and pulls out a rough purple crystal. "A lady I met in town gave this to me. Said it has healing properties. I didn't have anything for you for your birthday, so thought this would be nice." She hands it to me. "I want you to have it."

"What's it supposed to heal?"

"I don't know. Your hands, for one." She says gently touching my fingers. "What happened to you?"

"I hurt myself in the forest."

"You have to be more careful, honey." A shadow crosses her expression. "Actually, I thought this might help with...you know. Not that it's been an issue lately, right?"

I swallow hard. "It hasn't."

"I know I haven't been around much again lately. But...you haven't had any more of those...episodes? Think that specialist maybe cured you?"

All he did was offer a few explanations as to why it might be happening. Hardly a cure. But I don't say that. Again, there'd been no money for further testing to investigate the specialist's hypotheses.

"I've been fine."

"Good," she sighs. "Good." She picks up her keys from the counter. "Did Dan give you these? I think...I think he gave me a lift home last night. I had a couple—not much." She dodges my eye. "He was being overly cautious, you know?"

"Of course." The words are tight on my tongue. I set the crystal onto the kitchen counter. "Thanks for this."

"Oh, yeah. It's pretty, and I know you like that kind of stuff. The lady was real interesting. I guess her family's new to town. Gorgeous black woman. Just stunning."

I hesitate. "Did she say her name?"

"Yeah...it was a real interesting name." She opens a compact from her purse and checks her reflection one last time before leaving. "Magenta something. She had a crystal just like this one around her neck on a chain."

Heat rises in my chest. *Alexa's mom.*

"I gotta run, hon. School go okay? It started this week, didn't it? Or was that last week?"

"Yesterday, Mom. It started yesterday. It's fine."

"Good. You're so smart." She pats my cheek. "See you later. Uh...maybe not tonight, I'm not sure. Might have to work late." We don't meet each other's eye. "But you're such a big, strong, independent boy, I know I don't have to worry. And Dan's there if you need anybody—"

"You better get going Mom, or you'll be late."

She holds the keys up. "Right. Bye, love." And she's gone.

I quickly get ready for school and head out the door. As much as I try,

I can't stop last night from coiling through my mind. *Found buried in a low ditch. Abandoned. Eviscerated. Signs of wolves and—*

Something else.

SEVEN

SCHOOL. ALL THE students are huddled together in groups, shooting fleeting glances to each other and the outlying property along the school's grounds, the death of Sophie heavy on everyone's minds. The morning passes in a blur, the lunch bell startling me, marking the end of Advanced Literature and Composition class. Students begin to file out of the room. I remain seated at my desk, staring out the window, my mind a million miles away.

"Jayden? You okay?" Ms. Cash. I have her again for senior year AP Lit as well as homeroom.

"Yeah. Sorry, Ms. Cash. I'm going." Dazed, I pick my pack up off the floor and start to stuff my books inside.

She leans back against her desk, arms crossed. "It's about Sophie, isn't it."

I give a weak smile and zip up my bag. "I'm okay."

"It's okay to not be okay too, Jayden. Just remember that."

I nod. As I stand to leave, I notice out the window a group of students gathering near the track. An announcement earlier had stated anyone interested in trying out for the cross-country team was to meet today at lunch. I'm about to leave when I recognize down below, long dark curls. Alexa. She stretches, bending low, her lithe form illuminated by a rare ray of midday sunlight.

"If you need anyone to talk to..." Ms. Cash offers. "I'm here. All the staff is, Jay."

"Uh, thanks." Distracted, I shoot her a smile.

"Okay, then." She pats my shoulder and leaves the room, the click of her heels echoing out into the hall until she's gone.

Even from this distance the sight of Alexa catches me in the gut like a sucker punch. I can't help but watch her. She starts to run. Fast. Faster. Her body impossibly strong, overtaking the others on the track. And she continues, long after others slow their pace or drop off the track, fatigued.

"Checking out the new girl?" A voice interrupts my thoughts.

"Brody?"

"Yeah...I saw you standing in here on your own, so came in to see what had you so engrossed."

Embarrassed, I turn away from the window. "Was just watching the cross-country tryouts."

"It's not the tryouts yet. Just some warmup practice leading up to it later this month." He looks out the window to the loop of track. "The new girl...she's pretty fast, huh? Pretty, pretty too."

"Yeah." I zip up my bag and sling it over my shoulder. "I hadn't really noticed until you mentioned it."

"Right." He gives me a sideways smirk. "Glad to see you made it home last night. Miriam was pissed Mom and Dad let you take your bike."

"I wanted to ride." We head out into the hall skirting the cafeteria to head outside.

"Well, I just hope the authorities come up with an answer soon as to what happened to Sophie. Put it to bed. Half the town thinks there's a murderer on the loose and the other half thinks—"

"Werewolves." Sam's face haunts me. The way he was staring vacantly out the window. His fist on the wheel. The anger in his voice.

"I was going to say regular old wolves, but yeah, there's definitely some of that other talk going around too." He shakes his head. "It's getting old, Jay. Real old. All that werewolf and vampire shit. Geez."

"Though something got to her." I clench my jaw and push the doors open out into the fresh air.

Inadvertently, or not, we wind up near the track. Alexa stands off to the side drinking from a water bottle, coffee skin not even damp from sweat. She looks strong. Beautiful.

Brody and I watch some more runs. As much as I try to not focus on Alexa, my eyes keep drifting back to her as she dominates the track. The runners break before the bell sounds, filing back into the school to change for afternoon classes. Alexa catches my eye as she picks up her bag to head inside. She starts to head our way.

"I got to go, Brode. See you later." I jump off the bleachers and start walking.

"Uh, sure." Confusion laces Brody's words. "But...I think the new girl is trying to get your attention. She's headed this way."

I don't look in Alexa's direction. I don't want her to see how badly I want to talk to her. Not after hearing Sam spill his heart. He likes her too. Liked her first. "I got to go, man, or I'll be late for class. Catch you later." I hurry back into the school, my heart tangled in my chest, and find my next class. Science. I walk into the room.

Great.

Kam and his posse take up most of the lab tables. He scowls at the sight of me but says nothing as Mr. Sorenson, the science teacher, is at the front of the class. I slouch into a vacant seat at an empty table.

"Come on in," Mr. Sorenson ushers the last of the students in as the final bell rings. He closes the door and launches into the usual preliminary introductory to the course for the term and addresses the tragedy of Sophie and how we all must pull together.

I stare out the window as he speaks, to the jagged tips of the treetops brushing the sky. I can almost feel their boughs scraping my skin, the dense void of night. Sinister, rasping breath, heavy in the air. The sticky warmth of blood. *Stop!*

The classroom door opens. I startle in my chair at the sound. Mr. Sorenson shoots a concerned glance my way before addressing the person entering. "Welcome, please find a seat. Name?" He picks up his attendance chart.

"It's Alexa. Johansson. Sorry I'm late." Her eyes land on me, the empty space beside me. I turn my head back to the window, heart ratcheting in my chest. The seat next to me scrapes back, then there's the sound of a bag being placed carefully onto the floor. She has brought in with her a whiff of fresh air mixed with another fragrance. Vanilla.

Mr. Sorenson drones on but I don't hear, hyper-aware of Alexa sitting beside me, the rustle of her papers, the swish of her clothing as she crosses her legs and adjusts position in her seat. Her perfume scent.

Mr. Sorenson strides among the lab tables passing out sheets with a list of forest specimens detailed on them. "Today we're going to take class outdoors. We'll be finding different specimens out in the forest and recording their attributes and data as per your worksheet criteria. It's review from last year in preparation for this term. Partner with your neighbor, gather up your notebooks and let's head on out. It's a rare afternoon of sunshine, so I thought we all could benefit from time outdoors."

"Mr. Sorenson, is it safe? I mean..." a student asks, voice trailing off.

The class is quiet, waiting for a reply.

"Of course." Mr. Sorenson surveys the class, his face softening in sympathy. "We're sticking to the edge of the woods, going as a group. Don't venture too far and you'll be all right, okay? The chief said there is no reason yet for anyone to be concerned. Vigilant, yes; afraid, no. Not until they complete their investigation. Now let's head on out." He gestures toward the door and the students rise, gathering up their belongings.

"Jayden?" Alexa's voice is soft.

My mouth goes dry. I focus on the notebook I have lying open in front of me.

"Looks like we're partners," she says, a question suspended in her tone. "If you want. Or I...I can find someone else."

"No. I'm good." I snatch up my sheet of paper and head for the door. Sam's face is all I can picture, the wetness on his cheeks as he wiped it away. *Stop it. You didn't know Sam liked her—that he saw her in the backwoods. You didn't know—*

Alexa comes up beside me as we vacate the hall for outside. "Is everything okay? You seem bothered by something..."

"Nope. Just focused on school."

"Is it because of that girl? Are you still—"

"I'm okay, Alexa." I don't have to look at her to picture her eyes, intense and deep, drawing me in. The memory of her in the weak porchlight, night air around her, rain clinging to her like a second skin.

I swallow hard.

When we reach the forest, everyone breaks off into the low woods, pausing to examine flora and fauna, making notes of the physical attributes of their surroundings. I take note of where Kam and his pals are lurking for their research and go in the opposite direction.

"Hey, wait up!" Alexa pushes through the underbrush behind me.

"Sorry." I stop. The rest of the class is some distance away. I hadn't even realized I'd been moving so fast, walking so far. "I guess we shouldn't go any further from the group."

"Sure...okay." She holds my eye for a moment but when I look away, she sighs, running a hand through her hair, then skims the paper Mr. Sorenson handed out.

I chance a glance back at her. A ray of sunshine spills through the branches, catching the gloss of her hair. She puts the end of her pen in her mouth, considering the information on the page, then begins looking at the foliage around her. Her eyes suddenly slide up, meeting mine. "What?"

"Nothing..." I can't focus. I should be looking at the paper or the forest trying to identify plants, detail their traits. But all I can detail is the length of her lashes around the pool of her eyes, the way they brush the top of her cheeks when she looks down. The curve of her lips on the pen. "Alexa...you met my friend, Sam," I splutter.

"Who?"

"Sam. In the backwoods. Behind your house. He's one of my best friends. He said you guys really hit it off, so..." I fidget with my pen. Maybe I'm saying too much, being presumptuous. But an invisible spark runs between us. Surely, she feels it too. I need her to understand. "It's kind of an unwritten rule, if your friend likes a girl..." I don't know how to continue. "I mean, I'm just saying this in case I seem...distant. Because...the other night, at your place...it just seemed we...connected."

She studies me, a look of confusion on her face. "Jayden...I don't know anybody by that name. I don't know a Sam."

I give an uncomfortable laugh. "But you met him. He's a member of the Quileute tribe in La Push. The reservation borders the backwoods of your property some distance away. I guess you were out exploring, and he saw you. You two talked."

"Uh..." Alexa sets her paper on a stump nearby. "Jayden, honestly...I don't know what you're talking about. I haven't met anyone in the woods. I'm not out there often. I mean, there's one place I found when we moved here...a hill, not far from a meadow filled with wildflowers, that I go to sometimes..." Her eyes grow distant, as if searching for a memory. "But my father doesn't let me go much past our property line anymore. So...I don't get out often." She cocks her head, curious. "Your friend must be mixing me up with someone."

"You're pretty hard to forget." My words catch in my throat.

Her brow puckers as she considers. "I..." She exhales, her fingers twining in the length of her curls. "Maybe he and I met somewhere else," she states decidedly. "And he's remembering that. But I'm sorry, I just don't remember anybody by that name."

"But—"

A raven startles in a nearby tree, massive wings swishing through the air over our heads, its caws loud, accusing. A cold tingle slithers down my spine. *Watched. We're being watched.* I turn my head sharply, surveying the tangle of branches around us.

"Jayden, Alexa!" Mr. Sorenson calls suddenly. I turn to see him pushing through the underbrush behind us. "You two have wandered too far. Come on back this way."

Wandered too far. The words slice into me. A pressing sense of claustrophobia sets in. The branches too low, too dense. The wide ferns and snarl of bushes obliterating any trail. It reminds me of the darkness.

"Jayden, what is it?" Alexa whispers.

"Hurry along, you two," Mr. Sorenson calls, retreating in the direction where the others are scattered.

"Jayden?" she persists.

The forest holds a presence. I feel it. Hidden among the twining boughs.

"I need to get you out of here."

"Jayden? What—"

I take her by the arm and guide her ahead, my body close behind her, protective. The skin of her arm is warm and smooth. She stops suddenly. My body—so close behind hers—glides into the full length of her. Neither of us moves. My heartbeat heavy against her back. Her hair brushes my face.

As quick as I'd felt danger, the feeling ebbs away. The twitter of birds fills the space with innocent sound. The woods adjust as the sun filters in brighter. Maybe there's nothing at all. Maybe just my imagination.

But being so close to her—*that* feeling—is real.

We stand like that for a minute more. I almost forget why we are this way. How we came to be so close together.

"What is it?" She says at last, turning to face me, concern etched on her features.

Reluctantly, I step back to put space between us. "I'm sorry...it was nothing. Just a trick of the senses."

The woods tower around us like a fortress. She scans the forest, looking uncertain. After a moment, her gaze returns to me.

"I'm sorry if I scared you," I apologize.

"Don't be." It's not cold, but her breath catches in the sunlight like phantom air, a fall chill already lying below the sunshine. We stand, just looking at each other.

"God...Alexa..." Her expression softens at the tremor in my voice. "I've never seen eyes like yours before. Never. They're...beautiful." I want to take the words back as soon as I say them, afraid they sound like some used line. But it's true.

She lowers her eyes, self-conscious, a smile tracing her lips. "Thank you."

"You really don't know Sam?" My voice is hoarse. Hopeful.

She shakes her head slowly. "I don't."

"Good," I manage.

"Wow." A sardonic laugh causes Alexa and I both to jump. "Blowing off class with a little backwoods romance, eh?" Kam emerges from the forest, two of his friends in tow.

"Not now, Kam." My body instinctively tenses.

"Well, don't let us interrupt. We're just out...looking for *specimens*," he taunts. His eyes run over Alexa. "Welcome to Forks, new girl. When you're tired of the cold ones, you should come find me. I've got a nice warm body for you."

"Don't talk to her that way," I snap.

"Don't talk to her that way or what, Death? You're gonna what? Use some of your sensei's trailer park moves again?" I don't dare correct him on the term for a taekwondo instructor: Master. He'd have a heyday with that one.

He feints a punch but doesn't do anything more. He remembers. The crack of a foot to his jaw.

Dan taught me well.

As if reading my mind, Kam runs a hand along his jawline before taking a step back. "Just watch it, Blue," he says, his eyes locking onto Alexa's. "Anything he kisses winds up dead." He arches an eyebrow and takes another step back just as Mr. Sorenson appears once again.

"All right, are we having a party back here now, or what?" Mr. Sorenson lectures. "Come on you guys, the hour is almost up. Time to be getting back. Next time stick to the designated area on class outings."

"Sure thing, Mr. Sorenson," Kam pipes up. "Just came out this way to see if these two were lost."

"I bet," Mr. Sorenson chides. "Come on. Get going."

They lead the way back, Alexa and I falling behind. "Sorry about that." Shame sears my cheeks. "Kam's an old thorn in my side."

She walks in silence behind me on the narrow trail. "What did he mean by *cold ones*?"

"It's from that *Twilight* series. He's just being a jerk."

"You mean vampires?"

"Just forget about it, okay?"

"Why would he call you that?"

I stop. "Aside from being pale, you mean?"

"I don't think you're pale." She stops walking, those intense blue eyes skimming my face. "There's nothing wrong with how you look. In fact...there's more than nothing wrong."

A lightness fills my chest. A fire. "Well, thanks for that. I think more of the reason he keeps calling me that now is that some people think I look like Edward Cullen, or rather the guy that played Edward Cullen in the movies." A flush heats my face. I don't want her to think I'm fishing for compliments.

"I've noticed. At least based on all the posters plastered around town here. I read the books but didn't see the movies. I wanted to, but my mom always thought I was too young for them and by the time I was old enough—" She stops, a shadow crossing her face. "Well...life threw me an unexpected curve ball. Then hot vampires were the last thing on my mind."

"What *was* on your mind?"

"Survival."

EIGHT

"SURVIVAL?" I TRY to get Alexa to look at me, but just then the rest of the class suddenly seems everywhere, everyone swarming out of the forest.

A girl with titian hair tied back tight in a ponytail comes up to us. "Jayden, there you are. I didn't get to talk to you earlier. You were in your own world." She turns to Alexa. "Hi, I'm Faye."

"Alexa," Alexa responds.

"Anyway, did you hear? A bunch of us are doing a memorial type thing for Sophie down at La Push tonight. No adults allowed," she says conspiratorially. "You guys in?"

Alexa looks at me. "Uh, sure. Jayden?"

"I'm working until seven."

"Come on...ditch Thriftway," Faye encourages. "Let someone else stock cans on a shelf tonight."

"I don't ditch work, Faye."

"Fine. Come after then. I think it will do everyone good to get together and celebrate her life, you know?"

"Yeah, no, of course," I say.

"We could go together," Alexa offers. "You could pick me up when you're finished work."

"Students, come on! The bell is about to sound," Mr. Sorenson urges.

"Alexa, I don't have—I don't have a car." I don't want to feel embarrassed but suddenly I do. Embarrassed not to be able to pick her up. And who knew when Mom would be home with her car, or if she'd be home at all for me to borrow it.

"Oh, well I can use my dad's truck. I'll pick you up."

"You guys figure it out. See you tonight at the beach!" Faye calls and trots back in the direction of the school.

Alexa raises an expectant eyebrow at me. "Will that work? Me getting you?"

"Don't come to my place! I mean—I know where your home is, so it's—it's easier for me to just come to you instead of me explaining where I live," I say evasively. I can't let her see my home. What would she think of it? Of me? "I'm not located in town either, so…I'll ride my bike out to your place since I know where you are, and we can go from there."

"Okay, sounds good. See you when you finish work."

"Wait! Alexa, what did you mean earlier? By 'survival' being all that was on your mind?"

Her eyes distance, a look passing across her features. "I was in a really bad car accident, Jayden. A couple years ago. I almost died. We've moved around a lot since then. It's been hard on my parents. Hard on me."

"A bad accident? God, I'm so sorry to hear that."

"Yeah. I don't really like talking about it though, so…" Her eyes cloud over. "Come on, we better get back." She starts heading toward the school.

I jog to catch up, a million questions on my mind, but when I reach her, the bell sounds and a surge of students flood from the building. She shoots me a smile, but there is a haunted emotion behind it. "I'll see you tonight," she says, "when you finish work. You finish at seven?"

"Yeah. Seven." I want to ask more. Know more. Know she's okay. But she's backing away, into the crowd, further and further away from me. "See you tonight," I call, but she's already gone.

* * *

Shift ends at last. Before I can slip out, my manager approaches.

"Jayden, got a moment?"

"Sure."

"Casey called in sick. You free to stick around 'til closing? I know you're wanting the extra cash for your college fund."

"Uh, actually this time no, Steve. I...I got a thing I have to be at."

"Really? It's not like you to turn down work."

"Yeah, uh...it's kind of important."

"All right. I'll find someone else then," he sighs. "This important thing wouldn't happen to be important to all the other Forks High seniors, would it? Seems a lot of people are either sick or have 'important things' to do tonight."

"There's kind of an informal memorial for Sophie, so..."

"Gotcha," he says. "Okay then. You take care, you hear? I'll cover."

"Thanks, Steve."

I turn to head down the aisles of food to the front automatic doors when I spot Miriam hanging out at the entrance. "There you are," she says when she sees me, giving me a quick hug in greeting.

"Mir! What are you doing here?"

"Well, I thought I'd wait until you were done work and give you a lift to the beach for Sophie's memorial. Come on! It started a while ago. Brody and everybody are already there." She walks around to the driver side of her car and opens the door, two surfboards strapped to the roof rack. "What are you waiting for? Let's go!" Her smile is so bright. All these years she'd been the sister I'd never had. Been there for me, teasing me, waiting to help me out. A couple months younger, but as protective as an older sibling.

"Mir, I can't. I'm meeting someone and going with them."

"Oh." Her face falls. "Who?"

"Alexa. The new girl."

"Oh," she says again. "She's coming? She didn't know Sophie."

"I know. But you and I both know it will be a party as much as a memorial. It will be a good chance for her to get to know some people."

"Right." Miriam focuses on the keys in her hands before pinning a smile on her face. "Guess I'll see you there then."

"We shouldn't be too long getting there."

"Mm-hm." She jumps into the car and fires up the engine, casting me an absent half wave as she pulls out of the parking lot.

It's still early enough in the season to be light at this hour. A sense of anticipation fills me as I pedal toward the distant road where the mansion is located. The familiar route feels like a salve. How many times I'd pedaled it before, craving the sanctuary of those abandoned walls. A nervous apprehension fills me to see what it looks like inside now. All those years of dreaming my way through fiction curled in the windblown corridors and now my own story seemed to be unfolding. One with Alexa.

I hope.

When I arrive at the front drive, candles burn on the patio and along weathered stumps dotting the perimeter of trees. I rest my bike by the front porch, taking in the swags of dried herbs suspended from the porch's ceiling.

Before I can knock, the door swings open. "Jayden, welcome." Magenta Croy stands in the doorway, dressed in a long black dress, a blood red crystal dangling from her neck down to her midriff. "Come in." She steps back and gestures into the front foyer. Her deep, dark eyes study me as I cross the threshold.

It's strange coming through the front door. Seeing the walls with their crumbling plaster patched smooth. Seeing the elegance. Pictures transform the mansion's shell into a place of warmth. And wealth. An odd sense of homesickness passes through me. For the drafts, the empty spaces.

Alexa appears on the sweeping staircase and that lost feeling morphs into anticipation—an aching need to feel at home here. With her.

"Have you met Lester yet?" A mischievous smile twitches the corner of Alexa's lips.

"Met who?" There is sudden movement beside me as what I thought was a playful butler mannequin, whirs forward. "Oh! Uh... What the—?"

Ms. Croy gives a secretive smile. "Alexa...your young man here has no coat for Lester to take, as you two are leaving."

The mannequin whirs back into place, its head and arms swiveling stiffly.

"That's...ha...pretty cool." I look at the details of the mannequin's features.

"He's been with me for a long time," Ms. Croy purrs. "One of my firsts."

I crumple my brow in confusion. "You made him?"

"Mom used to work as a Special Effects artist in Hollywood long ago," Alexa says, coming down the stairs.

"Yes, and Alexa always likes to intrigue people with the remnants of that time." Ms. Croy rolls her eyes and arches an eyebrow.

"He's pretty cool, Ms. Croy. And your work sounds like it was pretty cool too." I run a hand over the cocked arm of the mannequin, a serving cloth draped dramatically across its forearm.

"Just call me Magenta, dear. And yes, it was 'cool.' Still is. I've traded building robotics and props for movie sets to building mechanical prosthetics and such for the medical field." She sweeps across the foyer, rearranging some crystals on a low table.

"Wow. Impressive." I fight the feeling of inadequacy that bubbles up. "Do you work together with your husband on that? I heard he's a neuroscientist or neurosurgeon?"

A slow smile stretches across Magenta's face. "He's both. And we do work together. On some things." She cups a crystal in her hand, a dark look passing across her features. "And he's not my husband."

"Oh, I'm sorry, I just assumed—" Embarrassed, I look to Alexa for help.

"Mom and Dad never married," Alexa states simply. "So, partners, I guess is the word. Dad helps Mom with some of the innovations she's developing for neuroprosthetics and she helps him with his research. Their two fields are symbiotic, so they work well together."

Magenta offers a thin smile. "We're Alexa's parents. That's the most important aspect." Her demeanor brightens as she sweeps toward the revitalized kitchen. "Tea before you go?"

A thread of spiced incense smoke rises from a dish on a central dining table.

"Uh, I'm good, thanks. Alexa? You want—"

"No. We're going, now. Thanks, though, Mom." Alexa smiles at me as she pulls a coat from a vast closet.

Magenta drifts back into the dining hall by the foyer. "Very well then. You're taking your father's truck, correct?"

Alexa nods, zipping up her coat.

"Do be careful." A drop of worry pools in Magenta's dark eyes.

"Of course, I will." Alexa's face stiffens.

"Have a nice time." Magenta's smile widens and she ushers us out of the house.

"Thanks. It was nice to see you—" I stammer, "Whoops!" My hip catches a low table with a large crystal balanced at its center. I catch the gem in time before it topples to the marble floors of the entrance.

Magenta doesn't even flinch. "Yes, do be careful. Our home is boobytrapped with those things."

I handle the rough texture of the crystal, placing it back on its stand. "I really like them," I say. I think of the one at home. The one Mom gave me. The one Magenta gave her. I hesitate. "What does purple do? The purple crystals?"

"Amethyst aids with healing substance dependencies." Her eyes alight on mine, probing.

I quickly look away.

"And it helps promote healthy...sleep," she finishes.

"Mom...we have to go. Jayden?" Alexa interrupts. "You okay?"

I chance a look at Magenta, her onyx eyes on me. Intense. As if she can read right through me. Before I can say anything, she turns with a swish of her dress. "Be home by curfew, Alexa—twelve sharp. Do not be late." She casts a warning scowl Alexa's way.

"I won't," Alexa responds, a hint of frustration shadowing her face. "Ready?" She says to me.

I nod, an uneasy feeling creeping up my spine as I watch Magenta disappear down the sweeping hall. *Does she know about us? About Mom and me? How?* My heart skips in an erratic rhythm as we climb into the cab of Alexa's father's truck. The interior has a faint chemical smell. A scented artificial pine freshener swings from the rearview mirror.

"So, you're kind of like Cinderella, huh?" I tease. "Midnight curfew."

"Ha, yeah. You could say that," she sighs in exasperation.

"And what do you turn into if you don't get back in time?"

"Clearly, nothing pretty." She rolls her eyes and turns the ignition. "Guide me with directions to La Push." She grips the wheel, her irritation with her mother dissipating. She starts to radiate an air of excitement. It's contagious. The wind funnels in the rolled down windows as we pull out onto the road, the damp air rich with the scent of possibility.

* * *

We reach the beach, a slew of cars parked in half-haphazard rows in the open lot. Waves crest in broken lines, large rock formations jutting from the sea like rugged mirages. There's been a good turnout for Sophie's memorial. Some juniors and sophomores have joined. I recognize a few student faces from Port Angeles as well who I'd met over the summer on the beach—people who must have known Sophie too. Either that, or they caught wind of a party happening tonight. A big bonfire sparks in the sand, bodies clustered around it. Music thumps from somewhere, competing with the crash of the waves. Voices and laughter fill the air with ebullient sound.

"What is it?" I ask, swinging the door open to jump outside.

Alexa remains seated, a hesitant look on her face. "I don't really know anyone yet."

"Come on, I'll introduce you. It's a small town, so everyone kind of knows everyone." We get out and meld into the crowd.

"Hey, man." Brody slings a loose arm around my shoulder, his breath already heavy with booze. "I'm crashing at your place tonight if anyone asks, okay?"

"Got it." I try to brush off the tension in my chest.

"Thanks, man," he slurs. "Hey...Miriam brought my extra board and wet suit for you, if you wanna hit the waves." He gestures to the breakers curling in the fading glow of daylight, cloud heavy on the horizon.

"We'll see. I'm with Alexa tonight."

"Gotcha. Hey," he says to Alexa in greeting. "K, gotta go, man, I'll catch you later. Hey, Colleen! Wait up!" And he's off into the night.

"To Sophie!" Someone hollers, and the crowd raises their bottles and cooler cans to holler, "To Sophie!" in response.

"Rest in peace," someone else chimes in.

I recognize some of Sophie's good friends gathered in a circle, eyes red rimmed as they reminisce and try to drink their sorrows away. But most seem to have forgotten why they came, a strong party vibe overtaking the night. A table with a blown-up photo of Sophie has candle vigils in glass cylinders that are already burning low, flames wincing in the coastal breeze.

"Where do you want to go?" Alexa calls over the music.

"Want to take a walk?" I suggest.

"That'd be nice."

As we thread our way through the crowd, I pause to introduce Alexa to various people. It feels weird. I usually hang back from the crowd, preferring the solitude of the waves.

I recognize some of the youth from the reservation. "Jayden, what's up?" A tall guy with long, dark hair pulled back in a low ponytail bumps my fist. "Haven't seen you in a while."

"Not since you stole my wave last month," I joke. "How are you, Cole?"

"Good." He surveys the crowd. "Sophie's tragedy is turning into quite the rager, huh?"

"Seems so." I look past his shoulder scanning the group he's with. "Is Sam here?"

Alexa glances over at me at the mention of Sam's name.

"Nah, he didn't want to come." Cole takes a sip of his beer. "He's been pretty distracted lately."

"I heard. He mentioned something about helping out around the res.

Young blood needed, or something."

"Maybe," Cole says noncommittally. "Could be helping, I guess. Though, he's kind of gone rogue. Out on his own a lot. He's not been himself, lately."

"Oh? How so?"

"Just been acting strange and stuff. Kind of cagey." Cole's cool eyes survey the crowd with detached interest.

"Cole! Dude! What's been going on?" Another guy staggers up and Alexa and I are jostled back. The two start BS-ing about the surf.

"Jayden, can we go?" Alexa touches my arm.

"Yeah. Of course." Cole's words burrow into my gut.

"What is it?" Alexa asks.

"Ah...nothing. Just...I've been a bad friend, is all." Guilt washes over me. "I haven't seen much of Sam this summer. I should have checked in with him more." Again, I picture him sitting in his truck. His vacant stare out the front windshield. But he'd been fine at the Fosters. He'd seemed himself. But I should know more than anyone that looks can be deceiving. That secrets can be covered. I clear my throat.

Overhearing us, Cole elbows me. "Why don't you text or snap Sam if you're wondering where he is?"

"Right. I could do that." Half the time I forget my phone somewhere. The other half I can't be bothered. All social media has ever done is leave me depressed at the glittering lives other people lead or the confusing conflagration of news about the world and its slow demise.

And truthfully, I don't have much to say most of the time, so why be attached to a phone?

The breeze has picked up, furling Alexa's hair into the wind. She pulls her coat closer around her and smiles at me.

I return her smile and reach into my back pocket. Tonight, the phone somehow was remembered, I'm thankful to see. Because I want to check on Sam. What's up, man? U should get out to First Beach. I hit send.

Alexa waits for me, and we stroll down the beach, our shoes removed, damp sand between our toes. We find a rocky outcrop to settle on to watch the last of the sun's weak rays meld into the sea. A dark formation of cloud piles high, thunderously dark. "Looks like rain tomorrow. Again," I observe. "You'll have to get used to it in Forks."

"I like the rain." Alexa leans back on her arms.

"Good thing you moved here then," I joke.

She laughs. "I find it cozy when it's raining out. I love curling up with a good book and reading while the weather is pure insanity outside."

"Really? Me too. That's my favorite thing. Especially in your place. There are so many nooks to sit with windows overlooking the forest..."

She looks my way. "And how would you know? About those nooks?"

"Uh...I can just tell. From its architecture." I clear my throat.

She looks back at the setting sun, the film of cloud dulling its rays. "You have an eye for architecture, then, because you're right. There are a lot of great places in our home for that."

A wistful pang flutters in my chest. Where would I go now when I needed time alone? When I needed an escape? But then the thought of sitting in one of those nooks—now warm with heat and cushioned seats, no doubt—and the thought of sitting there with Alexa ignites hope. About a better future.

"What are your favorite books?" she asks.

"I like the classics. The language...the protracted suspense. The originality. All the ideas hadn't been used up yet when they were published. They were fresh. Their own. I gravitate towards Gothic. Though I think that could be why my imagination runs away on me, sometimes. And I don't always have the most restful sleep." With that, I feel I've said too much. Become too exposed. I clear my throat. "You? What do you read?"

"Well, I'm the opposite. I don't do Gothic or anything horror. I love Romeo and Juliet-type scripts. Doomed love and all that. Though happily-ever-after is okay too. I love romance. Like a lot of girls, I guess." She keeps her face forward, her fingers self-consciously holding her hair back from her face in the toss of ocean breeze.

My heart stutters. We're sitting close. The breeze between us cold, yet all I feel is warmth while next to her. "Romance is good." My voice is hoarse. I don't know what to say. I want to get this right. Being here.

With her. Feeling the way I do when I'm around her. *Like I'm someone else*. She doesn't know anything about me like the other girls here. Doesn't know the kid I was. The damage done. I'm just a blank page to her. A story not yet told. And that feels good. A fresh chapter.

"Have you lived here your entire life?" she asks.

The warmth fades. "Yeah." I don't want to talk about my past. Don't want to talk about my life and its broken bits.

"What about your parents? Are they both from here?"

I adjust on the rock, uncomfortable. "Uh...my mom, yeah. She's from here."

"And your dad?" Her inquisitive eyes turn on me.

"Uh...to be honest...no idea. Never met him. I know nothing about him."

"Oh. I'm sorry. I didn't mean to pry." Embarrassed, Alexa returns her gaze to the coastline, the sun now consumed by darkness, swallowed into the sea. The plume of dark cloud spreads wider, blotting stars. Overhead, the moon drifts, as if dodging the cloud.

"Don't be sorry. It's not your fault." Not my fault. Not my mother's. Maybe he was a nice guy and couldn't stand my mom's drinking. Or maybe he was a monster who caused my mom's drinking. Or maybe he was nothing at all.

My fists clench and unclench.

"Well, I think you're lucky to grow up in one town," Alexa says. "We've moved around a lot. At least, we have these past couple years." Her voice trails off, a note of melancholy threading her words.

I know she means they moved around a lot the past couple years since her accident. Her thoughts about it are palpable, but so is her reluctance to speak about it, so I don't ask.

The wind picks up, a trace of vanilla lifting from her hair into the tangle of coastal scents. "Your dad is on sabbatical here?" I ask.

"Yeah. Doing some kind of research. And Mom can work on her stuff from anywhere. She's on the frontline of developing technology and bionic models for medical use. The big house helps. Keeps us all separated. I can get away from their work. And Dad has his lab out back.

I just claim a wing inside somewhere to myself and disappear into another world with a book, when I need to. I guess the same way you do. Seems we have something in common."

"Yeah." I laugh, a pang hooking my chest. Books in common. Not lifestyles. "I'm kind of surprised your parents chose Forks for sabbatical. I mean...your family seems a little out of our league." I keep my eyes forward.

"They have favored small towns since my accident." She stops herself. I wait for her to say more about it, but she doesn't. "I guess they just needed some quiet. Life was turned upside down for a while, I guess." She scrapes at some lichen clinging to the rough rock. "But before the small towns, we were always in central hubs where the big medical science institutes were. My mother likes the outdoors, though. The wilder, the better. She...she draws energy from it." She lapses into silence.

"And what do you draw energy from?" I ask. The wind catches between us. A vanilla infused loop of magnetic air.

A smile traces her lips. Even in the darkness, with the silver cast of moonlight, I can make out the intoxicating blue of her eyes. "This," she says, gesturing to the swirl of waves buffeting against the rock. "Being here...with someone like you."

The breeze displaces her hair, so it flits across her face as she turns toward me. Slowly, gently, I trace the strands back from her cheek. She inclines her head toward me, the ocean of her eyes inviting me in.

"Jayden! Hey!"

I pull back at the sound of my name. A surfer splashes out onto the beach below where we're sitting. "Want to come grab a wave with me? I brought a board and suit you can use."

"Miriam? Hey!" I call in response, my heart still ricocheting from the moment before. "The surf looks great, but not tonight."

Miriam shakes her long blonde hair out from her hooded wetsuit and props her board in the sand. "You sure?"

I nod. "Yeah. Another time?"

"Okay." She lifts the board over her head and makes her way down the beach back toward the thump of music, casting one last glance back our way. In the distance the crowd has grown more chaotic, groups cavorting on the sand, some dancing, the movements manic in the firelight. Laughter and shouts carry through the night.

"She likes you," Alexa observes.

"Miriam? No. She's like a sister. She just likes to tease me because I used to have a crush on her when we were kids. I proposed to her when I was seven. She won't let me live it down."

"If you say so," Alexa says softly.

"I know so."

"Mm. Sometimes we're oblivious to the most obvious facts."

We watch Miriam head down the beach, she glances back at us again but turns around quickly when she sees us staring after her.

Then I see it. A figure standing alone where the beach meets forest. Watching. "Sam?" I whisper. I stand up. The figure steps back into the shadow of forest.

"What is it?" Alexa twists to try and see what I'm looking at.

"I could have sworn I saw—"

"Well, well, well. If it isn't the two lovebirds," a voice interrupts. Kam sidles up the back of the rock behind us, two of his posse shadowing behind.

"Kam, what are you doing here?" Instinctively, I tense, moving so that Alexa is safely behind me. Though it's not her I'm worried about. Not her he'd bother.

Kam places a drunken hand theatrically across his chest. "Remembering my old girlfriend, of course. Like everybody else. Except you, that is. Why are you here? To give another girl the kiss of Death?"

"Kam...don't," I warn.

"What's he talking about?" Alexa rises to her feet beside me.

"Kam dated Sophie. After they broke up, she kissed me once at a party. It was nothing. I know it and he knows it. Come on, Alexa, let's go."

"What's the hurry? It's a party, after all." Kam raises a bottle to his lips and takes a long pull of beer. "Come on, we're all friends here in this town. Alex, is it?"

"Alexa," she says through gritted teeth.

"Alexa...hmm." He staggers slightly where he stands. "How'd you get so pretty, Alexa? You're the prettiest girl on this beach—in this town. And Death here thinks he's the only one for you? He thinks he's the only one for *all* the girls here. They all just think he's so goddamned *gorgeous* with his vampire looks. But he ignores all of them. They aren't good enough for him. Then the one he does kiss...winds up dead in a ditch somewhere. Insides torn out."

"Kam, that's enough!" I bark. "Alexa, let's go."

"Do you know anything about vampires, Alexa? *Real* vampires? They seduce their prey before feeding on them. Yeah." He nods exaggeratedly.

I take Alexa's hand and help lead her down the jagged rock onto the beach. Kam and his friends jump down onto the sand beside us.

"Let's just go, Alexa," I urge. "He's just—"

Crack! A fist connects with the side of my face.

"Stop it!" Alexa screams.

Stunned, I stagger, my hand touching my face where a stream of blood courses from my lip. But the next punch, I'm ready for. It's as if I'm in the clearing behind the trailer park. Dan with me, running through the moves. My arm automatically lurches up to block the next punch, and the next as the three of them descend on me.

For a panicked moment, I'm seven again. Ten. Twelve. Fourteen. On an empty side street with Kam and his friends surrounding me.

But not anymore. I spin, my foot connecting with Kam's chest, launching him backwards. I block another blow from behind, jam an elbow into a set of ribs just as another fist flies toward my face from the third guy. I block it just in time, landing a punch solidly in his midsection.

"*Stop!*" Alexa cries again.

A chant strikes up down the beach. "Fight! Fight!"

I'm distantly aware of people running toward us. Some are cheering, others are hollering for us to stop. I want to stop. But the fists keep coming. I hold my own, a strength rising inside me like a ferocious beast.

Dan's tireless training. Committed to muscle memory.

I strike hard.

Fast.

My body feels inhumanly strong with adrenalin. As if fueled by something else.

Others arrive. Brody grabs Kam and pins his arms behind him with the help of another guy. More jump in and wrestle the other two friends of Kam's away. Panting, I wipe the blood from my lip.

"Hey, is she okay?" a voice says.

"It's the new girl," another voice says.

Dazed, I turn around, trying to spot Alexa in the gathering crowd. Then I see her. She's on her knees, her body supported up by one hand, the other gripping her forehead.

"Alexa!" I push past the people and drop to my knees beside her. "Alexa, are you okay?"

"I need to get home," she chokes. "Please...I need to leave..."

I try to help her stand but her weight collapses against me. Without hesitation, I scoop her into my arms and cradle her against my body.

"You all right, man?" a voice asks.

"Just get out of my way," I bark.

"Jayden, let me help you." It's Brody. "Is she okay?"

I don't say a word, just push through the crowd toward the parking lot in the distance. Everybody parts to let me pass. I see Miriam, standing by her board, pale in the moonlight. She doesn't speak as I stride past her. My muscles are on fire. Alexa is heavier than expected for her slight form. All muscle. But I don't feel her weight. Or the bruises culminating on my body. Just the adrenalin licking through my veins.

When we get to her truck, I gently set her down on the open truck bed.

"Where's your keys, Alexa? *Alexa?*"

"My pocket," she manages.

I reach into her pocket, feel the warmth of her body through the fabric. Hot, as if fevered.

I settle her into the passenger seat, jump into the driver's side, and twist the ignition. A trail of people have gathered around, worriedly watching us depart. I don't pay them any attention, quickly reversing the truck then stomping on the gas pedal to tear down the narrow road out of the park.

"Damn!" The digital clock on the truck's dash says 11:47pm. I increase the speed, the dark shapes of the trees whipping past.

"Slow down, Jayden," Alexa says, her voice weak. "Slow down or you'll get us killed."

"I'm sorry," I pant. "Your accident. Of course. I'm sorry, I forgot. I didn't mean to scare you." I ease off the gas pedal. "I'm just worried about you. Are you okay?"

"I just need to get home."

"What happened to you back there?" The adrenalin keeps sparking in my body. My foot on the gas pedal instinctively wants to press harder, gather as much speed as possible. Tear through the night. Tear the night down.

"I don't know. I just suddenly didn't feel right. It's okay. I'm okay."

"You sure?"

"I'm sure. It happens sometimes. Since my accident. Sometimes, I'm just not right."

"Your parents are going to kill me!" My hands grip the steering wheel so hard it feels as if it will break. "Your mom was really adamant you be home by midnight. And here I am bringing you in late. Coming to your property with blood all over my face." *Again.*

"Jayden, it wasn't your fault, what happened. I'll explain. Don't worry. Are *you* okay?" She shifts in her seat to look at me, lifting a hand to trail down the side of my face. I wince at her touch, the bruise deepening, blooming across my cheek and jaw.

"I'm fine," I say tersely. "He's had it out for me since I was a kid. It's just been a while since he's actually tried to fight. He caught me off guard."

She's quiet a moment. "He keeps saying everything you kiss dies. Why?"

"Just because of Sophie. Because he likes to keep making me out to be some dumb vampire. Because he doesn't want me to be happy. With you." I glance over at her profile in the darkness.

"*Are* you a vampire?"

I slam on the brakes.

Mist gathers in the headlights as we both sit there, breathing hard from the sudden stop.

"Is that what you think?" I can't even look at her. But then my mind goes into overdrive. The stress. The adrenalin. I feel my body tense as if running. Running through the dark woods at night. Waking up, half clothed, blood all over my hands, my face. I squeeze my eyes shut and rest my head on the steering wheel.

"I'm sorry." She places a hand on my back. "Jayden? I'm sorry, okay?"

"Why are you asking me this? Alexa…" I lift my head to look at her. "Why would you ask such a thing?"

"We haven't talked about that night. When I first saw you."

"You said you weren't afraid of me. You said—"

"I'm not. Afraid." Her eyes are steady on me.

"Alexa," I sputter, astonished she'd even ask it. "I'm *not* a vampire. If you really think that you *should* be afraid. This isn't a page of fiction here."

"What happened that night then? Why were you in the forest covered in blood? Looking like it wasn't the first time it's happened."

"I need to get you home," I stammer. "If you think—"

"I don't think that. Obviously, I don't. It just sometimes seems— sometimes feels like—you're holding something back from me."

Like the fact that I live in a trailer park. With an alcoholic mother. That I have some kind of weird disorder that has me wake up disoriented in the woods, exhausted, as if I've been running for my life. Running from my life. That you're too good for me, Alexa. That you're out of my league…

"Aren't we both holding things back?" I say it, then want to take it back when I see the look on her face. She barely knows me. She doesn't have to tell me about her past. Her life. Her accident. Same as I haven't told her. "If I'm keeping things from you, it's not that I'm a vampire. Or a killer," I emphasize. "If you're starting to think I had something to do with Sophie—"

"I don't." She exhales slowly and puts a hand to her forehead as if in pain. "I'm sorry. I'm just not feeling right. Of course, I don't think those things. From the moment I saw you, I knew you were a good person, Jayden." Her voice is drifting as if losing focus. "Something about your eyes. The expression on your face. I knew you were someone who would understand me. Instinctually, you know? Despite how you looked that night. It wasn't scary, no. You looked sad—scared...as if you'd just lived through something horrible. It was weird, but I felt nothing but concern for you when I saw you. It was like I already knew you. It was like..." Her voice grows softer. "It sounds so crazy but...it was almost...like love at first sight."

"Love?" A euphoric rush fills my senses.

"I'm sorry, I'm not even thinking straight. I—" She grows silent, her face suddenly paling. "Jayden," her voice tremors. She lifts a shaking hand and points toward the front windshield.

I follow her finger to the empty road ahead of us, mist heavy in the headlights. I freeze. An enormous animal looms in the darkness, crossing the road, all fours stealthily marking the ground beneath its feet. It's large head swings toward us, amber eyes reflecting in the beam of the headlights, then lopes into the forest on the other side of the woods and out of sight.

"What was that?" Her voice quivers.

I stare into the darkness where the creature has disappeared, my chest tightening. "A wolf." The biggest wolf I've ever seen.

NINE

"IT CAN'T HAVE been a wolf," Alexa protests. "It was way too big!"

The engine falters, stalling. I wrench the key in the ignition. It sputters and coughs but doesn't turn over.

"What, are we in a frigging horror movie here? Come on, start!" I anxiously scan the black depths of the forest. The tendrils of mist have deepened, lowering further into the gloom making the forest depths harder to see. It trails across the windshield like a damp wraith.

"Jayden, we have to get out of here." Alexa's voice worries me, her fright layered with something else. I glance over at her quickly.

"I'm trying, I've got to—" Finally, the engine kicks to life. I cry out in relief and punch my foot to the gas pedal. We surge forward with a rumble.

It's hard to see the road, the mist thick as gauze. It lifts a bit the closer we get to town. Finally, I see the turn-off to Alexa's road. She's silent in the seat next to me.

"Alexa?"

She doesn't respond.

"Alexa?!"

The mansion's drive appears, and I swing the truck through the open iron gates. It's after midnight—by twenty minutes. Magenta paces the length of the front porch. She swoops down the drive as we pull in. Dr. Johansson emerges from the house, the truck headlights washing his face in light. His complexion is paler than mine. And stone cold.

I brake and jump out of the truck scrambling around to the other side. "I'm sorry we're late," I begin to babble. "We lost track of the time but she's not feeling well, she needs help—"

"Where is she?" Magenta demands.

I wrench open the passenger door. "She started feeling weak at the beach and collapsed—" I stammer.

Dr. Johansson lifts his daughter from the truck, his eyes pausing momentarily on my bruised and bleeding face. The blue of his eyes startles me. The same shade as Alexa's. "You need to go."

"Will she be all right?" I persist. "She said sometimes this happens since her accident—"

"She told you about her accident?" Magenta interrupts.

"Yes, but... I'm sorry, I would have brought her home sooner."

Dr. Johansson strides to the porch steps and inside, Alexa limp in his arms.

"You need to go now," Magenta states firmly.

"I'm so sorry. Can I—?"

"Go. Now." She stands, the mist circling her, threading across her black dress like a curse. "There's nothing more you can do. We will take care of her." She whirls away, her dress billowing, and darts up the porch, into the house, closing the door firmly behind her.

I'm alone, night air pressing in all around me. The mist has brought with it an eerie silence. A presence. I retrieve my bike from beside the porch and wheel it out onto the winding road, switching on my bike light. My heart feels heavy. Gouged. The image of Alexa's still face seared into my mind. I start to peddle, the porch lanterns from the mansion fading behind me so there's nothing but the thin beam of my light to divide the utter blackness of night. All I hear is my breathing, hard and heavy as I pedal faster and faster. Another thought creeps into my mind. The creature caught in the headlights when I was with Alexa. It's huge body, shaggy coat.

Feral eyes.

The mist has turned to rain, the road slick as I carve my way out from the dense trees to open road, the forest running beside me. I can almost hear a howl woven into the rain, but I know it's just my imagination. Maybe I'd mistaken what I saw. Maybe it hadn't been a wolf. *What if it was a bear?* They roamed these woods too.

No.

I know what I saw.

At last, the dull lights of the trailer park blink into view. I nearly wipe out in my haste to get home, wrenching my handlebars left into the park's entrance. I pull up alongside our mobile home, panting. To my surprise, Mom's car is parked out front.

I jog up to the front door, fumble with my key, and swing the door open.

"Honey?"

I stumble inside. She's standing at the kitchen counter, stopping what she's doing when she sees me. "What happened to your face?"

"I was in a fight." I brush past her to the bathroom, shutting the door behind me and hunker over the sink, breathing hard. I look up at my reflection. My right eye is swollen half-shut, a shadow of bruising lines my cheek to my jaw, redness flaring around it. I twist on the taps, let cold water spill into the sink's basin and splash it over my face, washing the dried blood from my mouth.

I stay there for I don't know how long, standing in front of the mirror, scrutinizing my face, my eyes. *What is happening to you?*

Finally, I open the door. Mom is perched on the edge of her chair, waiting. Her eyes are clear. Focused. For once, herself. I can't remember the last time she's been like this.

"I didn't think I'd be seeing you back home so soon."

She drops her head. "I can pull myself together sometimes, Jayden."

"Yeah, well—not usually." I don't mean the words to come out dagger sharp, but they do. I lumber into the kitchen. The purple crystal still rests on the counter where I'd left it. I shove it aside and open the freezer to pull out a frozen package of peas for my face.

"Do you want to tell me what happened?" she ventures.

"Really? You want to play mom now?" I stalk to my room and sit on the bare mattress, my sheets still a tangle on the floor from the previous night.

"Jayden?" She's in my doorway.

"You want to know what happened, Mom? The same stuff that's been happening for years. Kam and his friends targeting me for no good reason. But you wouldn't know anything about that."

"I did know, Jayden, I just didn't know what to do—"

"So, you did nothing?"

"Dan said he had it handled. He was going to help you—"

"Dan's not my father!" I shout.

She flinches and falls silent.

"I wish you could predict things for yourself like you used to predict for everyone else, so you could keep safe." Her face looks pained.

"What are you talking about?" I spit, wiping a fresh trickle of blood from my mouth.

"It was like you had premonition. If something bad was going to happen, you'd be there ahead of time to stop it. With me..." She didn't have to mention the situations she'd got herself into with some of the men she'd bring home when I was younger. "But also, with others. If something bad was going to happen, you'd always be there trying to stop it."

"Yeah, well. It never did stop, did it."

"But you tried. You were never afraid to try and stop something awful before it happened. I just wish you had that same sixth sense for yourself. To keep you away from all the Kams of the world."

"Yeah, well, I don't." The annoying prickle of tears sears my eyes. "Please...just leave me, Mom. I need to be alone."

"I'm sorry, Jay. So sorry..." She sniffs then straightens, a gloss of emotion wetting her eyes. "I'll give you your space." She turns away, closing the door behind her. Moments later I hear the familiar clink of a glass bottle, my gut contracting. The front door opens and shuts. But there's no use. I can't stop a train wreck I hadn't started. Just because it paused for one night. It would have started again anyway.

Her car guns to life then there's the crunch of gravel as she pulls away. I cry. I haven't cried since I was a kid following a beating from Kam, or the fear of Mom not returning. Or returning *with* someone.

I lie back on the bed, let the tears roll silently down my cheeks, across the bruised flesh and bone. I wonder how Alexa is doing. If she's all right. Maybe I used to predict when something bad was going to happen. Maybe I used to walk into the middle of danger to try and make it stop. But where had that gotten me now? Who had I saved lately?

Exhaustion floods my body, a weariness bone deep. From the eye that isn't swelling, I notice the robe tie still strapped to the bed post. I reach for it and hold its rough fabric, too tired to bother with it.

Too tired to care.

*   *   *

I dream of a face. Beautiful, mysterious. Blue eyes, electric and haunting. A face so familiar yet strange. Her long, dark curls blow in the wind as she runs fast, faster, leaping over fallen logs, moss bitten rock. Powerful, strong, serene. But the dream changes to a different face, unfamiliar and frightened. Short pixie hair framing narrow cheeks, hazel eyes wide with terror. A scream silenced on her lips.

I dream of a forest, ragged and dark. Rain-soaked boughs hooding the ground as this unfamiliar girl runs. She screams. Screams again. Her voice echoing through my head, shrill and high.

Until suddenly, it stops.

*   *   *

I jerk awake, panting hard. Darkness shifting above me, shadows of cedar, fir, and hemlock; the twisted shape of maple; billowing sheaves of aspen and alder. I'm on my back, arms sprawled, ankle twisted beneath me.

As if I've just fallen.

I don't move, the moist earth cold against my skin, rivulets of rain soaking through my shirt, drizzling onto my forehead, trickling across my sore cheek, my swollen eye.

Below the hiss of rain there is silence. Pregnant. Full. As if moments before the air was filled with siren sound.

"No," I whisper. Then scream, "*No!*"

It's been two days. Two days since I wakened in these woods, my heart racing. Not months. Not weeks. Two days.

Too soon.

Tentatively, I test my ankle. It survived the fall. *Did I fall?* I don't feel blood on my hands. Not this time. But my entire body is bathed by rain. So maybe—

No. Don't go there. Don't let yourself think.

I've never dreamed before. Not like this. Not when wandering.

I grind the balls of my fists into my temples, ignoring the flare of pain where the bruising has spread.

My heart slowly steadies as I try to gain my bearings. I push myself to my feet and stagger forward. Something startles in the bush behind me, a flurry of wet leaves.

Then silence.

Nausea springs up out of nowhere and I double over, retching into the darkness. Fear spirals from temple to gut. Instinctively, I pause, listening for heavy footfall. The memory of the wolf caught in the headlights, eerie in the fog, in its size. It's ethereal shape sharp in my mind—gray coat, moving like the mist itself.

But there's nothing. Just rain pattering upon drooping leaves.

I stagger forward. Lost. Wandering, but awake.

I continue until finally, I come upon a parking lot connected to a trailhead and follow it out to a main road, dawn staining the sky. Traffic is light, but still, I skirt to the side and merge back amongst the foliage at any sign of a passing car. Like a fugitive. Like someone who is being hunted.

Or the hunter.

At last, I reach the trailer park. No one stirs. Dan's trailer blinds are pulled tight, though his vehicle ticks as if recently running. Mom's car isn't home. Not that I expected it to be. The front door to our mobile is unlocked, the door a fraction open. Cautiously, I nudge it wider. It's empty inside. *It was you. You who left it open when you left.* It's the only explanation.

I pause by the kitchen, the purple crystal shoved aside from the night before. "Healing properties, my ass," I curse. Grabbing it, I return to the front door and hurl it into the ditch across the thin lane. It lands with a satisfying crack against stone. I glance toward Dan's trailer to see if I've disturbed him, but the blinds don't open. Nothing stirs.

I close the front door and stumble to the bathroom. My face looks bad. There's dirt in my hair, a twig. Shirt and pants torn, covered with mud. I realize I'm shivering. Cold. Blood rims my lips. I trace my fingers over my mouth. *I've bitten my tongue.* At least I think I have. *Or has the split in my lip from Kam reopened?* I rinse my mouth out, spitting red into the sink when I notice the small clock in the bathroom. 8:01am.

"*Shit!*" I'm late for work.

Quickly, I shower, lathering the filth from my hair, my skin. I pull on my work clothes and try to tame my snarl of hair. There's nothing I can do about my face.

Jumping onto my bike, I pedal to the Thriftway as if a wraith trails behind, ditching my bike outside the store to rush inside.

People stare. Whisper.

"What the hell happened to you?" Steve steps in front of me at the end of an aisle.

"I'm sorry I'm late," I start.

"I can see why you're late. Get back here." He ushers me into the area that's for staff only. "We can't have customers seeing you like this."

"Right. I hadn't thought about that."

"You need to go home, Jayden."

"Steve...you can't do that to me. You know I need the money."

"Your college savings can wait, Jayden. You need to go home and take care of that bruise. Can you even see out of your eye?"

"It's fine."

"Well, it's not going to be fine for service here. It's making customers uncomfortable."

"Can't I just do some work in the back? Please?"

He exhales a drawn-out sigh. "Fine. You can help with some paperwork."

He guides me toward his office. "Sit down." He gestures to a cracked vinyl chair. "First things first. Are you all right?"

"I will be." The fluorescent light flickers. I hear footsteps running across soft earth. The winded pant of a person running. A girl. Memory snagged in the circuits of my brain. *A dream. It was just a dream, Jayden!*

"Who did this to you?" He unfolds his arms gesturing to my face as he moves to the other side of his desk and sits down.

I'm quiet a moment. "It's nothing, Steve. Things just got out of hand at the memorial last night down at La Push—"

"Is that how to honor Sophie? With a brawl?"

"It wasn't like that."

He picks up a pen and holds it between his fingers, considering. "If you need help, you'd ask me, right?"

I swallow and nod. "I would."

He waits, giving space for me to say something more. I don't.

"Okay, then," he sighs. Leaning forward, he shows me some papers, explaining what to do. By the time he leaves, my head is pounding. I've barely slept. And when I did sleep, I was on the run. My body unrested.

Fatigue swallows me whole.

Steve pokes his head back into the office minutes later. "Jayden?"

"Yeah?"

"Go get some coffee. Get alive. A fresh pot is in the break room."

"Thanks." Relieved, I push back the chair.

The break room is empty, quiet but for a small television propped in one corner playing the news softly in the background. I pull out a mug and fill it with fresh brew. I'm not listening to the natter of the news anchor. I'm back in the woods, the rain in my face. Then back further to Kam and the beach. Fists raining like hail. Alexa, her eyes, her voice. Her body, limp in my arms.

"For the small town of Forks, already rocked by the death of seventeen-year-old local, Sophie Wilkinson, comes another unexpected tragedy. Body of eighteen-year-old, Lindsay Sutton, was found early this morning by officials in the forest just outside of Forks small township. Her injuries are similar to the ones Sophie suffered not two days before. But the bigger question is who, *or what*, that killer may be."

A buzz fills my head as a photo flashes onto the screen. Pixie hair. Narrow cheeks. Hazel eyes.

The mug of coffee shatters onto the floor.

TEN

I CAN'T TAKE my eyes off the screen, the picture of the girl still featured in the top corner. The news anchor continues with her report.

"Previously, officials cited wolves as being the most likely suspect in Sophie's death with recent sightings in the past weeks of a rogue pack exhibiting signs of unusually aggressive behavior toward locals and tourists venturing into the backwoods. Sophie would be the first known attack by the wolves, but authorities still have questions as to whether wild animals indeed are the ones to blame for the death. More information should become available following the coroner's investigation into both bodies. Friends of Lindsay who were with her in Forks, say she was visiting from Seattle, Washington in preparation for the town's annual Forever Twilight in Forks Festival next week—"

I can't listen anymore. I lumber from the break room, out into the storefront. Steve is standing near one of the locals, a few other people gathered around. The local is Tim Wells, a restaurant owner in town. He has his phone out in front of the group, streaming the news.

"Authorities are advising the people of Forks to use extra vigilance when out in their community and to stay away from heavily forested areas unless traveling together in large groups. Though concern has been that the recent deaths were caused by a pack of rogue wolves, police are investigating the possibility of homicide. People are still encouraged to be cautious if they see any wildlife in the area and to report anything suspicious—"

"I feel sick," a woman says, a hand pressed to her mouth. Someone puts a comforting arm around her shoulders.

"Jayden, you okay?" Steve glances up at me with concern. He excuses himself from the small group. "Tim's wife just called and told him to turn on the news. Did you hear?"

"I...uh...Steve...I'm going to go, like you suggested. I'm not feeling too good."

"You don't look good," he notes. "Go on home then, that's not a problem. Get some rest. Maybe see if you can get that face looked at."

"I'll pick up an extra shift later."

"Don't even worry about that right now. We'll make sure you make up the lost income. Just get on home and heal. You're not back in until Monday or Tuesday after school, right?"

I nod.

"Let's change that to Friday. I promise I'll fit in the hours missed for you when you're one hundred percent. If you're still not healed enough by then, I'll find something in the back for you again, away from customers. Sound good?"

"Yes. Thank you." Dazed, I ignore people's stares as I make my way down the aisles and out into the front parking lot and the rain.

I grab my bike but don't head home, instead pedaling to Mocha Motion for some espresso. I need to wake up. I need clarity.

I need to remember.

The barista is a girl from town who graduated last year. "Oh my gosh, Jayden. I heard you got jumped last night at La Push. You okay?" But I don't pay her any attention.

Pixie hair. Hazel eyes.

The barista eyes me warily when I don't answer. "What will it be for you today?"

I mumble my order and wait impatiently, eyeing the townsfolk going about their business. My heart bangs in my chest, wild, on edge.

"Jayden...Jayden? Your espresso is ready," the barista calls uncertainly.

"Thanks," I mumble and take it. Grabbing my bike, I push it down the road, veering off so I'm not as visible to passersby.

Pixie hair. Hazel eyes.

The face haunts me. I must have seen her before. *But where? In town? At La Push, last night? Before—*

My breathing comes hard. I toss the scalding espresso down and crumple the cup.

A familiar figure comes sweeping down the street in a long midnight blue dress, umbrella erected against the tumultuous weather. I try to shrink back behind the buildings, but she pauses. "Jayden?"

"Ms.—Magenta. Hello." Self-conscious, I raise a hand to my bruised face. "Is Alexa okay?" Suddenly, it's all I want to know. Nothing else matters.

"Much better," she replies. "I apologize for the...haste in which we dismissed you last night. Our priority was making sure Alexa was all right."

"Of course."

"But—I did not have the opportunity to ask after you. How is your face? Alexa told me what happened."

"It's fine. I'm not bothered by it." I lower my hand from my face. "Alexa's recovered, already? I'm so glad to hear that. She was so weak—"

"She simply needed to rest and recharge," Magenta says, a distant look in her eye. "She'll be all right." Her coal dark eyes drift down the road, avoiding mine, a sadness ghosting her expression.

"I don't doubt she will be. She's strong. I've seen her run. She doesn't even break a sweat. I was so caught off guard when she collapsed last night."

"Yes, well. She's only human. Good days and bad days," she dismisses, a distracted look on her face. She turns her eyes back to me. "I have something to help your face. Why don't you come home with me? Then you can see Alexa. She's been asking to see you."

My heart swells. "Oh, sure, thanks. I'd like that." I straighten my bike to ride.

"I meant I can drive you," she offers. "I doubt you want to be pedaling alone through the woods at this time. Not with the current news..." she trails off.

Across the street I see Chief Hanson climb out of his cruiser to talk to someone. "Uh...I'll be okay to ride. I just have someone I need to talk to first."

She follows my gaze. "All right then. If I'm not back before you arrive, Alexa will let you in." With that, she gathers her dress in one hand to lift it slightly from trailing on the damp ground and proceeds down the road, disappearing into one of the shops.

When the chief finishes his conversation, I quickly dart across the road, pushing my bike. "Hey, Chief Hanson! Can I talk to you for a moment?"

The chief turns to face me. "Jayden, good to see you." He crosses his arms. "What the heck happened to your face?"

"I was jumped at a party last night." I pull up alongside him.

"You better get that looked at—it looks pretty bad."

"I'll be fine," I sputter. "I wanted to report something. The news said we are to report anything suspicious."

"Oh?" He uncrosses his arms, his eyes sharpening with alert. "What is it?"

"When I was driving home from La Push last night, I saw something." I close my eyes for a moment, remembering the glow of the animal's amber eyes caught in the headlights. I shudder. "I know there's been a lot of speculation as to whether Sophie was attacked by wolves—"

"Less speculation now, Jayden. There's been another death very similar to Sophie's," the chief says. "I've personally not witnessed anything like it. We're keeping a look out, and meanwhile you are to keep yourself safe—"

"No, you don't understand. I said I *saw* something!" I'm breathing hard, as if I've been running. The adrenaline pumping through my veins.

"Well, what is it then? What did you see?"

"A wolf, sir. A big, big ass wolf."

He raises his eyebrows. "Jayden, we know there's been an increase in wolf activity in the area, and we do believe there is an alpha leader that has influenced the pack toward unusually aggressive behavior, but—"

"No—this wasn't any ordinary wolf. It...sir, it was the size of a grizzly. The biggest one I've ever seen."

The chief looks into the distant forest, his hand stroking his chin. "Well, grizzlies aren't typically in these parts, Jayden. Though, it's not unheard of. Some have been migrating over from Montana—"

"You don't understand, it wasn't a grizzly. It was a wolf. A very big one, and—" I want to say sinister. But I can already see the look in Chief Hanson's eye.

"Jay, listen..." He puts a hand on my shoulder. "You've had an active imagination ever since you were a kid. Maybe from all those books you like to read? And I hear from Ms. Cash you are the best student she's ever had in Literature, so... That's not a bad thing—" he says when I start to interrupt, "—to have an imagination. Listen, it was dark last night. You were driving home from a party. There was probably drinking at the party."

"I don't drink."

"Fair enough. I didn't think you did." A sympathetic look crosses his face. "Look, your eye is quite swollen. It could have affected how clear you were seeing, and the fog rolled in heavy last night—"

"But—"

"I'll look into it, okay? I promise. We already know wolves are active in the area, so we'll keep an eye out. But I'll also keep an eye out for any bear activity too. See if any grizzlies maybe migrated down to the area. Sound good?"

I don't move. Just stare at him.

"Jayden, the whole town has been shaken by this. And the timing couldn't be worse with the festival starting next week. It's our biggest priority right now—to get to the bottom of what or who is behind the deaths." He glances down the road. "It's early, but I can already see them starting to arrive and set up camp." He sighs.

"Who?"

He gestures toward a group of tourists gathered around a poster listing upcoming events for the festival. "Look, I can't go into the details of the crime scene, but aside from what the wolves left behind, it looks like maybe...human hands were responsible for this last death. Hands." He opens his up as if to show an example. "We don't want to scare away the tourists while we're trying to sort through everything. We're doing our best to find out what happened, okay?"

"Yeah. Okay." I'm already distant, taking a step back. Something inside me closes.

"I don't doubt you saw something, Jay. It's just what you saw that's the question, okay? But I'll keep a look out, all right?" The radio on his belt crackles to life. He gives a final pat of my shoulder and responds to the call.

Gritting my teeth, I swing my leg over my bike.

"One sec," the chief says into his handset. "Jayden? You never did tell me who did that to your face. Who jumped you?"

"It doesn't matter."

"It *does* matter. And I have my suspicions," he says. "Stay away from Kam. He's bad news."

Like I didn't already know that.

I shove my bike forward, pedaling hard. Down the road I spot a group from the Quileute tribe outside the Sporting Goods shop. I recognize Cole.

"Cole! Hey!" I pull up to the group.

"Geez...your face," Cole drawls. "They messed you up bad."

"Forget that." I shake my head. "Have you talked to Sam? He never got back to me last night. I—" I want to know if that was him I saw along the forest's edge when I was with Alexa. I want to know if he's okay. "I need to speak with him."

"He ditched his phone a while back. He's spending time in the outback. I told you that. Like I said, I don't see him around much. When he is around, he's spending close time with one of the elders." Cole seems bored and turns back to his friends.

"But—I just saw him a few days ago, for my birthday. And he came out to help us search for Sophie when she went missing. He seemed fine—"

"I don't know man, okay? You'll have to ask him what gives when you see him next." Cole and his buddies start to move off. "See you around, Jay."

Fury bubbles up inside. Sam is one of my best friends. I need my friends. They are my family. Why hadn't he told me he would be off the radar for a while?

One of the tribe members, Chance, has hung back. He glances quickly toward the others, their backs turned as they walk away. "Look, Sam's been developing and deepening his cognitive map of our territories and the resources within it. Like how it was done in old times—by connecting directly and deeply with nature, being part of the land. He's preparing. He's ready to find his own guardian spirit now. It's a rite of passage. Don't take it personally. He needs time alone right now."

I give a nod of thanks. But it doesn't take away the sting. I don't understand. Sam was like my other brother. Brody and Sam. We'd been close since childhood. Why hadn't he just told me that himself? That he needed time? That he was doing something important?

I take a deep, calming breath. The Fosters. I still have the Fosters. And Dan.

The rain intensifies, drenching me to the core. Another thought comes to mind. Alexa. *I have Alexa now too.*

I hope.

I jump back onto my bike and make my way out of town toward the mansion. It's cavernous wings like my other home. Just this time, without cold drafts and hollow halls. This time with warmth. And someone to...love. *That's what she said, wasn't it?* That seeing me had been like love at first sight. In the car. On the way home from La Push. *She said that.* A giddy feeling washes over me.

I pedal harder.

ELEVEN

THE MANSION LOOMS in the low cloud, rain cording the mullioned windows. I set my bike against the porch, panting from the exertion, oblivious to the cling of my soaked clothes, and jog up the steps to knock on the door. It opens and Alexa's face appears.

"Jayden!" she cries in surprise.

"Hi," I pant. "I saw your mom in town, and she said it would be okay to come see you." The ridiculous sensation of overwhelmed tears burns at the back of my eyes, and I take a steadying breath. Just the sight of her. Those blue eyes.

Her hand flutters self-consciously to her hair, adjusting a curl. "I'm so glad you came. I was worried about you."

"I was worried about *you*," I counter. "You scared me last night. You...you look well. Like last night never happened. I'm glad to see that."

"I'm sorry I scared you. Hey, I'm fine now..." She reaches forward to touch my arm when she sees the worry flexing across my face. "Really, I am. Come in."

I follow her across the threshold into the warmth of the foyer, the scent of spiced incense infusing the air with pleasant invitation. I can't stop running my eyes over her, making sure she's okay.

"How's your face?" She lifts a hand, as if to gently touch my face, but stops. "It looks so bad," she whispers.

"I don't pay it much attention. It's not the first time my face has looked like this."

"He's such a jerk, Jayden. But you put him in his place. Him and his friends."

I nod then look around, wanting to change the subject.

"Thank you," Alexa says. "For standing up to him for me. And for taking care of me afterward."

"Of course." A shyness settles between us, and we stand awkwardly for a moment, not knowing what to say next.

"Do you like cinnamon tea?" she asks, to break the silence.

"I don't think I've had it before."

"Come on." She gestures through the grand dining area and I follow her into an immaculate kitchen, its colors and appliances changed from how I remember, the cabinetry foreign with its refreshed face. She places the kettle on the hob and leans against the counter, looking out into the forest. "Jayden...what do you think that was that we saw last night?" Her voice is low.

"You mean when we were stopped on the road?" A tension washes through me at the memory.

"I feel like I'm a little hazy on all that happened after I started to feel unwell. I don't remember everything, but...I feel like I remember that."

For a fleeting moment I wonder if she remembers the word *love*. That seeing me was like love at first sight. My heart lurches but I don't ask.

"We saw a huge bear or something, right?" Her eyes stay focused on the forest with a distant look.

"It looked like a wolf." My voice is hoarse suddenly, anxiety building in my veins as the night comes back to me. The cold shadow of woods. And after. Rain upon my skin instead of the hood of her father's truck.

I shift, trying to dispel the discomfort building within.

"It was bigger than a wolf," she protests softly.

The kettle suddenly whistles, breaking the moment and she busies herself reaching for deep mugs and filling tea balls with loose leaves, the fragrance of cinnamon filling the air as she pours boiling water on top.

"Let's let these steep," she suggests, carrying them out to the dining table. I watch her set them down, last night heavy between us.

"Would you like a tour of the place?" she offers. "There's something I want to show you."

We wander down the halls. I can't get over how different the mansion looks. Alexa's family only moved in this summer yet had already transformed the place. Period décor and architecture fill each room, harkening a previous century, featuring ornate furniture made of dark wood, upholstery lined with natural patterns of fanciful blooms and fauna. Trailing down the different wings, I notice where there had been a hole in the wall now patched and papered over. Fresh paint brightens the corridors and plush carpet lines the floor beneath our feet. I know each room. This whole floor. The boards that squeak. The hidden nooks. I know all its secrets. Or rather, I did. Once. The familiar has become unfamiliar. A brocade area rug here, the curved feet of a thick coffee table there, low couches filling the once empty spaces. Each room holds an eclectic array of obscure statues hidden by darkness, random arrays of crystals, candlesticks, indistinguishable trinkets and tchotchkes. A grandfather clock eyes me from the end corner of a hallway, its steady metronome oddly ominous.

We climb an expanse of stairs and meander down more wings, passing a gable, a comfortable settee nestled to overlook the wild landscape outside. I pause, a wistful knot forming in my stomach.

"Jayden? What is it?" Alexa pauses in wait.

I remember. I was only maybe ten, curled up in that space on the bare floorboards, my jacket pulled over me, reading a copy of Mary Shelley's *Frankenstein*. Mom was on a bender with some tourist she'd brought home that seemed as if he'd never leave. Maybe he liked my mom in the beginning but he sure as heck didn't like me. Turned out he didn't like my mom either, in the end. I'd escaped many a day and sometimes a night to this very spot, the gable narrow enough to feel safe, almost cozy, when I brought a blanket and old pillow. I'd sit, tucked against the wall, and read about that patched together monster, feeling I could relate. As if I too were made of something else. Someone else. Made of pieces of another life. Always on the outside looking in at the happiness of others.

"What is it, Jay?" Alexa comes up beside me, her voice soft.

"Nothing. This just reminds me of something."

"What?"

"Someone else," I say. Someone else who was young and weak. Someone who was unable to defend himself or stand up to anyone. Who was afraid. Unhappy.

Sensing I don't want to talk about it, Alexa waits in silence for a moment until I stir and indicate I'm ready to move on. I feel her steal glances at me as we idle down the vast hallway, but I can't meet her eye. I don't want her to see in mine any ghosts from the past.

Paintings line the hallways, an eclectic array of artwork. Vibrant scenes amid threatening skies swirl across canvas as if touched by magic. The dark eyes of a lord, or the surreptitious glance of a maiden fleeing a distant castle. There are celestial arrangements spanning one panoramic canvas, its meaning hidden but felt. And an involved diorama of the human brain, synapses lit with sparkling thread.

"Your parents have...interesting taste in artwork. Quite the variety."

"Genius comes with eccentricity, I suppose," she responds, contemplative.

"Well..." she says at last. "Here we are. This is what I wanted to show you." She draws in an anticipatory breath and opens a pair of double doors.

"Oh...wow!" I breathe when I see what's inside. Bookcases line the walls, floor to ceiling. Russet furniture clusters in the center of the room, forming a comfortable reading area in front of a lit fireplace. The fire pops as a log shifts within the hearth, sending a shower of sparks. Above the heavy mantle, a large painting looms. A grim face stares from the swirl of oils, brooding eyes. There's something familiar about the face.

"Prince Vlad Tepes, Drăculea," she says when she sees me studying it. "Otherwise known as Vlad the Impaler."

"Why would your family have a portrait of the man who inspired Bram Stoker's *Dracula*?" Curious, I walk closer to examine the face in the painting; the length of dark, wavy hair beneath a beaded hat that looks to be banded with pearl, a ruby red gem at its center. And the eyes. The coldness in them. A shiver passes through me.

"Dad's a collector of things," Alexa replies absently. "*Dracula* was one of his favorite pieces of literature."

"It's one of my favorites too," I confide.

She walks over to a section of books. "Here's his collection of Gothic novels. I remember you saying that the classics are your favorites. The Gothic genre, to be precise."

"It is," I stutter in awe. I stride over to where she's standing and run a finger along the dusty spines of the worn novels, reading over the various titles. "*The Picture of Dorian Gray, The Strange Case of Dr. Jekyll and Mr. Hyde*—this book was amazing— *The Fall of the House of Usher...*" I pause when I come across *The Modern Prometheus*, the original title for *Frankenstein*. I pull it out, running a hand over its cover. A tremor of despair courses through me at the memory of reading it. The plot a sliver in my heart. *For it's a father, essentially, who left his creation. To suffer the whims and cruelties of the world,* I think. "Everyone thinks the monster in this story is the creation. But it's the one who gave him life that is the real monster. Sometimes it's the creator, the parent, that causes the most harm." By not being there at all. Or if they are there, the stupor sound of glass bottles clinking late into the night. Slowly, I replace the book on the shelf.

Alexa's eyes are soft as she watches me. "You really are a book nerd," she jokes. "You look like you belong on some athletics team, but something tells me you'd far rather be curled up somewhere reading than chasing around some ball on a field. That these stories...matter to you, somehow."

My lip curls in a faint smile. "You got that right." I continue skimming the titles in awe. "My Literature teacher says that sometimes intellect can make you feel separate from others. Because you see the world in ways that others don't. Think about things differently. I guess some people run deeper than others. Not saying I'm an intellectual or anything," I backpedal, flushing.

"I can tell you think about things differently. See things differently. And I like that about you. And your teacher is right. Intellect can separate you from the rest of the pack, so to speak." There's empathy in her voice. An understanding. "When everyone else doesn't seem to have the thoughts you do. The feelings you do. The ideas. The dreams...the understanding...it can be lonely."

She's right. I think of the boy huddled in the nook of an abandoned mansion, searching for meaning in the pages of a book because none seemed to exist beyond the world of imagination.

Searching for love.

I feel her eyes on me, the radiator warmth of her body close by. The sweetness of vanilla mixes with the musty elixir of literature. Intoxicating. Rich. The scent of promise. I'm afraid if I look at her now, she'll see how raw I feel. How exposed. How ready I am for someone like her to open me up and read my story. Become my story.

Instead, I continue running my eyes over the titles, spotting what looks to be an original edition of *Dracula*. I reach for it, gently sliding it free from the other titles.

"Be careful with that one," Alexa warns. "Like I said, that's my father's favorite. He's read it a million times. It was somewhat of an obsession of his for a while."

"I wrote about it once. A comparative essay on *Dracula* and *Frankenstein*. What constitutes a monster..." I carefully place the book back onto the shelf and take a deep breath.

"Anytime you want to read something, just tell me. I'm sure my father won't mind."

"That's kind of you." I gaze up in awe at the endless collection of books. How had I never seen this room before? Or had it become a library after? There had been some rooms that remained locked even when it was abandoned. Rooms I couldn't enter. Perhaps this had been one of them. Even so, the bookshelves undoubtedly would have been empty had I discovered it. But still...it was a room I would have wanted to shelter in. Line with the small collection of stories I owned.

"What is it?" Alexa asks. "You have that faraway look on your face again."

"It's nothing," I assure her. "Whatever I'm thinking, this is a million times better." I step away from the bookshelves looking everywhere but her, not ready to face the vulnerability of my heart yet. I look around the room, taking in the rich mahogany shelving flickering in the firelight, the rows of imperious books, weak afternoon sun dusky through the arched window. I'm suddenly overwhelmed by the opulence of the room. My heart sinks a little. *She's out of my league.* She just doesn't know it yet.

But I do.

My eyes fall upon a violin hanging from the wall on a curved hook, bow tucked behind the strings, a few loose hairs gleaming in the wavering light. "Do you play?" I ask, gesturing toward it.

"I do." She smiles.

"Will you play for me?"

"Oh..." She walks over to it, easing it from the wall. "It's been a long time, Jayden. I might embarrass myself."

I come up behind her to look at it. I can't help but notice the breadth of my size next to hers. The way her head would fit perfectly beneath my chin against my chest if I pulled her into an embrace. She looks strong, yet in this light, fragile, somehow, an aura of delicateness hanging about her. A shyness has entered her posture as she holds the violin.

"Don't be embarrassed. At least you can play," I encourage. "Come on...I'd love to hear you."

She draws a deep breath, raises the violin to her chin, then slowly slides the bow across the strings. A melancholic note emanates from the instrument with such surprising emotion, I'm caught off guard. Time seems to suspend as her arm gradually moves faster and faster, fingers sliding up and down the strings as the bow moves across them, a complicated tune emerging that is loaded with passion, anger, revelation, loss. A whole story spun by music; wordless, spellbinding. A tangled web of hope and desire, yearning. And hidden rage. Hidden fears.

As if it's my story.

When the last note dies away, I can barely breathe. "What was that?"

"Something I made up myself," she says, carefully replacing the violin on its hook.

"How long have you played for?"

She runs a finger down the length of the violin, her hand curving over its hourglass shape. "I just started playing last year. At my father's encouragement, I picked it up one day. It...it just came naturally." Her brow knits slightly as if puzzled by her ability still, a fleeting expression that crosses her face then is gone, as if nothing more than a passing shadow. "I guess I just had music in my soul already. At least, that's what my father said." She lets her hand fall.

"That is amazing. *You're* amazing."

"Thank you."

An awkward silence stretches between us. We're standing so close. The air between us electric, charged.

"Mom will be home soon. We should probably go back downstairs," she says at last, taking a step back. "And our tea will be ready to drink by now."

"Sure. Okay." But I don't want to leave the library. It's as if we've stepped into another dimension. One that contains just her and me. "Thank you for bringing me here. It's incredible."

She smiles. "I knew you'd appreciate it with your love of books."

Out in the hall, I drift further down the corridor, looking at the artwork as she's closing the library doors.

"It's this way, Jayden...to get back downstairs."

"Right, sorry." I turn to rejoin her when I notice another door ajar. I stop. Sets of long, dark hair rest atop a variety of Styrofoam heads. I take a step back and look at the array of hairpieces. The room stretches further, deeper. Surreptitiously, I nudge the door open wider. Along the back of the room, I see what looks like a workshop. Prosthetic arms and legs lining the shelves and a work bench with an open model, wires and circuits running through it. An elaborate computer system is set up behind the worktable. Sheaves of flesh-like silicone wrap the exterior of the prosthetics.

"That's my mother's workroom," Alexa's voice interrupts my thoughts. "It's private. We shouldn't be in here," she hedges.

I hadn't noticed that I had wandered inside, my eyes roving over the bionic pieces.

"This stuff is amazing," I say. On the computer screen, an image repeats over and over about the working mechanism of the arm that lies on the table.

"It is. But again, we better get out before my mom gets home. She's always scared someone will knock something over and break it." Alexa runs a hand over one of the headpieces at the front of the room.

"What are those for?" I ask.

She laughs. "Some are Mom's personal weaves."

"Oh," I sputter, embarrassed.

"It's not like you just stumbled upon her stash of lingerie, Jayden," she laughs. "It's just hair."

"Yeah, well—hair is kind of a personal thing for a woman," I stammer.

Alexa laughs again. "I don't know about that. Either way, some are just leftover props from her Hollywood days. And some she creates for cancer patients. She's in this room so much..." She glances around her mother's workspace thoughtfully.

"This stuff she's doing looks really complex." I gesture toward the large computer screen and electronics, the prosthetic open on the table, its complicated interior on display.

"She's the best out there, if not a bit unconventional with her workspace. She should be at some bioengineering firm, but she's happier working independently. She just ships finished products off or shares proprietary technology she's developed to further the advancements in prosthetic limbs. She's a genius. Both her and Dad. As I think I've mentioned...rather begrudgingly." She laughs. "They're working together to develop breakthroughs in whole brain emulation. But yeah," she trails her hand down the length of one of the weaves, "Mom is a combination of the natural and the digital. She lives in this world of technological advancement, but then she's into herbs and crystals and...stuff." Her voice trails off.

"She sounds like an interesting person."

"She is," she says, an odd note in her tone. "Come on, our tea must be getting cold by now."

She shuts the door behind us, and we meander back down the hall. Suddenly, I'm hyper aware of her beside me, our arms brushing. My interest in seeing how the house changed replaced by my interest in her. An intense interest.

"Are you close with your mom?" She asks out of the blue.

"Uh..." I keep my face neutral, afraid she'll see all the pent-up hurt that has accumulated over the years on that subject. Afraid she'll see the truth. "Close enough," I evade. "Why?"

"I don't know." She's quiet a moment. "I know my parents love me. They'd do anything for me, really...but...there's a distance there."

"Maybe it's because they are so involved with the work they do." Better than because they are so involved with a habit. A destructive habit.

"Yeah, maybe..."

Outside, the rain has rolled into thunder. A flash of lightning sparks in the window.

"How come you aren't taken yet?" she asks suddenly.

"Excuse me?"

Alexa stops walking. "By a girl," she says, her eyes lifting to meet mine.

"Oh..." A ball of emotion wedges in my throat when I look at her. *Because the girls here have grown up with me. They know I'm not some sophisticated vampire living with a wealthy family in the woods, as much as I might look it now. They know I'm not some fantasy.* But it's not just that. "Haven't met the right one yet. At least, I hadn't..."

She smiles. "Too picky?" she teases.

"Maybe," I drawl. "A lot of the girls are superficial. Too into themselves or their social media accounts. I'm kind of old school, I guess. I like real. Authentic. When I read about times before..." I glance back to the doors of the library room. "I think there was substance to be found then. True romance."

Her smile widens at the mention of romance.

"I think you'd agree," I say, taking a step toward her, "because that's *your* favorite genre."

"It is my favorite genre," she concurs. "Especially in the classics. Because it was different then. The build-up...the anticipation." She takes a step toward me too.

"You know, I dreamt of you last night," I say, my voice growing husky. "You were running. Strong. Beautiful..."

"Yeah?"

"There was something different about you in the dream." I picture her running through the verdant woods, shaded by night, lush foliage framing her form. I stop, suddenly remembering how the dream had morphed into a nightmare. The girl with the pixie hair and hazel eyes. I turn my head away. I don't want her to know about last night. About me. Wandering like some feral creature through the night.

A crack of thunder erupts overhead, lightning illuminating the hall, bathing Alexa's face in an angelic glow, then everything goes dark but for the dim storm glimmer through the windows.

"There goes the power," Alexa sighs, but her voice holds a note of soft anticipation.

Her voice steadies me. Brings me back to the moment.

"Perfect mood lighting..." I murmur and reach up to trace the contour of her cheek.

She's standing so close. Shadows caress her features, her eyes a magnetic hue in the flickering light.

The sound of tires biting through the rain up the drive cuts through the storm. Then the sound of a car door being slammed.

Alexa takes a step back, the moment broken. "That'll be my mom. We better go. I don't want her finding us up here by her workspace. She'd kill me for bringing someone up here."

We race down the corridors and sweep of hall, down to the front foyer in time to see Magenta hurry inside, her dark blue dress even darker with damp. "The spirits are angry today," she proclaims, shaking water from her umbrella and depositing it with a bang into a holder by the door. "Oh, hello Jayden. You made it here. Good. How are you, dear?" she says to Alexa.

"I'm good, Mom."

"I smell cinnamon tea. Delightful. I might make myself a cup too. Thank goodness we have a gas range with this power outage." She sweeps past the dining room and out of sight into the kitchen.

Alexa and I head toward the dining table and pull out chairs to have our tea. Somewhere in the back of the home a door slams, distant footsteps growing louder down the corridors.

"Magenta?" a voice bellows. "Another damn power outage in the middle of my work!"

Alexa flinches at the gruffness of the voice. "Dad. He can't work in the lab without power."

"What does he do out there?" I ask.

"Whatever neuroscientists do? Research. Studies. Experiments." She shrugs. "He's always out there."

"Sven," I hear Magenta call, a note of warning in her voice. "We have company."

I see her cross the kitchen and disappear from sight. A low murmur of voices rises. Alexa shifts, uncomfortable. "Maybe we should take our tea to one of the lounges." She stands but sits back down at the sound of her father's voice.

"I don't want that boy in our house." It's Sven, his voice lowered but still audible. "Alexa's had more episodes lately. They're becoming closer and closer together. It's a bad idea to have her taking visitors right now. What if—"

Magenta's low voice cuts him off, but her words are unintelligible from where we're sitting. Despite myself, I strain to hear as another burst of thunder rattles the windowpanes and a glorious disturbance of light blanches the room in a ghostly flare.

"Maybe we should go to a place with less windows," Alexa says anxiously. But I know it's not the lightning she's anxious about. It's the terse words simmering in the hall.

But the voices have gone quiet, the only sound, the storm and rain outside, and a clock ticking somewhere.

Magenta appears moments later. "Jayden, I said I'd help you heal that bruise of yours. So, let me do that. After that, I think it might be time for you to head home. The storm is worsening." Her face is lined with worry. Tense.

"Oh, okay. Thank you."

"Just wait there. I'll be right back," Magenta says.

Alexa looks uncomfortable, an apologetic expression on her face. "I'm sorry you had to hear them arguing—"

"It's okay. Think nothing of it. You were just unwell last night. I'm sure he's just being protective."

"Too protective, if you ask me," she objects.

Magenta reappears, carrying a basket with an odd assortment of items inside. "Sit here, Jayden. The light is better." She gestures to a chair by the window.

"Aren't you supposed to avoid windows during a lightning storm, Mom?" Alexa protests.

"He'll be fine," Magenta clips. "Come sit," she says to me.

Obliging, I move to the seat she has proffered, watching as she lays out some items on the table.

"I'm going to apply a Witches' Magic Healing Poultice to the affected area—"

"Mom!" Alexa objects.

"Pardon, apply a *poultice* to the area." Magenta shoots her daughter a dark look.

Alexa shakes her head and crosses her arms, pacing to the far side of the dining room.

"Whatever works," I say willingly. "Should I really believe it will work? I mean, with a name like that..." I examine what's in her hand.

"Is not belief in something, what makes it real? The mind is the most powerful source in the body," she chides gently, brandishing a confident hand as she applies the poultice to my bruise. I try not to flinch.

"What's in it?" I ask, crinkling my nose.

"A blend of arnica, calendula, witch hazel—thus the name—" again she shoots her daughter a look, "comfrey and rosehips. And of course, a little magic." She winks at me.

"Stop it, Mom," Alexa simpers. "Please."

"Embarrassed by your heritage, Alexa?"

"An online coven hardly counts as heritage, Mom."

"Then you need to understand your roots a little better. Online or not, it's about the bigger picture." Magenta fusses over my face then disappears into the kitchen to fetch some hot water from the kettle. She pours the liquid over some kind of tea.

"Online coven?" I ask around the poultice.

"Let's just say the gods failed me, so I took matters into my own hands," Magenta says. "Regardless, this concoction is used by midwives and natural healers. It works."

"He's not giving birth, Mom."

Magenta rolls her eyes and continues busying herself with my face. Another rumble of thunder causes the windows to tremble in their casings.

"You're a witch, huh?" My skin tingles beneath the poultice.

"Not your white western version," she states. "I'm afraid it was ghastly sitting on Hollywood sets and seeing how ancient traditions get trounced upon for the sake of entertainment."

"It's not done with malicious intent, Mom," Alexa says.

"No, no, of course not. And some of those stories are highly entertaining indeed," Magenta agrees while dabbing at my face. "But people should be just as curious to learn about the real stories behind the fictitious ones. Real practices and traditions. The history of different beliefs. Beliefs of those who came before." Another rumble of thunder sets the mugs of tea rattling on the table. "My goodness, that storm is close."

We remain in silence for the rest of the time Magenta works on my face. With my good eye, I glance over at Alexa still standing across the room, arms stubbornly crossed, her face turned to the window.

"There," Magenta says at last. "Take this home with you and apply it throughout the night."

"Thank you." I stand as she clears her items away, gathering up her basket.

"I can drive you home," she offers. "It's too dangerous for you to be riding in the storm." A flash of lightning illuminates her dark skin, giving her an eerie essence. Almost ethereal.

"I've ridden in storms before. I'll be fine. I like it, actually," I admit. "It makes me feel alive."

Magenta cocks her head, regarding me. "You could be a magnet for the electrical currents with the metal on your bike."

I shake my head. "The trees are taller. Lightning would strike them first."

"Foolish boy," she clucks. "Let me put your poultice in a sealed bag then. One moment."

I walk over to where Alexa is standing. "I'm sorry about that," she whispers.

"Why? I'm feeling better already."

"I mean the whole...she's not a witch. The coven just draws on old traditions. Celebrates traditional worship of spirits."

"What did she mean when she said the gods failed her?" I ask, my fingers gently probing the bruise around my face. Was it my imagination, or was it already feeling better?

"Because they almost lost me." Another fork of lightning cleaves the air.

I hesitate. So many questions, but I know better than to ask. Not yet. "But they didn't lose you. And you look...I mean you don't even have a scar."

"I do." She runs a finger down the length of her chest. "Here. And here." She points to the back of her head beneath a tuft of long hair. "There are others. Just faint lines now."

"I'd say that's pretty lucky, all things considered."

"True," she acquiesces. "But it's not an appearance thing. They don't say it, but I feel like maybe I'm not the same as I was before. That I changed." The throaty rumble of thunder congests the room with sound before another boom sets the chandelier swinging.

"If how you are now causes them any sadness, then I can only imagine how amazing you were before," I say softly.

She smiles shyly then glances back out the window. "You shouldn't go out in that, Jayden."

"It's okay. Look, the rain is already stopping. It means the storm is moving on." Together we wait in silence for the next peal of thunder. Sure enough, it comes delayed longer than the last one. "Almost sixty seconds that time. It's moving farther away."

"Here we are, then." Magenta returns, her poultice bundled tightly in a sealed plastic bag. "Leave it on all night." Her dark eyes meet mine, probing.

Unsettled, my mouth goes dry as I take the package from her. "I will." My heart skips a beat. *If I can stay in bed.* I try and fight the image of dark trees, the haunted forest. The girl from the news report.

"Goodbye, Jayden." Magenta moves toward the staircase. "Alexa will see you out."

"Thank you. For everything." I don't meet her eye, afraid she'll be able to see right through me, read my thoughts, and instead retreat to the front door and step out onto the covered porch.

The sky overhead is an eerie gray, the clouds full and writhing in a sharp wind that has picked up.

"You sure you'll be okay getting home?" Alexa worries.

My phone vibrates in my pocket. I ignore it, focusing on her, those blue eyes. I don't want to go home to an empty trailer. Don't want to be alone tonight. I want to touch her, pull her close, breathe in her vanilla scent. But I don't. Instead, I take a step off the porch. "See you in school on Monday?"

"Yeah." She steps back toward the door.

"Alexa?" her father's voice calls sharply from inside.

"I've got to go." Her face is haunted by a trace of sadness as she shuts the door.

Taking a deep breath, I hurry down the porch steps and grab my bike. I fish my phone out of my pocket and see I have five missed calls. Four from Brody and one from Miriam. A text from Brody reads: Swung by your work to see how u were doing after last night. They said u went home, so went there. Where r u? U good? Call when u get this. Dinner at 6 here. Don't be a no show.

There's one voicemail. It's Miriam. "Jay? I just wanted to see how you're doing. Brody said you weren't at work or at home. Just want to make sure you're okay. Come over tonight for dinner, okay? Mom's making your favorite. Just text when you get this. Or call. I'm here if you need to talk."

I feel a surge of warmth. I don't have to be alone tonight. I glance back at the closed front door of Alexa's house, a pang hollowing my chest that it won't be her I'm with, then shove my phone back in my pocket and jump onto my bike, the wind biting against my skin as I pedal down the drive and out onto the road, the trees shifting heavily above me.

All I can think about is Alexa's face, her eyes in the storm light. The feel of her skin beneath my fingertips when I traced the contour of her cheek.

The wind feels good against my skin. My bruise even feels less painful, my swollen eye opened a bit better to see. I swing down the narrow winding road, the memory of the search for Sophie rising in my memory, the ghost image of that night featured on every familiar twist of the road. Again, the face of Lindsay Sutton surfaces. *How do you know her face?* I search my memory, trying to recall the faces of the people congregated at La Push. Trying to remember—

Someone steps from the bushes onto the road in front of me. I slam my brakes, panting hard, almost toppling my bike. "Hey! What gives?" I cry in frustration. Then I recognize the person standing in front of me. "Sam?"

"Were you just at the mansion?" His voice is low. Tense.

"Alexa's? Yeah. Why?" Frustration burbles up. "I've been trying to reach you, you know. I was worried about you after seeing you that night out on the road. You were acting strange, man—"

"Stay away from her, Jayden. I mean it."

"What? Why?" The frustration turns to anger. "If this is because you think you had some nice conversation with her in the woods—she doesn't even remember who you are!"

"Just stay away from her! If you know what's good for you—"

Behind me a truck rumbles down the road at breakneck speed. I wrench my bike off the road just as the truck rounds the corner and speeds past. "Holy shit!" I fall back into the ditch, my bike landing beside me. As the truck races away, I recognize its cherry red color. Dr. Sven Johansson. "Where the hell is he going driving like that?" I push myself up and tear some brambles from where they have attached to my jacket. A distant boom of thunder resonates through the air, a blink of lightning tinging the cloud. "You okay, Sam? Sam?" I look around but there's no sign of him anywhere. "Sam!" I shout, breathing hard.

Nobody emerges from the woods.

"Fuck it!" Furious, I haul my bike up from the ditch and jump back on, my heart a steady rhythm in my chest. Anger, the blood in my veins.

I careen down the road, wind in my face, the sky pulsing above. It's too early to go to the Fosters. And I don't want to go home.

I pedal blindly, not paying attention to where I'm going, clouds restless above, the roads still slick from the recent rainfall. Showers tumble onto me at various intervals from the laden trees. My body moves on instinct, until I stop. The forest is silent around me. *Why here?* I'm back at the trailhead I had stumbled upon last night. The trailhead that led me out of the woods. My muscles twitch, as if guilty of betrayal. *I don't want to be here.* But something stops me. The sigh of wind the only sound, and the distant tenor of storm. The rest is silence. Peace. These woods are the woods of my childhood, my dreams—before last year when I turned sixteen and they became the woods of my nightmares. Waking alone, lost. Then waking on the threshold of horrific nightmares, as if they were real. As if I was the one—

I'm not.

I steady my breathing. I set my bike behind some bushes and trace across a narrow boardwalk, heavy with moss. I don't know where they found Lindsay Sutton, but it obviously wasn't here. No police tape marks the area. No signs of investigators scouring the underbrush. The gravel parking spaces lie empty. Nobody wants to be roaming these woods right now. Not yet. Not when there are rogue wolves prowling the forest depths. Or a killer. Maybe one and the same.

Maybe not.

I stop walking, imagining the yellowed eyes of the wolf in the headlights. I imagine that I see its gray coat skimming the leaves in the distance. *You've had an active imagination since you were a kid.* That's what Chief Hanson had said. But Alexa had seen it too. Hadn't she? But she didn't remember it as a wolf. *Did she?*

My fingers trail the damp foliage as I tread the narrow pathways, across broken boardwalks and mulched trail. *What am I looking for?* A sign? Proof? That I was here? I suddenly need to know where Lindsay Sutton was found. Where Sophie Wilkinson was found. Had I been anywhere near them? Had I maybe seen something? The scream from my dream echoes in my head. Surreal. Alive. As if I heard it.

Before it went silent.

My senses are on fire, the fresh scent of rain filling my nose. The crispness of pine and cedar. The loaminess of the earth. The pungence. The shades of green and pale crimson, plum, gold, and every hue in between. Every detail of the forest seems imprinted on my olfactory senses, on my retinas. The detail in each leaf. It takes me back to science class with Alexa. The proximity of her, the look in her eye.

The sense that we were being watched.

I run a hand across my eyes, an ache coagulating in my head. It was a bad idea to come here. *As if I consciously chose to.* Emotions twist inside me. The need to be within the forest. That sanctuary I used to escape to. Mixed with the fear of what secrets that very sanctuary holds within its dark center. And the worry that someone will find me wandering here and ask why. Yes, why Jayden? *Why is it that you wander?*

A guttural sound escapes my throat, the world closing in. I fumble with my phone to check the time. Impossibly, already 4:02pm. Too early to arrive for dinner at the Fosters but they wouldn't mind. I turn and make my way back toward where I hid my bike but pause at the sound of tires crunching down the gravel strip of road at breakneck speed.

Sinking into the folds of the forest, I hunker down onto my heels, waiting. Hoping whoever it is will move on. I want my solitude. My sanity. I swipe a hand under my nose and swallow hard. And wait.

A red truck screeches to a halt in the deserted parking area.

"Dr. Johansson?" I whisper.

He jumps out of the truck and paces the length of it, a hand pressed to his head in anguish. He kicks the tire of his truck then lets out a loud sob, sagging against the truck bed, his head against his arm.

Confused, I push back further into the bushes, peering at him through the narrow space between fronds.

"No! No, no, no, *NO.*" he cries.

Something about the misery in his voice triggers a pain just as deep inside me. The raw anguish. The despair. He chokes on his sobs, unable to catch his breath. He walks to the lip of the woods and sinks to the ground, pushing the heels of his hands into his eyes to quell the tears, his body shuddering with each gasp of air, emotion a live beast within his core.

Gradually, the sobs subside, and he sits, his head hanging, sniffling the last of his grief. Finally, he raises his head to look out over the forest. Even from where I hunker, I can see the bereft contour of his face, the hollowed-out pain.

It's odd. Crouched here in hiding, sharing a private moment of such raw agony with someone. Like dissecting a heart. The inside laid bare where normally all you would see is a steady beating, a steady pulse of life—not see the internal mechanisms at all. The complexity of emotion.

Why is he so upset? What loss has he suffered? At home, Magenta and Alexa wait in the lavish comfort of their residence. Alive. Well. It may not be a perfect love between them all, but it was still love. Togetherness. A chasm creeps open in my own chest when I think of home.

I firmly will it shut.

Dr. Johansson slowly rises to his feet, drawing one last shuddering breath before climbing back into the cab of his truck and turning on the engine. Carefully, he pulls away, and proceeds gradually down the pitted gravel, the gusto of his arrival burned out.

The minutes following his departure, all I can do is squat there, alone in the forest, leaves still veiling my face, staring at the space he'd just occupied. *What the hell just happened?* What weight in the doctor's heart would cause such grief?

Slowly, I push past the heavy brush and lift my bicycle from its hiding spot, wheeling it to the gravel road. The doctor's presence lingers, the sound of his sobs full in my mind.

Trying to brush it off, I swing my leg over my bike and make my way to the Fosters, watchful for the red truck. But as I pedal through the narrow track of forested road, my mind starts to be watchful for other things too. A stray wolf. Ghosts slipping through the forest. Anything that might offer me a sign. *What happened to those girls?*

TWELVE

"OH, YAY! YOU got my message. I'm so glad you came!" Miriam exclaims as she opens the front door of their home. "We were worried about you." Her eyes run over my face taking in the bruises and swollen eye. "Are you okay?"

"Yeah." I shrug out of my coat and offer a weak smile. "I'm fine."

"Whoa," Brody says as he comes into the front entrance. "They did some damage, huh? Though, it actually looks a bit better than I thought it would."

"Alexa's mom had a special treatment for it." I trail after them into the open living and kitchen area, Mrs. Foster busy bustling about the kitchen.

Miriam's brow puckers. "When did you see Alexa's mom?"

"Jayden, come in!" Mrs. Foster exclaims. "I'm so glad the kids got ahold of you. I'm ahead of time here, so dinner is almost ready. Can you smell it?"

"Enchiladas?"

"Yup. Your favorite." Mrs. Foster glances up from her prep work, her face falling when she sees my face. "I thought you were maybe in need of some cheering after I heard what happened last night." Her eyes roam over the bruising.

"I could always use cheering," I deflect.

"Well, come in and get comfortable." Her voice wavers a bit, but she doesn't grill me any further on what happened.

"Where's Dad?" Brody asks, grabbing a piece of chopped tomato off a plate.

"He won't be making it back in time to eat with us, unfortunately. Something came up with work at the City Hall. He'll be home later." Mrs. Foster licks a finger and surveys her dinner preparations. "I think it's time you three washed up and took a seat." She glances up when Brody rinses his hands and heads for the patio doors. "Uh...we'll be eating inside tonight, Brody."

"Oh, right." Brody looks out at the sky. "The storm."

"It's not that," Mrs. Foster hedges. She pulls the enchiladas from the oven and plates them, adding tomato garnish and sour cream. "Until they know more about Sophie's death and the death of that tourist girl, I'd feel better if we spent more time indoors. You all will need to be mindful of your surroundings—stick closer to home. Until they figure out for sure what happened." Her eyes flit to the back window.

"I agree," Miriam states, carrying plates to the table and setting them down. "I have no interest right now in wandering around."

Mrs. Foster glances up at me. I dodge her eye and quickly wash my hands then take a seat.

"Do they really think the deaths are related?" Brody asks, picking up his fork.

"Brody, wait for Mom," Miriam lectures. "And of course, they're related. They said the wounds were similar."

The room feels muggy. Like storm air. I pull at my shirt collar.

"You all right over there, Jayden?" Mrs. Foster asks.

"Yeah, I'm good." I still my restless shifting, my teeth clenched in place. I clear my throat, glancing up at Brody and Miriam. "Uh, hey...do either of you think that girl—the one they just found—do you think she was at the beach last night?"

Miriam scrunches her face. "No. Why?"

I fiddle with my cutlery. "I just thought maybe she looked kind of familiar."

"Never seen her before," Brody says, covertly forking a mouthful.

"Besides, why would she crash a memorial? Be kind of weird."

"Yeah, right." Agitated, I take a sip of water. "But if someone came down to the beach, they may not have realized it was a memorial going on if they didn't notice the photo and candles. There were lots of people there. And it's a big beach."

Mrs. Foster joins us at the table. "You think you saw her before, Jayden?"

"I must have been mistaking." I force my voice to hold steady. "After everything that happened with Kam and his friends... I guess my memory is kind of hazy." I try to ignore the memory of those eyes haunting my dream. The scream—

"Listen everyone, it's not an excuse for Kam's behavior," Mrs. Foster interrupts my thoughts, "but he *is* going through some personal stuff right now. His mom left recently. She's gone back to live on the reservation."

"How's Mr. Slade taking it?" Miriam asks, reaching for her glass of water.

"I don't know." Mrs. Foster sits back in her chair. "I don't really know the family that well. I just remember Wesley, Kam's father, back when they started dating. It took some convincing to get her to move off the reservation to go live with him. She was happy with her life there. But he was smitten, and I guess so was she. It's too bad. Seems Kam could use having a mother figure in his life."

"Why do we even care, Mom?" Brody looks bored. "We don't really know or care about that family. And Kam is a prick."

"Mind your mouth, Brody." Mrs. Foster scowls at her son. "I'm just saying this because," she continues, her focus returning to me, "it might be best to learn to walk away when people are bothering you, Jayden. If Kam and his friends start coming around—"

"I didn't really have a chance to just walk away. I mean I tried to." I set my fork down. "He kinda jumped me."

"I'm just saying...do your best to avoid confrontation."

"He just *said* he tried to walk away," Brody cuts in.

Miriam's eyes dart from her mother to me. "Kam used to bother

Jayden all the time, Mom. He only stopped a couple years ago."

"Because Jayden started beating the piss out of him when he even tried." Brody spears another mouthful of enchilada.

"I understand the need to defend yourself—I do. But it's much better if you could just walk away, as hard as that may seem," Mrs. Foster insists. "Don't get caught up in that mentality of fighting back and hurting someone just because they hurt you. It only serves to perpetuate the cycle. In the end, it makes you no different, so you must try—"

I feel the blood pumping through my veins. Steady. Strong. "With all due respect, Mrs. Foster...you're not my mother."

Everyone falls silent.

"Excuse me." I slide my chair back and head to the Fosters' bathroom to get my bearings.

"*Mom,*" Miriam rasps in a frustrated voice as I leave.

I close the door to the bathroom and lean against the counter. Bruises color my hands where they connected with my attackers, the fingertips still torn and raw from whatever the hell happened on the night of my birthday. A lump forms in my throat. I swallow hard and raise my head to meet my eye in the mirror. I'm slightly surprised to see my face looks better, the swelling on my right eye is not quite as bad as it was before. I trail a hand down my face. Maybe Magenta used a little magic after all.

There's a soft knock at the door.

"One sec," I call then flush the toilet as if I've used it and turn on the sink, studying my reflection one last time, trying to collect myself.

When I open the door, Mrs. Foster is standing there. "I'm sorry," she says. "I didn't mean to lecture you."

"I know you meant well," I respond. My heart moves in my chest. As if slightly broken.

"I know I'm not your mother, Jayden. But I love you like a son. And I'm worried about you." A sheen of emotion glosses her otherwise strong eyes. "There's a look in your eye that I haven't seen before. You had it when you came here on your birthday. A distance, Jayden. An anger. And these past few days, you've looked so...tired and spent. Distracted."

"You know I don't sleep well," I deflect, running a hand across my jaw, sniffing defiantly, trying to avoid her eye. "And last night I was out late and ran into trouble, obviously. That's all."

She studies my expression. "Jayden...I know you had that wandering episode on your birthday. We talked about it. Please tell me you haven't had another one. So soon—"

"I haven't," I lie, lifting my eyes to meet hers to try and convince her. "I'm fine."

A sadness crosses her face as she holds my eye. We both know she sees through me. "Okay then."

We stand there for a moment. Neither of us moving.

"If you were in trouble...you'd tell me, right?" Her voice catches.

"Of course, I would."

The sound of plates being loaded into the dishwasher breaks the moment. Mrs. Foster takes a step back. She wipes her hands down the side of her apron, a nervous habit of hers. "Well then, let's get back and finish dinner before it gets cold."

A physical sharpness daggers my chest. I don't want to lie to her. I don't want to push her away. But I feel cornered. Like some wild animal. Fangs bared.

*　*　*

After dinner Brody wants to watch a movie.

"The first *Matrix*? Again? Isn't there anything more—oh, I don't know—*current* to watch?" Miriam sighs, collapsing onto the couch next to him.

"What, you want to turn on the news again for something current? Hear again how they're making artificial rain in Dubai? That's good stuff. Human rain makers of the gods. Because the world is one big wildfire thanks to human idiocy—we're just lucky our little peninsula has been spared these past years. We need that manmade rain. Oh, wait...but then that'd cause mass flooding due *also* to—wait for it—human idiocy. Degradation of the earth. Well? Shall we? Turn on something current? Depress ourselves? Or how about we tune in for an update on that war going on overseas?" He raises an eyebrow.

"Never mind, you know that's not what I meant," Miriam sighs with a wave of her hand. "You win. Let's go back in time and watch your old movie fantasizing about the future. Much more interesting. Still depressing and dark, though." She rolls her eyes.

"Ha! Good! Okay, *The Matrix* it is. It's one of my favorites, you know that. Jayden, you in? It's either that or *Terminator.*"

"Ew, no," Miriam complains.

"Sure." I hate *The Matrix*. All the digital sequences streaming down the screen. The plugged-in minds. It's too close to the reality of the times if you ask me. Brains already controlled by technology. We keep inching that much closer to the virtual reality portrayed in the movie. And I want no part of it.

"You know he's just being nice, Brode," Miriam chides.

"I'll put on something else, man. Just say the word," Brody says, but he already has the movie loaded, the credits running.

"Nah, I'm good. You go ahead."

"You'll stay though?" Miriam implores, moving her long blonde hair over one shoulder.

"Why not." It's not like I have anywhere else to be. But I wonder what Alexa is doing right now. I wish I could pedal back to her place, find a spot on one of those antique lounge settees with her, and put on a *real* classic movie. Or maybe just curl up in her father's library together and read something from his incredible selection. If only he'd allow me to be there tonight.

The sound of his sobs catches in my mind. *What was he doing out there? At the trail? Why was he so upset?*

"Want popcorn?" Brody vaults the back of the couch and pulls out a bag of Jiffy Pop from the pantry, popping it into the microwave.

"No, I'm good," I reply absently.

"There's space over here, Jay," Miriam says, patting the cushion beside her.

"I'm fine here," I mumble, not paying attention, my mind a million miles away. Distracted, I stare at the movie for a minute as Carrie-Anne Moss's character, Trinity, is pursued over roof tops in the opening sequence. "You know what guys? I think I'm going to head out."

"Really?" Brody returns to the couch with a bowl brimming with popcorn.

"Yeah. Where's your mom? I want to thank her for dinner."

"I'll get her." Miriam rises to her feet.

"Don't stop the movie, Brode. I'll catch you later," I say when Brody reaches for the remote.

"Okay," he says around a mouthful of popcorn. "See ya." He lifts his fist to bump mine, his focus never leaving the television screen.

Miriam returns with Mrs. Foster, who waits for me at the front entrance. "I can give you a ride home, Jayden. I don't feel good about you being out there while the police are still trying to figure out what was behind the deaths." Mrs. Foster wrings her hands together.

"I'll be fine." I slip on my shoes and quickly lace them together. "Really. I want to ride. It's not even dark yet."

"Why don't you just stay here?" she offers. I feel her eyes on me and know what she's thinking. She can keep an eye on me then. All night. Make sure I don't leave the house.

"I think I'll rest better in my own bed, thanks."

She exhales slowly, unable to argue. "Okay, but head straight home so you don't get caught in the dark."

"Mom, you have to stop treating us all like kids," Miriam objects. "Jayden will be fine."

"I'll be sure to head home," I promise. But I already know I won't, my body on edge. I need to ride. Clear my mind.

"I'll walk you out," Miriam offers.

The storm has blown over leaving behind the scoured scent of clean air. It fills my lungs, damp, pure.

Miriam follows me to where I laid my bike. "Our place."

"What?"

"Here. This is where you proposed all those years ago," she teases.

I glance at the tangle of branches overhead, the worn circle of brick beneath our feet where a patio was once placed. "I guess it is." I shove my hands in my pocket and breathe deep the raw air. "Little known fact to that, you know, is that you broke my heart two days later." I feel a smile twinge at the corner of my mouth. "You said I made a better brother than future groom." I pick up my bike and let it rest against my side. "Broke my seven-year-old heart, you did. I was so devastated, I never loved again," I joke. It was true. I never really did have an interest in anyone after that childhood crush. Not until now. Not until Alexa.

"Well, as it turns out...I *have* a brother." She twines a finger through a length of her hair. "So, am not in need of another."

"Well, too bad. Because you're stuck with another one anyway." I smile and swing my leg over my bike.

"Jayden—" She covers one of my hands on the handlebars with hers.

I glance up at her, confused by the tone in her voice, the pressure of her hand on mine.

"I wish you didn't see us as that now. Brother and sister." Her voice drops. She moves closer.

"Uh..." I pull my hand gently away from hers. "Miriam..."

A ray of fading sunshine has ventured into the cloud. Wan and thin, its twilight casts her face and long blonde hair in a golden hue. She looks beautiful. Hopeful. Crushingly close.

But she's not who I want to be close to. Not now.

"We aren't like that, you know that," I say lightly. "It's always been our joke. That I proposed when we were kids. That we were to be married."

"Would it be so bad if we ended up together?"

"I—I don't think it would be bad, it's just...that crush was a long time ago," I stammer. Maybe not as long ago as I like to think. But still—

She takes another step closer. The fresh coconut ginger scent of her soap catches my senses.

"Miriam—there's someone else."

Her face falls. "You mean Alexa? The new girl?"

"You've seen us together." My hands on the handlebars grip tighter. My throat suddenly feels dry at the mention of Alexa's name, a yearning rising deep in my chest.

"Jayden, you've known her all of what? Three days?"

"I know it sounds crazy—"

"Uh, yeah. Just a little."

"You have to believe me. There's just something about her. I can't get her out of my mind."

Miriam takes a step back and hugs her arms across her chest as if a chill has suddenly touched her. "You barely know her."

"It doesn't matter. I know enough."

"We've known each other for *years*," she objects. As if that means anything when it comes to matters of the heart. As if time is the only requisite. If that was the case, she and I would have already—

"We have known each other for years," I say softly. "And I love you, Miriam. Because of that. In a million different ways. But we aren't kids anymore. I outgrew my feelings. You did too. Remember? You broke off our engagement two days later." I try to make her laugh with that.

She doesn't smile. "I suppose that's where you're going now? To see her?"

"I wish I was," I say honestly. "But I can't. I just...need to get out and clear my head. There's a lot of ghosts rattling around in there lately."

"Funny."

"I didn't mean—god, I didn't mean to sound so flippant. Obviously, Sophie and that other girl are on my mind. How could they not be? I just...there's been a lot going on with me lately. I need to work through some stuff."

Her face softens. "It's been hard. This week. For everyone." A genuine look of trepidation crosses her face. And sadness. "What's happening to our town?" She takes a deep breath, her arms loosening their clutch across her chest. "Look, I'm sorry if I made you uncomfortable." She turns her face away, an embarrassed look straining her expression. "I just saw you with Alexa and..." She takes a deep breath. "The truth is...I didn't like it."

"I'm sorry. I didn't know...that you...I mean—until now, you never gave me reason to think—"

"And what if you did know? Would that have changed anything?"

I shake my head. "No. Mir—I...we're family. That means so much to me. You have no idea."

She nods her head, her lip lifting in a pained half smile. "I better get back inside."

"Sure. I'll see you soon?"

She's turned away from me, already walking toward the house, still holding herself as if the air were frost bitten. "Yeah," she says. But she doesn't turn back around.

A strange sense of regret washes through me. A loss. Because I know things have changed between us.

That they'll never be the same.

THIRTEEN

WHEN I LEAVE the Fosters, I already know where I'm going to go. La Push. Maybe being there will jog my memory. Make me remember a girl with pixie hair and hazel eyes.

Or not.

Still. I need to know why that face was in my dreams before it ever hit news stations. Before it wound up dead in the forest.

The wind has picked up again, the memory of rain heavy in its gusts, the light fog, tiny pinpricks against my skin. I pass the shadow of road where Alexa and I had stopped suddenly, where the grayness of the wolf had moved through the mist. Where she'd said seeing me was like love at first sight.

Where she'd asked, "*Are* you a vampire?"

I'd almost forgotten that part.

A knot twists in my stomach. *Why had she asked me that?* Had she really wondered? *Why would she wonder that?*

A movement in the forest startles me and I push on, fearing what might be behind the barricade of broken woods as the evening light deepens to darkness.

My breath comes in short, fast bursts as I zip along the winding road, the scent of the sea now salting the air, the distant drone of surf detectable in the wind.

At last, I arrive, the beach vacant but for the tumbling surf and the mysterious sea stacks rising from its depths like narrow, mystical kingdoms. Their stark silhouettes haunt the horizon. I deposit my bike against a jumble of driftwood. The table that had been set up for Sophie still stands, legs slightly askew. Her photo has been removed, but the remnants of the candles in their glass casings remain, drooping, forlorn, forgotten. As if already years have passed since those candles glowed. Since Sophie's face lit with laughter. Time is a tricky thing. One moment here. The next, gone.

As if maybe never here at all.

I retrace my steps from when Alexa and I arrived and try to recollect the faces that passed by us as we pushed through the crowd. *Was that girl here? The pixie haired girl? Was she in the crowd?* Without realizing it, I have drifted down the beach to the rock where Alexa and I sat. I climb its rough face and perch on the same spot, reliving the sensation of her beside me. The ocean has grown wild, the surf rising as if angry by the arrival of something. I glance back at the length of sand, running over the memory of people dancing in the distance. *Where did I see that face?* My mind stops when my eyes land upon the edge of woods where I thought I'd seen Sam. If that had been him, why was he just watching? Why hadn't he come to join the revelers? I saw him, so he would have seen me. *Why didn't he come and speak to me? At least wave?* Instead, the figure had melted back into the forest. As if never there.

Suddenly, I feel aware. Of a presence. Sand spirits whisper across the surface of the beach, the displaced grains emulating the movement of wraiths. The air fills with the sound of wind, a haunted breath. The rock beneath me seems to vibrate with the power of the sea, trees moving like black banners against the night sky. It reminds me of when Sam brought me to a tribal drum circle; what they taught. That everything in nature has a spirit. I feel those spirits now. In the stone, the sky, the sea. In the cedar and fir, the hemlock; in the whispering western white pine and drooping maple vines. Once, I'd been with Sam to the tree graveyard at the mouth of the Quillayute River. There you could feel that connection to the physical world and its spirit—the thick skeleton of trees tumbled together like old bones, their tangled trunks atop black sand, a spectral mist winding over their pale cambium skins. As if in mourning.

I feel it now. The pulse of nature. Its spirits.

Who was I to be angry at Sam if he needed time? If he was on a personal quest? And who was I to be angry at him at a time when his people were fielding the ridiculous rumors of werewolves responsible for the killings. I know how sacred wolves are to them. Like the Adam and Eve of their creation. The first of their people from the Time of the Beginnings. Wolf blood in all of them. So, when the authorities suggested Sophie's death may have been caused by a pack of rogue wolves—

But then Chief Hanson had suggested her injuries didn't appear to be from a wolf attack alone. That human hands might have been at play. *Human hands.* An intelligent being. Not that wolves aren't intelligent. They are. But still...

A sharp iron taste fills my mouth. I didn't realize I was clenching my teeth, had bitten my tongue. Blood trickles across my lower lip. I spit and wipe the back of my hand across my mouth, feeling the tension of the last week culminating in my marrow.

And Alexa...

My heart snags. *If Sam feels anything for her like what I feel, who am I to be angry at him for being pissed at me?* For that same flame of jealousy had sparked in me—just for a split second—when he said he'd spoken with her in the forest. Seen her eyes. *What claim do you have on her?*

None.

But she doesn't remember him. *So, she said—*

A howl starts up behind the tree line. Forlorn. Alone. Then another. And another. Wolf cries fill the sea spun air, its tone changing as more join the chorus. From sad to sinister. Or maybe a warning.

Get off my land.

Or maybe I'm just interpreting the sound as sinister because of the weight in my heart. The weight of the town, bearing crimes so heinous, they are hard to comprehend. It's one thing to think nature acted primal on its own land. Another to think a person could have been involved.

I rise to my feet and follow the waterline, far from the edge of the woods and the cacophony of cries, back to my abandoned bicycle. I straighten it, and head for home, the cries fading into the night.

* * *

Back at the trailer park, all is quiet. I don't know how long I was at the beach. Longer than I thought, the silence of the outlying town belying the deep throat of night. At home, I park my bike against the side of the mobile and unhook the plastic bag Magenta gave me, carrying the poultice inside. Fatigue settles into my bones, but my mind won't stop whirring. I haven't slept in days. Not properly. Two of those days fraught with midnight wanderings.

Inside, I shoulder my way into my room, placing the poultice on the shelf beside my bed. I gather up my sheets from the floor. I'd never bothered to put them back after that fitful night tied to my bed. But now, I want comfort. Warmth. I leave the bathrobe tie where it is. I'll use it tonight. Just to be sure.

I head to the bathroom to quickly clean up before bed and stop when I catch my reflection in the mirror. I trace a hand down the bruised side of my face. It looks even better than it did at the Fosters. I stare in wonder at the change. *It can't be.* I walk back to my bedroom and pick up the poultice, turning it over in my hands. *If Magenta's concoction works this well, then—*

The crystal!

Grabbing a flashlight, I lumber out the door and across the lane to the dip of gully by Dan's trailer, scanning the thatch of tall grass and weeds nesting in the damp ditch. The crystal wasn't big. I could palm it in my hand. And the purple was deep, dark, like stone. It would be like finding a needle in a haystack. *If only I hadn't thrown it away in my fit of rage.*

"Whatcha doin', kid?" A familiar voice asks. Dan steps from his trailer porch, lighter flickering to life as he places a cigarette between his lips.

The lighter goes out, and his face falls back into darkness but for the amber stub of cigarette glowing at his mouth.

"Something I need is in here," I mutter.

"Yeah? And what's that?"

"Just—I threw something away while being stupid."

"Seems we often throw away the most valuable things while being stupid," he muses. He draws deep on his cigarette. The ghost of smoke plumes around him in the diffused light of a distant porch lamp sputtering further down the lane.

"I heard what happened." I feel his eyes on me in the dark, studying what he can make of my face in the dim swath of light. "You don't look as bad as I thought you would."

"Yes, well..." I push aside armfuls of tall grass, the light scouring the tangled roots. "Seems I've been blessed with a little magic."

"Seems so." Dan exhales. "Superhuman healing powers."

"No, not *me*—I got a poultice from a friend's mother."

"Hm." He sidles over to where I'm groping through the grass.

A frantic flutter of wings brushes overhead, the eerie shapes of bats chasing through the mist, their shadows caught in the light. "Dan, is there a nest or something around here? These bats—they're everywhere near your trailer."

He takes a slow drag of his cigarette, exhaling a vaporous cloud. "Must be." The sound of his lungs languorously filling then exhaling fills my head as I paw around the undergrowth. "And its roost. Bats roost, not nest."

"Same thing," I grump.

"It isn't." His voice is low. He's silent another minute, then: "Too bad about that girl. Another one dead."

A cold tingle runs the length of my spine at the mention of the deaths. "Yeah." *Pixie hair. Hazel eyes.* I paw through the ditch with growing desperation.

"Here, let me help. Whatever you're looking for, you obviously want real bad." He stubs out his cigarette and climbs down into the ditch. "Give me the light. What're we looking for?"

I hesitate, embarrassed. "A crystal, actually."

"You don't say," Dan chuckles. "Well then, a crystal it is. What size? Color?"

"About this size." I gesture cupping my hand. "And it's purple. Dark. It's going to be a nightmare trying to find—"

"You mean this here?" He bends over and scoops something up in his hand.

"Uh...yeah. How—"

"Just caught a glint of it in the light." He drops the crystal into my hand. "Whatever you want it for, hope it works." He hands the flashlight back to me and steps up out of the ditch.

"It's supposed to help with sleep issues."

"Hm." He turns his face upward, as if lost in thought, gray stubble silver in the trace of light. "Let's hope it helps you then."

"Let's hope." I climb out beside him, an odd niggling tugging at my gut. A culmination of everything the last twenty-four hours has served up.

"Well, it's late, so you better head on inside," he says after a moment.

"Thanks for your help. Night, Dan." I turn toward home.

"Hey, kid? Good on you. For using your defenses to fend off those guys."

"Yeah, well...someone taught me well."

Dan gives a small laugh. "With or without my training, I think you'd be pretty hard to beat these days. Good night, Jayden." With that, he swings open the screen door of his trailer and disappears inside.

I stare at the rectangle of closed door, suddenly wanting Dan to come back outside. To talk. To train. To be with someone. But the door remains closed.

Sighing, I retreat to my mobile, the door creaking shut behind me and drift to my room, placing the crystal beside the poultice. Straightening my sheets, I quickly dress down to my boxers, and rope the bathrobe tie firmly around the wrist of one arm before lying back against the pillow, the poultice crooked against my face.

I breathe in. Out. In. The ceiling overhead flickers with the wavering porch lamp diffusing in through the window from down the street. A wan glow. Like firelight. It dances and moves across the blank plaster, as if alive.

Breathe in, out, in.

A clock ticks somewhere. From the living room, maybe. I don't remember where all the clocks are in the mobile, I spend such little time here. The place has a deserted feel to it. As if hope slipped out the door long ago. With me. With my mother. With—

I don't wonder about him often. My father. Who he might be.

I think of Alexa's father, doubled over in grief beneath a canopy of trees. The worried bark of his voice in his concern for Alexa the night I brought her home from La Push. What would it be like to have that? Mr. Foster was great. And Dan. But to have someone in my life that was my own father.

I swallow the hard lump that balls in my throat. The corners of my eyes moisten with emotion. I don't move to wipe them.

No! I won't think of it anymore—who my father might be. Somewhere, someone romanticized about what it would be like to be reunited with their missing mother. I had that. A mother.

Not everything we yearn for turns out to be what we want.

The flickering reflection of light dances across the ceiling. Hypnotic. Alive. Like spirits telling a story. My eyes grow heavy. *Breathe...in, out, in...*

*   *   *

When I open them again, it's still dark. The spill of porch light on the ceiling snuffed out. The room like a tomb around me. The poultice has slipped from my face, my right arm almost asleep from where it's pinned over my head, tied to the bed. I reach over and undo the knot, rubbing the place where the tie chafed my wrist, and sit up. An odd sensation courses through my veins. An energy. A spark. I get up and pull on my jeans and hoodie, treading out into the living area. It's empty. As expected. Night shadows fill each corner of the room. I open the mobile door and step outside. The mist is low but thin, a skein of stars burning in the atmosphere, a million miles away. The moon is slung low against the trees, the dark shape of a bat flits past its sullen eye.

I step down a step. And another. Then dart back up to get my shoes. I need to walk. Run. There is a thirst, a desire. To be free.

I'm awake, I tell myself, as I start down the lane and break into a light jog. *This is a conscious choice to roam. I'm not asleep. Not wandering. I'm awake!* A euphoric sensation courses through me. An adrenalin. A hunger. For the woods. The air. For—

I know what I want.

I start running. Fast. Faster. A line of sweat beads down my temple as my feet pound the pavement, arms pumping, heart pumping, mind throbbing with awareness. I've never run like this before—that I've been aware of. The speed, the power. As if I've been in training. *What have you done those nights of wandering?* I shake my head hard. I won't think about that! *It doesn't matter anymore.* The steady rhythm of breath, locomotive strong. The woods brush by beside me, the pavement hard beneath my feet until I veer into the forest, the loamy mulch of earth soft against the soles of my shoes.

It's instinct.

Desire.

A *need.*

I won't stop until I find what I'm looking for.

Only a flicker of warning flashes within. A moment of fear. Conscience. Only for a split second do I think it's not right.

Then that moment is gone.

FOURTEEN

THE WOODS ARE familiar, even in the darkest hour of night. I'm never lost. Not fully. Instinct always leads me to a trail, a swatch of road, a clearing or riverbed to follow home. It's as if I belong deep within the hinterland. And at night it is no different.

But this path, I've trailed it a million times before. Since I was a child. The tall peaks of the mansion's roofline appearing through the trees, black against the deep night sky.

My heart is pounding. Blood coursing through me with a need so great, my muscles seem to vibrate and hum. I reach the forest's edge on the cusp of the mansion's untidy lawns. I want to go inside but stop myself, pressing back into the shadow of woods. An unexpected despair fills me—despair tinged with an unexpected rage. Helplessness. *This was my place.* But the rage dies the moment it starts when I look at the porch. Think of her face. That moment our eyes connected—frozen in time.

I need to see her.

But I can't. Not at this hour. Not with her parents' protective eye. Not when she'd been so weak not that long ago after the beach, Sophie's memorial. But in her hallway, there'd been that almost kiss...

I pace in place, a simmering cauldron of emotion churning within.

Selfish to come here. To even think—

An exterior light flicks on at the side of the outbuilding. I hunker deeper into the woods, watching. The outbuilding's side is windowless, its long rectangular bulk half hidden by overgrowth that has encroached upon the manor's property. Moments later, two figures exit from the building's side door and the exterior light flicks back out. But I see them, in the pale streak of moonlight, Magenta and Dr. Johansson huddled together in close conversation.

"I've almost figured it out, Magenta, if you can just hold things on."

"There is little time left, Sven. Very little time. If you don't get—" A loud crack in the backwoods stops her midsentence.

They both freeze, eyes scouring the black line of woods. The boughs shift in the wind, dark silhouettes moving softly. Dr. Johansson tilts his head upward as if sniffing the air. It smells storm clean, scented with rain. Clear. He adjusts his collar and clears his throat. "Let's get inside. The wolves—"

"Yes," Magenta hurriedly concurs, and they crisply cross the lawn and disappear inside the mansion's dark interior.

I wait for them to turn on a light, but the windows remain dark.

Some distance away behind me, another branch snaps and there is the stealthy movement of something through the underbrush that stops as suddenly as it started. I wait, muscles tensed for whatever lurks beyond. *Wolves? A murderer?* I hadn't even thought of the dangers of the forest when I left. Instead, I'd felt invincible. As if nothing malevolent had just terrorized our tiny town with the deaths of those girls. The foolishness of it makes my blood run cold. The fire that had filled my veins dissipates. I stand, tense, waiting in the shadows. Waiting for whatever's out there to find me.

"Jayden?" It's a whisper. A voice. Soft. Feminine. Carried on the currents of air.

"Alexa?" Confused, I strain against the darkness, trying to see.

"Up here!"

I glance up at the low boughs overhead, perplexed.

"No, up *here*..."

I turn to the mansion, running my eyes over the rows of dark windows until I see one on an upper floor, a figure standing there, night dress glowing phantom light in the haze of moonlight.

"What are you doing here?" Her voice is soft. Secretive. She glances behind her.

A pale glow of light flickers on in a window several rooms down from hers. We both wait in silence until it goes off again. Heart in my chest, I creep forward, my toe touching the edge of lawn. "Can you come down?" I call softly.

She hesitates. "I really shouldn't."

"Please. I need to see you."

"Jayden...it's the middle of the night..."

"I know. I'm sorry. I just—" I run a hand through my hair, my heart thumping steadily in my chest.

She hesitates. "Hold on a sec, okay?"

Restless, I pace the edge of the property just out of sight, in the shadow of trees. The minutes tick by, night lengthening. Her absence grows longer, the night darker, the moon lost behind the tall reach of evergreens and languid leaves of vine maples. I begin to feel antsy, the breeze picking up, boughs swaying like spirits. I notice on a low stump hidden along the perimeter of the property, a glass hurricane holder containing a nubby candle, wick blackened, ivory wax spilt like frozen lava, a swag of dried herbs laid before it, parched leaves rustling in the stir of air. I'm wondering what it's for when the back porch slides open, and Alexa steps out. She's changed into ripped jeans and a comfortable sweater, her hair knotted in a loose bun. My heart surges and I watch her for a moment, heart palpitating madly, before crossing the swept grasses to her.

We stand staring at each other, unsure of what to say. Nervousness moistens my palms.

"I'm sorry...I didn't want to bother you," I say at last. "I just...I'm not some creep, I promise. I just needed to see you." I bite my lip, willing myself to stop, hating how vulnerable I sound. My heart twists; suspended on a wire. She could take it or cut it down; its beats like wings, quivering in air.

"It's okay. I'm glad you came. Truth is...I was thinking about you too."

Moonlight brushes up against the blue of her eyes, turning them to silver.

"You were?" My heart soars. Nervously, I glance up toward the darkened windows, worried her parents may hear.

She lifts a hand, it hovers near my face, drawing my eyes back to her. My muscles liquefy at the proximity of her touch. "Your face," she says. "It looks better. Mom's poultice helped."

Reflexively, I lift my hand to touch where the bruising was around my eye, my fingers brushing against hers. "Uh, yeah. I must thank her. Whatever was in it really was like magic."

She lets her hand fall, knotting it together with her other hand. She looks away to the snarl of branches, the gray pall of night, a troubled look on her face.

"I meant it figuratively, of course," I stammer, sensing I've upset her somehow.

"Of course," she echoes.

I don't know what to say, what to do. I didn't have a plan. No script on how things would go when I got here. I just needed to be here, my place of refuge. In the refuge of her presence. "Want to take a walk?" I blurt.

She glances back at me. I see her thoughts churning, assessing. Or maybe they're my thoughts I think I see reflected in her eyes: The dark of night. The recent deaths. The drift of wolves in the dark perimeter of forest—

"I mean...only if you're not concerned," I stammer.

"You mean afraid? Why would I be? I'm with you."

Though she says it, I know it's more than that. *She's* not afraid. Whatever is out there, it doesn't worry her. Her eyes are steady on mine, like pools of moonlit mercury.

She slips her hand into mine, her fingers threading tight. Exhilaration erupts in my veins, the misty air suddenly charged with a thrumming bolt of anticipation.

"Let's go," she whispers.

* * *

The road's black tongue is speckled with moonlight. Once past the mansion's drive, we break into a run down the damp streets, bumping against each other, suppressing laughter until we are out of her parents' earshot, a fortress of trees between us and the mansion. I feel manic in her presence—a glorious high.

"Come on!" she cries. "This way!" She veers off the road onto a wide trail where the trees have separated, the path lit by the mystical hue of celestial light. I follow her, up, up, higher, higher, until we crest the top of a hill along the mountainside.

Panting, I double over, resting my hands against my knees.

"Tired?" she teases. She stands strong, doesn't look winded at all. Her hair has fallen loose again, it tumbles around the relaxed gray of her sweater, tufts of wind tossing it in various directions. She looks wild, beautiful. One with the night.

"Never." My heart is thundering. Alive. And not just from the running. It hasn't felt this charged in so long. Maybe ever.

Below, the lights of Forks burn like scattered cinders. From this vantage, we can see the glistening serpentine skin of the Sol Duc River— or maybe it's the Calawah or the Bogachiel River, it doesn't matter which, I'm disoriented, turned around, giddy with adrenalin and something else. In the distance, mountains loom like the shadowed face of chieftains watching over their tribe.

Alexa turns her face upward to the myriad of crystal stars above.

"Pretty incredible up here, isn't it?" I say.

"You've been to this spot before?"

"This forest...these hills...they've been my backyard." My oasis from life. Until—

No. I won't think about that now. The deaths. The waking in the middle of the night, blood trickling down my fingers—

"Sounds like you were pretty lucky growing up. With all this."

"Lucky. Yeah." My throat tightens at the simplicity of that word. Lucky to have a forest to run to when life got too hard. But that's where my luck ran out.

Until I met her.

I watch her drinking in the world before her, feeling a catch in my heart. With sudden realization, I'm painfully aware that I'm afraid to lose her. Though I don't even have her.

"This place...this land...it feels alive. Like the trees are watching," she says, her voice hushed. "There's a lot of legend around here, isn't there." I think of Sam, his people. The ancient land beneath my feet. "Yes. But those legends belong to the Quileute." There is a hollow in my heart for my own stories. I have none. Just voices from literature whispering through my soul.

Her eyes skim the razor shadow of trees, their dark crowns stark against the starlight. "Do you think werewolves are real?"

The breeze lifts, branches creaking eerily in its wake. In the distance, an owl hoots a forlorn note. "No. That was a twist on the Quileute's creation story, and it has hurt some of the elders deeply." But my mind returns to the image of the wolf lumbering across the street, its fur one with the heavy mist. Uneasily, I glance toward the shadowed labyrinth of forest.

"I don't mean their tribe," she hedges. "I mean in general. Do you think they exist...somewhere?"

"Of course not," I say, but an inexplicable chord of uncertainty tugs at my chest.

"And vampires?" She stares down to the valley below where Forks glitters like spilled magic.

My heart skips a beat remembering how she'd asked, *are you a vampire?* "No." I feel her mind casting back to the first moment she saw me hovering in the shadow of night.

"I'm not thinking of when I first saw you, Jayden." It's like she's read my mind. "I won't ask you why. I don't need to know."

I swallow hard. My fists clench and unclench nervously.

"I just need to know I can trust you," she whispers.

My breath exhales in a rush. "Of course, you can. You must know that. Or you wouldn't be here with me now, on this hill. Right?"

Slowly, she turns around, her eyes on me, vulnerability softening her face. "Because if you were...a vampire...it wouldn't matter to me."

"Are we being real here?" I stammer. But the look in her eye stills me. She moves toward me, a wisp of silk in the wind. "I'm just saying, it's you I see. And I don't care what other people say about you. It doesn't matter to me."

I realize now it's more than Kam's vampire insults she's heard. She's heard about me. My life. The boy from the outskirts of town.

I feel raw, exposed. My soul naked in the chilled air.

She knows and she's still here.

I hesitate. *She doesn't know everything.* Doesn't know about the boy who was bullied beyond words, left to bleed. Unable to fight back. All she knew was this boy. This man. Strong. Capable.

What would she think if she knew the truth? That a part of that boy was still inside me? Was still...afraid.

"That's why your mom gave my mom that crystal." The words feel rough against my tongue. To say it. To acknowledge the ghosts of my existence. *Amethyst aids with healing substance dependencies,* Magenta had said. "She knew?"

"In part..." She stops and looks away.

And it helps promote healthy...sleep, Magenta had also said. Did Magenta know about my nights too? *Did Alexa?*

Me. Outside in her yard, night thick amongst the trees. How she saw me for the first time.

Does she know? About the night wandering?

My mouth goes dry. I don't want her to know. It's one thing to be from hard times, another to be—

A freak.

The word rattles around my mind and I squeeze my eyes shut willing the voice in my head to stop.

Alexa moves close. Closer. I don't notice until she's standing before me. "Jayden...I know what it's like to have people talk about you. Judge you. I know what it's like when people are mean."

"How?" is all I can manage. My heart surges uncontrollably at her nearness.

She crosses her arms, rubbing her hands up and down as if chilled, and angles her body away from me.

"Alexa, what is it?" I place a hand on her shoulder, gently turning her to face me.

"It's nothing."

"You can tell me." I need to know. My secrets are laid like cut crystal in her hands, ready to shatter my heart if she decides I'm not enough.

She draws in a deep breath and steadies her gaze on the low moon cratered in the sky. "It was after my accident."

I'm quiet, breath bated, for her to go on. For her to share a piece of her story. To be vulnerable too.

"I told you I almost died. Maybe even did for a bit." She pulls away from me to walk to the edge of the slope, the shadowed valley silent below her. Her body is in silhouette against the moonlight. She's quiet for a long minute, her arms still clutched across her middle, fingers fiddling with the side seam of her sweater.

"What happened?" I encourage gently.

"I was with a friend. An older friend." She lets out a long breath. "Truth is, we were dating. But I'd just found out he was seeing someone else at the same time." She swallows hard. "We were arguing about it. He was driving." Her words come out broken, as if each breath is a shard in her lungs. "We...went off the road. It—it happened in Sweden, where my family was living at the time—where my father is from." She draws in a shaky breath. "We landed in a cold fjord." She hesitates. "The fact that it was so cold probably saved my life because we were trapped underwater. I should have drowned. Like he did..."

"God, Alexa...that must have been awful—"

"I don't remember being in the water." But she's there. In her mind. Her body starts to tremble slightly.

I step toward her, placing an arm around her shoulders, wanting to protect her from the memory, the pain.

"I don't remember much about it at all. Or what happened afterwards.

All I remember is that after that, nothing was the same. I woke up...changed." Her body grows still beneath my touch. "The kids at school started to treat me differently after that. Before, I'd been...popular, I guess you could say. But after..." She stops. "There were...rumors."

"What kind of rumors?"

"About how I survived."

"I don't understand."

"It doesn't matter," she says brusquely. "It was just kids being mean, you know?" Her lip curls slightly, hurt and anger simmering just below the surface. She turns to face me, cerulean eyes glistening silver in the moonlight. "All the towns we moved to afterwards, I never really trusted myself to get close to anyone again. I kept to myself. But then I met you..."

My heart catches in my chest. I don't have words. I don't know what to say. My small world filling with the expansiveness of her presence. The fact that she needs me as much as I need her.

Her mouth lifts in a sad half smile. "I'm sorry. I'm not being very fun right now."

"I don't need fun."

"No, I mean it. After what happened to you on the beach with those guys...you don't need me complaining about some silly rumors and mean people from my past."

I don't want her thinking about Kam and his friends and what they did to me. I don't want her to see me as the weak kid I was. "I can handle those guys at the beach."

"Right. And you did."

Gently, she lifts her hand and traces her fingers down the side of my face near the faded bruising. She may as well be made of fire. Her touch blazes across my skin. I catch the vanilla scent of her, faint among the damp musk of the woods. Desire ignites within.

"Guess we're just a couple of misfits in a mean world," she murmurs.

"You're not a misfit," I say, my voice rough with emotion.

"You're not a misfit either, Jayden James." She leans forward, resting her head lightly against my chest, her arms winding around my back. "And for the record," she says softly. "You aren't a vampire. It's confirmed."

"Oh?" I can't even think straight, my arms finding their way around her, mapping the contours of her waist as I draw her closer.

"Vampires don't have a heartbeat." She doesn't have to say more. I know she can hear and feel my heartbeat loud and clear as it threatens to burst right out of my chest.

"Why me?" I whisper into the curl of her hair. "Why choose me to let in?" I can't erase the first night I saw her from my mind. She was a goddess on the porch in her nightgown, sheer moonlight striking the beauty of her face. And I was the beast, hiding in the woods, body and soul torn.

She runs her face along the hard lines of my chest. "Because when I saw you...there was something about you. Call me a hopeless romantic because...maybe it's the setting...or those infernal *Twilight* books...or the fact that 'your' face is plastered all over town as the image of every teenage girl's fantasy—the boy that will love you back, no matter what your secrets." She laughs softly then goes quiet. "Or maybe it's because I needed somebody...and it looked like maybe you needed somebody too." Her hand moves to rest against my chest, grazing the edge of muscle beneath my hooded sweatshirt.

"I did need somebody," I whisper hoarsely. "I needed you."

Our conversation drifts into silence, replaced by the deep physical awareness of one another. All I can focus on is the feeling of her fingers on my chest, the scent of her hair, the pressure of her body pressed close to mine. I take a steadying breath. "I've known you for three days, but it feels like I've known you for a lifetime," I whisper. Like a secret. Afraid the universe might hear and think me not worthy of having her.

I move a strand of hair from her face. "You... you feel like home to me. Where I belong." I want to say *love. You feel like love.* But the words hang on the tip of my tongue not ready for that kind of vulnerability yet, though the thought releases a maelstrom of emotion within.

"Remember how I said I like *Romeo and Juliet*?"

"Doomed love? Yeah. It was rather inspiring," I joke.

"Did I not say star-crossed lovers?"

"I believe you did not," I tease.

She laughs. "In those five days together, they lived a whole lifetime of love."

"Do you have vials of poison in your pocket for us then?"

"Ah, but Juliet faked her death, remember? Romeo mistakenly thought her dead. Yet she lived." She smiles. "If only he had hung on. Waited. He could have known love with her yet."

"Hm."

"I think what that story taught me is you don't always need time to know how you feel about someone." Her voice is low, inviting. I try to read behind each word she says. "And if Romeo hadn't acted impulsively, if he had worked through his grief instead, Juliet would have wakened, and they would have been reunited."

But they would have been ruined by their families, I can't help but think. Their circumstances still standing in their way. *Ruined by drink. By a rundown mobile home. Ruined by the truth.* I feel my smile fall.

She doesn't notice my expression in the dark, her eyes faraway, a sadness stealing across her face before she angles her head to look up at me, an intensity behind her eyes. "I don't want us to be a story that somehow ends."

"You say that as if you know something. About our ending..." A hollowness opens in my chest. A panic. Because now that she's here, I can't imagine life without her.

"I just know that in real life, not all stories have a happy ending."

"Then we make one."

The air sighs and settles around us. It's the deepest part of night. The time before dawn. I can feel the shift in the atmosphere. All I know is that I don't want our story to end either—don't want this night to end. With her, everything feels bigger. The vastness of life surrounding us. The trees, the mountains, the distant rivers and sea. The stars overhead. *The possibility...*

Whatever darkness might be lurking far within the forest's depths, or in the corners of the universe, it doesn't exist here between us. Not tonight. I don't want her to stop looking at me this way, as if I'm the fantasy she's always dreamed of. I don't want my feelings to stop. Or her feelings. I don't want my old life back. I didn't want it to begin with. There are no words for what she means to me. *Already.* In such little time. Tentatively, I tuck a strand of hair behind her ear then cup her chin in my hand, tilting her face toward me, searching her eyes. "Alexa...what are you doing to me?"

She steps back and takes my hand, sinking to the ground, guiding me down beside her. We lie like that, beneath the starlight, looking at each other. The ground beneath us is cold and soft, the dampness of the earth causing goosebumps to ripple, making me more aware of her touch when she runs a hand across the line of my collarbone, her fingers trailing the perimeter of skin above my hoodie's neckline. I move toward her, hesitating, to make sure she wants me to. She smiles softly. Eyes on hers, I lean in, trailing my lips across the smooth skin of her cheek, along her jaw and down the side of her neck, pausing by the hollow of her throat. It's not been like this before for me. With anyone. I hadn't wanted anyone in this way. Not for a long time. *Not ever.*

My past held a handful of kisses and fumbling touches upon the moist bed of coastal sand, always instigated by the other person. I'd always find a reason to stop. It felt too vulnerable, being close. Too exposed. At first, I thought it was because I still felt like the beaten boy, but as my body changed into something stronger, sharper, I realized that wasn't it. It was that my heart was linked too inextricably to my desire. I needed to *feel* something and know that they felt just as much. I needed to know they wouldn't walk away after. Though a happy ending isn't promised, I feel in Alexa's touch that it's what she wants.

And I want it too.

She pulls my head up, her lips catching mine, and all thoughts melt away.

We are lost like that. Time losing meaning, as if the only place I've ever been or ever wanted to be, was here in her embrace. Her lips are soft, warm. Inviting. Everything I imagined. And more. A molten passion flames inside as I thread my fingers through her hair. When she pulls back at last, it's a physical loss. A part of me missing. I lean forward, seeking her again, but she drops her head, her hand pressed against my chest.

"Jayden, I need to stop."

"What is it?" Our foreheads rest together, my lips still wanting to find hers, our quickened breath mingling together.

A buttery dawn has started to striate the horizon with muted sepia light.

"I—I need to get home." She pulls away from me and sits up, wrapping her arms around herself.

"Are you okay?"

"The sun is rising. I need to get home. Before my parents find me gone."

But it's more than that, I can tell. "Is it like what happened to you at the beach? Are you feeling all right?"

"I'm fine." But she says it too quickly.

We rise to our feet, clots of moss and grass falling from our clothes as we brush ourselves off.

We descend the rocky trail in silence, avoiding the snarl of roots, her cool hand in mine.

The forest shadows are pocked by shimmering light as morning grows. Finally, we reach the strip of drive up to her home, quietly treading up the worn asphalt and around to the back. We step onto her back porch, a shyness settling between us, as if the spell of night has been broken by the rising sun. It was easier to be vulnerable beneath the cloak of night. But here, in the light, everything becomes clear to me yet again as I watch her, sunlight sliding over the richness of her skin, the gloss of her hair, the mansion stolid behind her, her palace. My once upon a time kingdom of escape. A kingdom that was never mine, in the end.

She's too good for you.

My skin still burns where she touched it, the taste of her lips still sweet on my tongue. But day is coming, night already feeling like a dream. The magic chariot becoming a hollow gourd.

"Jayden, I'm sorry. I didn't mean to ruin our night."

"You didn't."

"You mean it? It looks like something's bothering you."

"It's nothing." I try and memorize her face as it looks now, an overwhelming sense of dread seeping into my heart, a worry. *She won't be yours forever. Not all stories have a happy ending.* I know that better than anyone.

Impulsively, I step forward, wrapping my arms around her, inhaling the rich fragrance of her hair. As if she were returning to her tower and I to the barren lands beyond.

"What is it?" she coaxes gently as I pull away.

"Nothing. Just my imagination—always in story mode. Sometimes it runs away on me."

She reaches a hand to caress my cheek. "I like that about you. Life is more interesting with a little imagination." She takes a step back and glances up to the darkened windows. "I better get in before my parents notice I'm gone," she whispers.

"Okay." I take a step down from the porch as she turns to go. "Alexa, wait—" I jump back onto the porch and cross the distance between us, my fingers catching her elbow. It feels like a plea, a desperate attempt to grab onto hallowed fairy dust before it scatters in the wind.

She turns to face me. "What is it?"

I love you. "Nothing. Just...I had a good time tonight."

"Me too." She kisses her finger and presses it to my lips then disappears inside.

I stand staring at where she once stood. There's nothing more I can do, so I go.

Each moment I'm away from her feels like a lifetime.

Each moment I'm away from her, too long.

It's not until I'm making my way home through the forest that I remember what she said about why she wasn't afraid of seeing me on the wooded edge of her property that first night—how she compared me to the *Twilight* fantasy boy. *The boy that will love you back, no matter what your secrets.*

She must have forgotten. It wasn't the girl who had secrets.

It was the boy.

FIFTEEN

MY MIND IS still with Alexa as I trudge through the dense thicket. The way she felt wrapped in my arms. How her fingers blazed a path down my skin. The depth of her eyes.

But the further I venture from her, the more uneasiness settles in, the worry that I'll lose her. *Because something's not right with me.*

A dull thud begins to tap at the base of my skull. I realize I haven't slept in a long time, my limbs heavy with a gathering lethargy. *How many hours has it been since I slept? Really slept?*

How many days?

Despite the sunshine sifting through the veil of branches, the forest feels cold, damp. My instincts waver as I swat at my neck where a leaf trails a clammy tendril. The earth smells pungent, loamy. Like rot. I stop for a moment to gain my bearings. Beneath my feet, the soil sinks, slick from recent rain, oozing soft earth over the toe of my shoe. I draw back at the sight of a vibrant splotch on the ground, glimmering red. Like blood.

Pixie hair. Hazel eyes.

I blink, swipe a hand across my eyes. *A leaf. It's only a leaf. Autumn come early.* I stomp on the frond scattering its shimmering sheen of dew, and rub my eyes again, lumbering forward. *I need to get home.*

The air moves with serpent stealth through the leaves, a sigh like whispered words. *Jayden...*

I stumble to a stop, heart stuttering at the sound. "Who's there?" I shout. Nothing. Just the hushed exhalation of wind. I shake my head and rub my eyes again. Exhaustion weighs my bones as I push forth, the forest seeming denser somehow, brambles and brush impeding my every turn. But I'm not lost. I'm never lost out here.

You were there...

I freeze. In my periphery, I think I catch a length of long blonde hair. *Sophie?* My muscles clench instinctually, breath jagged in my chest, as I slowly turn my head.

Nothing.

Just a wisp of holodiscus. *Oceanspray.* Cascading pale flowers fluttering like a wild mane.

A vile nausea surfaces as I stagger forward, glancing back one last time before picking up my pace, fast, faster, until I break into a run. Branches and leaves claw at my face, my wooded sanctuary turned prison, secrets oozing from the forest floor. Secrets I know nothing about.

Or do I?

I emerge from the forest and cross a ditch, climbing up onto the road. I stumble along the road's shoulder when I hear a voice.

"Jayden? What are you doing here?"

"Mrs. Foster?" I turn to see a blue Tesla pull up beside me, window rolled down.

"It's almost seven—on a Sunday morning. What are you doing out so early?"

I press the heel of my hands to my eyes, try to quell the thoughts strangling my brain; try to go back to the euphoria of holding Alexa. *Calm the fuck down,* I chastise myself. *It was your imagination. Your exhaustion. Your—*

"Are you okay?" Mrs. Foster asks, her eyebrows scrunched with worry. "Were you—"

"*No!* I mean, I'm awake—was awake. All night." I can tell from her face she's worried I had another episode. "I wasn't—it's not what you're thinking."

"Get inside. I'm going to drive you home."

"I'm fine, really—"

"Please." She leans over and opens the passenger door.

Reluctantly, I climb inside. She pulls a leaf from my hair, her face a mask of concern. "Jayden—"

"I promise you, I know what I was doing. It wasn't like that."

"Okay." But she's not convinced. She puts the car in drive and pulls forward. We drive in silence for a few minutes. I can feel her thoughts churning.

"At least your face is looking better." She glances over at me. "Much better. I'm surprised. I guess the bruising was superficial."

I turn to look out the window, my face away from her.

"I have an early morning showing on Robin Hood Loop, so was headed to the home to get it ready—lights on, fireplace going—that sort of thing. Lucky I was out so early and found you."

"Lucky." I keep my eyes on the line of trees zipping past.

At last, we near the entrance to the trailer park.

"Here is fine to stop, thanks, Mrs. Foster." It's not like there are any secrets. The Fosters have known since I was a child where my home is. The whole town has. But seeing the mildew streaking the rooftop in the early morning light is more than I can bear. I don't want her to pull up alongside the mobile. The weeded flower pots. The patchy square of lawn. I don't want her to see the sad little lane in the morning light.

And she doesn't wish to humiliate me. She knows. She eases over to the side of the road. "Listen, Jayden, I was thinking...I talked this over with Kent too. We think maybe it might be a good idea for you to come live with us for a while."

"Oh, thank you—and Mr. Foster too—it's nice of you to offer but I'm fine. Really."

"You had that episode recently..." She trails off. I know she's wondering if I've just had another despite what I said. "And I know your mom hasn't been around much—"

"It's fine. Everything is fine."

"Jayden, I've seen her a couple of times recently, so I know—" she stops. "I know that maybe she's not in the best situation right now."

"She goes through spells. Some worse than others. It will be all right," I say, and open the door.

"We just want to make sure you're safe. With everything that has happened in town this past week—the thought of you being alone here concerns us."

I stare off into the distance, my heart in my throat. "If—when—Mom does come home, I don't think she should be alone at the place. She'd be safer with me around."

Mrs. Foster considers what I'm saying, a pained expression on her face. "You're a good son, Jayden. Just—the offer is open, okay? So, anytime, just come. If you want."

It's not the first time she's offered. When I was a kid, I'd lie to her sometimes when she invited me to come stay with them for an extended period. I'd say Mom was home and sober when she wasn't. Though I loved the Fosters, I didn't want to be anyone's charity. I had too much pride for that. But I did sleep over when I was young. A lot. And ate meals at their place several times a week, never declining a bag of 'extra, won't be eaten otherwise' leftovers she offered to send home with me. It was unspoken between us. They cared for me in ways my mother never had. But I could care for myself now.

"Jayden, you're sure you're okay?"

"Just tired," I say, closing the car door. "Thank you for the ride."

Her face is lined with worry as she pulls away.

*   *   *

The trailer is quiet. Too quiet. I lie back on my bed, thinking, wondering how Alexa is feeling. She'd been so silent when we hiked home. So distant. Something had been wrong, but what? Because before that—

My heart skips a beat at the thought. Our bodies tangled together on the damp hillside, hands in her hair. I'd never felt so close to anyone.

Ever.

My pulse quickens at the memory, warmth thrumming with each beat. It's embarrassing, how I can't contain my emotions when I'm around her, how my heart beats uncontrollably when I'm around her. She knows. She heard it when she rested her head against my chest.

It's confirmed. You aren't a vampire.

My brow knits. I sit up.

Restless, I walk to the bathroom, stare at my face. The face of a fictitious vampire. I examine the hard chisel of my cheekbones. *Vampire.* It was a joke that wouldn't go away. A taunt. A threat. I know Alexa didn't mean it like that. But ...

Why are you here? To give another girl the kiss of Death? My fists clench at the thought of Kam. I close my eyes, the night on the beach coming back to me. I can almost feel his fist strike my face.

My face.

I open my eyes and look at my reflection again.

All evidence of that night on the beach, nearly gone. Healed.

As if it never happened at all.

I lumber back to my room, grab the poultice from its spot on my mattress where it had fallen from my face last night. I pick it up, turn it over in my hands. *A blend,* Magenta had said, *arnica, calendula, witch hazel, comfrey, rosehips*—I smell the poultice. It's herbs. Plants. Nothing more. *Right?*

The muscle twitches in my jaw. *You don't look as bad as I thought...Superhuman healing powers.* I pace the room, Dan's voice echoing through my head.

Don't be ridiculous.

Sweat beads at my temple. I hurry back to the bathroom, knocking over the jar that holds my toothbrush, my mother's toothbrush, my hands clenched on the sink's edge as I examine my cheek, jaw, eyes. Not even a hint of purple. Black. Green. Not a single shadow of bruising. The once swollen eye stares back at me, panic behind its pupil.

Well? What is it? Magic or vampire blood? What was the cure? My mind churns, chest rising and falling hard as I push back from the sink, confused. I run my hands down my face again.

You've had an active imagination ever since you were a kid. Chief Hanson.

"Stop!" I shout at the mirror trying to silence my thoughts. Pushing away from the bathroom vanity, I hurry down the narrow hall and wrench open the front door, vaulting the few steps to the ground. I grab my bike. I need to clear my mind.

Cloud has spilled over the sunshine, turning the sky Forks gray.

Normally, all I want is woods and wind, sea and sand to escape my thoughts, but right now I want to see people. Be surrounded by the mundane. The normal. *You're just overtired,* I try and convince myself. *The stretch of sleepless nights are getting to you. You're not thinking straight.*

I push down on the pedals, pump hard, harder. My legs tense with the need to ride, run, escape. Escape my thoughts.

When I reach town, I'm startled by the number of people thronging the streets. Then I notice a sign and remember. *Of course.* Less than a week until the annual Forever Twilight in Forks Festival. Each year, tourists arrive early from all over the world to tour the place where the romance began. It has been like this for years. The only thing that stopped it one year was the pandemic blip of closures. But it's back, full throttle. Our town eager to receive the never-ending fandom. Eager to share its piece of the mystery. It's disorienting, all these people, but I get off my bike and wheel it among them, absorbing the thrum of excitement that pulses in the streets—a pulse that will swell as more fans arrive in time for the festivities. What I notice, also, is a strong police presence. Members from the precinct scatter the crowds, asking questions of some of the locals, eyes sharp on the faces of the tourists, many who probably haven't followed the news. Don't know about the deaths. Their love of the franchise too consuming to notice or care about the real drama unfolding in the town.

A murmur of excited voices rises as a truck drives by; loaded on its bed, the wedding arch used in the movie *Breaking Dawn* from the *Twilight* series. It makes its way down the road enroute to the location where it will be set up for the festival. The very arch that Bella Swan and Edward Cullen promised a life of eternity to each other beneath. Ridiculously, I feel a pang. The thought of forever with someone. That kind of intense love. I hadn't known I craved that for myself. Needed it. Hadn't known until...

Alexa.

Just the thought of her quickens my pulse. I grip the handles on my bike and continue pushing it down the street, allowing myself to be pulled into the fervor of tourist excitement, away from the delirium of being at home alone with my thoughts.

"Oh. My. God."

I'm stopped from my progress forward by someone grabbing the back of my hoodie. I turn to see who has stopped me.

"Oh my god, it *is* him!" A college aged girl covers her mouth, her eyes wide as a circle of friends near her clamor around.

"You are *way* more handsome in real life!" another exclaims.

"Uh—" I take a step back, angling my bike between them.

"Edward Cullen? No way!" another girl squeals. People nearby turn to look over.

"Is it Robert Pattinson?" someone whispers.

"Can't be...shouldn't he be like—in his thirties or forties or something?"

"Edward is forever young—in body!" someone enthuses.

"Oh—no—I," I stammer. "I'm not the actor—or the vampi—"

A woman has leapt over beside me, her phone poised in the air. "I need a selfie!"

"Dear God," I breathe, glancing around for an escape. This happened before, to a lesser extent. The year when I started to change, fill out, my body and face chiseling away the boy, and Dan's training, strengthening my muscles...the resemblance to the movie star had started to emerge. And now, at seventeen—

Another girl smushes herself against me, an arm wrapped tight around my waist. She is vibrating with excitement.

"Ladies, ladies..." a familiar voice interrupts. I shoot a desperate glance over to the voice and see Chief Hanson. "I see you have found one of our locals, here. He *does* bear quite a resemblance, but he's not the real deal."

"A local?" a girl twitters. "I am *so* moving here."

"If he's a local, we have to go check out the reserve," another one insists. She's wearing a Team Jacob shirt.

Still the girls gather around, their ages varying. Among the small crowd, two women with gray at their temples flash smiles for a selfie.

"Okay, that's enough," Chief Hanson says good naturedly. "I think Jayden here has somewhere to be. Enjoy the town and the festivities this weekend." He bids farewell to the tourists and they fall back, still twittering away.

The chief slings an arm around my shoulders and guides me away. "You might want to keep a low profile this week, young man, unless you want to help the town's tourism and be the Edward cosplayer at the Welcome to Forks part of the festival this weekend. You're really growing into the role here." An amused smile lifts his face as we stop further away from the road and its swarm of people. His brow knits when he looks at me, a perplexed look crossing his face. "You're looking better. I thought your face would be messed up for a while the way you looked the last time I saw you."

"That might have been helpful for this weekend," I deflect and give a weak laugh.

"Guess so," he concurs with a laugh, and lets it drop. His eyes turn wary again as he turns to scan the numbers of people moving along the street and parkways.

"Have they figured out anything more? About the deaths?" A cold sensation courses through my body at the thought of the murders.

"Not yet. But we're working on it. This..." he gestures to the abundance of tourists, "complicates things."

I swallow hard and glance down a side road. I see the tavern where my mom works. Mrs. Foster's Tesla is parked outside. *Crap.*

"You just stay vigilant yourself, you hear?" Chief Hanson says, his radio crackling to life. "Avoid the woods. Keep an eye out for anything suspicious in town." He responds to the radio request then gives a slight smile. "Maybe wear a disguise or something for this week. Or you could be in trouble."

"Got it."

He pats me on the back and heads off, speaking into his radio transmitter.

My eyes drift back down to where the Tesla sits. I push my bike down the short drive. It's early, the tavern parking lot empty except for Mrs. Foster's car. Then I hear voices, hushed. Angry.

"Chantelle, you have to let me get him seen again."

"No." My mother's voice.

"I think he's having more trouble. You said the doctor said it was just stress related—"

"I said, no. He's fine." I recognize the slur in her voice. My knuckles whiten on the handlebars.

"Look, why don't you let him come stay with us for a while? Until he's feeling more himself again—"

"Jus' because you paid for him to go to Seattle...to see that...quack—doesn't mean you own him. He's not your family. Not your son."

"Chantelle, there could be a murderer on the loose and we're not comfortable with him being all alone at the—"

"He's a grown boy, Jill. Have you seen him? Strong. Yeah. So how about you mind your business now."

From behind a tall bush, I see them standing near the backdoor of the tavern where it leads to the kitchen. "I'm thankful for what you did," Mom continues, "but it's enough now. He's fine." With that, Mom staggers a bit and reenters the tavern, shutting the door behind her. Her shift won't be until later, I know. She usually works night. Spends the day drying out doing God knows what.

Mrs. Foster lets out a long exhale, her bangs puffing with the force of it. She clenches her key fob tight in her fist and stalks back to her car, climbs in, and cruises out of the parking lot and down the street.

So that's how I was able to go to Seattle. A mix of emotions twine through my gut. Gratitude. But also, humiliation. Anger. I don't want to be someone else's burden. It couldn't have been cheap. And all that time Mrs. Foster had known and not said anything to me about it. Maybe she was just trying to protect my pride.

Still.

She hadn't been honest with me. She'd known. And she didn't say a word about it until Sophie's death. What was it she'd said? *Sometimes people who wander can hurt others. They aren't in their right mind. They don't even know what's happening.*

Was she doubting me? Even a little? My innocence?

I sling my leg over my bike. I need to get out of town. It wasn't the distraction I was hoping for today.

"Excuse me...are you that vampire in the movie?"

I turn and find a young girl, maybe eight or nine years old, looking up at me, an information brochure in her hand for the upcoming festival.

"You've watched the movies?" I look up to see if I can spot her parents. "Aren't you a bit young for vampires?"

She shakes her head.

"I'm not him, I'm sorry."

"But you look like him," the girl insists.

"I know—"

"You have the same sadness. And you look lonely. All alone. Like he was. Before he found Bella."

"Caitlyn!" a voice calls.

"I have to go." The girl runs off to find her parents, blending into the crowd.

I stare after her, her words hatching a heaviness in my chest.

Up on the road, people walk by in clumped groups. Family. Friends. Together. Laughter lighting their faces. A strange emptiness clenches my gut as I glance back toward the tavern. For a life I'll never know. Not in the way I should.

You have Alexa now, I remind myself and my heart stutters with hope.

"Jayden? Hey, man!"

"Brody, what are you doing here?"

"Got called into work this morning," he sighs. He's wearing a golf shirt with a name badge of the sporting goods store he works for. "I'm just on break. A bunch of us were supposed to be hitting the waves this morning, so I'm choked I had to come in." He tosses a paper coffee cup from Mocha Motion into a trash bin.

"Oh."

"I invited you, but you never check your phone."

I pull out my cell and see three text messages from him. "Yeah, sorry."

"I don't know why you even bother having one," he laughs. "Half the time you don't even have it on you."

"I know. I got it when I was applying for work, so potential employers could get ahold of me. After that, I thought it would be important to keep for work, but..."

He laughs. "Steve's a good guy. He just tracks you down when he wants you in for a shift. Speaking of, I just saw him. He said if I see you to get you to call him or drop in. He saw you and said something about you looking better—which you are, by the way. Holy shit, man, you healed fast." He lets out a low whistle. "Anyway, he wants you to come in for tomorrow. Guess you'd switched your schedule or something for later this week? The store is really busy with all these extra people." He surveys the crowd.

"Okay, thanks. I'll give him a call."

"You okay?" He swings his eyes back to me. "You look kinda jumpy."

"Nah, I'm fine." I catch a glimpse of my reflection in the window of a car that eases down the drive toward the tavern. *I have a heartbeat. A reflection.* I swallow hard. "I think I'm just...really overtired or something."

"You look it. Are you going to head home to rest?"

"No. I'm...itching to get away. Do something. Anything."

"Well, my board is all waxed and ready to go if you want to hit up First Beach. It's just sitting outside the shed under the cover. Or you could use the one you usually borrow. Just get Dad to let you into the shed. He should be home. The suits are still hanging on the hooks outside, if you want to grab the one you use." He shoves his hands in his pocket. "You should go, Jay. Have some fun. Looks like you could use some."

"Thanks, man."

"No problem. Catch you later." He bumps my fist with his and swivels on his heel, heading back to work. "Oh, hey!" he calls, turning back. "You seen Sam lately?"

Sam's face drifts across my mind. Hostile. *Stay away from her, Jayden. I mean it.*

"It's usually his favorite time of year," Brody continues, "what with all the tourist girls." He laughs then immediately sobers. "Though some whack jobs are starting to seriously talk about werewolves. The talk got worse with the second death of that other girl. Guess that would have pissed him off. It's one thing to pretend to be a sexy stud werewolf, another if people equate you to a killer, huh?"

"Yeah." The amber eyes of the wolf in the mist wanders through my mind.

"You all right, bro?" Brody narrows his eyes, scrutinizing me.

"Uh...yeah. Sorry. I guess Sam's on some spiritual quest or something. I saw Cole and Chance with some of the others from the tribe—that's what they told me. That's why Sam's not been around much."

Brody shoves his hands in his pocket. "Don't know why he didn't just mention it to us, though. He's been getting to be like you—not returning texts. Disappearing."

"He's ditched his phone."

"Still. Could have told us before falling off the radar like that."

"It's a personal thing if I understand it right. The spiritual quest. Private to his culture. Or private to him, anyway."

A light rain starts falling, fine as mist. Brody looks bothered, his usually jocular face tightened by a trace of pensiveness. "Feels like things have been changing, you know? With our group." He doesn't meet my eye. "Some kind of drift."

I thought I'd been the only one drifting. Wandering. Losing my way, a little. But while lost, it felt like I'd found something too. Found Alexa.

Before I can say anything else, he says, "I better head. You go. Surf.

Have fun in La Push. Though, you might want to go undercover. These tourist girls catch sight of you, and you'll be in trouble." He gives a light chuckle, then turns, giving a jaunty wave as he heads off. But the lightheartedness is missing. His posture stiffer than it should be.

A pit gnaws at my gut watching him leave. He's right. The group has been drifting. I hadn't noticed because I'd always felt like I was drifting but realize now how alone I'd be if the rest of them drifted away too. Or Alexa...

An emptiness seeps into my heart, a fear. This is the danger of caring. The danger of love. Because losing it can leave you shattered. One thing I'd learned in life is if it's too good to be true, maybe it is. Maybe it won't last.

Suddenly, all I want is to be lost in the waves. Alone, surrounded by nothing but sea. Just me against the surf. No other demons to haunt me. Nobody to let down. And nobody to let *me* down either. I sling my leg over my bike and ride across the rutted grass, away from the stream of people, pausing briefly at the Thriftway. I spot Steve outside, checking a display.

"Steve!" I call.

"Jesus Christ, Jay," he says when he turns around. "I thought maybe it was just the distance playing tricks on me but look at you. How the hell did your face get back to normal in, what, twenty-four hours?"

"A friend's mom gave me some stuff for it." I swallow hard, my toe scuffing the ground where I'm straddling my bike. "Brody said you wanted to see me?"

"Yeah." He gestures to the crush of people inside buying food. "The tourist numbers are even more insane than usual this year. If you're healed up, I'd really like it if you could keep your shift for tomorrow. I know I said to come in Friday instead, but if you're good, we could really use you. I checked the schedule. You were originally supposed to be in tomorrow—Monday—then Thursday. But why don't you come in after school Tuesday too—pick up the shift you missed yesterday. I know you want the extra work."

A wind picks up, laden with the soft spit of rain. I feel restless. I just want to ride. Run. Climb a mountain and stare at the stars. Be with Alexa. Leave the world behind. Together.

Instead, I say, "Sure."

"Great. See you tomorrow." He disappears back inside the sliding doors.

* * *

At the Fosters, I grab Brody's board and fasten it to the board rack on my bike then grab a suit that fits me off one of the hooks. I don't knock on the door to see if Mr. Foster is home. I'm worried too that Miriam might be in there. I can't face the awkwardness of seeing her right now. Not after our last time together. As I wheel my bike out of their yard, I pass the tangled arch of boughs over the broken circle of brick where she and I last stood. The place where my seven-year-old self proposed, sure that Miriam was the only girl for me. Sure we'd be together forever.

A twinge of nostalgia surfaces, the ghost of laughter filling the yard, the mist shaping spectral images of us as kids—or so it seems. *Me, Miriam, Brody.* Lost in the haven of friendship. With them I could forget for a moment where I came from. Who I was. Brody was always there to hang out with. And Miriam always had my back—was always there for me.

But something had shifted. When she turned away. The sanctum of childhood ties untethering.

And there had been Sam too. The four of us against the world.

I blink back the burn of emotion that pricks my eyes. Nothing stays the same. Not forever.

I hover a moment longer in that space of broken brick, the yard filled with its ghosts of memory. The people we once were, slowly disappearing. Becoming phantoms of the past.

I push my bike forward and head off onto the street toward La Push.

SIXTEEN

WHEN I REACH First Beach, there are more cars than usual parked in the parking lot, the beach dotted with people. Many are likely tourists who have come for the festival, eager to see the strip of coast where Jacob shared his tale of the 'cold ones' to Bella for the first time.

The sea stacks seem to waver in the haze, the mist deepening, rain cold against my skin. I hope the weather drives people away. But then again, it's Forks. If you come here, you must know what to expect with the weather. I push my bike off to the side, away from the main parking area, and strip down behind a jumble of logs, wriggling into the wetsuit, then hoist the board over my head. I hit the beach, keeping my face half concealed so no tourists will spot me or confuse me for what they came here for—*a fantasy*—and head toward the curl of waves. I'm not alone. Other surfers bob among the swells, black as seals, patiently waiting for the right wave. I launch into the water, paddling with my arms further out to the sea, nothing but the sound of gulls wheeling overhead and the slosh of cold Pacific against my board and face. A wave comes and I duck dive, wanting to pull myself out further, farther, my head spinning with thoughts. Another wave foams down toward me, and again I dip beneath its power. *Pixie hair. Hazel eyes.* I surface, sputtering, coughing up a dredge of sea. Unsettled, I pause, resting on my board, looking back at the span of beach, the formidable forest pressing around it, trees sentry strong. *It has to have been here that I saw her.* I'd barely been anywhere else except school. *And the woods. Don't forget that. Wandering.*

I choke on another onslaught of sea as it crashes overhead, momentarily disoriented as gray water fills my vision. I open my eyes, a shred of kelp caught twirling in the bubbled depths. A face.

I surface, gasping for air. *What the hell?* My fingers grip the sides of my board, frozen, my heart slamming against my chest. *It's just your imagination. Breathe.* I suck in air and plunge my head below the water, scanning the void beneath. *Nothing.* I pull my head out of the water, shoving hair off my forehead, sucking in the misty air, suddenly feeling like a child again, remembering Sam with me, Brody, and Miriam, splashing in the surf. Their parents were on shore keeping a watchful eye, Sam's father with them. Sam told us about Dask'iya', the kelp haired child snatcher—how she'd kidnap children and take them up the Quillayute River to Yaq'ilis creek to cook. I don't know whether Dask'iya' was supposed to live in the sea or on land, but the thought of her kelp hair had made me fear the water for a long while after. Made me afraid of what lay beneath the gray surface. But eventually that fear passed. Because there was more to fear on land than in the sea. Legends, you could run from. Bully boys and the stark loneliness of an empty mobile in a trailer park, you could not.

Still.

I could have sworn I saw eyes just now. *Hazel eyes...*

I push myself off my belly to sit on my board, bobbing in the lull of waves, the breakers distant before and behind me. *You're overtired. It's just your mind playing tricks. There's nothing there.* I close my eyes, instead the memory of a dream surfacing—the one with the pixie haired girl, eyes wide with terror, a scream silenced on her lips. And waking up. The forest floor boggy beneath my back. *Was I there? Did I see something?*

I can't shake the growing alarm building in my chest. I glance back toward the strip of beach, remembering the summer. The nights by the beach fire. Sophie's hair swinging in my face.

I rub my eyes with my fingers, saltwater stinging. *You were out then too. When Sophie died. How could you not have known? How could you not have seen or heard anything?*

"Because the forest is *huge!*" I shout. "Because I *wasn't there!*"

Then why do I feel like this?

"Jayden?"

I look over through the sting of seawater to see another surfer paddling my way. I hadn't noticed anyone out this far with me.

"Are you okay? I heard you shouting." Miriam. Wet blonde hair slicked back from her face. Concern in her eyes. Always the rescuer. Always the one to find me broken. The one to save me.

"I'm fine." I sniff hard, wiping the heel of my hand across my nose.

"You don't look it."

"So, everyone says." I push back down to my belly and begin paddling away. In the distance, a wave gathers height. I keep focused on it. I don't want Miriam to see me like this. My head spinning out of control.

"Be that way then." Her voice gets lost in the drone of sea, the splat of rainwater against the ocean's skin. But I hear the hurt in her voice. I've never seen Miriam vulnerable. Until she turned away from me that night, leaving me standing in the broken circle of brick under the boughs of yesteryear. And now. In her voice. I turn back to apologize, but she's already paddling away.

It's just that I don't need to be saved anymore. And it felt good to be the one who could protect for a change. When I held Alexa against my chest when she was faint at the beach. The way her head rested against the crook of my neck. And how she held my hand when we descended the hilltop last night, gripping it as if her life depended on it. Depended on me. I'd never felt like that before. The one to be the protector. And it felt nice. To be the one not needing anything.

But I *do* need something. And that need burns in my veins.

Love. Alexa's love.

The wave in the distance has drawn nearer, a culminating wall of water, the peak not yet white with curl. The waves are bigger here, far from the shore. Their imposing strength and size like gods. Their wrath just as merciless. But in it, there's a cleansing.

"Come make me pure, you son-of-a-bitch," I whisper as the shadowed depths gain speed.

I think I hear my name being called. The voice filled with worry. Fear.

My body is all instinct now. I paddle hard, shoulders and forearms burning, climbing the face of the wave, board and body gathered by its force. And it begins. The crest of white, growing, widening, arcing into a tunnel. On the other side of that tunnel is life.

Get through it. Or die.

I spring to my feet, body balanced. One single focus. Like a rite of passage. A meditation. A single thought that blots out all others. *Survive.* And when I do survive—ride the wave—nothing else matters. It's just me and that tunnel forward. The water closing in behind me. As if what came before is washed away. All that's left is what's ahead. I'm suspended in that glorious space of time, all the way to the brink of shore. My mind clear, singularly focused. At peace.

The wave deposits me in a churn of surf near others who tried to catch the remnants of its power closer to shore, respectfully keeping their distance from where I dominated. I let the water surge over my face, floating on my back for a minute, board tethered to my ankle. The sweet rush of oblivion.

"Are you trying to get killed?"

I push myself up, fighting to hold onto my foothold in the shifting sand as the water froths around me.

Miriam is sitting on her board, angry, a few meters away.

"You were out there too." I shove my board forward and jump on, paddling.

"Not that far. And I know when to duck out!" she admonishes.

Well, I know how to survive. An inexplicable fury starts to broil in my blood. I paddle hard, leaving her behind.

* * *

The sky is streaked twilight blue, nightfall moving in. In the distance, the beach has thinned to no one, the rain intensifying, the surf becoming increasingly inhospitable close to shore. Further out, waves tear through the narrows between the sea stacks. My body is spent, exhausted—on one level. On another, it's more alive than ever, synapses firing like the Fourth of July. I don't want to go in. Until I see a lone surfer still bobbing some distance away, watching me.

"Just go home, Miriam," I mumble to myself. But I know she's there. For me. Making sure I stay safe. As if she could save me.

The water has turned black in the loss of daylight. It's near impossible to see, rain driving from the heavens with a vengeance. But I don't want to stop. The face in the sea, the face from my dreams, washed from my memory in these hours out fighting the surf. A blissful reprieve. But life starts closing in again when I glance back to see Miriam knocked from her board and climb back on. I can't stay out here forever.

It's like the sea feels the shift in my spirit, the heavy waves dulling to lolling swells. The absence of ferocious breakers creates a stillness like silence as the rain lightens. I sit on my board allowing the swells to lift me high then ride down their long backs as they gently rush away. I wait for one last heavy one to roll in. But it doesn't. I stare out at the distant horizon, impatient. Waiting. For one last escape.

"Jayden, aren't you going to come in? It's getting late."

I turn. Miriam is belly down along her board a short distance away, paddling toward me.

"Why did you come out here, Miriam? You don't like it out this far."

She pushes herself up to a sitting position, jaw set. "Because I've spent the afternoon watching you dodge death. Now that that's over, you're still out here, so... Kind of wondering what the deal is."

"You don't need to wait for me. I got here myself, I'll get home myself." I wipe a hand under my nose, rain mixing with the seawater on my face.

"Jayden—"

"I said I'm fine. Just go. I'll drop the board and suit off when I'm back in town."

She turns away, her jaw muscle flexing. "What is with you?"

"What do you mean?"

"Since your birthday...it's like you've changed into someone else."

"That's not true—"

"It *is*, Jayden. In fact, ever since last year you've been turning into someone else. When you started getting all like—that." She gestures flippantly at the expanse of my chest, the tautness of muscle beneath my suit. "With it came a change in you."

"I'm not myself because I got in shape?"

"In shape? I can see every—every cut of your abdomen when you take your shirt off." She stops, seeming embarrassed for a moment, but it passes. "And Mom was right. If Kam or the others bother you, maybe you should just walk away."

"These," I jab at my stomach, "are from training with Dan. And Kam gets what he deserves if he comes near me."

"Jayden, it's one thing to defend yourself, it's another to be out for blood."

"Excuse me?"

"At the beach! You weren't just defending yourself, you wanted to hurt him. And his friends. You didn't just try to put them down, you were hitting hard, Jay. Like, *hard* hard."

"And they weren't hitting me just as bad?"

"Apparently not. Because I saw Kam and his friends today. They don't look so good. And look at you. Like nothing even happened."

"You saw my face yesterday, you saw what they did—"

"Never mind."

"Yeah...never mind," I spit. "Because when someone puts you down for as long as they have—for as long as he has," I say, Kam's face searing to life in my mind, "you have an anger that simmers inside. For so long, I didn't have a voice—a way to defend myself from all his bullshit. From any of life's bullshit! You begrudge me for striking back? For finally saying *enough*?"

"No...of course, not. You know that. I'm sorry. I didn't mean it like that." Her face softens. "I know he's been awful to you. I just didn't like seeing you like that. I'm not used to it. You've always been so..." She searches for the words. "You're just a good person, Jay. The best. Always looking out for everyone and doing the right thing."

"It doesn't feel like it. It seems like everyone else is always having to look out for me. You especially." The thrum of fury dissipates. Memory thick in my veins. "And I appreciate it. I do. What your family has done for me—"

"And we do it gladly, Jay. We love you." Her voice catches. She sucks in a breath, biting her bottom lip. "It just seems like you're distant lately. Especially this week. Something's changed in you."

"Look, I'm fine. I'm just going through some stuff right now. Some personal stuff."

Her face deepens with concern. "Mom said you might be having some health trouble."

"Health—? No." The last thing I want is for Miriam to see me as some psycho wandering the night. Unable to control myself. "I'm just a little stressed, maybe." Stressed. Yeah. Stressed there's something wrong with me. That maybe she's right. That I am becoming someone else. *Something else.*

"Don't worry. She didn't elaborate," she says, seeing my discomfort. "I just don't like seeing you this way."

"I'm fine."

"So, you keep saying." She pauses. I can see her considering whether to say what's on her mind next. "Maybe...I don't know...is it that girl influencing you?"

"It's not Alexa, Miriam. If anything, she's changed me for the better. When I'm with her I feel understood. Alive."

She gives a sad smile. "And you don't with us?"

"That's not what I mean," I stammer. "It's just—Alexa's got nothing to do with it. I promise."

"You've bitten her."

"What?" My heart stops. Goes cold.

"I said you're smitten with her." She looks at me, an odd look on her face. An inquisitive look. "What? It's true. I said it before, and I'll say it again—you seem consumed by her, yet you barely know her."

I exhale, slowly. "Sorry, I misheard." I rub a hand across my eyes, feeling edgy. "Time isn't the only measure for feelings, Miriam. And how would you know if I'm consumed by someone?"

It's like I've hurt her. Again. Her eyes sharp. Wounded. "Because you've never paid anyone the attention that you're giving her. Everyone has noticed. I heard you even snuck off during science class together. And someone saw you running through the night together last night too."

"What? Who?"

We sit like that. Eyes on each other, a discomfort and tension between us that never existed before. Because despite everything, I still need her. Need her forgiveness. For what, I don't know, but I feel like I need forgiving. And without her, I don't have family. Not in the same way. To share in a piece of the Foster family, I need all of them. Together. But more than any of them, Miriam had always been there for me, ready to take my side. Ready to fight for me, if needed. I need her laughter. Her to have my back. Her approval.

I need her.

The sound of a blow—that distinct expulsion of air—breaks the moment. We both twist on our boards to look out toward the sea. Not far from us is the unmistakable shape of a dorsal fin, cresting the surface.

"Oh...wow," Miriam breathes. "Ka-ka-wad." *Orca.*

"The wolf of the sea," I murmur.

We look at each other. The shared memory of gathering around a drum circle when Sam's father shared the story of the orca's origins. Of the great white wolf that walked into the ocean and became the Orca. I think of the gray wolf emerging from the mist to cross through the headlights of Alexa's father's car. Its yellowed eyes intent on me before it disappeared into the forest. Watching.

I break Miriam's gaze and scan the surface looking for signs of others, but none appear. "It's all alone." An odd stirring shivers through my chest.

Miriam scours the length of sea. "You're right. It's not with its pod.

It's not the season they usually pass through here, though. I wonder how it got separated." She leans forward, squinting to see through the rain. "Oh my gosh, look!" She draws her feet up on her board, her face in awe. "Is it—white? That's so—they're so rare."

The ambient gray of the rain-soaked skies and the gathering evening make it hard to distinguish sky from sea. But the tall dorsal looks paler than it should. White instead of black. Like a spirit haunting the horizon.

It releases another blow, spray spewing into the air then dives deep, out of sight.

"It's like we just witnessed a miracle," Miriam breathes. She looks over at me, her face a bright spot in the rain with its awestruck glow.

A calm enters my soul. Out here, in the distant waves, everything that has haunted me is stranded on shore. Out here, I feel more a part of the world than when I'm in it. As if I too, am nothing more than spirit.

SEVENTEEN

ON SHORE, I go behind the pile of driftwood where I left my bike. I fumble through the waterproof bag strapped to the bike rack and pull out my clothes. The rain has softened again to mist. I peel the wetsuit down to my waist and, using my shirt, rub at my skin to wick away the moisture.

"Oh—I'm sorry," Miriam stutters, rounding the logs. She turns around, awkward. "I didn't know you were changing."

"I'm not naked here. It's not anything you haven't seen before." I toss the shirt onto the handlebars and fish out my pants.

She glances back at me, her eyes drifting down the length of my torso. "I'll—I'll wait for you by the car, okay?"

"Mir, I told you I'm good for getting home. I've got the rack for the board."

"I'll just mount it to the car and take it home. No sense you having the extra ride past our place."

"It's fine. I like to wash it after borrowing it anyway. Return it as I found it." I look up to find she's still staring at me. She turns away.

"Sure. Whatever," she says. "Just seems easier to ride with me. I mean, you must be tired after being out there so long. Especially in those waves."

This awkwardness between us—it's unfamiliar. I grapple with finding words. "Uh...sure. Okay then."

Her back is to me. I can't help but notice the curve of her form in the fitted wetsuit. I guess I wasn't the only one who had grown up. I clear my throat and focus again on my clothes. "Aren't you going to change too?"

"I'm—right. Yes." She gives a nervous laugh. She grabs her things and moves off to a covered area of brush.

I wait for her to disappear out of sight before peeling my wetsuit down further, struggling to pull my legs free. Worried she'll reappear with me exposed like this, I glance up, catching a flash of her fair skin in the deep twilight between the branches. I hesitate, caught off guard at the sight of her, then turn around, nearly toppling over. I fall back hard against the logs.

"You okay over there?" she calls.

"Uh, yeah. Just...these things are always a bitch to get out of." I make sure to keep my eyes pointed toward the sea, guilt at having seen her, warming my cheeks.

She laughs. "That they are." Minutes pass. "Is it safe now for me to come out? You decent?"

"Almost." I hop on one foot, hoisting my jeans into place. "Okay...I'm...good?"

She comes out from behind the branches just as I finish fastening the snap of my jeans. My shirt is still askew, riding up, belly exposed. I pull it down and snatch up my hoodie.

"Oh—I...sorry." She stands there, peering at me lengthwise, her arms clutching her shed wetsuit to her chest.

I clear my throat again. "No, I'm sorry. I said I was ready. You came out...faster than expected." I run a distracted hand through my hair. "Shall we go?"

"Yes...yeah. I'll...let me warm up the car."

As the car idles, I help her strap the boards to the roof rack, our arms bumping here and there as we maneuver them into place. "Sorry," I mumble, my arm brushing hers. I step out of her way.

"Just collapse the back seats and put your bike in the trunk," she instructs, tightening the straps over the boards, her glance drifting to me.

As I load my bike into the back of the trunk a flash of light brightens the cloud.

"More lightning?" Miriam groans.

"Looks like it." I hop into the passenger side of the car as she climbs in behind the wheel.

"Good thing you're getting a ride then." She looks over at me and smiles.

"I guess so. Thank you." I hold her eye. "For everything. Truly. I was feeling really off today. Just...couldn't get out of my head. Being out there in those waves...and talking to you—seeing that whale—I feel...better. More myself."

"I'm glad." She glances down to where her hands are fiddling with the keys. "You look after me too, you know."

"What?"

"Out on the water, you said it seems like everyone else is always having to look out for you. But you look out for me too. By making me laugh when I need to. Helping me with a difficult piece of literature for school. By showing up just when I need you, all the time. It's like you have a sixth sense. So, I want you to know, it's mutual, this needing each other. It's not just you."

"Thanks, Mir. I needed to hear that. You have no idea." She slips the keys into the ignition and drops her hand to the gearshift. I place my hand over hers. "You're a good friend. Always have been."

Her face falls slightly, and she sits back in her chair, pulling her hand from mine. "Any time." She draws a deep breath, and only after I return my hand to my lap, does she reach back down to shift the car into gear.

* * *

We drive in silence. The strip of road scything through the thick forest. Plumes of inky cloud have obliterated any moonlight, the road dark and heavy with atmosphere. Lightning flickers, sparking the sky at random intervals as we wind toward town.

We pass the place where the wolf crossed. I can still see the shag of its gray coat. The amber burn of its eyes. Still hear Alexa's voice, *love at first sight*. Another flash of lightning takes me back to the hallway near her father's library, the storm light catching the blue of her eyes. The electricity in the air seeming to connect us. Like a sparkling thread. And the clearing on the hill, the pressure of her body against mine...

"You falling asleep over there?" Miriam's voice jars me back to the present.

My head is tipped against the cool glass of the passenger window. I sit up straighter, feeling disoriented. "A little, I think. Sorry."

"It's okay." The dark shape of trees passes by the window, broken by houses. "I like that you trust me enough to sleep."

"Of course, I do." I give a slight laugh. "I've slept over at your place enough times these past years. I would hope I could trust you."

She smiles, a streetlamp lighting her face in brief passing. We have already reached town. Clearly, I dozed off given our location now. I straighten even further in my seat.

"I meant vulnerability," she says. "That I'm someone you trust enough to sleep in front of. Without worry or judgement."

"Yeah...well...I'm pretty tired. I don't get much sleep anymore."

She glances at me then back to the road. "How come?"

"I just don't." I shift, uncomfortable. I don't want to talk about it. But I'm grateful for the few moments of sleep. Grateful that I could relax in her presence. Rest. *Rest and not wander.*

The Foster's home comes into view. "I'll just drop the boards off and continue on to your place to take you home."

"No, I'm fine from here. Thank you. I've been out in storms a million times—haven't become a science experiment yet." A rumble of thunder reverberates ominously in the distance. "Let me get these." We've climbed out of the car. I reach up to undo the boards.

"Don't worry about them, Jay. I've got them. Just get yourself home since you won't let me take you. I want you safe."

"No, I want to wash—"

"I know you do. But I mean it." The lights in the house are on, her family visible behind the windows, together in the kitchen. "Mom will kill you if you even try and stay to clean these. And kill me if I let you. Not in a storm like this."

"Thanks, Mir. For everything."

She keeps a measured focus on the boards, avoiding my eye. "You better get going," she says. "I expect it's going to get worse before it gets better." A stark cloud overhead whitens for a dazzling moment in a burst of lightning.

"I expect you're right."

She chances a look at me then, her eyes drifting from my eyes to my mouth. I know that look. Though I've never seen it before on her face. Not for me. My seven-year-old self stirs somewhere deep inside for a moment, the hint of that old yearning for her from when we were kids. It flashes through me quick as the lightning.

A clap of thunder sounds, closer this time, and the feeling slides away, back into the past.

"Good night, Miriam."

"Good night, Jay."

I start for home, the weight of the air full around me. The promise of rain. The promise of worse. There is a restlessness inside. One that in the ocean's grip, I had—for a moment—released. But it has returned. A discomfort in my own skin.

But also, there is a need.

I reach a fork in the road. I hesitate only for a moment, then veer down the lane that takes me not to home but into the bowels of the forest. To the mansion.

To Alexa.

* * *

It's hulking form in the clearing of lawn looks foreboding. As if torn from the page of a novel. All five floors of windows are hooded in darkness but for a distant gleam behind the mullioned glass of a single pane on the first level. I don't know what time it is precisely, but it's late evening. The storm giving the impression of midnight.

Not too late for a visitor, I try and convince myself. I set my bike down by the steps of the porch and take the stairs two at a time, stopping at the front door, my heart hammering. I raise my fist to knock but stop at the sound of voices inside. Shouting.

"No! Sven, this cannot continue anymore. It's become too much!"

"How can you say that? You've seen for yourself! Look at her!"

"It has to stop!"

"Then let me do what I need—"

"Enough! Please! For her sake as much as ours. It's for her own good!" There is emotion in Magenta's voice. A desperate sadness. Grief. Like Dr. Johansson in the woods.

I lower my fist, confused. I step back along the porch, out from beneath its cover to scan the dark windows overhead. Alexa's room is around back. I tiptoe off the porch and round the side of the house, the shouting growing fainter. The windows in the back are dark. The tree by Alexa's window stands stark, a grotesque arm, illuminated in the brief moments of lightning. I creep the length of the house until I'm beneath her window. Behind me, the woods are in utter darkness, eeriness permeating the shadows.

"Alexa?" I call in a hoarse whisper.

The backdoor of the manor opens and slams shut. Quickly, I duck behind the tree's thick bole. A streak of light pierces the sky followed by a sharp crack of thunder. Dr. Johansson, hunched against the storm, trench coat clutched tight, hurries across the weeded lawn to the back outbuilding. He disappears around the side. There is the resolute sound of the side door slamming shut. A light flickers on behind the tightly drawn blinds of the lone window. Moments later, Magenta emerges from the mansion, dark dress flapping in the growing wind. She marches across the lawn and she too, disappears into the outbuilding. Indiscernible shouts begin again from within. I glance up at the darkened window of Alexa's room then over to the porch, its screen swinging on its hinges, a forlorn squeak in the ghostly air.

I glance back at the outbuilding. Magenta and Dr. Johansson are deep in the throes of their disagreement, and from the sound of their voices, show no signs of stopping. Cautiously, I cross the lawn, tall grass brushing against my jeans, and step up onto the back patio, one hand gripping the metal of the screen door, silencing it mid-swing. The glass of the door behind reveals a lounge, a heavy hearth hunkering over a low flame. Quietly, I pull the handle of the door, push it inward.

The house creaks in the growing wind, boards settling into place, or perhaps shifting out of them. Inside, the fire pops and a log shifts within the hearth, sending a shower of sparks. The air holds the must of time and the faint scent of cinnamon tea, vanilla. I inhale the faint sweetness of Alexa then stop, uneasiness creeping up my spine at having entered without invitation. I glance back toward the outbuilding.

I should go. At least make my way round to the front door to knock or ring the bell, not be here, like this, uninvited. I inch back toward the porch door when I hear a squeak on a floorboard above.

"Alexa?"

The soft fall of footsteps echoes above.

"Alexa?" I call again, edging toward the staircase.

It has to be her. Who else could it be? It's just the three of them living here.

Palms sweating, I inch into the front hall, grab hold of the banister, and lightly hurry up the steps. I'm greeted by shadows in both directions. Treading lightly, I follow the hall toward the library, pausing by the nook where I sheltered when I was younger, ghosts of yesteryear stirring in my heart. Swallowing hard, I continue on until I near the library, a faint pool of light seeping from beneath its closed doors.

"Alexa?" I call lightly, my hand touching the solid wood of the door.

"Jayden? Is that you?"

Relief floods me, and I push the doors open to see her curled in a blanket on one of the couches before a low fire. "Hey," I say softly.

"What are you doing here?"

"I hope it's okay...I let myself in. I was going to knock, but—" I stop, uncomfortable at having heard her parents arguing.

"I'm sorry if you heard them." She looks away toward the fire, sadness ghosting her face. "They do that a lot now."

"Have they always?"

"Not so much before my accident. But yes. After. Not like this, though. It's been worse lately."

"I'm sorry. It must be hard." I glance back out toward the hall. "Will they be upset if they come in and find me here?"

"They'll probably be a while yet." A loneliness has crept into her voice. She huddles deeper into her blanket. Slowly, I cross the room and lower myself onto the couch near her feet, my eye catching the forbidding visage of Vlad the Impaler looming above the hearth. I look away from the ominous eyes of the portraiture. "Is everything okay?" There's something different about her. A distance.

She shrugs slightly. "I don't know," she whispers.

"What happened?"

"My dad wants to put a lock on my bedroom door. Keep me in at night. He noticed I was gone last night. I don't know if that's what they're arguing about, or what, but..."

"I'm so sorry. I didn't mean to get you in trouble." My heart palpitates. If her father finds me here now, he'll be beside himself. But more than that...the thought of not being able to see her whenever I want, twists like a blade. Because last night was the first night in a year that nighttime felt different. Like a dream instead of a nightmare. "Why would he do that, though? It sounds a bit extreme."

"He's worried. Those girls' deaths..."

"Of course. Right. But still—"

"He was worried the first night I saw you too, that he found me outside—" She stops when she sees me tense. "I didn't tell him about you. I never said a word then or after."

"I know."

"But he doesn't want me out. Not at night. And I've not listened."

I reach forward and take her hand, threading my fingers through hers. "I just hope he doesn't move you away because of what's been happening in town. I promise it's a safe community—usually."

She exhales a sad sigh. The firelight catches the crystal shimmer of her eyes as she watches the flames flicker and glow. "It's not the first town we've lived in where there's been a death...a disappearance. An accident...or suicide. A case unsolved. A person who never returns." She sighs. "The world has its shadows—demons that people are running from. The world's...their own. It's everywhere. It happens no matter where you go. And we've moved...but you can't escape it. I don't know what my parents think about Forks now. All I know is I don't want to move anymore. Not now. Not since I've found you."

I slide closer to her, holding both her hands in mine. "I don't know what I'd do if you left." I can't even begin to think about life as it was before. In the few days I'd known her, it was like something inside me had awakened. Nothing else mattered. Not my past—the bullying, Kam; not my mom or the lonely life I'd led in that dreary trailer park.

No, nothing bothered me anymore. Except one thing.

The night wandering.

But with her I'm not wandering. Not lost.

I'm becoming something stronger.

"We could run away together." It comes out of nowhere. I don't know what I'm saying. "Like Romeo and Juliet."

Alexa chuckles softly. "Their plot to run away didn't turn out as planned."

"No...but ours could." I can almost hear Ms. Cash's comments about wasted opportunities if I never returned to class, the flutter of scholarship papers blowing in the wind. The life everyone imagined would set me free. But they were wrong.

Because I'd still be me.

And with Alexa, I feel different somehow...

She leans forward, breath sweet with cinnamon from the half empty teacup on the table beside her. "It's our last year of high school. Then we have our whole lives. To be together. If we want... If you want... Anything is possible." Her eyes are shining.

"Just don't leave before we get that chance." My voice is rough with emotion.

Don't leave me here. Alone.

She leans toward me, firelight dancing between us as she touches her lips to mine. I watch her, the pure cerulean of her eyes before she closes them, the ebony curls shining in the firelight, the mocha warmth of her skin.

Stay with me forever.

"Alexa?" Dr. Johansson's voice resonates down the hall. Alexa pulls back, her hand light on my chest. "You need to go." Her eyes look worried, but there's something else. Something I can't quite put my finger on. And still, a distance.

"Are you okay?"

"Just go," she pleads, her voice soft. "It wouldn't do either of us good if he found you here with me. Not after last night."

I rise hurriedly and cross the room as the sound of footsteps echo from the stairwell. Down the hall, Dr. Johansson's shadow lengthens from around the curve of corridor.

There's no way out but down the same set of stairs that Dr. Johansson just ascended. *I need to hide...*

I stumble down the hall in the opposite direction of his looming shadow, my hand lighting upon a doorknob, I twist it, push it open, slip inside and ease the door shut, heart pounding. I inch back from the door and turn, bumping into something. I spin around to confront whatever it is, only to discover a long, dark silhouette of hair in the brief illumination of storm light through the window. I stifle a yelp at its appearance, gripping the figure hard, then relaxing as my fingers flex into nothing more than Styrofoam. *Magenta's office.* The busts with the wigs, dark hair upon ghostly mannequin heads, the rows of them creepy in the flashes of light. Like an army of bodiless ghouls. A screen saver squiggles across a large computer screen at the end of the room. The last place I want to be caught is in here, among Magenta's private prosthetics and props. I fumble my way back to the door and crack it open ajar, peering through the slit of the door to where light tumbles from the open library doors.

"Come, Alexa. It's time to rest. I'll help you to your room."

There is no protest from Alexa and moments later she emerges, leaning heavily on her father's arm.

Why is she walking that way? What's wrong with her? For a panicked moment, I wonder, irrationally, if he drugged her so she'd sleep the night away without the temptation of trying to leave.

Muscles tense, I wait until they have disappeared out of sight, their footfall ascending the staircase to yet another floor. After a moment passes, I slip out of Magenta's office, quietly closing the door behind me and lightly hurry down the hallway to the winding staircase, glancing upward before slipping down the expanse of stairs, hugging close to the banister. A light glows from the kitchen, spilling out over the dining hall to the front foyer. The back lounge still sits in shadow, so I retreat back to where I entered, the fire's embers now burning low. I cringe at the sound of the patio door, hinges protesting as I inch it open. My only hope is the howl of wind and percussion of storm has hidden the sound amongst its fury, or that the sound has been lost in the expanse of vacant rooms. I slip along the perimeter of the mansion toward the front to retrieve my bike, noticing candles have been lit along the porch rail, wax slowly dripping down the fat pillars like tears.

"It would be wise for you to not come again at night."

I nearly jump out of my skin at the sound of a voice. Magenta rises from where she is seated in the shadows.

"I'm sorry...we were just talking," I stammer. "I didn't mean to disrespect your household rules by—"

"This isn't a good time for our family right now. It would be best if you gave Alexa some space."

My heart constricts at the thought of not seeing Alexa. Of not being welcomed at the dining table to drink cinnamon tea. Of not being able to approach her window after nightfall, hoping to see her framed within the glass, waiting for me too.

I lift my bike from where it's lying by the porch, my fingers flexing on the handlebars. "I don't understand." I try to find the words. "I—I have only the best intentions with her, I promise."

"Jayden...she's not well."

"But—"

"She needs some time. That's all."

"Is she okay? I mean…will I see her in school tomorrow? We only just met, and—and school has just started, and—" *and there's so much left for us to discover about each other.*

"Our hope is she will be better soon." Her gaze slips beyond me to the distant bulb of the moon. "But for tonight, she needs to rest." She glances over her shoulder to the dark windows behind. "Did he see you?"

"The doctor? No, he didn't."

"Good. Go, now."

I sling my leg over my bike, my foot on the pedals. "I know he wants to lock her in her room at night. That's wrong. And her being out last night…that was my fault. Please don't punish her for it by trying to keep her locked in."

"It's for her own safety," Magenta states.

"They'll find who's behind the deaths soon. Chief Hanson and his team are being thorough. Just don't…I promise I won't come back at night."

"Good." Her dark eyes glitter. "It's for the best."

She moves toward the front door, pausing before she opens it. "I'm glad to see my poultice worked. You look…better." She opens the door and disappears inside before I can say anything more.

*   *   *

Dark winds gust along the streets, funneling through the treetops with a melancholic moan, the eerie bay of wolves haunting the deepest depths of the woods beyond. I pedal hard until I'm out of the forest corridors and on the main strip, my mind churning. *What was wrong with Alexa? What hasn't she told me? What did Magenta mean by her being unwell?* My heart constricts thinking about how she'd been faint at the beach and tonight, how she'd leaned heavily against her father's arms. It couldn't be anything serious, surely. I'd seen her run on the track at school, tireless and strong. How she crested the hilltop with me, her body lithe and powerful. And her eyes…always clear and bright in that impossible shade of blue. *She has to be all right.* I try not to let my imagination spiral down a dark tunnel. Besides…she'd alluded that we had all the time in the world. *It's our last year of high school. Then, we have our whole lives. To be together. If we want… If you want… Anything is possible.* Her voice swirls through my head.

"Anything is possible…" I breathe. I need to believe that. I need it to be true.

An increase in traffic due to the upcoming Forever Twilight festival provides reassuring light from passing cars as I make my way past the outskirts of town to the trailer park. I slow when I round the lane, seeing the old Ford parked out front.

Dan is puttering in the ambient light of a distant porch lamp, appearing to tend his scant garden, but I know better. He's restless. He has his own demons that keep him up at night.

"Jayden," he says in greeting as I pull up alongside the mobile.

"What are you doing out here at this time, Dan?"

He nods toward my mobile. "Just keeping an eye."

I exhale slowly. "She's not alone?"

"She is now," he assures me.

I take a breath, bracing myself for what's to come. "Thanks, Dan."

"Sure, kid." He gives a nod and retreats toward his front door. "If you need anything—"

"You're right across the street. I know. Thank you."

He opens his door. "You know, it's been a while since you came knocking for some training. If you want to do a round of sparring—to keep your abilities sharp—I'm here. It's good for the mind too, you know."

"I know. And I will," I promise, and watch him disappear indoors.

Tentatively, I open the front door to the mobile, the sound of the television the first thing to greet me.

"Jay? Is that you, honey?"

"Yeah, Mom."

She's sitting on her chair, afghan draped across her legs. Her eyes are makeup heavy, the scent of liquor a cloying perfume in the air. "I'm glad to see you. I was hoping you'd be home soon."

"Heard you had company," I say, dumping my coat on a hook by the door.

"Mm. He's gone now." She has a cigarette dangling between her fingers. She takes a long drag. "Besides, I just wanted some time with my boy. See how you were doing."

"I'm fine, Mom."

She reaches for the remote and switches off the television, stubbing out her cigarette. "You sure? I heard—thought—I better check in. It's been a while since I checked in on you about all that trouble you were having before. With sleep and everything."

I open the fridge and scan the few contents inside, suppressing the urge to confront her about the Fosters paying for my trip to Seattle. "I'm fine. Besides, you could have checked in sooner. But you've been off doing your own thing."

"That's not nice, Jayden. Don't exaggerate. Someone keeps that fridge stocked here, you know."

"Yeah. Me." I firmly shut the fridge door.

"They let you bring home groceries from work as a perk?"

"I pay for it, Mom."

Guilt flushes her face. "I'm sorry. You're working to save for college. You shouldn't be paying for that." She reaches for her purse, extracting her wallet, her hands shaking as she fumbles with the few weathered bills inside.

"Mom...don't. You don't need to give me that," I protest, a sadness filling my chest at the sight of her fingering the only bills she has. "Save that for something else. Like for calling a plumber. That leak under the kitchen sink has started again."

"Has it?" Mascara smudges darken her eyes. "I'll have to give Larry a call then. See if he can get by this week."

But she won't. By morning she won't remember about the leak. Maybe she won't even remember the conversation.

She looks up at me, her eyes glassy with drink or with tears, it's hard to tell in the wan light.

"I'm trying, Jay," she says. "I really am."

"I know, Mom."

She gets up and makes her way over to me, wraps her thin arms around me. "Why don't you get some sleep. You need it, okay? I'll be right here if you need me. Keeping an eye to make sure you stay safe in bed all night."

"I'm not a kid anymore. I don't need to be watched."

"No, I know. But sometimes when we're grown, we need someone watching over us too."

I think of Dan out in the chill air, his eye on the mobile before I got home. "True."

"Maybe in the morning I could make you your favorite breakfast?"

"I outgrew Pop Tarts like ten years ago, Mom. You won't find any in the cupboards."

"Oh. Well. I'll make you a nice cup of strong coffee. That will see you through your day at school. It's back in now, isn't it?"

"It is. That would be nice." I give her a peck on the cheek goodnight, trying not to breathe in the sad smell of her, then retreat to my bedroom. Not long after, I hear her stagger to the bathroom and then to her own room, her door clicking shut.

I sit on my bed, the lump of crystal on the bedside table glinting in the light filtering in from the window. The pathetic bathrobe tie looks like a bitter snake stretched across the bed, its tail still wrapped around the bedpost. I'm exhausted. So little sleep. I lay back on my bed, one hand gripping the tie, ready to knot it around my wrist. But the exhaustion is too consuming. I'm asleep before I can secure myself to the bed. Asleep before I can clear my mind.

In my dream there are voices calling my name. Lanky branches hang low, brushing against my stubbled chin, night pressing in all around. I startle as Sophie steps in front of me, long hair draping across her shoulders down past her breasts. *Come find me,* she says. So, I follow the river of her blonde hair through the dark woods, her laughter echoing through the forest, a chilling, haunted sound. *Stop,* I say. *It's too dangerous.* But she keeps going, faster now, edging further and further away. Suddenly she screams, her body disappearing from sight. I run to find her, pawing through the tangle of branches and leaves until I see a body lying in a low ditch, face down. I roll her body over to see if she's all right, but vacant hazel eyes look back up at me, pixie hair framing the narrow face. *Too late,* the girl says. I stagger backward, then turn and run, tripping on a root, sprawling to the ground. *Get up,* a familiar voice says. *Get up,* it says again, this time more urgently. I lift my head to see Alexa standing there, moonlight streaming across her face like an ethereal veil. *What did you say?* I ask. She crouches over me, mesmerizing blue eyes searching mine. *I said, wake up.*

I jerk awake as if shaken, sweat beading my forehead. I'm lying on the floor beside my bed, the bathrobe tie draped loosely over the side. I sit up, scrunching my back against the bedframe, tucking my knees up to my chest, breathing hard. I fumble my fingers across the top of the bedside table until I feel the jagged edges of the crystal, and clutch it, drawing it to my chest.

The dream was so real. *As if I was walking through the forest. As if I was there with the girls before—*

Breathe. In. Out. In.

Out...

It's sweet relief that I'm still here, in my room.

Only darkness outside.

EIGHTEEN

THERE'S COFFEE IN the morning. And eggs, shiny and slightly undercooked, but Mom looks so pleased that she's prepared me food, I make a deal about saying how good they are. Then I dress and head for school, hoping to see Alexa.

But I don't see her.

I watch the field track to see if she joins for the continued cross-country prelim tryouts, scanning the faces as each student sprints by. There's no sign of long wound curls, or coffee cream skin. No intoxicating blue eyes searching the crowd for me too. At science, I arrive early, claiming the same lab table where Alexa and I sat together, waiting impatiently as the other students file in.

A sinking feeling fills my chest when Kam and his friends walk into the classroom. But it stops when I see their faces. Bruises color their cheeks, the skin around one of the guy's eyes bulges with swelling. Another holds his arm across his stomach as if protecting an ache in his ribs. Kam has tape across his nose, his eyes smoldering coals, as they pass me. I don't miss their double take. The shock at seeing my face. Unscathed.

The class is unusually quiet as it waits for Mr. Sorenson to arrive, just a whispered murmur moving through the room. I can feel eyes on me, and on Kam and his friends. Anyone who wasn't there at the beach, knows about it. The altercation. Sweat dampens my armpits as I catch the incredulous glances of some of my classmates. I don't know what they're saying but I know they're saying something. About me.

Mr. Sorenson finally enters the class, announcing that we won't be continuing with our forest exploration in light of the second death that happened over the weekend and the ongoing investigation into the murders. He doesn't linger on the subject other than reminding students the counselor is available to help us sort through any emotions we might be feeling about the recent tragedies. He drones on, but I don't listen, absently opening my textbook, pretending to follow whatever page he's discussing, hyper aware of the vacant seat beside me.

When class ends, Kam and his friends brush past, Kam pausing long enough to fix me with a cold stare. "This isn't over, Death," he says just loud enough for me to hear.

The other students file out, shooting curious looks my way before merging into the hall.

"Is there something I can help you with, Mr. James?" Mr. Sorenson glances my way, straightening a stack of papers on his desk.

"No, sorry. I'm going." I rise to my feet, gathering my books. I sling my backpack over my shoulder and move toward the door, pausing by his desk. "Actually, there is one thing. We cover human biology this year, right?"

"Mm-hmm." Mr. Sorenson flips open his laptop and clicks on a few buttons. "Why do you ask?"

"I was curious...about the body's healing capacity."

"In what way?" He glances up.

"Is it possible to recover from severe swelling and bruising in just twenty-four hours? For it to be gone almost entirely two days later?" I suppress a nervous urge to clear my throat.

"Hm. I suppose the body is capable of just about anything, but generally it needs time to heal. That being said, some surprising things can happen, certainly. Why do you ask?" He adjusts his glasses and skims over my face with his eyes. He obviously hasn't heard about the altercation on Friday. I'm sure the news of another death in town would have taken precedence in his mind either way.

"What about natural healing...concoctions? Could homeopathic treatment accelerate the healing process?"

"Again, it's entirely possible. Natural treatments have a long history of effectiveness. Individual cellular proclivity and the general health and constitution of a person plays a role in the healing process as does the selection and combination of any treatment, natural or otherwise. We will be covering human anatomy and physiological responses in further detail later in the year." His eyes are questioning as I take a step toward the door.

"So, miracles can happen."

"Yes, they can. And they do," he muses. "Many a mysterious thing has happened in life."

Like a poultice. A face wiped clean—*if not my conscience.*

A miracle...

Manipulated not by some god but by a man—or woman. *Who could trust that?*

And a teenage boy who suddenly feels like he has fire in his veins...

"Are you all right, Jayden?" Mr. Sorenson is looking at me curiously, his brow wavering with concern.

"Yes, sorry. I'll look forward to those classes then. Thank you." I leave before he can ask me anything further. Out in the hall Kam is loitering around with his friends. They don't say anything to me as I pass. The rest of his group—the ones that weren't part of the beach attack—look at me with a mix of awe. But I don't miss the look in Kam's eye. I know he means what he said.

This isn't over.

*   *   *

When the final bell rings, I gather up my books from my locker, scanning the halls for Alexa's face one last time. Maybe she came late. Maybe she switched classes. Maybe she's here after all...

"Hey man, heard you were ripping it up out at First Beach yesterday." Brody angles up beside me. "Glad you got the board and went. Just wish

I could have been there with you."

"Did Miriam tell you?"

"No, she didn't say anything about it, except that she gave you a lift home. But the others I was supposed to be there with saw you. Sounds like the waves were pretty incredible. And you, always the furthest out from shore, playing in the danger zone."

"Yeah, well. It was therapeutic."

"I'm sure it was. Hey, some of us are heading over to Sully's to grab a burger. Want to come?"

"I can't." The thought of sitting there, acting like life wasn't slowly unraveling, is impossible right now. I don't offer any more by way of excuse, but Brody knows better than to push me.

"Well, okay then. Guess I'll see ya later." He does his usual fist bump and sidles off.

I need to get out of here. Get on the road. *It would be best if you gave Alexa some space.* Magenta's voice. Warning in her tone. But I can't give space. I need to see her. Need to know she's okay.

I sling my backpack over my shoulder and beeline for the exit.

"Jayden, you got a minute?"

I grit my teeth and turn around. I just want to get out of here. "Sure, Ms. Cash. What's up?"

"There's an Advanced Literature and Writing group that's planning on meeting after regular hours every Wednesday, if you're interested. The plan, among other things, is to discuss and analyze the structure of bestsellers, starting from the classics—and to talk about writing tips for those interested in creating their own stories. It will help when it comes to exams time at the end of the year. It could be helpful too for scholarship applications. And we'll be looking at places where you could submit your work for consideration of publication. You might want to think about joining." Her eyes are sparkling as if she's just delivered the best news ever. Which, normally it might have been. A chance to be with books and brains. A chance to dream about the future. Dream about getting out of town. Except this town is where Alexa is. And right now, that's all that matters. "I know you're quite fond of the classics. We'll be covering Gothic horror as well, I might add—your favorite."

"I'll—I'll think about it. Thanks for telling me." I turn to go.

"Jayden, is everything all right?"

I nod, without facing her. "Uh—yeah. It is. Thanks...for letting me know about the group."

I hurry away before she can say any more, though I can feel her eyes boring into me as I head down the hall for the exit.

Outside, I grab my bike and jump on, ignoring the few people calling my name to say goodbye. All I can think about is Alexa. An unsettled feeling stirs within at the thought of her. An instinct.

Something isn't right.

I careen down the roads, my eye toward the belly of woods on the town's perimeter when suddenly a familiar voice calls my name.

"Jayden..."

I brake, turning to see Sam's grandfather, gray hair billowing around his shoulders in the tumult of afternoon wind.

"Sir..." It's reflex, this shyness when around him; his deep-set eyes reserved within the leather of his face. His voice holds a quiet intensity whenever he speaks, especially when recounting the legends of his people. I don't know him well but have felt the depth of his spirit by just being around him when visiting Sam at his father's. There is reverence in his aura. A harkening to another time, greater spirits.

"I have not seen you in a while," he says.

"No...I...I've been a bit preoccupied this past year." I moisten my lips, the mystery of my nights rising to the surface like poison.

"Do you and my Sam still spend time together?"

"Yes." *Not like we used to. Not like before.* "I haven't seen him much this past summer. And recently..." I trail off, a question hanging in my words.

He looks past me down the street. "He's been troubled. This summer..." His words edge into silence for a long minute, unfinished. "And this week...he's been preparing for something important."

"I heard he's on a spiritual quest?"

"Preparing for it..." His eyes drift to mine. "I was hoping perhaps you knew what had been troubling him as of late. He has been away much these past couple months. And when home...shadows haunt him." He pulls his gray sweater closer around his broad chest.

"Maybe the deaths—"

"It started before those. This summer...something changed. And now, with these deaths...he possesses an anger. A...restlessness."

"He's offended, sir...about what some people have been saying about the deaths. The...whole werewolf thing again...but this time—"

He lifts a hand and waves it in dismissal. "What they're saying now is nothing new. There will always be fools amongst us. Those who cannot decipher which stories are true." He returns his eyes to the distance, watching the tourists who have chosen to brave the town's unsolved deaths as they move along the streets. "I suppose, though, with the recent danger, perhaps it gave him reason to turn his mind toward his taxilit. If ever there was a time to feel the need..." His voice trails off and he takes a few steps, drifting further down the walk. He pauses, turning to face me. "You look like something haunts you as well. There is change about you." His gaze is steady on me, now, eyes inquiring. When I don't respond, he says, his voice resigned, "Perhaps, for both of you, it is nothing more than your youth that leaves you restless."

"Perhaps." But it's not.

And he doesn't look convinced.

He gives a slight nod. "Should you see Sam before we do...please ask him to return home. We are...worried for his safety."

"I will."

"Thank you." He turns to drift down the street, his gray hair and sweater merging with the low cloud.

I watch him fade among the tourists, my stomach twisting. I'd been so preoccupied with my own unrest, I had been oblivious to Sam's. A sliver of guilt slices through me. Maybe Miriam thought I'd been there for my friends as much as they'd been there for me, but she was wrong. If Sam had been drifting away since the summer, I hadn't noticed. Because *I'd* been drifting away for the past year.

Further down the road, I see Kam and his friends swarming the parking lot of Benelli's Burgers. They haven't noticed me yet, nor has the cluster of tourists coming my way, so I flip up my hood and jam my feet on the pedals, reeling down the streets.

I know I shouldn't go to Alexa's. I know I should give her space as Magenta requested, but I can't be away from her, my gut tensing at the thought of not seeing her. And there's that feeling. As if she's in danger.

When I reach the mansion, I don't pedal up the drive. Instead, I continue past, ditching my bike in the cover of some bushes. I hesitate, not sure what I'm doing. *I just need to see her.* The woods are thick, underbrush choking the forest floor, but still, I push through.

I feel criminal, somehow. Like I'm doing something illegal. But Magenta was clear. **Give Alexa some space.**

What are you doing, Jayden? I ask myself. It feels wrong. Like I'm spying. But a bigger part of me feels tense. Protective. *I need to know she's okay.*

Mom had said I had premonition.

Miriam said it too.

And I feel it now. A prickling in my skin. A restlessness. Unease.

And again, the feeling. *Something isn't right.*

I blend into the trees, drifting behind low boughs until I'm behind the manor, scanning the length of property, the vacant windows. I want to run, move, stride right up to the door and pound on it until someone opens it, until I can see for myself that Alexa is okay. She's fine. It's nothing. *A virus. Maybe a residual problem leftover from her accident.* I'm not afraid of what those issues might be. Even if her parents don't want me near her right now, I just need to know she's all right.

So, I wait.

*　*　*

Hours pass, and my sharp surveillance wavers. The nights of sleep deprivation begin to wreak havoc on my mind. Caught somewhere between vigilance and sleep, my mind drifts. Sophie...Lindsay...slip across my mind, eyes vacant, bodies gaping, open. Eyes wide.

I jerk awake, realize I've dozed. I push myself up from where I've slumped to the ground against the rough bark of a tree. For a moment, I think I see someone pushing through the underbrush but it's just the movement of branches in the stir of air.

I wait. When there's nothing, I slide back down the base of the trunk. Waiting. Watching. Time ticks slowly on.

There are whispers.

The sound of breath in the breeze.

Stalker...

I startle, my eyes flying open. I'd fallen asleep yet again. But there'd been a voice. Hadn't there? I swear I heard someone speak. Frantically, I glance around.

Nothing but trees.

Maybe it was just my conscience talking—grappling with the absurdity of standing out in the gathering dusk, cold mist starting to curl through the air. I shiver where I stand, darkness thickening around me.

This is insane. Just go home. Nothing is out here. Everything is fine. Alexa is fine. I climb to my feet, brushing clots of moss from my pants, heaviness guilting my heart for being out here at all, when the rear patio doors open. Magenta rushes outside, her long dress swirling about her ankles. She raps on Dr. Johansson's lab door, which opens moments later. I can't make out what words are exchanged, but he quickly follows her back to the mansion, the outbuilding door left open in his haste.

I push aside the veil of Douglas fir that hangs before me, curiosity filling me with inexplicable guilt. *What are they talking about? Where is Alexa? Is she okay?*

As I wait, breath bated, twilight drops to night, deep and dark. Mist has filled the air, blackening like cloud, blotting the moon, leaving the forest in complete shadow. The only light, that from the lab.

I'm almost ready to give up, come again tomorrow, when I notice movement in the forest where it brushes up against the rear wall of the outbuilding.

Someone *or something* is there.

NINETEEN

I FREEZE, UNABLE to move. Unable to speak, as a shadow merges with the light that spills from Dr. Johansson's lab.

The sight of him fills me with sudden rage. *Why is* he *here?*

My fists clench in place, a possessive fury bubbling up.

Sam. *One of your best friends,* I remind myself.

But still...

I stand frozen, immobile. I don't know what to do, the shock of seeing him tangling in my mind.

Before I can grapple further with my thoughts, the patio doors of the mansion burst open. Magenta hurries outside and off the decking into the susurrant grasses, a flood of lamplight carving through the night air before her. I shrink back under the cover of the boughs as Dr. Johansson emerges next. I watch the door behind them, waiting for Alexa to appear.

She doesn't.

Magenta and Dr. Johansson move quickly across the property, into the tangle of woods, their spotlight carving through the thick trunks of trees.

I want to follow. See where they're going. I glance back at the mansion to the low-lit windows of the first floor. *Is she still inside?*

And Sam. I jerk my head back toward the outbuilding, searching the dark perimeter for his form. Nothing but the gentle stirring of heavy boughs, the whisper of grasses.

As if he hadn't been there at all.

Did I dream seeing him? A heaviness weights my mind. I stumble on some roots, my jeans snagging on thorns, and advance toward the outbuilding. "Sam?" I call, softly.

The glare of Magenta's lamp has disappeared, swallowed by the dense cloak of forest and mist.

I reach the outbuilding by way of the forest edge. "Sam?" I call again.

I listen for footfall through the forest. The snap of a branch, the rustle of leaves.

Nothing. The mist heavy with secrets.

Confused, I turn back toward the mansion, running my eyes along the length of it then stop suddenly. In the center of the yard stands a wolf. *The wolf.* Amber eyed. Large as a bear. It watches me intently, mist suspended around it like a mirage.

My heart lodges in my throat, the instinct to run flexing in my muscles, but I know to run would be foolish. Instead, I creep, imperceptible movements, toward the open door of Dr. Johansson's lab. A few more steps. Then I can slip inside. Shut the door.

Wait.

The mist grows heavier, the wolf's gray coat becoming part of it, as if absorbed by air, until I can no longer see it. I don't know where it is. Heart pounding, I reach the lab's doorway at last, the slit of light spilling onto the grass in front, refracting back in the wall of mist. I lunge inside, slamming the door behind me, gripping the doorknob to hold it in place. *As if a wolf could open it.* "You're safe," I sputter out loud, trying to convince myself. There are two deadbolts above the door. I flip them closed, the click of them locking into place giving small relief.

Because I'm trapped.

With nowhere to go.

TWENTY

IT'S SILENT IN Dr. Johansson's lab but for the low hum of overhead fluorescents. I lean against the door, my hand still clenched on the knob, heart pounding. I listen for the heavy tread of animal footfall outside, sinister breath, or a deep throated snarl.

Nothing.

So, it was real. The wolf. Not a figment of imagination that night. I press my back to the door, beads of perspiration dampening my forehead.

I've never seen one so big.

Still breathing hard, I turn around slowly, my eyes combing over neatly arrayed items stacked on pristine shelving. Charts line the walls, detailed diagrams of the brain, neurons, synapses, the paleomammalian cortex, high resolution somatotopic maps—*whatever that means.* 3-D models, one, a life-sized body, propped on a stand with a detailed intricate network of thread-like nerves running from the simulated brain stem, the spinal cord, connecting to all the organs, muscle, tissue and bone. Despite myself, I'm curious. I release my death-hold grip of the door, and drift to examine the charts.

How brilliant Dr. Johansson must be. The complicated models, the exhaustive list of names and functions with lengthy titles or explanations make no sense to me other than the rudimentary recognition I have from high school classes and reading.

The ominous ticking of a clock mounted on the far wall draws me back to my senses about my current situation. Beneath the clock, a row of computer screens sit, screen savers swirling. I glance back toward the door. Locked tight. What if Magenta and Dr. Johansson return? *My other fear.* My eyes flit to the square of window, blind pulled snug against the pane of glass. There is no movement there. I wait, as if expecting the creature outside to lunge through the glass. But of course, it doesn't.

It's a wolf, Jayden, not some monster.

Exhaling, I try and steady myself. Everywhere I turn are more charts, models, computers, walls—no other exit. Stepping back, I bump against a computer, it blinks to life ready for a passcode to be entered. I stare at it for a minute, tempted to try my luck at unlocking it. As if I could. And as if I'd understand any of the scientific world that would be revealed to me if I did.

Some papers lie beside the computer with *SciLifeLab* letterhead marked on the top, the content typed in another language. There are random pamphlets from the *Allen Institute, Delft University of Technology, Neuralink, DARPA,* and a sealed envelope mysteriously labeled *2045 Initiative.* I trace a finger over the papers then step away from the computer, scanning the walls, racking my brain on what to do next when I notice a bulletin board tucked behind shelving of brain models, newspaper articles pinned to its surface. Glancing one last time toward the door, I slip over to the board and run my eyes over the articles. The words are in a different language, the city captioned Stockholm. There is a photo of a car being pulled from a lake, its top smushed in. Another photo is of someone on a stretcher. I swallow hard. *I was with a friend who was driving...*

A boyfriend, I remember, my mouth dry.

...and we went off the road... We landed in a cold fjord. The fact that it was so cold probably saved my life because we were trapped underwater. I should have drowned. Alexa's story comes back to me. But seeing the picture causes my gut to turn over. It's one thing to hear it, another to see the destruction of the steel, the crushed hood, the caved in roof, frigid fjord waters spilling from it as a crane lifts it free from the depths. Desperate to understand the article, I scrutinize the words,

trying to make sense of the unfamiliar script. What I presume to be the date, reads two years ago.

My eyes trail over other images that comprise the article. There's a picture of someone lying in a hospital bed, linked to tubes, cords—an assortment of medical equipment. I recognize the long, wound curls spread across the thin hospital pillow, the photo too grainy to make out any detail of the bandaged face.

"Alexa," I whisper, touching a finger to the newsprint.

My eye catches a color printed family photo included in the same article of Alexa with her parents. A before picture, obviously. Before the accident. Dr. Johansson looks happy but serious. Magenta beams, and Alexa—face full of vibrant youth—beams back.

But there's something different about her. Something...not right. She was two years younger, but it's something more. I lean closer. From behind, I notice another article tucked almost out of sight. I reach up and slip it free. There is a picture of Alexa, looking how I know her today. She looks beautiful, strong. The article is dated four months post-accident, its title, *Mirakel Dotter*.

"Mirakel Dotter." I run the words over my tongue. "Mirakel dotter...mirakel dotter... miracle...daughter?" A shiver runs down my spine when I voice the phonetics of the foreign words. Reflexively, my hand drifts to my face, skimming the flesh above the cheekbone, the perfect eye socket. Smooth. Unblemished by pain or swelling. Healed. "Her recovery was a miracle..." With trembling hands, I replace the article as it was behind the other, so its discovery won't be noticed, my mind spinning.

Outside, there's a sound. Something brushing past the door.

Hairs rise on the back of my neck. I can't breathe. My heart pounds, too loud for the silent room; the hum of the lights, the resolute tick of the clock, the only other sounds. Slowly, I chance a glance back at the door, then to the window, praying that whoever—whatever—is outside doesn't try to come in.

Then there's a voice. A mumble through the walls. A question hanging in its intonation. A voice that is familiar.

"Alexa?" I stumble over a carefully laid array of neuroscientific books in my haste to get to the door. I press an ear against its cold steel, listening. *You're imagining things. It's not her.* I look at the tedious clock. It's only approaching 9:30pm. *What if it is?*

My mind fills with the image of the wolf standing in the mist, watching me. *What if it's still out there too?*

Flipping off the light so I won't be noticed, I cautiously undo the locks and ease the door ajar, peering into the thick fog of night. Every sense is alert, alive. The bleak air cloys, pellets of water cling to my skin. There's nothing but the heavy hush of mist.

Carefully, I step outside, leaving the door open as I found it, hoping Dr. Johansson won't notice someone was inside. Apart from the light, I have left everything as I found it. *The books!* I realize too late that the carefully stacked books I tripped over were knocked askew. There's no time to go back, for in that moment the voice sounds again.

"Mom? Dad?"

Alexa. I scan the thick air trying to see her. "Alexa? It's me—Jayden. Where are you?"

There's no response. My brow knits. Instinctively my fists clench, muscles rigid with the feeling that something is about to lunge at me. *The wolf. Fangs bared.* I squeeze my eyes shut, the sensation so profound.

"Jayden?" Her voice is melodious. Close. There is confusion in it.

"I'm here," I stammer, inching forward into the thick night.

The mist is just as heavy as it was moments ago, but it's like she appears, fragment by fragment, or my eyes adjust, because suddenly I see her standing not too far away. She's barefoot, dressed in pajamas that are gossamer light.

"Are you okay?" I ask.

She doesn't answer, looking behind her at the thatch of hidden forest, trunks twined with the oppressive haze. "Why are you here?" Her voice is a whisper.

"I was worried about you," I whisper back. "Your parents...they're gone. They went into the woods. And...and there's a wolf here somewhere, so you need to get inside—"

"You can't see me like this." Now there is emotion. Packed and poignant, threaded with intensity.

"See you like what?" I step toward her, her face lost in shadows.

There's something about her stance. It's unsteady. Shaky.

"Let me help you." I reach to touch her elbow. "What are you doing out here?"

Her eyes drift toward the manor—just a thick shadow in the murky haze—then away. "I don't know."

"Alexa..."

Even in the dark, the bright blue of her eyes is intense. Or maybe I'm just imagining their color in the dull mist...needing things to be normal between us.

I thread my fingers through hers. They feel cold, as if she's been walking a long time through the mists. "I need to get you back inside. The wolf—"

"Something is happening to me," she whispers.

"What?"

"Something...is...happening..."

There's a snap of a branch deep in the underbrush. The fiery light of a lantern carves through the mist. I can hear the sound of muttered incantations.

"You have to go," Alexa whispers. "She can't find you here with me. Not like this." She looks down at the dewy nightgown, moist against her skin from the damp air, as if noticing it for the first time.

"I'll come back," I promise. "To make sure you're okay." I hold her face close, search her eyes.

"I'm sorry, Jayden," she whispers. One solitary tear collects and fades within her eye. "I don't want you to see me like this—"

"Like what, Alexa? See you like what? Because I don't care what it is. What you're not telling me. I just want to be with you. If you're not well—"

"Go—"

"—it doesn't matter. Please. Alexa—just tell me what's going on!"

"Please...before she sees you..." Gently, she pushes me away and disappears toward the manor just as Magenta sweeps into the yard, her lantern carving a path through the mist. I press back into the depths of the forest and watch through the veil of trees as Magenta too, heads straight for the manor and out of sight.

Stealthily, I push my way through the undergrowth, keeping aware of the sounds around me, listening for any footfall indicating the wolf is still present. Or Sam. I silently pray he's gotten away. That danger doesn't find him. But the feeling is mixed with a deep-rooted anger. That he was even here at all. Watching.

It's difficult to navigate, the damp air heavy as zombie breath. But I'm grateful too, for its cover. It takes some time to locate my bike in the dense night, but once I do, I head home, each curve in the road committed to memory. I could navigate it with my eyes closed, I don't need to see. I don't need anything at all.

Except Alexa.

*   *   *

Back at the trailer park, I ditch my bike and head inside. The mobile is empty, though the ethanol scent of Mom lingers. I pace the narrow length of the mobile, my hands raking through my hair, trying to make sense of my convoluted thoughts. *She'll be okay. Let it be. It's just something to do with her accident. A blip in her health. She'll be okay. You weren't even supposed to be there. You weren't supposed to know.*

But I can't convince myself.

Slowly, I calm down, the erratic thud of my heart steadying. I wander into my room and sit on my bed, picking up the purple crystal from where it's fallen to the floor. I lie back, massaging my temples and stare at the ceiling in the half-light coming in from the hall. The tension of the evening unravels. The spying. The wolf. The entrapment in the lab. Alexa, distant and distracted, the gloss of a tear hovering behind her eye.

Exhaustion beats my brain, as it always does the minute I stop. I start to drift off, my leg jerking in protest, jarring me from sleep. With anxious fingers, I reach for the robe tie and loop it around my wrist, my mind running back to Alexa, her gossamer light pajamas, moist with mist, her ethereal presence in the haunted night.

My mind runs over the articles tacked to Dr. Johansson's wall. The car like a crushed tomb. The girl in the hospital bed. The *Mirakel Dotter.* And the girl before. Something had stood out in that photo. *What was it?*

I sit up.

Poking half out from underneath my bed is my cell phone. I kick it out from underneath and stare at its dark rectangular face, snatching it up to try to get on the internet. It's suddenly deeply important to look at those articles again. Look at the photograph. Know what the article says about her.

There's a text from Steve: Where are you?

Shit. I missed work. I've never done that before. I rake my hands through my hair.

I have to send him a message. But first things first. I need to look up those articles about Alexa's accident. I hit the Safari button. No wifi. Of course.

"*Damn* it!"

I rush into the hall and clamor out the door to sprint across to Dan's, dodging the erratic path of a stray bat as it swoops low over the doorstep of his trailer. I bang on his door, desperate.

"Heard of just knocking?" he asks when he opens. "I thought the park was on fire." He steps aside so I can come in.

"Sorry, it's kind of important." I rush over to the squat desk where his laptop is sitting. "What's your password?"

"I'm well, thank you, and you?" he mocks, sidling over and punching in the access code.

"I'm sorry, I just—saw some articles that were in a different language and I want to know what they said."

"What's it about?"

"Someone I know." I sit staring at the google search page. "Can I get translations done on here?"

"Yeah. You just google 'translation' or 'translate' then it will have a box you can type in and it will convert it to the language you want. Come on, Jay, you're seventeen and you're asking a fifty-seven-year-old about the wonders of the Net. See something wrong with this picture?"

"Yeah, no, I know what to do. I'm just not thinking straight. I don't use the internet often. Not if it's not school related."

"I know. It's weird." He picks up a cigarette and flicks a lighter, going to his door to stand on the stoop to smoke.

"You know, if you ever want to open a Dojang somewhere, someday, you might want to ditch that habit," I mutter. "No one is going to want taekwondo lessons from someone with emphysema."

"Do I look like I have emphysema?"

Distractedly, I glance his way. He casually takes another drag, his powerful form hulking in the doorway.

"No."

He shrugs. "Well, then."

I type into the search engine *Mirakel Dotter.* Some obscure links appear. I scroll and scroll, narrowing the search to Stockholm and finally an online version of the news article I saw in Dr. Johansson's lab appears with what looks like links to a few other associated articles on the accident.

Dan drifts back in, shutting the door behind him. "What language is that?" he asks, peering over my shoulder.

"It's Stockholm, so Swedish. Alexa's dad is from Sweden. They spent some time there."

"Alexa," he turns the name over on his tongue. "This the same girl you were rushing off to see the other night?"

"I don't know what you're talking about."

"You've been more nocturnal than usual again these days, Jayden." He's drifted to the far corner of the trailer, setting himself down on a lumpy couch in the slide-out space.

"What do you mean?"

"I see your comings and goings."

"Yeah, well...they aren't all for a girl."

"I know."

My hands hesitate over the keyboard, an uncomfortable knot forming in my stomach. I glance back at him, his eyes steady on me.

"Go on," he says. "Continue what you are doing."

Slowly, I turn my eyes back to the screen, trying not to wonder what he meant. Trying not to wonder about the truth behind those words. My knuckles are white as I click on the article that shows the picture of the car being dredged up from the icy waters.

I copy and paste the article and find a translation box on another page, dropping in the text.

My eyes skim over the words, catching on one section.

> The car was submerged for one hour with the girl and the body of her friend trapped beneath the frigid water.

"One hour," I murmur. "How does someone survive being underwater for an *hour?*"

"What's that?" Dan gets up from the couch and saunters over to my side.

"Nothing." I try to angle the screen away, suddenly protective.

"Jayden, what is it?"

"Have you ever heard of people being trapped underwater and surviving?"

"In cold water? Yes. It's something to do with the hypothermic state the body goes into. It slows the blood. There's stories of people who survived, who are brought back to life. I believe there's a saying: 'you ain't dead until you're warm and dead.'" His eyes drift to the window. The blinds are open. Nothing but darkness and dismal trailers and mobiles lined in loose rows outside, yet it looks like he's looking into a different world. A faraway one.

"You know something about this?"

"Just have heard about it." His hands start to fidget, he pushes them into his pockets. "It's called the 'twilight zone.' The time when the body begins the process of dying."

I shudder at the image, and return my eyes to the screen, my body angling to block the article from Dan.

"You're using my computer but won't let me see what you're reading on it?"

"I'm sorry…I just—"

He reaches over and swivels the laptop toward him. "*The girl has since been identified as Alexa Johansson, daughter of acclaimed neuroscientist and surgeon, Dr. Sven Johansson and neuroprosthetics engineer, Magenta Croy,*" he quotes. "*Medical staff were able to resuscitate her using cardiopulmonary bypass, a critical care process that gradually rewarms the blood and organs. However, Alexa still faces a long journey ahead, her long-term prognosis yet to be determined. A mere 30% of patients have survived accidental hypothermia with cardiac arrest—*"

"That's enough." The breaths are sharp in my chest as I struggle for air, emotion blooming inside.

"You all right, kid?"

"Yeah."

"How about I give you a minute," Dan says. He places a hand on my shoulder then fishes another cigarette out of the packet in his pocket and disappears outside, closing the door behind him.

I stare at the screen, at the image of the car, water draining from it like some kind of leviathan, then at the hospital picture. I fumble to navigate to the *Mirakel Dotter* article written just four months later with the photograph of Alexa, standing strong and alive. The before picture of her with her family. Something about the picture niggles at me. She looks different. *But how?* It's not just that she's younger.

Hands shaking, I try more than once to successfully copy the text to the translation box.

The medical community is in awe of the recovery of Alexa Johansson, daughter of top neuroscientist and surgeon, Dr. Sven Johansson, and biomedical engineer, Magenta

Croy. Staff were concerned earlier this year when the pair decided to remove their daughter from hospital care to continue her recovery at home, with both parents taking a step back from their demanding careers to care for their daughter. The two joined forces after Ms. Croy left an illustrious Hollywood career in Special Effects to train and specialize in the cutting-edge developments of neuroprosthetics.

I skim over the details that recap the last article about the accident until I reach the end, unable to stomach reading the specifics of Alexa's injuries again.

Medical experts remain in awe of the speed of Alexa's recovery, as many believed her return home earlier this year was a palliative move. Her remarkable recovery is seen by many as a medical miracle. Dubbed the Miracle Daughter by residents of Sweden's esteemed Karolinska Institute, Alexa is pictured here, having regained full physical and cognitive abilities with only minimal effects showing from the trauma she experienced just a few short months ago. Sources would like to discover the secret behind Alexa's miraculous recovery, but the family is requesting privacy at this time. They will continue their work in innovation for medical advancement but are planning to continue their sabbaticals overseas while their daughter continues to focus on her recovery.

That's it. No other articles. Without the family available for more interviews, it seemed interest died, and the *Mirakel Dotter* disappeared from the news without further trace.

I click the computer off and sit back in the chair. Miracles. By God or by man? *Or by a woman?* I rub my temples. Alexa's injuries were nothing a poultice or herbal teas could have fixed. I scrape back the chair and go to the door, opening it to find Dan standing in the lane, smoking, his eyes tracing the outline of moon peering through the thick patch of cloud.

"Find what you were looking for?"

"I don't really know what I'm looking for," I confess.

"Answers, it seems," he says, stubbing out his cigarette. "Sometimes the answers aren't what we want, you know?"

"Yeah." I step down from his trailer and head toward the mobile. "Thanks for letting me use your computer."

"Not a problem." He watches me and as I approach, shoots a closed fist out toward me. Reflexively, I block it, my body crouching into a fight stance.

"What was that for?" I sputter, relaxing when he makes no further move.

"Reminding you to be ready. For anything, Jayden—the unexpected. And that doesn't just mean physical danger. Emotions are just as vulnerable. You're here looking up information about a girl instead of just asking her. That should tell you something. You should know someone before you serve up your heart to them." There's a sadness in his eye as he looks away from me into the shadow of trees.

"Yeah, well, maybe I don't want her to know everything there is about me either."

"That should tell you something too."

I give a tight laugh. "Trust me, it's better that way. Either way, it's too late for my heart not to get involved, Dan."

"I see that," he says, pushing his hands deep into his pockets. Overhead, a pair of bats flit past the faint sheen of moonlight, their silhouettes darkly tangled together before parting. "Just be careful."

"I let you in, you know," I say, walking backward toward my mobile, watching him. "Sometimes you just have to trust someone. Like I trusted you. From the moment I met you. Yet to this day, I don't know everything there is to know about you either."

He gives a slight nod of his head, his mouth tensing in consideration. He turns toward his trailer, slowly retreating up the front step.

"Well...like you said...maybe it's better that way. Good night, Jayden."
He goes inside, closing the door behind him.

Frustrated, I head inside and beeline to my room. I sit on my bed and
knot the bathrobe tie tightly around my wrist, my mind whirling as I lie
back. I fight it, but sleep comes quick, my body desperate to rest.

* * *

I dream of being trapped in a car, underwater. I'm in the driver's seat
and turn to see beside me Alexa's profile, dark, curly hair drifting upward
in the wash. She turns to face me. Even with the water murky between
us, she looks beautiful, her eyes a beacon of blue. I lean forward to kiss
her. As if that would save her. Save me. Both of us trapped, unable to
escape. She leans toward me too, her lips parting. But she isn't trying to
kiss me. She's mouthing something.

Help me.

TWENTY-ONE

AT SCHOOL THE next morning, Brody bumps up against me while I'm getting books for morning class. "Man, you look like death warmed over," he cheerfully observes.

A shudder runs through my body, Dan's words ricocheting through my mind, *There's a saying, 'you ain't dead until you're warm and dead.'* Alexa, entombed in a glacial fjord, her body cooling, heart slowing to a stop...

I slam my locker shut. "Gee, thanks." I shoulder my bag and stride down the hall, scanning each face I pass, searching for the shock of blue eyes, the cascade of curls. "You're the last person I expected to refer to me as Death."

"Hey, what gives? You know I didn't mean it like that," Brody objects, hurrying after me. "What's got you in such a mood?"

We head into math class and plunk down into seats. "Nothing. I'm sorry."

"Look, all I meant is you don't look so well. The only thing that links you to 'death' or a vampire is your *devastatingly* good looks, okay? Looks that remind everyone of the most popular vampire to ever have graced the Hollywood elite." He smirks as he shoves open his textbook. "Seriously though...Kam been bugging you again? I thought he'd have left you alone after the last time. People are talking about how beat up he and his buddies are...and how you walked away unscathed. Everyone saw you get worked over, then you show up yesterday like nothing happened." He leans closer. "Though we both know that's not true. You were messed up. You just got lucky, somehow, in healing fast." He skims his eyes over my face again, a trace of puzzlement crossing his expression.

"It's not Kam," I respond.

"You better watch your back though, Jay. I mean it," Brody says, his voice low. "There are rumors that he has it out for you. He's embarrassed about how you took over the fight and whooped their asses bad. He wants revenge."

"I got that impression." I picture Kam's face as he passed me yesterday in science. *This isn't over, Death.* I sit back in my chair. The rest of the class is gossiping, waiting for the bell to ring and the teacher to appear. I feel their eyes on me. "Funny how he calls it revenge when he's the one who attacked me first."

"Doesn't matter how it went down. It's what he wants. Just watch your back, okay?"

"Always do." I run my knuckles across the stubble of my chin, trying to ignore the weight of peoples' stares. As if my threatened demise were some script for entertainment. I shove back my seat. "I gotta go."

"What?" Brody's brow puckers. "It's only the second week of school. You can't skip out yet. It's not like you."

"It's too crowded in here," I state, casting my eyes around the room. Everyone stops murmuring to each other, watching me.

I grab my books and head for the door just as the bell rings and the teacher, Mr. Bekker strolls in. "Where you headed, Jayden? We're about to start."

"Something came up." I shoulder past him and out into the hall, drawing in big breaths once I round the corner of the hall. *What are you doing?* I know I shouldn't be rattled by Kam. I can handle him.

But ghosts haunt me. That boy still lives inside. The one pedaling home to an empty mobile not knowing which road was the safest route home. And it wasn't the wildlife I was trying to avoid.

I go to my locker and grab my things, hurriedly stuffing them into my backpack then slam the locker shut and hustle toward the nearest exit.

"Are you leaving?"

I stop and turn around. Miriam stands, backpack on her back, coat on. "Yeah."

"Why?" Something about the look in her eye makes me hesitate. A look of disbelief.

I clear my throat and glance up at the hall clock. "*You're* late."

"Yeah, I know. I slept in." Her expression holds a question.

"Your mom didn't get you up?"

"She was gone for an early showing. Dad was early to City Hall, and Brody had basketball tryouts. So, no. I had bad dreams last night. Guess I missed my alarm." She hasn't moved, one hand still gripping the strap of her pack.

"Guess you better get to class." I clear my throat and hold my ground.

"Jayden...this is the year that counts. All your scholarship potential finally gets its chance. Why now? Why when you finally have the opportunity to achieve all your dreams are you skipping out? Are you trying to self-sabotage?"

"It's just the first part of term, there's lots of time to—"

"She's not here, is she."

I exhale, my heart stuttering in my chest. I know who she means. "I don't think so, no."

"That's why you're leaving. Because being here without her just isn't worth it anymore. Because she's all that matters to you right now." There's a hardness to her tone that I'm not accustomed to.

"It's not like that, Miriam. I'm worried about her. Besides, it sounds like there's a mark on my back."

"Yeah, I heard. Kam. He's not going to do anything here, Jayden. And do you really want him to see you running away?"

I gesture down the hall. "He's not here right now, so guess he won't see me."

"Nice." She shakes her head and starts walking toward her locker.

"And I'm not running away. Like I said, I'm worried about Alexa."

She stops, her back rigid, then continues slowly to her locker.

The thought of her angry or disappointed with me is like a blade through my gut. Already, I feel like I've drifted from the people who were my world before I met Alexa. And I don't want to lose them. But somehow, it feels like I am. Like an irrevocable shift has begun. "I'll be here tomorrow, all right? I'm not going to blow this year."

"You better not. Ms. Cash thinks you're good enough for Harvard. Good enough to get a scholarship to get there. Or any of the other elite schools. Isn't that what you want?"

"Yeah...it was."

"*Was?*"

"I don't know where I'll end up." Where will Alexa be? Will she still be walking the mansion halls? Or will she be off to college somewhere? Maybe a place that also has a good Literature and Writing program— one I could look into. Or would her family be packed up and headed to some other remote town? They'd moved so much already since her accident—

Sources would like to discover the secret behind Alexa's miraculous recovery...

A cold shiver leaks down my spine.

"Guess you better go, then," Miriam says, her voice heavy with disapproval. I snap back from my reverie, her eyes on mine. "Because it's like you've already gone anyway." There's hurt in her tone. A thread of frustrated anger.

Defeated, I turn to walk away, not sure how to respond. "I'll see you around."

"You didn't ask about my bad dreams."

I turn. Her back is to me as she stuffs her coat into her locker, extracting the binder she needs for her first class.

"What were they then?" I ask. I do care. I need her to know that. That I'm still here if she needs me. At least, I want to be.

She shuts her locker resolutely, a hand resting on the cold metal. "The killer got me. He took me. I woke up in the forest all alone. At least I thought I was alone, but when I looked around someone was standing there." Her hand slides down the locker before she moves it to wrap around her other arm, her binder clutched to her chest.

A lump forms in my throat. I swallow hard. "Who?"

"You."

"So, I'm the killer now?" My voice catches and I close my eyes. A face flashes in my mind. *Pixie hair. Hazel eyes.* I shudder.

"No, you were trying to save me. But you were too late." The air between us is charged. Her lip quivers slightly then stops, her eyes sharp. "My heart had already been ripped out."

I remember her look on Sunday night, the storm raging overhead as we took the boards off the top of her car in her driveway. The look in her eye triggering the memory of my crush. The memory of wanting her.

"Mir...I'd always save you. I'd never let anything happen to you." My voice is soft. "Just because I finally found someone...doesn't mean I've forgotten what you mean to me."

She half smiles, a sweet sadness haunting her face. "Guess I had...forgotten. Or never realized, until it was too late. What you meant to me." She toys with the edge of her binder.

I don't know what to say. Neither does she. She shakes her head and tucks her binder under her arm, turning toward class. I watch her go, an inexplicable loneliness filling my chest.

"I hope she's worth it, Jayden. Worth who you're becoming for her." She stops in front of a closed classroom door. "But I guess you've been becoming someone else for a while now. Maybe it's got nothing to do with her at all."

"Look, I'm sorry if I've been distant this past week—this past year. I've been going through some stuff. But I mean—I've always been a bit of a loner anyway, you know that."

"Not like this. Not with me." Her eyes shimmer with emotion then harden, resolute.

She opens the classroom door and disappears inside, shutting the door behind her.

"Shit." I've become the champion of hurting Miriam and she's the last person on earth I'd want to hurt. She'd been the only one with guts to stand up for me over the years. The only one who I didn't have to hide my truth from. She knows all the sordid details of my life. But she doesn't know about the wandering. What would she think of me then? The boy who wakes up in the middle of a dark forest covered in blood. The boy with the memory of a dead girl he's never met.

I stumble backward then gain my bearings, hurrying out into the fine rain falling outside. I grab my bike and start to pedal, my mind in a vortex of emotion. I'm still lost in thought when I pass the Thriftway. Outside, Steve is unloading boxes for a seasonal display. My knuckles tighten on the handlebars as I veer into the parking lot and coast to a stop beside him.

"Shouldn't you be in school?" he says when he sees me.

"Taking a personal day."

"Is that what you were doing yesterday? Taking a personal day then too?"

"That's why I'm here. I want to apologize for missing work. I—it just totally slipped my mind, to be honest."

"That would be a first for you." He puts down a box and strides through the automatic doors to the inside of the grocery store. I follow. He pauses in front of another display, picking up an inventory list. He glances at me from the corner of his eye as he leafs through it. "Look, maybe it was too soon for you. Your face may have healed, but maybe you just need some more time."

"It's not that...I just—forgot." I take a deep breath as his posture stiffens.

"Okay, well. Let's not forget again, okay? I need you in. The tourists are crazy right now—all here for the festival. And you need the work, Jay, if you're going to save enough for college, right? That's what you've been saying."

"I know."

"Then be here later today. I offered you it as a make-up shift, remember? Four o'clock. Don't forget this time."

"I won't. Thanks, Steve. And again, I'm sorry."

"Just don't let it happen again, okay?" He stops what he's doing to look at me. "We're all rooting for you, you know. Everyone in this town wants to see you succeed. Just make it happen."

"I will."

"Good."

Behind him I notice a group of girls pause, whispering to each other. One of them slips out her phone, raising it in my direction. "Do you think it's really him?" one of them whispers loud enough that we hear.

Steve sighs. "I'll put you in the back this week. Until the festival ends after the weekend. Better go before you get mobbed."

"Thanks." I hurry out to my bike, pulling my hood up over my head to conceal my face from the rush of people in the parking lot and those meandering down the street. I head back the way I came, passing the school, then further, past the Forever Twilight in Forks Collection at the Rainforest Arts Center, a bunch of fans coming and going from the building. I notice the '52 Chevy pick-up brought in years ago to represent Bella's truck in the *Twilight* movies parked outside the Chamber of Commerce in preparation for the weekend, a flock of tourists gathered around, snapping photos. I pedal harder to pass by quick.

I'm going to have to keep a low profile around town until the festival ends and the tourists move on to other places. Next year, I won't be here for the festival. Next year I'm supposed to be in Cambridge at Harvard if all goes right. Or somewhere equally exciting. And next year, I'll be that much older, my face changing, with any luck, so I look less like someone from a movie and more like myself. Maybe next year, I'll be someone else entirely.

The tourists aren't bothered by the rain, so I steer off the main drag, ducking down side roads until I'm on the outskirts of town. On impulse, I maneuver my bike down the lane that leads deeper into the forest cover and past the mansion. I slow at the base of its drive. The tall iron gates are closed. Dr. Johansson's red truck is parked in the driveway, but it looks like no one is home. Not that it ever looks incredibly inhabited when they *are* home. But still. There's a stillness about the place that disconcerts me.

I push onward, weaving along the roads, the streets narrowing the deeper I get into the forest, further and further from town, until I reach the Bogachiel River. I ditch my bike and wander out onto the stone riverbed alongside the rushing water, hunkering down on my heels, watching the steady flow of water. Some tourists meander down a trail some distance away. I stay far away from where they are, following the flow of water until I'm alone. Around me the forest breathes, mist rising from the dripping foliage as the rain stops. Weak rays of sunshine touch glossy leaves. Old Man's beard hangs in thick swatches from weathered bark. Further up the banks the river is rougher, thundering from shallow falls in a frothing torrent. I pause, watching its power and beauty. But my mind turns to the bodies of the two girls found deep in these woods. Someone had dragged them through the thick underbrush, away from town. Because surely, they hadn't wandered deep into the backwoods on their own. Only someone with a lot of experience with this wild terrain would be able to navigate the forest depths at night.

Someone like me.

I shake the thought away, a frosted edge of fear spiking my spine. I run my hands through my hair, my mind a tangle of thoughts, then smooth them down my stubbled cheek, my fingers exploring the contours of my face, feeling for any pocket of bruising still healing beneath the surface. Nothing. The news article about Alexa floats into my mind, her body lying in the hospital room, bandages covering her face, tubes linked to her lifeless arms. Then her face in the *Mirakel Dotter* article. The face I can't stop thinking about every minute of every day. I think of poultices, spiced tea, muttered incantations...of candles wavering on their wicks, dotting the property behind the mansion and the rails of the porch. *Was it witchcraft?*

I give my head another shake and stand. "Don't be insane," I whisper to myself.

But something feels off. About me.

About everything.

Not for the first time, it feels like the forest is watching. That it knows all the answers.

Some hikers make their way up the trail toward where I'm crouched. Quickly, I rise and push my way through the heavy undergrowth back to where I've ditched my bike and make my way back to the mobile. There's nowhere to go, the town teeming with people ready to celebrate the story of vampires and werewolves. Of eternal love. There's irony there. In how I fit the part. Yet here I am, alone in an empty mobile. Wanting the very love that only fiction can promise.

At least I thought it was fiction. Until I met Alexa.

At home, exhausted, I sit on my bed and scoop up the purple crystal, holding it in my palm. Wedged into the back of my mattress are the remains of the poultice. I pry it free, its scent still heavy as I draw it near and unwind the gauze, inspecting the contents inside. There's nothing special. Just a paste that has dried flecks of herbs peppering its surface. *How then?*

I place it on my nightstand and lie back, gripping the crystal tightly so its edges dig into my skin. I wonder where Alexa is. If she's okay. I wonder when I'll be able to see her again.

My eyes grow heavy, the toll of the past week—the past year—the past seventeen years—gouging me, leaving me tired. Spent. I'd already felt different enough before waking on my sixteenth birthday in the bowels of the forest, shivering and afraid. This summer, I'd felt almost human— normal—the wanderings temporarily stopped. My ability to fight back had made Kam withdraw. It was just me working toward my future and surfing. Hanging with the crowd on the beach, even if I felt apart from everyone else.

Then my seventeenth birthday. Like an anniversary of all that was wrong with me. Waking up, in the middle of nowhere. Broken. A day later, a confrontation with Kam. The cycle starting again.

But that's when you met her.

And though she couldn't fix me, my heart had suddenly felt whole.

That was something.

Something big.

She hadn't looked at me like I was someone to pity. She looked at me different. Like she understood. With eyes that saw only the best of me.

Like I was some god fresh from battle. Not like some freak who wandered from his pathetic life because he was too stressed to handle it.

Like love at first sight.

I drift off to sleep. At least, I think I do. Because I see her. In my room. An ethereal angel in the doorway, blue eyes bright as the coastal seas when sunlight touches its surface.

I jerk awake. The room is empty, my hand a vice on the crystal. I release it, rubbing the welted indents it left behind and wipe the back of my hand across my mouth, sitting up. The bedside table blinks 3:30pm. I rub my eyes, still heavy from sleep. The rest was like an antidote, my mind feeling clearer than it has in days. I look at the bathrobe tie draped listlessly down the side of the bed. I hadn't needed it. I hadn't moved an inch.

Maybe day is now my time to sleep.

Like a vampire.

I cringe at the thought and push myself up quickly to get ready for work.

* * *

Steve puts me in the back in the stockroom to do inventory. I'm grateful to not have to face customers or dodge the lustful eye of some fan obsessed with a dream.

On break, I drift into the empty coffee room and slump into a seat, unwrapping the cellophane on a muffin. The television is on, a local newscaster covering the festival preparations and the cautions being taken by local authorities to keep things safe.

The news anchor chatters on. "There have been more sightings of the rogue pack of wolves initially implicated in the deaths of local Forks girl, Sophie Wilkinson, and Lindsay Sutton, a tourist visiting Forks from Seattle for the Forever Twilight in Forks Festival. The wolf pack is said to have migrated from outside Olympic territories from the north. Autopsy results of the girls' bodies are expected later this week in hopes of shedding more light on the true cause behind their tragic deaths.

Meanwhile, authorities continue to urge caution for locals and visitors while accessing park trails, warning people to be vigilant about wildlife, and to remain on the lookout for anything or any*one* suspicious—"

"Hey." Jason, who works the deli, walks in, pulling a hair net from his head. "What are you doing in here all alone?"

"It's the break room—taking a break." I keep my eyes fixed on the television.

He rolls his eyes at my response. "Well, 'scuse the hell out of me." He opens his travel mug and pours some coffee in from the pot on the counter. "All I was meaning was I figured you'd be out taking advantage of tourist season—like the rest of us. You out of anyone would be the one to get lucky, looking the way you do."

"What's lucky about that? To be wanted by someone because they think you're someone else?" My stomach clenches when I say it. *Hadn't Alexa made some comment?* Said something about why she wasn't afraid of me the first night she saw me? She'd said, *maybe it's the setting...or those infernal Twilight books...or the fact that 'your' face is plastered all over town as the image of every teenage girl's fantasy...*
The boy that will love you back.
No matter what your secrets.

"What's with you?" Jason shakes his head, his eyebrow lifting at the expression on my face.

She didn't mean it like that...she wouldn't. I'm not some fantasy to her. It's different with her. It's more than that.

I crumple the muffin in its cellophane, my appetite gone. "I don't want to get 'lucky' with a tourist. That isn't connecting with someone. Body, heart, and soul."

He shoots me a derisive look and heads toward the door. "What century are you from, man? Hook-ups are what it's all about."

After he's left, I chuck the muffin into a garbage bin by the door and head to Steve's office where he's set up some paperwork for me to finish. I look out the window at the people moving around the street with an air of excitement, the sordid news of the past week only an echo to those whose lives aren't directly affected. The disconnect of humanity, from its collective whole, from each other. Their interest more in fiction than the heartbreaking news. But I understand that. I do. Because fiction is better, it's filter pure. It makes sense, it's moral made clear. The heroes get to be heroes and the villains find their match.

If only things were so in the real world.

* * *

When my shift ends, it's dark outside. The town hasn't slowed, people milling around in animated groups, lights strung up, the few bars and restaurants thronging with people. Forks, the hottest spot in the US during the week of the Forever Twilight festival. Or so it seems.

I pull my hood up over my head and go to retrieve my bike from where it's locked to a post, overhearing a group of girls cloistered outside the Thriftway, pizza slices in hand from the takeout pizzeria next door.

"What if it *was* wolves?" one of them asks.

"That would be too cool," another says. "Because the report a couple days ago was saying *maybe* it looked like human hands were involved. Like, what if it was a person who turned into a werewolf?"

"Oh god, Jeanine, you are such a die-hard. Jacob protected Bella. He wouldn't rip a girl open. That's disgusting."

"He might, if he thought it was protecting his true love."

"Gross," a third girl comments. "I'm not going hiking during this trip. I don't want to see any wolves."

"So, if a guy that looked like Jacob came up to you right now, you'd turn him away?"

"Ha, no. If a guy like Jacob came up to me then all my dreams would be coming true. Or Edward, for that matter. I'd take either."

They start laughing.

Grimacing, I jerk my bike from its spot, hop on and veer down the street. Posters of scenes from the movie and the cast of legendary stars flank the windows of the businesses lined along the main strip. I catch a glimpse of one where the actors who play Edward and Bella face forward, arms around each other, looking moodily at the camera. For a split second it's like looking in a mirror. Only it's a different girl who would be on my arm. One with her own confidence and power. One who had fought her way back from the brink of death. An intelligent, nuanced person who had consumed my heart in a matter of days. Hours. Not some damsel in distress. Because if anyone needed saving, it was me.

I steer toward home but at the last minute change my mind, taking the fork in the road before disappearing down the deserted stretch that leads to the trailer park and head to Alexa's. My heart accelerates with a rush of anticipation.

But the gates are still closed when I get to the mansion. They stand, foreboding, their spiked tips piercing the air meters above me. The bottom floor is dark. On the second floor, I recognize the length of window where the library stands just a few windows over from the gabled nook where I would sequester away from the world. Lamplight touches the library curtains, the memory of Alexa sitting curled in a blanket on the couch strong in my mind, firelight ringing her with magical aura.

I stand by the gate, watching the window, hoping to see her, when the front door opens. Magenta steps outside, bending to light the candles that line the porch steps and rails. She trails into the yard toward where the other candles sit unlit in their glass casings. She sees me and pauses. "I thought I told you not to come, Jayden."

"I'm sorry, I just need to know she's okay."

Magenta continues her path to the candles, solemnly lighting them one by one. "She's not here right now."

"When will she be back?"

She doesn't answer, pulling her long shawl close around her shoulders. "You should get home. Another storm is expected tonight."

Frustrated, I grip the bars, the iron cold in my grasp. "Will you tell her I was by? That I came to see her?"

She looks my way, her face lost in shadow. "Of course."

"Thank you."

She moves back across the unkempt lawn to the manor, her dress trailing behind her as she climbs the porch steps. She glances back one last time before opening the door to go inside. "I know she means something to you, Jayden. And it has meant a lot to see her so happy with you." She pauses as if considering her next words. "Sometimes, the best thing we can do for our loved ones, is let them go." Her voice is ringed with sadness.

"Let her go? I—" *I don't want to.* "If she needs time—I'll wait."

"Perhaps you shouldn't." Her voice is a pent-up storm of rain and broken light. She disappears inside.

A chasm opens in my chest. *What the hell does she mean?* I feel like I'm suffocating. The gate standing between me and everything I need. My place of comfort. The place where love was dreamed of.

Found.

There's movement in the second-floor window, someone pulling the library curtain aside to peer out. I swallow hard and look up. Alexa stands there, a blanket wrapped around her shoulders. I can't see her expression, but I swear I see her eyes. Feel what they contain. She reaches a hand and touches the glass. I uncoil my fist from its grip around the gate, spreading my fingers to mirror her gesture. We stare silently at each other, the cold night between us. She glances quickly behind her, and the curtain slides back into place.

"I don't understand," I choke. "Why are they keeping us apart?"

Something startles in the dark thatch of woods behind me, across the narrow strip of road. Remembering the hulking form of the wolf, I pedal off, my face damp from the misty air. I retrace my route, back out to the long stretch home. I need to see her. *I need to find a way—*

A group of tall shapes step out from the shadows ahead of me, blocking the street. "What the hell?" I brake to a stop, breathing hard from the exertion of pedaling so fast. I reef the handlebars around to retreat in the opposite direction, when several more step out from behind to surround me.

"Kam..." I recognize his groupies before I see him. He steps out from behind them, a baseball bat tapping his open fist.

"Going to mess you up tonight, Death, since you made a fool of me on Friday night."

"Kam," I hedge. "We're past all this. It's been over between us for a while. Let's forget Friday—"

"And suffer the humiliation of vampire boy besting me? I don't think so." He moves closer in steady, incremental steps, the bat tap tapping menacingly against his meaty palm with slow, metronome precision. "What *do* the girls see in you anyway? You're a late bloomer, got to give you that. But I remember your scrawny self. The outside might have changed, but not the inside." He flips the bat to the other hand. "So, you're strong now...but how will you hold up against this?" He brandishes it toward me, causing me to flinch. "As I thought," he laughs.

My heart thunders, a reverberating echo in my head as the group closes in.

"You won't get away with this," I stammer.

"Hm. Always did before." He paces back and forth like a panther eyeing its prey. "And let's not forget too...there's some psycho on the loose. Lots of bad things been happening to people around here. Real bad. And they don't know whose doing it. *What's* doing it. So...something bad happens to you?" He makes a show of looking around at the silent fortress of forest. "Empty woods. Nobody here to see what happened. And after what *you* did to *me* last time..." he gestures to the bruises swelling his face. "Who's going to believe *I* was the one who attacked *you* when *clearly*," his voice is laced with sarcasm, "you have the upper hand." He takes a step forward. "We've been waiting. Patiently. Took longer than expected for you to make your sorry route home from work. Thought maybe you stopped at the Fosters for your foster family time," he mocks.

"Guess you'd know a little something about that since your mom left," I quip.

His face darkens and his eyes narrow. "You know nothing about me. Or my family."

Two guys rush me from behind, pinning my arms behind my back. A third helps them as I struggle, nearly knocking the other two off their feet.

"Don't worry," Kam sneers. "I won't mess up your pretty face—not too bad." He raises the bat. "But the rest of you? No one will see *this* damage." He lowers his voice, "It will be our little secret..." and swings.

I shove hard, pushing off center the guys holding me, the bat missing me by sheer millimeters. Using the bodies of the guys pinning me from behind as leverage, I lunge up and kick hard, connecting with Kam's forearm.

"You bastard!" he splutters, dropping the bat. He grips his arm then comes at me all fists, connecting with my ribs and stomach.

Unable to use my arms to block him, I strike again with my foot, connecting with his pelvis. He drops to the ground, fumbling for the bat. He grabs it and swings, the wood cracking against my shin. I cry out in pain, fire burning up my leg then a disturbing numbness. He lands another fist into my stomach, then, with the other hand, lifts the bat once more, level with my ribs. As he flings it backward, ready to strike, someone charges from the bushes and grabs the bat, twisting Kam's arm and shoving him to the ground, yanking his arm upward behind him, a firm hand on Kam's shoulder one press away from dislocating it from its joint.

"That's enough." Dan's voice is low and threatening. "These woods *aren't* empty. They have eyes. *My* eyes."

Some of the others lunge forward but Dan reacts quickly, blocking their fists and forcing them into submission. He defends without laying a single punch. I shake my arms free from my captors fighting the electric urge to crush their noses with a palm strike. My muscles quiver with pent-up rage.

"Leave it, Jayden," Dan warns. "Let this scum slither back to the burrows they came from."

Kam has gotten to his feet and unexpectedly makes a move toward Dan who simply sweeps Kam's legs out from under him, a fist hovering above his face ready to deliver a solid blow. "I said that was enough," Dan seethes.

Two more swing at me but I block them and—unable to resist—feel the crack of my fist against their faces.

"Jayden!" Dan admonishes. "Leave it." He turns and torches Kam and his friends with a dark glare. "Enough—all of you! Or I won't be able to hold myself back. Or him." He gestures sharply my way as I try to gain control of my breathing, trying to calm the fury boiling in my veins. "And I can't be responsible for what happens next if you don't." His tone is low. Ominous.

"Fine," Kam spits. "But this isn't over. Not until I have my revenge."

"On a war you started?" Dan challenges. "Know when to walk, boy."

"Who you calling boy?" Kam postures. But his bravado comes at a safe distance as he scuffs backward with his group. "Come on," he commands the others. They amble off to cars parked along the ditches that I missed seeing before in the dark of night. Their doors slam and engines rev before they peel off and disappear out of sight.

"You okay, kid?" Dan clamps a hand on my shoulder.

"Yeah. Thanks." The adrenalin leeches out, my body shuddering with its release. My shin throbs.

"Better get home and give that some attention. Ice and elevation."

"I know what to do."

"I'm sure you do," he says.

I hobble to pick up my bike from where it has fallen. "Where's your truck?"

"Don't have it here."

I look up and down the road. "You were out walking? In the forest? At night?"

"Think you're the only one?" He glances into the deep shadows of the trees as if looking for something lost, then starts walking down the road toward the trailer park. "Coming?"

*   *   *

Back home, he comes inside my mobile and helps get me situated with a bag of ice. "You need anything you come on over, got it? I don't think those boys will be coming back tonight."

"Not tonight but they'll be back. As long as I'm here—in Forks." I rest my head back on the chair. "You told me not to fight back. I don't understand."

"No. I told you to stop once you were safe. Violence is not who you are, Jay. You don't need to do anything more than defend. With guys like that, throwing a punch won't stop them from coming. It will just make them thirst for more."

"Yeah, well, they thirsted even when I didn't punch back. I remember." I tip my head back against the cushion and close my eyes.

"Just remember to not be the monster," he says. "I saw the rage in your eyes, Jay. When you feel that kind of fury...you need to walk away. Otherwise, worse can happen."

"Sure."

"I mean it," he insists.

I open my eyes and look at him.

His body is tense, fists clenched. "You have to be careful with your strength—with the skills I've taught you. You don't want defense to turn into something more."

"I'm not going to *kill* him. Obviously."

"Things happen." He flexes his fists, clenching and unclenching, then exhales heavily and moves toward the door. "Keep that thing iced. I'll see you."

"Okay..." He's gone before I can say anything else. I tilt my head back again and let out a long breath. Because he was right. I was angry. Blind with it. The pent-up fury of the years coursing through my veins when my hands balled into fists.

I could have killed them.

Maybe.

"What's happening to you?" I whisper to myself. Because as I think it, I know it's not me. Not what I'd want. As if my body has a mind of its own. Instinct of its own. An instinct that's growing. Jayden James as I know him, disappearing.

Becoming consumed.

Becoming something else.

TWENTY-TWO

THE NEXT DAY I don't want to go to school. But the thought of not being there is worse. The emptiness of the mobile deeper than ever. Just me. Alone. Besides, I can almost see the disappointment in Miriam's face if I don't show up at school again. The echo of her words: *Are you trying to self-sabotage?* Her apparent disappointment stings.

But I may as well have stayed home. Classes pass in a blur, the information in one ear and out the next, my mind a million miles away. I dodge seeing Kam and his friends, the fear and fury of the other night becoming a backdrop to the noise in my head. Instead, I'm consumed with the image of Alexa. The memory of being on the mountainside, tangled in each other's arms. The taste of her lips on mine. And in her home—*my safe place.* Firelight behind her. The melancholic melody of the violin. The mystery of her. And again, *Frankenstein* in her hands, her quest to understand me, who I am, what I feel.

But then, there was that distance in her eyes.

Worry knifes my heart. I picture her outside in the mist. Her whisper, *something is happening to me.* A lump forms in my throat. *She's not here right now,* Magenta had said. But she was. *Why did she lie to me?* And what about the articles? The miraculous recovery?

Who is this girl I love?

Just thinking it—*love*—sends a burning hope through my body. A need. Never before have I felt so alive. I just need to see her and try to make sense of everything.

I fidget at my desk and move through the halls like a ghost. Even Brody seems to keep his distance, a worried look on his face when I don't immediately respond to his banter. When school finally ends, I wait until the crowds have thinned to grab my things to leave. I pass an open classroom door and see Ms. Cash inside with the Advanced Literature and Writing group meeting for their after-school college prep. Her face brightens when she sees me, and she beckons for me to join them. I pretend not to see her and hurry to the exit and out into the fresh air, leaping onto my bike, trying to ignore the throb of my shin beneath the loose fabric of sweatpants—the only thing I'd been able to pull on that would fit over the swelling. And that was the other thing. I hadn't healed. The contusion grew, the color deepening. Unlike my face last weekend. I'd tried to soak the poultice and bring it back to life, but it sat limp and soggy against my leg. By morning, nothing had changed—not for the better. I flex my hand on the handlebar where the crystal had dug into my palm all night. At least that had worked.

I cruise down the streets, blindly heading to the mansion. I stop outside, looking up at it. The gates are still closed, the curtains drawn. It's been a week since I stumbled onto the back property in the dark of night. A week since the night wandering started again. A week since I met her. So much has happened since then. The dreams. The deaths. The town changing in that one week. My *world* changing. Like the Capulets and Montagues. Romeo and Juliet. So much has happened in so little time. And there seems to be so much keeping us apart. I don't even know *why* or *what*, but something is complicating my chance for happiness. With her. Here.

I push down on the pedals and head for home. I don't want to see anybody from town or be seen. Don't want to be reminded by festival fans mistaking my face for someone—*something*—else, of the enduring love of two fictitious characters that were able to find an eternity together. Not when all I feel is the doom of my own love. If I'd been Edward—a vampire with the power to keep my love by my side forever—I wouldn't have waited. With her permission, I would have sealed our fate on the mountainside, the moon high above us. Made our own forever.

Then I wouldn't be alone. And neither would she.

* * *

Thursday passes, Friday...I go to school, blindly going through the day, then go to work, hiding in the back away from everyone. When shift ends on Friday night, I'm one of the first to leave.

"Jayden, can we talk a minute?" Steve sets a clipboard down at the back desk.

"Sure."

"I've known you for a while now—since you were fourteen, to be precise. The moment you were of legal age to get a 'real' job, you were on the doorstep here, ready to work hard. Ready to start saving for college, even then." He gives a dry sniff and crosses his arms. "You always gave me one hundred and ten percent since day one. But this week..." He cocks his head, studying me, his eyes kind. "I can only imagine how stressful it must have been for you to be...jumped...last week. I heard what happened at the beach. And I saw, obviously, how you looked afterwards. You healed, but I'm thinking maybe...you didn't. You know?"

"I'm fine, Steve."

"But you're not. You're really distracted, Jayden. That paperwork I gave you when you came in Tuesday, you normally would have finished in a couple hours. It's Friday, and you still haven't."

"I'm sorry, I'll get it done tomorrow."

"It's not that...you're staring off into space when I see you. Hanging out alone in the break room."

"I don't want to be seen with all the people here for the festival right now—"

"No, I get that. But it seems to be more than that."

"When I'm in tomorrow, I'll do better, all right?" I pick up my hoodie and twist it in my hand. "I gotta go."

"Okay, Jay. Just...let me know if you need more time."

"I don't. I promise. Tomorrow, I'll be...more present...for my shift."

"Okay."

I feel him watching me as I yank up my hood and head out the back exit into the night.

Outside, things are hopping. The festival in full swing for the weekend. I find my bike and bend over to unlock it when a group comes up behind me.

"About time!"

"Brody, geez, man." I stand up. "You startled me."

"We've been waiting forever for you to get out of there. What the heck?"

"Waiting? Why?" I glance past him and see Miriam, Murphy, and some other of Brody's surf buddies. People I spent the summer surfing with. People who are my friends too. If I was the type to accrue friends.

"Uh, Forever Twilight?" Brody rolls his eyes. "One of the biggest parties we get to have around here. Come on! It's tradition. You always get off early for festival weekend. We're all here, the only one missing is Sam."

"Yeah, well...I think I'll skip it this year. Seeing how I kind of grew into the part and all." I push my bike forward and straddle it.

"That's why we brought you these." Brody tosses a bag at me.

I reach inside. "A wig?"

"Yeah. Don't worry, it's not a mullet," he laughs. He snatches back the bag from where I'm holding it limply in my hand and jams his fingers in, extracting a pair of glasses.

"I'm not wearing those—"

"Oh, yes you are." He shoves them onto my nose suppressing a guffaw. "It helps cover all that sickening perfection that gets the tourist girls all hot and bothered. Don't worry, they aren't prescription, so you'll see out of them fine." He rummages around the bag some more. "And this...the final touch."

"Seriously, man?" I cast an eye at the others giggling as Brody sticks a thin swatch of moustache to my lip.

"Seventies porn star. Perfect," he declares.

I tug the moustache off my lip. "Over my dead body."

"Well, you just may end up dead if you don't disguise yourself," Miriam mocks. "You'll get mobbed to death by the fans thinking they've found their vampire in the cold flesh."

"I'll take my chances, thanks." I drop the moustache back into the bag and pull off the wig and glasses. "Listen guys, I'm not up for the festival this time. I'm sorry."

"You don't get to say no, Jay," Murphy says. "We've just waited half an hour for you to get out of work. This one here wouldn't let us take off without you." He jerks his head toward Miriam.

"Sweatpants, dude?" One of the others, Rex, gestures toward my pants. "Couldn't you have dressed a little better for tonight? You're kind of bringing down the look for the rest of us."

"Yeah, what gives with those? You've been in them for three days straight," the only other girl, Emily, asks. She's friends with Miriam. Crushing on Rex too, from the looks of it.

"I wasn't planning—look, tonight wasn't on the agenda for me. And I needed the baggy clothes. I hurt my leg."

"On what?" another friend, Justin, asks.

"Had a bike accident," I lie.

I catch Miriam watching me, her mouth set in a thin line. She knows me too well. I look away, my face burning.

"Whatever. He's trying *not* to get noticed by the ladies, you ass," Brody jokes and flips the wig back onto my head. "Wear it. It's not so bad. I promise." He claps me on the back. "Lock your bike back up. We're hitting the town." He hands me the glasses. "Just put 'em on and let's go party."

I tell myself it beats sitting around an empty mobile all night. Beats riding past the mansion, its walls locked away behind the iron gate, Alexa hidden inside. Like some princess locked in a tower. My gut knots at the thought of not being allowed to see her. But it can't last forever. Surely, she'll be back at school soon and we can make plans then—could secret away at lunchtime. I let my imagination take me back to the woods with her like we were during science class, a ray of sunlight catching in her hair. And the night on the moonlit hillside…

"Jayden? You coming?" Miriam asks, her voice tentative. Our last interaction hangs between us, a frisson of tension in the air.

I can't say no to her. It *has* been tradition. Alexa's not here, I remind myself. And sitting and stewing somewhere won't make her appear. Maybe actually doing something will pass the time faster to when I can see her again. "Sure."

* * *

Despite myself, I find I'm enjoying the night. The town is different. Alive. The pall of death has evaporated with the excited fervor of die-hard fans—most of whom haven't been following the news—though a police presence fringes the crowd keeping a watchful eye. But for some moments, it almost seems like the drama of the past week hasn't happened. That none of it has. In time, I find myself laughing and taking part in the festivities. Brody manages to smuggle us into the Family Fandom party. People mill around old props from the *Twilight* movie sets, life size cutout figures of the characters clustered on display along with mannequins sporting some of the *Twilight* fashions. Trays of hors d'oeuvres and 'blood punch' are circulated through the excited crowd.

"Don't mind if I do." Brody snags a glass from a tray.

Off to the side, a group of people gather around actress Vee Elle who has graced the town to sign autographs and add to the fan fervor. As we pass, her eyes slide to me in my wig and glasses, a look of surprised recognition crossing her face, then confusion. Of course. She sees the resemblance. I'm Robert Pattinson over a decade ago, dodging the crowds. To her, I'm a ghost from the past in a room filled with vampire wannabes. The crowd around her presses closer and I'm lost from her sight.

"Mm. Smell." Emily stuffs her wrist under my nose. "*Immortal Twilight* perfume. You like?"

Not too far from her, Miriam shifts uncomfortably and looks away.

"Uh, yeah. It's great." I push Emily's arm away and trail over to where Miriam is standing.

"Hey," I say. "I just wanted to apologize for earlier. I don't want us to be off with each other."

"I don't either," she says. But her arms are crossed, her eyes guarded.

"Hey, you two, there's more cocktails happening outside the Arts Center. Come on!" Brody surges past us, the others trailing behind.

"Guess we better go." Miriam falls into step behind them.

Sighing, I follow, trying to ignore the tension between Miriam and me.

* * *

The night is made for vampires and werewolves. A full moon skirts the treetops, the sky blessedly dry for the evening festivities, stars jagged in the sky above. When we reach the Rainforest Arts Center, someone deposits a drink in my hand. I sip it, glad to discover it's a mocktail, and survey the crowd.

"I still don't get it," Murphy says, examining one of the life-size cutouts of Edward Cullen and Bella Swan. "Why would a girl fall for a dead guy?"

"He wasn't dead," Emily protests. "He was undead."

"And that means...?" Murphy holds his hands up in a baffled gesture.

"It means he's *alive*—like his mind, therefore his soul, I guess...just not his body. That's why he was so cold." Emily steps aside as a bunch of girls gather around the cutout to take photos.

"So, alive but not alive. Real attractive." Murphy shakes his head.

The tourist girls drift over to a cutout of Jacob, tittering away.

"Sucks that Sam isn't here," Brody complains. "He'd never have missed the festivities before. It was his night to get lucky—his words, not mine!" he laughs as Emily punches him in the arm. "Come on, you know it's true." He nods his head toward the enamored tourists. "And I'm sure he did. He played that werewolf thing up big time. I just wish it hadn't been ruined by the shitstorm that happened this week."

"I thought I saw him earlier," Murphy says, trying to make eye contact with the group of girls.

"Nah, he's not going to be here." Brody shakes his head. "Not when he's been out in the bush doing his thing. It's too important to him."

"He shouldn't be out there," Emily worries. "Not right now. With the wolves or the murderer, or whatever is out there—"

"He knows what he's doing, Em," Rex chastises. "He could be back at home, for all we know. He's been drifting from us this past while. A few friends have." He casts a pointed glance my way. "And stop with the murderer angle. It's just those wolves that came down from up north. They've even said."

"Nooo. Follow the news much? They said it looked like more than wolves were involved," Emily protests. "Like, a person."

"*Human hands*, to be exact," Justin says. "Nobody said *person*, specifically. So, who knows? Maybe these woods *do* have secrets. Shadow hunters…immortals…blood sucking souls hiding in the forest depths…"

"Shut-up, Justin," Emily scolds. "You're sounding like one of the groupies now. There's nothing fantasy about a psycho."

"What?" He shrugs laughing. "It's Forks. Not exactly serial killer territory. There's got to be more to it. There are people that believe vampires are real. You know…who knows? Maybe vampires were real at one time, huh? Maybe some old thread of DNA has kept them around still. It's not so absurd if you think about it. Stories…they're passed along from generation to generation. Century to century. They had to come from somewhere. Some grain of truth. They may change over time, but something started them. Imagination isn't spontaneous. It's a culmination of all the other stories we've heard over our lifetimes."

"Oh, god, here he goes." Emily rolls her eyes.

"I mean, come on…" Justin persists. "People believe all kinds of strange stories. And stories form the basis of history. Religion. Before those stories could be written down, they were passed orally. Think about it! If a man could rise from death to become a spiritual savior—if a wolf could turn to human—why is it so hard to believe this? There are lots of stories that sound fantastical yet are the basis of firm belief. And seriously...there are parts of this forest people instinctively avoid, you know? Ask the lady at the flower and gift shop. She even said so on that documentary that was made on our town. What was it called? *Twilight in Forks*, or something. And she's not the only one who thinks that. There's just parts of the forest people don't go into."

Except me, I think. I've been all through its mysterious depths, seeking solace away from town and everything it contained. Solace from my life. And then there were the times I'd just simply woken up. Far from everything else, in the silent, dark heart of the forest.

"Okay, we're off topic here," Murphy interrupts impatiently. "Back to what I was saying—I'm certain I saw Sam. That's all. On the edge of the crowd. I thought I saw him then he was gone. So maybe he's here, maybe he's not."

"Why don't Jay and I go look for him," Miriam suggests, coming up beside me. "You guys stay here, so we know where to find you."

"If you do find him, I'm going to kick his ass," Brody vows, taking a lighthearted swig from his glass. "If he's at this without telling us, he'll have some explaining to do."

"Wait and see what he has to say first—*if* we can find him." Miriam lifts her eyes to meet mine. "Ready?"

"Sure," I hedge. I'm not sure I'm ready to see Sam. Not sure what I'll say when I do.

She lightly grabs my hand to lead the way, threading ahead of me through the crowd.

Once we're away from the others, she stops and turns toward me. "So, what was that about?"

"What?"

"Your expression when Murphy said he thought he saw Sam. You didn't look exactly happy about it."

"It's nothing."

"Right."

I glance over my shoulder, scanning the crowd. "I just...have some questions for him."

"Like what?"

"Like what he was doing lurking outside Alexa's home Monday night, is what."

"Lurking? What do you mean?"

"He was outside Alexa's house. Spying."

She scrunches her eyes shut and opens them again, a look of confoundment on her face. "I'm sorry...spying? And you know this...how?"

"I uh...I was...yeah, so the thing is..." I swallow hard, her eyes pinning me. "I was there too."

"Outside Alexa's?"

"Yeah."

"So...you were spying too?

"No! I was there to...I was just watching because—"

"Watching her house?" She paces a few steps. "Since when did you start doing that kind of thing?"

"Look, Sam was creeping around for no reason—"

"Sounds like it takes a creep to know a creep," she says, disgust lacing her voice.

"I wasn't *stalking* her!" *Stalker.* It was whispered in the wind that night. *Or was it in your head?* I swallow hard. "Look, I wanted to make sure she was safe, is all. I had a really bad feeling that something was wrong."

She opens her mouth then closes it, a shadow of hurt crossing her face. "Keep her safe from Sam?"

"No—something else. I just keep having this feeling that something's not right. That she's in danger somehow, but I don't know what it is."

"Well...you and your premonitions. Always showing up when something's about to go down." But she doesn't look happy about it. Not this time.

"Showing up after the fact, is more accurate. I'm never there in time. I just—I didn't want that to be the case with Alexa. I waited for hours just to see if she was okay."

I want to take back the words as soon as I say them but it's too late. Miriam's face breaks for a split second. If I didn't know her better, I wouldn't have noticed. But I do know her better. Better than anyone. And I've hurt her. Again. "Miriam—"

"You like her, Jayden. It's okay." She crosses her arms and looks past me to the throng of people. "It's just...what you do. For the people you care about. For anybody, really. You look after them. I get it."

"I like to think I try to. But I'm not so good at it. Stuff happens anyway." I shove my hands in my pocket and let out a long breath. "But this time...I think my instincts were right. There was a huge wolf on their property. The biggest one I've ever seen."

"A wolf?" She looks back at me. "You think it's one from that rogue pack the news has been reporting about?"

"It wasn't with a pack. It was alone. Both times. It wasn't the first time I've seen it. I saw it last Friday too, after Sophie's memorial. This one— *massive*—wolf. With these...penetrating eyes. It's scary, Mir. Just...stay out of the forest."

"Did you tell Chief Hanson? It might help them with their investigation."

"I did the first time." I swallow hard, remembering. "But you know they're on a different track now with the deaths. It's not wolves they're looking for anymore. Promise me you'll watch your back, at least."

She takes a deep breath and looks around the crowd again, avoiding my eye. "I'll be careful, Jay. And you be careful too. Of your heart."

"What is that supposed to mean?"

She sighs abruptly. "Jayden...this isn't some fantasy we live in, okay? You barely know this girl and you're already head over heels. It doesn't happen that way."

"It can."

"Yeah. In fiction." Her jaw is set. "Look, I get that she's really...gorgeous, or whatever, but keep your eyes open. There's more to love than that. It takes time."

"Well, gee. Thanks for elucidating that for me. I appreciate it. Don't fall for someone fast...got it. Instead, be patient and wait forever for the girl you like to notice you, is that it?" She flinches at the sting in my words. "Because *that* always works out." I can't keep the sarcasm from my words. "Sometimes the person you like doesn't bother to notice you until you like someone else. Or not until you happen to turn into that piece of fiction she likes so much. Start to look the part."

She looks away. "It wasn't like that."

"Wasn't it? Because before the Edward Cullen/Robert Pattinson resemblance became apparent, I was just the extra brother kicking around."

"Jayden..."

"Look, Alexa isn't going to hurt me, all right? She feels the same way."

She spits out a harsh laugh. "You don't know anything about her!"

"I know how I feel about her. How she makes me feel when we're together."

She shakes her head. "You're caught up in the fantasy of it, Jay. She's going to break your heart. And what you like about her...is that she isn't Forks."

"What do you mean by that?"

"I mean she's everything you want in life, Jayden. She represents the life you don't have here. Wealth. A life outside of this town. And she's holed up in that mansion you used to run to—the place you went to dream your life away—"

I jerk my head her way. "You knew about that? Me going there? Brody told you?"

We stand there staring at each other, neither of us speaking. I can tell she feels bad, but I don't care. It's as if she just stripped me bare. The pathetic kid hiding in the haunted wings of an abandoned manor, inventing a life in his imagination. Hiding from the world.

"Of course, I knew. Even without Brody telling me. I know everything about you. You know that. Same as you know everything about me. Everything that counts."

I see something just past her shoulder—the glimpse of a profile—threading among the partygoers. Rich skin, a tangle of long curls cascading down her back. I see her only for a split second before she disappears among the crowd.

"For what it's worth, it's not that I didn't notice you. In that way. Before," she says softly. "It's that you hadn't noticed yourself yet. And still...even after the new confidence you gained this past year...it's like you still haven't noticed how great you are. It's like you confuse even yourself."

I barely hear her though, my focus on the crowd, that flash of space where I'd just seen the long curl of hair, the sweet rich brûlée of skin. Breath catches in my chest.

"Look, let's just forget this whole conversation, okay?" Miriam glances haphazardly around, a shred of frustration lacing her words when I don't respond. "Let's just...find Sam." Her gaze skims the crowd. "I don't see him anywhere. Want to check over at—"

"I'll meet you back with the others, okay?" I don't wait for her response before I'm elbowing through the mob, searching each face.

"Jayden?" Miriam's voice hangs in the air behind me as the crowd surges around me.

"Watch it," someone grumbles as I push past.

I catch a glimpse of long, dark curls again and rush forward, catching the girl by the elbow. "Alexa!"

The girl turns, pulling her arm from me. "Hey, what do you think you're doing?"

The disappointment punches gut deep. It's not her.

"Wait a minute..." The girl scrutinizes my face. "Are you...?" She runs her eyes over the wig, bumped askew in my haste to get to her, the fake glasses slipping down my nose.

"Wrong person, sorry," I mumble and lose myself in the crowd just as I hear her cry out, "Oh my god, I just saw Robert Pat—"

I lurch out of earshot before she can finish, a frenzy of voices chorusing in the background trying to find the elusive star. But he's not here. Just someone living in his immortal shadow.

I hurry away, keeping my head low until I reach the Thriftway parking lot to retrieve my bike. Less people are in this area now, most having moved along to the heart of the festivities. I jump on my bike and thread down Forks Avenue, ducking down side lanes, passing by the tavern where Mom works. I stop, seeing Mom leaning against some stranger's car, arms entwined around his neck as he opens the door for her to climb inside. Even from here I can tell she's nine sheets to the wind. "Hey!" I call, but it's too late. I'm not close enough. The guy jumps into the driver's side, guns the engine and pulls out onto the main street. I try to catch the car, pedaling hard but it's too fast. An emptiness rips open inside. It takes everything in me to turn away, knowing my presence won't make a difference anyway. Won't stop whatever pain is coming. Won't stop her from hurting herself. And it won't be the first time. There's nothing I can do.

I'm too late.

*　*　*

The whole way home my eyes sweep the shallow ditches and cloaked forest, searching the shadows. But nothing happens. No one emerges from the darkness to ambush me. And no sign of Alexa. Anywhere.

In the mobile, I collapse onto my bed, my brain feeling like it's going to explode. Images crowd my mind. Alexa, Sam. Miriam. My mom. *Alexa...*

I don't feel sleep approaching. I don't notice it creep up on me.

Until I awaken. Alone. Surrounded by dark woods.

TWENTY-THREE

TO BE MORE precise, I'm running. Branches carving at my face. My hands flail in front to protect my skin from the razor tips of boughs. I trip and fall facedown, my lip catching the soft bark of decomposing wood. I push to my feet and run again, an unsettled angst tearing at my gut as if something is tailing me—fangs bared.

I break into a clearing, the moon hovering high above the dark silhouette of a house. My chest heaves with exertion, I'm breathing so hard I don't at first notice the sound of raised voices.

"Stop! Please!" someone cries out.

I rub the night from my eyes, blinking into the stream of moonlight cascading over the silver lawn. Two male figures scuffle together, grappling roughly in the darkness. "I'm not working so goddamn hard just to float your sorry ass." There's the slur of alcohol behind the words.

"Hey!" I call. I stagger a few steps into the clearing, still disoriented. I look around, trying to determine where I am.

"Get the hell off my property!" a throaty voice commands.

I hold my hands up in peace. "I'm sorry…I'm lost. I just…is everything okay here?"

"I don't need your help, Death! Get the fuck out of here!" I recognize the voice of the other person immediately. But behind the gruffness there's something else.

My heart accelerates when I realize where I am. The Slades. Kam's face looms into focus when he looks up, the moonlight catching his hard features. His father is even bigger. His face even harder.

"Mind your own business, boy," Kam's father barks at me. "And get the hell off my property."

"I am." I sidestep toward the ribbon of road. Their land is set back from town, a fortress of trees isolating them from the rest of the community. *Which way to home?* I just want to leave. It isn't my business. But as I go, I can't help but turn and see Kam cowering slightly, his hands raised to protect himself, his father towering over him.

"Hey!" I call. "That's enough!"

"You got something to say, boy?" The older man turns back toward me.

"Leave him alone." My teeth are clenched.

"I don't need your help," Kam sputters. He tries to straighten but it's evident he's hurt.

"He's your son," I state, holding Mr. Slade's eyes, which even from here I can tell are bloodshot. "That's enough."

I don't move as Mr. Slade lurches toward me, his footsteps unsteady with drink. "And who are you? Oh. Yes. The little James wimp, right?" he sneers, the flash of his teeth sinister in the moonlight. He staggers closer. "Not so wimpy anymore, huh? My boy teach you a thing or two over the years?" He gives a hard sniff and wipes his nose with the back of his hand. "Clearly, you didn't learn anything about minding your own business, though."

I glance over at Kam, he's breathing hard, his arm clutched around his midsection.

"What you doin' out so late in the night anyway, huh?" Mr. Slade steps closer. "Getting into trouble?" He runs his eyes over my face. "I saw you. The night that Wilkinson girl died. Yeah, that's right. I reported you to the Chief. Seems they didn't take that report seriously."

"I had nothing to do with what happened to Sophie."

"Didn't you?" he sneers. "What about when that other girl went missing? Were you out and about then too?" He chuckles softly then touches a finger to the side of his lip and taps. "What you got there? A little...something." He eyes me darkly. "You, what...split your lip?" There's menacing nuance to his voice, his eyes mocking.

My hand reflexively moves to touch my lip. I pull my hand away. Blood. I stare at it streaking my fingers in the moonlight.

"How about this?" Mr. Slade's slurred voice takes on a quality, smooth as silk, the hint of threat simmering behind each word. "You didn't see me tonight. And I didn't see you. Got it?" He takes a step back.

I glare at him, fighting the surge of fury and panic building in my chest. "I've got nothing to hide."

"Don't you?" his voice is snake smooth. "Not too different from your daddy, are you?"

"You knew my dad?" My heart stalls in my chest. Hope. Hurt. Confusion.

He takes a step back then another, his hard eyes never leaving mine until he finally turns away to cross the lawn. "Get your sorry ass into the house, Kameron," he demands and disappears inside.

I stare after him, a knot of emotion tightening between my ribs.

Kam glowers at me from across the lawn. Our eyes meet and hold, time sluggishly moving from one minute to the next. A welt of emotion sears inside. I don't want to care about this human. And yet—

"You okay?" I manage.

He doesn't say anything, doubled over slightly, gripping his midsection hard. It makes me think of something he said. When he ambushed me. *No one will see this damage. It will be our little secret.* "Is that what he does?" I ask. "Hit you where no one sees? Is that why your mom left? He hurt her too?"

"Shut-up about my mom!" he hollers. "And get the fuck outta here, freak. I don't need your help. I mean it, Death—go!"

For a moment I feel sorry for him. The years between us suddenly making twisted sense. The rage inside splinters, barbed pity surfacing in its place. It's one thing to have a bully in your life. Another, if that bully is your father. A father who he boasted about. The fishing trips, adventures. Maybe those happened too, but they had another side. No wonder Kam was who he was. What chance did he have to be any different than what he learned? *There's always a choice. You choose not to become what they are*, my mind screams. You choose not to drink. Not to abandon those you love. Not to carry their prejudices or pain. You choose to be the better person. The better generation.

You choose to lay your fist down.

I wonder if Kam will ever see that? That he has a choice.

Who was your *dad?* The thought ricochets around my head, twinging my temples with pain. *Are you like him too?*

I swallow hard and avert my eyes, giving Kam the dignity of looking away as he brokenly lumbers back to the house, slamming the door behind him.

The surrounding forest presses in as I try to collect my thoughts and orient myself, limping to the road, my shin throbbing. I hadn't noticed its ache in the woods, panic driving me forward, but it sears to life again with the adrenalin ebbing away.

I'm grateful for the moonlight as I limp the length of the road, making my way home, passing the odd house here and there until I finally reach the outskirts of the town's center, finding my way to the road that will lead me back to the mobile. The blood at my lip has dried. I probe my mouth with my fingers, trying to find its source. I must have split my lip when I fell.

It feels like hours but finally I reach the trailer park as the first gray of morning mists the heavy sky. Inside, I head to the bathroom, checking in my mom's room first to make sure there are no surprises waiting there. She didn't make it home. Not that that surprises me either. I know better than to worry about her yet. I can only hope the man she left with isn't somehow linked to the scourge that has combed the forest this past week. I can't even go there in my mind.

I shut her bedroom door, a weight in my chest, and go to the bathroom to rinse my face, trying to quell my thoughts. There's dirt on my clothes, blood crusted on my fingers from where I've wiped my mouth. I pull back my lip and inspect it. Two cuts line its inside, one on each side by the cuspids where my teeth have sliced it open. Probably on impact when I fell. I rinse my mouth with water spitting until no more pink shows in the basin, then climb into the shower, standing beneath the needled spray. I scrunch my eyes shut, trying to remember the night, remember walking out into the dark. My mind is nothing but an empty void. Nothing comes to mind. No memory. No dreams. Just waking, body in motion, the dark woods closing in around me. I can't even think of Kam right now or his father. *You didn't see me. I didn't see you.* As if *I* had something to hide.

I've got nothing to hide, I'd sputtered.

Don't you? ... Not too different from your daddy, are you?

I silence the echo of words in my head and twist the taps, stopping the spray. I stand there for a moment, water dripping from my forehead as I lean my head against the tiled wall, my mind a throbbing tangle of thoughts, before grabbing a towel and hurriedly dressing for work.

When I rush out to grab something from the fridge for breakfast, I find Mom, passed out on her favorite chair. She came home. She's safe. For now. How many times had I had to wait and wonder? Too many. Powerless to stop whatever came.

Gently, I pull the afghan over her and tiptoe outside.

* * *

The morning passes in a blur. I try to finish the paperwork and do my part behind the scenes until my shift ends. Try to avoid the look of concern etched in Steve's face when he checks on me.

When I leave work to grab my bike, Brody appears, a coffee from Mocha Motion in hand. "Hey! I just happened to spot you there. I'm getting off work in an hour. Where do you want to meet?"

"I don't, Brody. I'm sorry...I did the festival thing with you guys last night, so—"

"Yeah, and what happened to you? Miriam said you dicked off and didn't come back. We waited for you like you asked at the Arts Center but gave up after a while. You really need to start paying attention to your phone, man. It's actually kind of annoying when we're trying to contact you. You can't just keep us all hanging."

"Yeah, I know. I'm sorry."

"Okay." He runs a hand through his hair and glances around. "Man, it's insane this year, huh? I can't get over how many people have come this time. My manager is on fire today. Every hour he's paging Bella Swan, which gets the tourists all in a frenzy." He rolls his eyes. "I swear, some of the people really think we have vampires and werewolves in our forests. You know Drew? He just started working with me. Pasty guy, right? Looks more vampire than you. And not heartthrob vampire, know what I'm saying? He's like—freaking *freaky*, vampire. This girl walks right up to him to analyze his eyes. She comments on how dark they are and all. Says she'll be back to see if they change color. Nutzoid, right?" He gives a low whistle.

"What do you mean, 'see if they change color?' "

"Come on, man, you've seen the movies, right? We watched them together, didn't we?"

"Yeah, thanks to Miriam. Was her choice. I didn't want to watch them, so wasn't paying attention to every detail." I think at that time I was paying attention to Miriam. It was so long ago that we'd watched them. I shift, uncomfortably.

"All right, well, anyway, in the movie the vampire's eyes are all dark when he's hungry, right? Thirsting for blood. And once he's satiated, his eyes go this golden color. They lighten. Change."

I don't want to think about golden eyes. I don't want to think about eyes at all, because if I do, I might start thinking about hazel eyes on a stranger's cold face. But something about his comment sparks a disconcerted niggling in my mind. About what, I don't know.

"You all right, brah? You've got that freaky look going on again."

"I'm...I just gotta go, Brode. You guys have fun at the festival. I've had enough of it."

"Suit yourself." He takes another sip of his coffee and steps back. "Oh, hey. Coming at you. Three o'clock."

"What?"

He indicates his chin to a group entering the Thriftway behind me.

"You better duck out of here if you want to survive," he chuckles.

I chance a tentative glance behind to a group of girls gushing over something *Twilight* related as they head into the grocery store.

"Ooop, I better get going," Brody says, glancing at his phone. "Break's over. If you change your mind about hanging out today—"

"I'm done with the festival. Trust me."

"Fair enough." He pockets his phone and begins to sidle away. "Catch you later, man."

Before I can respond, two police cars go tearing down Forks Avenue, sirens wailing, lights flashing.

"What the heck?" Brody pauses mid-stride.

People stop and stare. The cars disappear from sight, their sirens growing fainter. After a few minutes when nothing else happens, people start to carry on with what they're doing, distracted by the festivities.

"Wonder what that was about?" Brody muses.

Steve darts out of the Thriftway, staring down the road in the direction the police cars just traveled.

"Steve?" I call, confused. "What is it?"

His face is pale when he turns to face me and Brody. "I just heard. They've found another body."

"What?" Brody's brow puckers in disbelief. "Where?"

"In the woods. Behind the Slades."

My blood runs cold. The sounds of the streets, the people, all blur together to form the buzz of white noise.

"Jayden? You okay, dude?" Brody drops a hand on my shoulder. "You look like you're going to pass out."

"Just don't feel so good all of a sudden." The words catch like cotton balls in the sudden dryness of my mouth.

"Hey, I know what you mean, Jay," Steve says, his face a mask of concern. "It's insanity, what's been happening. Listen, they'll find whoever is doing this, okay?"

"Do they know who it was that they found?" Brody tries to hide the shake in his voice.

Steve runs a hand through his hair. "I don't know the details yet. I don't think they even *have* details to share yet. I just got a call from one of my friends who lives down the street from the Slades' property. I mean, this must be a shock for Wes and Kam."

"Maybe he did it," I say, flexing my fingers. "Mr. Slade." I picture the darkness in his eyes, his tall form towering over Kam.

"Wesley?" Steve seems confused. "He's a good guy. No, it's not him. Just because you've had a run in with his son, don't assume things about his old man. He's been nothing but good. Just does his thing and minds his own business."

I know what Steve means. Until last night, I'd have thought the same. It's funny how little you can know about a person. How façades can tell a different story.

"Besides, it would be stupid of him to commit a crime in his own backyard," Brody points out.

"Look, the last thing our town needs is to start pointing fingers at one another," Steve says gently. "You should maybe go on home, Jayden. It's been a tough week for you all around. For everyone. Let the cops do their work. They'll figure it out. They'll make our town safe again."

"Sure," I say, but I don't go home. Instead, I circle the perimeter of town on my bike, my hood drawn, afraid to be alone. Afraid memories will surface of dark woods, my feet sprinting across the boggy forest floor. Running from I don't know what.

The festival continues, though the police presence intensifies. Some of the tourists look confused at the number of uniforms filing through the crowds.

In the parking lot of Sully's, I spot the group of friends from last night, Murphy and Justin, huddled around Murphy's truck, Emily and Rex sitting on the open bed, faces ashen.

"Hey," I say pulling in, angling my body away from where guests are entering and exiting the diner. "Have you heard what's going on?"

"You mean about the other body?" Murphy says, voice drawn. "Yeah."

They are hunched into themselves, nervous. Genuinely scared.

"What is it?" I demand. "What are they saying?"

"We don't know if what we're hearing is true but..." Emily starts. "It's another tourist."

"Not a local?" I breathe.

"Does it make any difference?" Emily asks, her face scrunched with disapproval.

"No—no, of course not," I stammer. "I just mean for the town. I don't think we could take another personal loss."

Emily draws in a deep breath and lets it out slowly, her eyes running over the tourists. "It was another girl. About the same age as Sophie and the last one. But that's not all..." her voice trails off.

"It was different this time," Rex fills in for her. "The girl's body was left untouched."

"Untouched?" I glance back at the tourists walking out of the diner. You can see that word has started to spread for they glance around anxiously before heading to their vehicles.

"Just two puncture marks," Rex finishes.

"Puncture marks? What do you mean?" A buzz starts somewhere in my body, a steady vibrating thrum.

"On her neck." Rex's face is ghost white. "The body was drained of blood."

I stare at him, unable to process what he's saying. "You mean like..." I stop, not sure what I'm thinking.

"A vampire," Murphy finishes.

"It's *not* a vampire," Emily says tersely. "They aren't real for Christ's sake."

"Yeah? Then how else do you explain it?" Murphy retorts.

"First wolves, now vampires." Emily slides off the truck bed. "I swear some sadistic psycho is messing with the people of this town. Trying to make some sick mockery of all this," she says, gesturing loosely to the *Twilight* posters in Sully's window. "I mean, why else? Why now? Why in this way?"

"Who knows...like I said before...maybe they *are* real," Justin says. This time he's not joking. "After this week...I'm starting to wonder."

"You are not," Emily chastises. "Don't be ridiculous."

"Well, how else do you wanna explain it? Bodies of girls found deep in the forest. I mean, hello! Have you seen how wild it is out there? And at night. Always at night. First it looks like a feral wolf got to the first two. Then maybe not, because there was evidence of *human hands*." He flips his fingers in quotations. "But now this? A body drained of blood with just two puncture marks on its neck?" The muscle in his jaw flexes. "It's too weird, guys. All of it."

"Okay, now I'm getting the heebie-jeebies. Like, seriously." Emily shakes her arms out as if trying to shed cooties.

Dark woods. Running.

What was I running from?

A voice haunts my thoughts. *What you got there? A little...something.* Mr. Slade. *You, what...split your lip?*

I touch my fingers to my lips, remembering the two cuts inside. *By your canine teeth.* Suddenly, I can't breathe.

"You going to be sick, bro?" Rex grimaces as he looks at me. "You're lookin' paler than usual."

"*I'm* going to be sick," Emily whispers. "This is so twisted. Can we just get out of here? I want to go home."

"Yeah, sure. Murph, can we get a lift?" Rex puts his arm around Emily.

There was blood on your mouth because you fell. That's all.

But it doesn't feel like that's all.

What happened last night?

Murphy jumps into the driver side and turns the ignition. "You want to throw your bike in the back, Jayden? I can give you a ride home."

"I'm fine." My fingers curl into balls, my short nails biting into my palms, my heart palpitating with cold fisted beats.

"Suit yourself."

The others climb into the truck and, in a cloud of fumes, peal out of the parking lot.

Some tourists pass me, uncertainty threading their voices. "You think it's real? Or just like...a staged publicity stunt?"

"Those cops looked pretty real to me. Even the locals look freaked. I think we should maybe get the hell out of dodge."

I jump on my bike and pedal away, not wanting to hear anything more.

Pixie hair. Hazel eyes. The last death. The last girl. I'd seen her before. *Where?*

I close my eyes and try to remember anything from the night before. A face. Eyes. Hair.

Nothing.

No memory of a face comes to me now. Not from last night.

And Sophie. Mr. Slade had seen me out that night too when she went missing. Not far from where she had been at a bush party.

"Don't...just don't," I whisper to myself as I careen down the road.

The festival goers have grown restless, shifty. People bristle against each other, mild panic shadowing their expressions as they move down the street to climb into their parked cars, glancing over their shoulders. Others seem to be reveling in the spreading news. One random girl stands, arms open wide by the lip of forest, a raptured look upon her face. *Come claim me,* her posture screams.

"Miriam!" I stop, seeing her weaving among the pedestrian-thick road.

"Jay, hey! I barely recognized you with your hood pulled so low. Recognized your bike, though. And, well...the rest of you," she trails off. I can't read her expression when she meets my eye, but she quickly looks away. "You heard what's going on? It's crazy!" She flips her long blonde ponytail from over her shoulder and surveys the crowd before her eyes once again settle on me. "You okay? You just took off last night."

"Yeah...sorry, I thought I saw someone."

"Was it Sam?"

"No." I chew my lip then stop, tasting the iron of blood from last night, the wounds still fresh. New warmth leaks inside where my tongue worries the thin fissures. I suppress the urge to gag.

"Oh," she says with clipped understanding. "You thought you saw...her." She draws a breath, adjusts her bag on her shoulder and straightens, arranging her features into a neutral expression, though a hint of hurt traces her lip with a line of tension. "For what it's worth, I saw her this morning at the Thriftway. She was looking for you."

"Alexa? She was? But...I was there. I was working."

"You were probably in the back. I told her you were likely there, but she said she'd wait and see you later. She asked where you lived so she could wait for you at your place."

"You didn't tell her, did you? Where I live?" I don't mean to say it as loud as I do, or as intensely.

"Geez, chill, Jay. I didn't. I figured if you hadn't taken her home yet, you had a reason. And I know what that reason is. It's not my place to hand out your address." She looks up, her eyes searching mine with that deep blue-gray hue that always reminds me of the ocean after twilight. "My question to you is, if she means that much to you...why don't you let her know you? Your life?"

"It's not like that—"

"If she's worth anything, she won't care, Jay." Her voice catches. Then her eyes slide past me to something behind me, her face tightening. "Jay, watch out—"

An elbow clips my ribs with a hard jolt. "Hey look, it's Death. Had another busy night, huh?"

I turn to find one of Kam's posse sneering in my face. Behind him are a few others, and Kam himself, at the back of his group.

"Hell, he's even got a bit of blood on his lip," snipes the guy who elbowed me.

Reflexively, I raise the back of my hand to touch my mouth, a faint trace of blood latticing the pale skin across my knuckles when I pull it away.

They all laugh except Kam whose smoldering eyes hold mine, eyes that are filled with contempt but something more.

"Piss off, Kyle," Miriam scolds. "Go find a sandbox to play in."

"Always hiding behind her skirt, aren't you," Kyle continues. "Since you can't get into it..." he taunts.

"As if I'd even wear a skirt, you ass," Miriam snipes.

"Guys, let's go."

I look up at the sound of Kam's voice.

So, this is it. I keep his secret and he'll leave me alone.

But as his eyes graze over mine, I see something behind their expression. Something other than contempt.

Fear.

He's afraid of me?

"Whatever," Kyle snips, but retreats with the others to amble down the road in search of other mischief.

"What *was* that?" Miriam says after they're gone, blended into the crowd.

"What?"

"Since when has Kam just left you alone? He didn't even instigate. You guys have some other run-in I don't know about? Some truce?"

"Something like that." I can barely hear myself think for the thunder of my heart. *He's afraid of me. But why? Because I know a secret about him? About his father? Or because—*

My thoughts fall into shadow, a tremor lacing my heart.

"Here." Miriam fumbles in her bag and extracts a tissue.

"What's that for?"

"Your lip. It's bleeding." She moves toward me, but instinctively I pull back. "I'm not trying to do it *for* you, for god's sake—unless you want me to. Here, just take it. Put some pressure on it. It's not bleeding too bad, but still. Get it on your hoodie and good luck getting the stain out." She stands, her hand outstretched with the tissue. "Jay?"

I don't want to go near her suddenly. I don't want to touch her. I can't help but look at the smooth line of her neck where her hair is pulled away, the gentle hue of delicate veins beneath her skin. *Two puncture marks. Body drained of blood.* A sick feeling churns in my stomach with the iron taste of blood.

I'd never—

—never!

She drops her hand, confused. "Why are you looking at me that way?" Her voice is soft, as my eyes roam the contour of her neck leading up to the smooth skin of her face. She steps toward me once more and I draw back further, an agonized fear fluttering in my chest, the haunted night scraping through my memory.

Dark woods.

Running.

"I gotta go, Mir. I'm sorry. I got to figure some things out."

I realize too late that she thinks I mean figure things out about her. My body language, the look in my eyes—all registering as some kind of confusion, some kind of emotional angst. About her. A flash of hope glimmers in her eyes. "Okay," she says softly.

But whatever I'm feeling, it isn't that. Not now. Not in this moment. Instead, what I feel is a sudden, vile, inexplicable fear of myself. Fear of being around anyone. Especially her.

What if...?

"*No!*"

"What?" She looks at me, perplexed. "*No*, what?" Jayden, what's going on?" She reaches out, placing a hand on my forearm, stopping me from leaving. "Talk to me."

"It's not about us, all right?" I don't mean for the words to spill out acrid and tart, but somehow, they do.

Her hand slides from my arm to her side, stung by my sharpness.

I swallow hard, forcing down the welt of emotion that burbles up at her expression. "Mir, go home where it's safe. Please." It's barely a whisper.

She stares at me in bewildered confusion as I jam my foot against my pedal and weave out into the traffic and away from town.

Like a bat out of hell.

TWENTY-FOUR

I GO HOME. There's nowhere else to go. My mind shrouds my thoughts with insane notions. I barge into the mobile, down the hall and to the bathroom, to stand in front of the mirror, hands shaking. The cold chisel of my cheekbones catches the light as I stare at my expression, mottled with emotion, eyes dark as deep wells—deep wells of secret.

Fingers trembling, I touch my lower lip, gently pulling it down to inspect the slits lining inside. The point of teeth. A film of blood glosses the tip of my fingers when I pull them away. *You're losing your mind.* But—

I back out of the bathroom, dizzy, needing air. I stagger to the weathered porch, fighting the tangle of thoughts that burn synaptic-hot.

Dark woods.

Blood. On my hands. My face.

The echo of a scream. But that was a dream. *Wasn't it?*

I drop down onto the top step, overcome.

Who am I?

What am I?

Hours pass, but I don't leave. Can't leave. My body weighted to the porch. Evening approaches, daylight sickening to the bruised light of an impending storm.

Dan comes home, his truck a cloud of exhaust as it pulls in front of his trailer. He jumps out and slams the door closed, lofting a heavy bag from the bed of the pickup. He stops, noticing me. "You okay, kid?"

"Yep." I try not to sound disconcerted but fail.

He sets the bag down and leans against the bed of the truck with his arms casually crossed. "Looks like you've got the weight of the world resting on them shoulders there."

"Yeah. Well. The world is pretty weighty right now."

He crosses the lane and sits on the stoop beside me. "I heard. About the girl."

"A tourist," I manage to say. I can barely meet his eye. A blackness wriggles within, nightmare cold.

He studies me. "You knew her?"

"No. And I didn't know the last one either. Just the first one...Sophie—" The name catches in my teeth. My leg jiggles harder, my knuckles dagger sharp as I clench my fists.

Dan's silent a moment, his mouth working in thought. "Well, whether you knew her or not, it's hell that it happened. To any of them. No two ways about it. And hell for our town. It's caused nothing but pain. Fear." He stares off to the culminating cloud, the tinge of turgid yellow. "Look, you've had a week, Jay. Period. The deaths...and that dick kid that thinks he's god of you or something."

I don't say anything, my mind ricocheting from one thought to another, heroin-hot.

After a moment, he sighs. "I know what Kam and his boys have been saying about you, Jayden. That they've called you *Death. Vampire.* If they're using this as an excuse to bother you more, it ain't right. The deaths, the cops will figure out. It doesn't need to concern you. As for those boys? They'll get what's coming to them. Fate has a way of righting wrongs. It's not your doing, you hear?"

"What if they're right?" I whisper.

He's silent beside me, his jaw muscle flexing.

"I know you've seen me leave, Dan. You said so yourself. I go out. At night."

He leans back against the siding of the mobile, his face lost in shadow.

"And I know Mom probably told you. About me. What I do."

"She's mentioned you sometimes sleepwalk, Jayden, yes. If that's what you mean."

"It's more than that. I..." I knot my fists in my lap. "I wake up in the woods. Alone. And I don't know where I've been. Sometimes I'm...covered in blood."

A long pause. "What are you saying, Jayden?"

"What if they're right? That I'm...a vampire." The words are cold rust on my vocal cords.

Silence stretches. One aching minute after another while I wait for his response, my breath corded in my chest.

"Listen, Jayden," he says slowly, his words carefully measured. "What I've learned in life is when people say stuff about you, sometimes there comes a point where you start to believe them." His words are slow. Considered. "The world is always going to be coming at you with judgment and assumptions. Names. Labels. *Wimp. Trailer trash. White trash. Vampire.* There will always be people who try to harass you or define you, or what you are, based on where you come from, what you look like, what you do." A solid hand finds its way to my shoulder. "But it comes down to what you believe about yourself. About all those things."

I drop my head, his words waking a well of magma hurt. I feel the desolate burn of it in the empty caverns of my heart.

"You sure as hell know what you're *not*," he says, gently. "And that's the weak little kid those bullies have made you think of yourself. Even now—long past any weakness. And you're not destined to be this." He gestures to the splintered siding of the mobile, the blackened veins of mildew seeping along the crevices. "You're not destined to be what you came from. You're destined to be what you believe for yourself. So, believe something good. Then act on it. This is the year you get to put things in place...to be in charge of your own future. Once you grad, you can stay or you can go. It's up to you. Don't let words stop you. Don't let anyone make you hesitate in thinking who you are."

"But what if something *is*...wrong with me?"

"All that's wrong is what you *think* is wrong. You are what you believe. What they've said about you...to you...I get it. Words get in your head. But then you need to get real about what those words mean. They're meant to make you feel like a pariah. But you're not. That's not you. That's just someone else's story about you. It says more about them than you. Write your own goddamn story."

"But the girl...the puncture marks on her neck..."

"Someone else's crime, son. Don't make it your own because someone wants you to think less of yourself. And are we even being serious here?" He slides his hand from my shoulder and fixes his gaze on me. "Surely, you can't be thinking that for real, just because of what they've said. Or because of what's happened to that girl. It's just some psychotic nuthouse who has a hard-on for vampires and figures what better place than the town of *Twilight* to torment. Come on. Let's be real here. They've been calling you 'vampire' for years. They've been calling you all kinds of names. So, what's the deal? Why are you taking this name so literally all of a sudden?"

"But my night wanderings—"

"Are just that. You, wandering at night. Like other people with the same affliction. From what I understand of it, this isn't new. You were doing it last year too. Anyone wind up dead then?"

"No."

"See my point?"

I shake my head, the absurdity of it dissipating. "I guess I let things get into my head."

"As we all do." He leans forward, the wan storm light casting his stubbled face in jaundiced hue. His eyes hold a distance. A buried hurt. I want to ask, but he rises to his feet. "Don't let names turn you into something you're not, all right kid?"

I nod. "Thanks, Dan."

"You got it." He claps my back and sidles down the stoop toward his truck, stopping for a moment. He takes off his ball cap and holds it in his hands, turning it, thought weighing his mind. "No matter what, Jayden, don't seek payback, you hear? Against Kam and his gang. Don't try and seek vengeance. All that will do is interfere with who you are. Who you want to be. Got it?"

I nod. "Sure."

"Good."

He crosses the lane, gathers up his bag, and vanishes inside.

I stare at the rectangle of his door then to the thick scrim of treetops beyond, lost in thought as twilight sweeps in, storm clouds thickening by the hour against the pewter sky.

Headlights swing into the lane, their obnoxious beams landing on me as a car pulls to a stop in front of my mobile. I lift a hand shielding my eyes from the brightness.

"Get in, bro."

"Brody?"

He leans out the window. "Come on! I tried texting you, but as usual..." He rolls his eyes. "Get in, we're all waiting for you."

I rise to my feet, hesitantly. "And we're going where?"

"Vampire hunting."

"Are you serious? No. I'm not doing that. I'm sick of even *thinking* about vampires."

I see movement in the blinds of Dan's trailer.

"Come on, we're all going. We're sick of sitting around here while our town gets terrorized. Seriously."

Against the glare of headlights, I spy dark shapes of others crammed into the car. "Who's with you?"

"The gang. Let's go." Brody settles back behind the wheel again.

I stride up to his window and see Justin in the front passenger seat. Rex, Murphy and Emily are squished together in the back.

Brody shrugs when my eyes return to him. "It'll be cozy, but hey. Cops are a bit tied up right now, so I'm not worried about being pulled over and ticketed for having one too many passengers. You coming?"

Emily leans forward with a strand of garlic bulbs. "It doesn't smell pretty in here, but I got us each one of these. You know... in case."

"Just this afternoon you were freaked by everything happening. All of you were," I point out.

"Yeah, well..." Rex clears his throat. "It's the hottest activity of the weekend. Tons of kids from school are heading out."

"And their parents are cool with that? Your parents?" I glance back at the shadowed windows of my own mobile. No one home to wonder where I am.

"Yeah, well, about that..." Brody stretches his neck, adjusting it one way then the other, then straightens his cap. "Mom and Dad think I'm at Murphy's for the night. Murphy's mom thinks he's at Justin's, and so on. You get the gist."

"Nice." I step back in disapproval. "This is the stupidest idea you've had in a long time."

"Come on, man." Brody gives me a look that says hypocrite. "Isn't surfing the furthest, gnarliest wave in a storm a death wish? Doesn't stop you. You think one sick dude will have anything on a whole shitload of Forks senior highs?"

"You mean one sick, bloodthirsty *it*," Emily mumbles, coiling her garlic rope around her arm like a wristband.

"Him, her, *it*—whoever or whatever it is, we'll let them know we aren't afraid." Brody slams the gear into reverse. "We'll drive 'em out of town. Take back our piece of the peninsula. Enough is enough!"

In the passenger seat next to him, Justin nods his head enthusiastically. "Fuck, yeah."

Part of me wants to go. Just to make sure nobody gets hurt. "Is Mir going?"

"Nah." Brody glances into the dusk reflected in his rearview mirror. "And I don't want her to. Too dangerous."

"Gee, thanks," Emily snipes from the backseat.

"I got your back, babe," Rex promises, unfurling an arm to hook around her shoulders.

I shake my head. "You guys are nuts. I'm not going."

"Alexa is." Brody says her name slowly. A tease. An invitation.

"Please tell me you didn't ask her to come," I explode. "Because the last thing she needs is to be out right now in the forest with some—"

"Hey, calm down! There will be a ton of us there. Everyone will be safe. Everyone except whoever is responsible for the crimes." He swings his eyes to mine. "We don't want to be victims, Jayden. No one in this town should be sitting in fear."

I glance up at Dan's trailer. I see the parted slat of blind, but I don't care. I'm tired of being a victim too. Been tired for too damn long. So tired, I don't even remember what sleep is anymore. "Understood."

I crawl into the backseat with the others and shove my way in beside Emily, my shoulder resting against the rear passenger window.

"Geez, man, a little room," Rex grumbles as everyone in the back shuffles to accommodate my presence.

I stare out the window as we pull away. The whole thing is ridiculous. As ridiculous as I was just an hour ago. *Vampire.* I feel my cheeks redden with having even aired that fleeting suspicion to Dan. How absurd he must think I am.

A ball of self-loathing wends through my veins. I glance around at the others, their faces shining with a mix of anticipation and apprehension for the night ahead. Whatever they're searching for tonight, I know what I'll be searching for.

Me.

TWENTY-FIVE

THE ROAD UNFURLS, a black tongue before us, the faint shimmer of fresh rain glossing its surface. Mist funnels through the crack in the window, brushing against my face, wraith-light.

The haunting voice of some unknown artist picks up on the radio, her voice seeping into my marrow with lyrics that slip like molten fire.

> *We are the monsters,*
> *We are the humans,*
> *We play the gods...*

"We kind of *are* playing God, aren't we?" Emily's garlic bulbs rattle on her arm next to me.

"Eye for an eye," Rex vows.

"We aren't going to *kill* anyone," Brody chastises. "We're just going to let them know our town can't be victimized like this. Sayonara, psycho. Even some fans from the festival are coming out for this."

"And we know this how?" I angle my shoulder closer to the cold glass of the window, the rope of garlic Emily pressed into my hand, knotted in my fist. In defiance of the quagmire of crazy vampire thoughts I had, I crush the garlic between my fingers. As if to be sure. Its juices trickle through the dactylogram swirl of my fingertips.

Almost as if in answer to my question, the song on the radio ends and a news announcer's voice fills the car. "In the wake of three suspicious deaths this past week, local authorities in the community of Forks, Washington are urging residents and visitors not to participate in an event circulating on social media inviting people to attend a so-called 'vampire hunt' tonight."

Vampire. I don't know whether to hate Kam for planting that thought in my head or thank him as now he seems to have bought into his own rhetoric. He'd look scared, hadn't he? *Of me.* Finally, found a reason to stay the hell away. At least for now. *Why did you even believe such bullshit?* And it wasn't just the vampire thing. It was the poultice Magenta gave me. My belief in its power—the momentary belief in her witchcraft.

An uncontrolled burble of sardonic laughter rises from my sour gut.

"Uh...what kind of laugh was that?" Rex balks, turning to me.

"Nothing," I say. "Just thinking about something."

"Oookay then." He and Emily share a look, amused laughter suppressed on their lips. "Cuz you kinda sounded a little creepy for a second there."

"Guys, quiet for a sec," Brody instructs, his hand pumping the volume button on the radio.

"Still reeling from the uncovering of two bodies earlier this week, the community has been shaken yet again with the discovery of a third body, found earlier this afternoon. With rumors of the first two deaths initially suspected to be the result of an encounter with a pack of rogue wolves, this latest death holds the hallmark signs of an attack by what would appear to be by none other than...a *vampire.* Though police won't make an official comment at this time, word is the body was drained of blood. The only sign of foul play? Two puncture marks on the neck. This all happening at the height of the town's annual Forever Twilight in Forks Festival, leading some to speculate this could be the possible doing of a serial killer who has a grim obsession with the franchise. The latest victim has been identified as Vanessa Chu, who was visiting Forks for the *Twilight* festival, from Vancouver, British Columbia. Friends traveling with Vanessa reported her missing early this morning after failing to return home from a bush party comprised of locals and fans that was held just outside of town. Police continue to urge people to stay in groups and avoid wooded areas for their own safety and to not interfere with their ongoing investigation."

"Too bad. She was good looking too." Murphy has his phone opened to a news article on the latest death.

"Yeah. Cuz *that's* the calamity—*she was good looking,*" Emily huffs, rolling her eyes.

I glance absently at the glow of Murphy's screen. The smooth face of Vanessa Chu radiates from the screen. Long, silken black hair. The smooth bow of mouth. *Eyes wide and staring.*

A serpentine cold stirs in my stomach. "Can...can I see that?"

Murphy tosses his phone to me. I grab the screen, pinch it larger. The image of her face is replaced by another image from my mind. *Ashen skin in filtered moonlight. The blue-gray ghost of bloodless lips.*

The phone drops from my hands as if torch hot.

"What is it?" Emily looks at me then to the phone, scooping it off my lap. "You know her?"

"I—I don't think so." My heart quivers in my chest, a palsied beat that rapidly stumbles faster and faster—

I swing my face back to the window, the dark fortress of trees passing.

A cell phone pings. "Change of plans, Brode," Rex announces. "Head to the old logging road. They've moved the meet location. Police broke up the other one. They don't want anyone out looking."

"You mean they don't want anyone else killed," Emily mutters.

"Relax, we'll be fine," Rex cajoles.

"You talking about the old logging road near where we searched for Sophie?" Justin twists in his seat to look back at Rex.

"Yep."

"Near Alexa's," I murmur.

"Uh...yeah. About that," Brody picks up speed and smoothly changes direction to head to the new location. "I don't know if Alexa will be there tonight."

"But you said—"

"Would you have come otherwise?"

His eyes find mine in the rearview mirror, I jerk mine away. Part of me wilts at the thought of not seeing her tonight, but the other part exhales with private relief. At least Alexa won't be out there.

In the woods.

With me.

My nails dig into my skin. I've already been down this road. *You're not a vampire!*

But—

Did I see something? Was I—my chest tightens, a tug of terror, as I think the thought—*there?*

What the hell is happening? These girls...these strangers...pixie hair...hazel eyes...long black hair...mouth darkening with death...*why are their faces seared into my mind?* And Sophie's scream, *"stop!"* haunting my mind.

As if I was there.

"Follow the logging road all the way up to the old connector route," Rex instructs. "You know, the one where the road forks. We hiked out that way when looking for that abandoned bunker we'd heard about, remember? The road was super overgrown then. Maybe impassable now."

"Jeez...that was years ago." Brody whistles. "Forgot about that."

"Wish we could have found it and gotten in there to have a look around, seen if there was any old military paraphernalia lying around," Rex muses. "Anyway, that connector is the place they're meeting. Far from any prying 5-O."

"What are you guys talking about?" Emily squirms in her seat. "What bunker?"

"You know how Washington has these abandoned military bunkers hidden around the forest?" Rex pulls her closer so that she rests her head against his broad shoulder.

"Uh, no..." she drawls. "I did not know."

"Well, our state is peppered with 'em. Some are listed, others just lucky finds. We'd heard about one that could be found if you hiked in from the old logging road. So, we went out looking for it a few years back, with Sam. Guess he'd seen it before. His family knows the lay of this land like no one. Sucks that we didn't find it, though. Geez...forgot about that. We gotta go on some of those adventures again."

"Like maybe when they clean up the little vampire problem we got going on here?" Emily admonishes, tucking her hands into her coat sleeves.

"That would have been frickin' awesome to see," Brody says, following the smooth lines of the darkened road. "But I was half glad we didn't find it. Can we say eerie? Jay...you remember that day?"

Overhead the clouds bloat black bellied sheaths across the sky. The wind is scented with storm, a heavy charge crackling in its vapor.

"Yeah," I mumble. I remember. But all I can think about are the dead girls. Faces drawn and cold. A tremble nudges through my body.

"Would make a pretty good vampire haven, a place like that," Justin says. "All hovelled up there away from everything. Sheltered from the daylight. Civilization."

Emily huddles into herself, shoving her shoulder deeper into the crook of Rex's arm. "Okay, you guys, I'm starting to think we should bail on this. I'm seriously starting to believe that we are in over our heads."

The boys burst out laughing. "We're not going to the bunker, babe," Rex soothes. "We don't even know where it is. Would be so overgrown, anyway. We'd never find it now if we couldn't find it then. I was just mentioning it as point of reference for the road we're meeting at. Just chill. We're good."

The night whispers past as we reach the road that leads by the old mansion. Alexa's home. We slip past it in silence. I look over to its towering form behind the closed gate. The second-floor library windows glow. I wonder if she's inside. If she can sense I'm near...

"I'm sorry, man. About the bait and switch." Brody eyes me in the rearview mirror.

"Doesn't matter," I mumble. "I'd rather her not be out there tonight anyway. It's reckless what we're doing."

"Not reckless when there's so many of us," Murphy points out.

"Personally, I think it's just going to turn into a big ol' party. So, I came prepared." Justin hoists up a bulging plastic bag. "Got me a six pack and a twixer. What did you all bring?"

"Ha, me too," Murphy confesses. "Figure the noise of us all will scare away any freakoids. When they see us dancing on their doorstep—that we're not afraid—they'll get the hell out. Betcha anything."

"You guys!" Brody shakes his head, amusement coloring his tone. "There will be partying, but there will be vampire hunters too. Especially with the festival Twihards coming. Whether it's cuz they're scared or seduced, I don't know. But they'll be there. Wanting proof. They'll take what they can get. Because where there are blood sucking vampires, lovelorn ones must be nearby too, right? Glittering in the moonlight," he chuckles.

"Sunlight, you mean," Emily corrects.

"Whichever," Brody laughs.

In time, we reach the end of the road and turn onto the pitted and rutted logging road, every lurch of the tire cinching my gut tighter and tighter. Presently, we pass a parked car, here and there, then more and more the farther up we meander. Other headlights fall in behind as more cars trail up behind us to join the search.

Brody finds an uneven patch of shoulder to pull off onto, parallel parking between two haphazardly angled vehicles. As soon as we step outside of the car, we can hear the excited tenor of voices, flashlights glowing like ghostly fireflies among the dense brush. We tread up the road and veer off to a clearing where people have gathered. The woodsy loam of the forest mingles with the cracked tang of liquor, the heady stench of cannabis, the perspiring exhilaration and fear of young locals from school and tourists itching for an excuse to gather, to party, to fight back in the face of an unimaginable threat. The potent scent of prey turned predator.

Brody pulls up short in front of me. "Miriam? What the hell?"

"Nice greeting, brother."

"I thought you said she wasn't going to be here." An unsettled worry scabs my heart.

"She must have heard *you'd* be here," Brody hisses in response. "She's been worried about you." He turns back to Miriam. "This isn't the safest place to be right now, Mir."

"Yet here *you* are. And on the contrary, I'd argue this *is* the safest place to be. Right smack-dab in the center of half the high school with all these lusty tourists. Safety in numbers. And there are plenty potential victims here that would willingly serve themselves up to some fiend, so I'm pretty sure I'm good."

"Unless it's the thrill of the chase that *it's* after," Emily advises sagely, snagging a bottle from Justin's six pack. She bats her eyes at him as he fixes her with a disgruntled glare.

Somebody leaps onto a boulder and addresses the crowd, giving a piercing whistle. "Hey! Listen up! There's plenty of time to party, but let's do what we came here to do first—hunt vampires!"

The crowd rouses with uproarious cheers, beer bottles raised in toast.

"This is our town, and we're gonna to take it back! Welcome and thank you to those of you who have come to help who are here visiting our town. Everyone, I recommend you search the woods in groups. Are you ready?" The crowd roars in response. "This is going to be an epic night! Let's do this!" The guy jumps from the rock and groups flock together, splitting off into the night.

"This has got to be the stupidest idea ever," I warn, the faces of the dead girls spidering my mind. "We're not dealing with some amateur." But no one is listening.

Miriam grabs my arm. "Jayden, you coming? Stick together, remember?" She pulls the hood of my sweatshirt up over my head to conceal my face. "Don't want anyone mistaking you for something you're not, right?" She holds my eye a moment then pulls her hands away.

I nod, but my mouth is dry.

Ahead of us, Brody and the others are already foraying forth into the woods.

She reaches down to take my hand and tugs me forward. "Let's go."

TWENTY-SIX

BRANCHES CLAW OVERHEAD like talons clasped and woven together, the whisper of wind soughing through the trees, the threat of storm on its breath. The muted rustle and scatter of talk and laughter from the other groups fans out through the forest, echoing through the woods with a campground frivolity, loaded with an undercurrent of gunpowder tension.

Rex has lofted up a long branch with a pointed edge. He shrugs when I look at him. "Makes Em feel better," he claims. "Closest thing to a wooden stake I could find. You know...to impale the vamp through his cold, unbeating heart."

"Right."

He creeps off, Emily close beside him.

"Exactly what are we supposed to do if we find one?" Murphy questions.

"Not die," Justin states.

"Great," Murphy says, teeth clenched.

"Come on guys, everyone else is trying to have fun with it," Brody insists. "What's with you guys? All quiet and cowering."

"We're not cowering, thanks," Justin protests. "Just...you know...hunting carefully."

"Look like a girl and you're going to get nabbed," Brody points out.

"Shut up, Brody," Miriam fumes. "Maybe the thing's got a thirst for teenage boys next."

"Funny, sis. Real funny."

Miriam makes a face at Brody and turns to me. "You okay?"

"I don't think we should be here."

"For the record, neither do I," she says, her eyes shadowed in the refracted glow from the flashlight.

"Why'd you come, Mir? Brody said you weren't coming."

"Well...I heard you were coming, so—"

"I can look after myself."

"I don't doubt that, Jayden. But you've been acting so—weird, lately," she sputters. "Like something heavy is on your mind. And the way you just took off earlier, yet again—" She doesn't meet my eye. She's crossed her arms across her chest. Protective. Uncertain. She lowers her voice. "If I didn't know you better, I'd think you knew something."

"What?"

She's quiet a minute, the others threading further and further away from us, deeper into the darkness. "Since everything started. The deaths. I mean, this whole year you've been acting different. Changing. But since Sophie died—" She pauses. "I mean, I get it. It's awful. And creepy. All of it."

"Then why worry? You get it."

She sucks in the dense wooded air. "I also thought maybe it had something to do with Alexa. Her family."

"What?"

"Since you met her," she continues softly, "you've not been yourself. I mean more than ever." She hugs herself tighter, as if fending off a creeping coldness. "And face it, Jay...they're kind of weird. Her mom, swishing through the town in those long dresses...that crystal she's always wearing... There's a rumor that she's a witch, did you know that? A witch, Jayden. Did Alexa tell you that?"

I stand silent, letting the shadows hide my face.

"I don't believe in witches any more than vampires," she adds quickly. "But she does seem...like something is different about her. I don't mean that in a bad way, but...there's just...something. And Alexa's dad...I mean, I hear he's done some great pro-bono work for the hospital here and all, but...why would an acclaimed neuroscientist and prosthetic's engineer come here for a sabbatical? That's what her mom does, right? Makes prosthetics?"

Neuroprosthetics, I think, but don't say it. Somehow, knowing the details of Alexa's mom's work doesn't seem like a plus right now.

"I mean...how can they advance their research *here*? Our tiny town, known for nothing more than its natural parks and—" she launches her arms in the air in a gesture of exasperation, "vampires and werewolves. It doesn't make sense."

My voice is low in my throat. "What are you suggesting?"

"Nothing. I'm not suggesting anything. I just—" She draws in a sharp breath. "It just seems like a lot has happened in so little time. Like a year has happened in this past week. The deaths. Your obsession with Alexa." The faint felt of worn emotion frays her words.

It did feel like a year had passed. A lifetime. But isn't that what love at first sight is like? A tumble of time wrapped into a moment? I wouldn't have believed it until I felt it. The crazy addiction to someone's presence. The intoxicating allure. Time was irrelevant. Then there was the juxtaposition of the high I felt with Alexa to the horrors the town had faced the past week—the night wandering spells intensifying. Waking up wounded and wandering. *My blood or theirs?*

I shake my head, rake my fingers into my temples, knotting my fists. I can't go there. Can't think about that anymore.

For I hadn't just lost my heart this past week. I'd lost my mind. *You actually considered that you might be a vampire.*

"Look at you." Her eyes slide over me, my body language. "That's why I'm worried. Because this past week you've not been yourself at all. Jumpy. Pulling away from everyone. You've missed work, school—the most important year of your life for it. And that afternoon at First Beach, surfing. You were fighting a battle out there on those waves. Don't think I didn't see it." Her eyes in the darkness find mine, the spectral glow of the flashlight wafting between us. "You don't look well,

Jayden. Those dark shadows under your eyes, I've seen them on you before. But this week they're worse." She gestures toward my face, her fingers hesitating just before me. I can almost feel her tracing the hollowed crescents beneath my eyes. She drops her hand. "Something's going on. Just tell me. Do you know something?" Miriam levels me with a look.

My fists clench and unclench at my sides. She knows me too well. Sees the pulse of my veins. The haunted aura.

Suddenly, I'm tired. Tired of the loneliness. The fear. The uncertainty of what's been happening to me. Trying to hide all the bits of me I don't want seen for fear that I'll lose the little I have.

"Have you ever felt like you're carrying a secret?" I whisper. "And you don't know what it is?"

Her breath is hollow in the night air. The sounds of the others have tapered away, the storm air pressing down amongst the trees with its leaden belly, snaking among the branches, muffling the adrenalin sound of the hunting parties. "I don't know what you mean," she says.

"The girls that died...not Sophie—the other two...it's like I'd seen them. They...their faces on the news...

"We went over this before, Jay. You probably saw them at the beach for Sophie's memorial. Or just around town with all the other festival goers."

"That was a fine assumption with the one girl. But the other?"

She doesn't say anything, her face lost in shadow. We're alone now, I realize. The others disappeared into the dark.

"I recognized them—as if maybe...somehow...I knew them. But I remember them as—" *Dying. Dead.* The words lodge in my throat, razor sharp.

She waits and when I don't say anything, probes, "As what, Jay?"

The echoes of screams haunt my head, nightmare sharp. Real or dreamt, I don't know. I don't know anything anymore. The pale circle of the last girl's mouth, the darkening lips. I swear I saw that—that the image in my head was real. And with Sophie, and the pixie haired girl...I heard cries in the dark, *didn't I?* Screams. Or was that all just a dream?

A dream that was— "It's like I was there."

"There...where?" Space hangs between Miriam's words.

I don't want to say it. I don't want to confess to her my worst fears. Maybe I wasn't a vampire but— "Like I was in the woods. When they died."

She sucks in the air, shaken. The air suddenly seems colder, fingers of rain beginning to leech through the trees, a steady thud, thud, thud, the sound suspiciously like a heartbeat. Steady. Strong. As if the woods are coming alive.

"Jay...I don't understand. How...?"

I don't say anything else, just feel the burn of tears gathering. I don't hide it as one leaks down my face—don't move to wipe it away. For once, I don't hide my vulnerability.

"Mom said you weren't well." Her voice is a whisper.

Not well can mean a lot of things. I see her mind touch upon the worst of it and flutter away, not wanting to go there. Not wanting to think dark things about me. Not wanting to believe.

Believe what? What is there to believe?

My hands flex into cold fists by my side.

The rain intensifies, hard pellets against deadening leaves, an eerie orchestra among the titan gloom of ancient trees. The loamy scent of gathering fall rises from the thick sponge of earth, summer decay wafting from where leaves have fallen to wilt and shrivel amongst the soil.

Miriam shakes her head as if dislodging an unpleasant thought. "You don't know what you're saying, Jay. Of course, you weren't there. How could you have been? It's because of the news. The detailed descriptions. You've always had such a vivid imagination. And you've always been prone to nightmares, right? I remember from when you slept over at our house...some nights you'd wake up screaming—"

"It's not nightmares." *It's real. Me. In the woods. Blood on my hands. My face. My mouth—*

"Come on, let's go find the others."

"I'm not going. You go be with them. I need to be alone." The rain is heavy in the trees now, a steady stream coursing from the branches above, my clothes adhering to my skin with damp. A low rumble of thunder echoes distantly.

"No—we're supposed to stay in groups, so let's go join ours. You can't be out here alone." She squelches across the sodden ground to grasp my arm, trying to make me follow her.

"No."

"Jay—"

I shake her hand off me. "I can't be around you right now."

"Jayden, you're being ridiculous. Let's go find the others." A shred of panic has pitched her voice a shade higher.

"Miriam, leave me. I have some stuff I need to sort out."

She hesitates. "Then I'm staying with you."

"You can't."

"Why?"

"*Because I don't know what I am!*" I shout, my voice getting lost in the steady cascade of rain, the thick veil of foliage and gathering mist.

My tears are hot and uncomfortable where they brim, mixing with the bitter rain. A strand of snot drips from my nose. I swipe at it with the back of my hand and turn away from her, hunched into myself.

"Jayden, what's going on? Please…just tell me. Let me be here for you." She reaches for me again, her hand on my shoulder.

I shrug it off. "Didn't you hear me? I said I think I was there, Miriam. When the girls died! I…I see their faces in my mind. I can hear them…and it's…" I suck in air. "It's excruciating."

"Maybe we should get you home," she says softly. "Maybe this is too much."

I turn to face her. "You asked me if I knew something, and I'm telling you. Why won't you listen?"

"Because I know you, Jayden James," she says, her voice breaking with emotion. "I've known you practically my whole life, loved you like a brother, loved you like—" she cuts herself off, heaving in a deep breath. "I know you. You wouldn't do something like that." She shakes her head. "I'm not afraid, Jayden. Of you. Of what you think happened. Because it *wasn't you.* I just know it wasn't. But we need to get you help.

You're obviously not well. You've had so much on your plate for so long. And the stuff with Kam—"

"This has nothing to do with that asshole—"

"Doesn't it, Jay? Because he's been on you for years, getting away with all kinds of evil, and calling you names. *Death. Vampire.* And then we get hit with a couple tragedies in town but it's not until a girl turns up dead and the news spins it like some vampire story...then suddenly you feel like you're the one to blame. Who do you think put that in your head? Kam, Kyle...their sick group. They said it right in front of me, Jay, and don't think I didn't see how it affected you. How it's *always* affected you. They tell you you're worthless and you believe them! They tell you you're nothing, and you believe them! They call you a vampire and you believe them. You—"

"*I was there*, all right? Last night. Kam saw me."

She stops.

"Behind his property. Where the body was found." My voice breaks, emotion cracking open and spilling. "I was out in that same area, Mir...and Kam saw me...his dad too. I...had blood...here." I gesture loosely to my mouth, my voice broken.

"Why were you out, I don't understand..." Her expression flickers in confusion.

"I don't know why," I whisper, my voice hoarse. "I swear to God, I don't know why."

She hesitates, a wariness entering her eyes, but still, she moves toward me.

"No, don't come near me," I moan, but I don't stop when she wraps her arms around me and pulls me close, my head dropping into her shoulder, the curve of her neck, my weary body heavy in her arms.

"You aren't a killer, Jayden. I won't believe it." Her voice is thick with emotion as she holds me tight. "I won't."

Drawing ragged breaths, my arms close around her, the comfort of her. In the thick dew of rain, I smell her skin. Coconut ginger soap, shampoo. Her. Just her. She smells like all the things I'd once hoped for and never found.

"You're never alone, Jayden. You need to know that. I'll always be here for you. No matter what you're going through," she murmurs into my chest. "Always..."

Her voice has a calming effect on me. My breath slows, the ragged intake of emotion tapering. "I know, Mir...I know." The panic and fear slowly begin to subside, my head clearing. *I've been a fool. Again. To even think for one minute that I was a vamp—*

"Jayden?"

I stiffen at the sound of my name. A voice. Not Miriam's.

And I know how things must look right now.

Miriam steps back from me as I drop my arms and straighten, my eyes combing the night for the familiar voice. For her.

"Alexa?" I catch her silhouette amongst the darkness of trees.

"What's going on?" Her voice wavers.

"It's nothing...it was nothing... It's not what it looks like."

"Isn't it?" Her words are weak, shattered. She takes a step back, melding with the darkness.

"Alexa, don't go..." I lurch toward where she was standing. "Alexa?" I hear movement among the thicket, beyond the veil of rain. "Alexa," I call, "wait!"

I shine my flashlight into the darkness, swinging the beam back and forth in search, pushing aside bracken and boughs in my way, then stop, hesitate. I look back at Miriam, her face unreadable behind the glare of her flashlight.

"It's okay. Go to her. I understand."

"I'm so sorry." I feel torn. I don't want to leave her, but—

"Don't be."

In the distance the firefly glow of the others' flashlights blink and glint amongst the foliage. Haphazardly, I glance toward them then back toward the shadows where Alexa retreated. Back and forth, my heart panicking with each second passing that I'll be too late to find her. "Will you be okay?"

"Yes. The others aren't far. I'll go join them. You go. It's all right."

"Thank you." I take a few hurried steps through the bracken then pause. "I mean it. Thank you. For everything, Miriam. Thank you for everything." Then I'm moving again.

I don't wait to hear her reply.

TWENTY-SEVEN

THUNDER ROLLS OVERHEAD, a long, drawn-out tenor. Rain streams down my face as I push through the slick underbrush, slipping in muck, branches snagging at my sopping clothes.

"Alexa!" I yell into the night. I don't care who hears me—what hears me. All I care about is finding her. My mind drifts in disoriented circles, darkness pressing in the further I foray. Branches overhead loom like the gnarled fists of giants against slivers of black-gray sky. Amid the thrum of rain slipping from heavy leaves, there is a sound like heavy footfall. I swing my flashlight toward the bushes beside me, catching the glow of two steady eyes peering through a screen of foliage.

Yellow eyes.

Watching me intently.

I fumble backwards, slipping, lurching to the ground as the creature lunges forward then away, my light catching its flank as it bounds through the underbrush.

"A buck," I pant, wiping a slippery streak of mud from where it's splashed onto my forehead, "just a buck." *This time.* My muscles clench at the thought of the mysterious wolf crouching in wait, amber eyes trained on me. Or trained on—

"Alexa!" My voice cracks with worry. *I need to find her.*

The muffled echo of the vampire hunters has been long lost to the sound of rain. The only illumination skimming the trees is from my flashlight, accompanied by the violent crack of lightning pulsing through the forest in patchy intervals.

I push forward, shoving low hanging branches aside, ignoring the cold slick of rain against my neck, the sodden pull of my clothes, drifting deeper and deeper into the darkness. The woods encircle me like a prison, heavy trunks on every side.

I'm not afraid.

Not for myself.

But for her...wherever she is...

My heart beats with steadfast intensity the farther I roam, muscles twitching with adrenalin. Presently, I detect a clearing among the thick canopy of trees, a glitter on the ground when lightning flares. Closer and closer I get until I see the ground isn't ground at all, but the restless surface of a large pond, water embossed with rippling waves. Then I see her, crouched on an outcrop of stone, staring down at the darkened depths in despair.

"Alexa!"

She glances up at the sound of her name. "Jayden, go back."

"No." Emotion forces the word from my lips, gruffer than intended.

She rises to her feet. "I mean it, go...please. I can't do this again. Can't be hurt like this..."

I half slide down an embankment until I'm level with the pond, crunching across strewn pebbles to the smooth gloss of slick stone where she stands, her body cast in storm shadow. "I don't want to be with anyone else, I swear. You need to know that. I know that last guy hurt you, Alexa, but I'm not going to."

She glances down to the pond. "Did he hurt me? Or did I hurt him?" Her voice wavers. "Because if we hadn't been arguing..." Her voice trails away.

"Then he wouldn't have lost focus and lost control of the car, I know. You both wouldn't have ended up in that fjord and he wouldn't have drowned."

She says nothing, her eyes trained on the pond's surface, her thoughts a million miles away.

"I won't be the guy that hurts you, Alexa. I promise. I'll never leave you." And in that moment, I know it to be true. This wasn't just a love at first sight story. Not just something to occupy my heart for a spell of time.

I want to find forever with her.

"Jayden..."

It's when she says my name that I remember what Magenta said, *Jayden...she's not well. Whatever that means.* Panic sparks in my veins that maybe she'll be the one to leave me. "It's not cancer, is it?" I blurt out. "Or something terminal?"

She blinks and looks at me, my flashlight filtering the air around her. "What are you talking about?"

"Your mom said you aren't well."

"Not well?" She scrunches her brow. "I'm fine. Stronger than ever."

"I don't understand—your mom told me to stay away. She said it was best for your family right now."

"God, no...don't stay away. I just need time tonight to think; sort myself out—"

I won't let her change the topic. "But I saw you leaning on your dad when you left the library at your home. You thought I'd gone but I was still there. And what about the night on the beach when you collapsed...?"

She closes the distance between us until she's before me, her hair buffeting around us both in the wind, like a swirling, silken veil of dampened curls. "Do I look unwell?"

Slowly, I shake my head, my heart clamoring at her proximity. She takes my hands in hers.

"She really doesn't mean anything to you?" she asks.

"Miriam? No. I mean, yes. She means a lot. But not like that. Not like you."

"I'm sorry I took off. Seeing you two together like that... You looked so..."

"Close. I know. But it's not like that." The scent of Miriam rises in my memory, the coconut ginger dampness of her skin and hair. "She's what I thought I wanted before. But maybe that's because her family was the only thing I had." The barb of yesteryear's loneliness rakes across my heart. "And I needed...someone."

"I'm not some crazy jealous person, I swear," she murmurs, moving closer to me until her head is resting against my chest. I feel the thud of my heart intensify, embarrassed that she probably can feel it too—can feel the power she has over me. "I just can't stand the thought of you with anyone else."

"It's okay. I understand that feeling." *Because I've felt it too...* Discomfort addles my brain as I picture Sam behind her home. *Why was he there? Why was he so fierce in warning me away from her if they weren't...something?*

I don't get to explore the thoughts more as her hand has found its way to the stubble of my cheek, guiding my face down to hers.

She tastes like rain and wind. Like a sweet secret.

There's something about the night; storms. The dark, wild restlessness of a world in hidden chaos. It's a reckless freedom that tears at the soul, allowing it to escape into wanton abandon. We're wet already, so it doesn't matter that the moss beneath us is filled with rain. Every sense is alive, the rain trickling from her skin into my mouth, our saturated clothes contouring our bodies so closely, it's as if they aren't there at all.

My body is alive, rampant with awareness. We peel away the layers, one by one. Legs entwined, the rise of her body beneath mine, the endless intoxication of lips, hands, skin, eyes...those eyes...

She's watching me as we kiss, our gaze locked, lightning splintering overhead catching her eyes in evanescent beauty, in fleeting sky-spun blue.

Between kisses, between intakes of air, we whisper in hurried need our plans against each other's mouths. We'll run away...we'll be together...we'll build a home on the banks of some sun-filled seaside oasis...we'll read, we'll write, we'll bask in literary glory...tell stories...make our own stories...maybe have children...marry...live each day, each month, each year...as one...

These are the hopes of youth. These are the dreams of two lonely hearts. This is the stuff dreams are made of...

But...

Afterward, I can barely breathe, my heart crescendoing and expanding within. I can't contain all that I feel for her, body and soul. It rachets within, feels as if it will split me open, to explode into the night. I'm in love. *So, in love.* My body a synaptic circuit of fire.

"I should go, Jayden," she murmurs into my shoulder. "Before my father notices I'm missing."

Her head is on my chest, the throb of my heart beneath her cheek, emotion bursting inside with each palpable beat. "Okay..." I try and quell my heart, even my breathing, but I can't contain it. Can't contain all that I feel. "But...how? If he's locking your door...how did you leave your place?" I try to bring myself back to earth, but I can't. Don't want to. I slide my hand up and down the contour of her hip and side, the perfection of her skin.

"The tree by my window." She sits up slowly, fumbling to gather her sodden clothes.

"In this weather?"

"It's okay. It's not the first time."

I run a hand through my mat of wet hair. "Why did you even come to the hunt tonight? It's dangerous to be doing what they're doing. Dangerous to be looking for trouble."

"Yet...you were there."

"Brody lied to me and told me you were coming—with them. I wanted to make sure you were safe."

"Well, I'm glad he lied. Glad you were here tonight." She casts me an almost shy look now.

I pull her back to me and kiss her, long and slow. "Look what you do to me," I whisper, guiding her hand to my chest, the pounding of my heart.

"And you to me..." she murmurs in return.

"Let me hear…"

She giggles as I roll her over and kiss her, down the gentle slope of her neck, my mouth hovering over its exposed skin as if daring myself to want more, then down the smooth plane of her breastbone, to the space between her breasts, the plush velvet of her skin, and listen…

Nothing.

Just the sound of wind…rain…the resonance of thunder…

There's noise all around, I reason.

I nestle farther, firmer, my hands laced with hers alongside her body, needing to hear her heart respond to me the way mine responds to her— the ridiculous, uncontrolled percussion of requited love.

Silence.

"I—I can't hear your heartbeat."

"It's there. I can feel it."

"But I can't—" That distinctive pulse.

She pushes me off her and sits up. "So what, Jayden?" she says softly. "You just saw how my body responds to you." She places a finger to my lips and smiles a mysterious smile.

"Let me try again."

"Why?" She playfully pushes me off as another roll of thunder resonates over the forest, the earth trembling at the sound.

I lean forward, my head pressed to her chest.

"Jayden—"

I clutch my arms around her pulling her closer.

Nothing.

No gentle bump against my cheek. No steady thrum.

I sit back and fumble for her hand, my fingers searching the underbelly of her wrist for a pulse, a coldness slipping into my soul. A quiet dread.

"Jayden, stop that—"

Lightning streaks through the sky in a crisp, jagged line, her eyes catching the light, their luminous shade of twilight blue. It's then that I remember what it was about the news article that bothered me—what niggled in my conscience long after I'd left her father's lab.

I search her eyes. "Do you wear contacts?"

"What? No..." She pushes my hands off her, laughing uncomfortably, and gathers up her clothes, pulling a damp shirt over her. "Why are you asking?"

Because your eyes used to be brown.

TWENTY-EIGHT

IN THE MOVIE the vampire's eyes are all dark when he's hungry, right? Thirsting for blood. And once he's satiated, his eyes go this golden color. They lighten. Change.

All I can think about is what Brody said in the parking lot outside the Thriftway.

"Jayden, what is it? Why are you looking at me that way?" Alexa is standing now, buttoning her jeans.

My throat is dry. *Overactive imagination*, I lecture myself. *Overtired... The night, the storm... Thinking I was a vampire...*

But—her pulse. *Where was it?* And her eyes...

"Nothing. It's nothing," I mumble.

She bends to pull her shoes on, one by one, then stands, her face glistening with rain, torrents of curls coiling around her shoulders. "I meant everything I said," she says softly. "About running away with you. Being with you. I want that, Jayden. I want it all. With you."

I'm numb, suddenly registering the cool temperature of the rain, the heat from our rapture leeching out of me until I'm shivering.

"Maybe this was a bad idea," she says, squatting down next to me, her hand on my shoulder. "You're skin's like ice."

"No..." The words catch on my tongue as I look at her. "It wasn't a mistake." My mind chugs like an engine. *You're not thinking straight. You're imagining things.*

But her eyes...

I can't bring myself to meet them. Maybe it was a misprint in the newspaper. A flaw in the ink.

But her heartbeat...

Maybe the storm is too loud, too intense, drowning out all other sound. She's a runner...runners can have low, slow heartbeats—heartbeats that would be imperceptible to the average ear and fumbling fingers in the midst of a midnight storm.

Don't fuck this up, Jayden. Like the rest of your life.

"I'm fine, I'm sorry." I get to my feet and pull on my clothes under her watchful gaze. "The truth is, I haven't slept in days. So, I'm...I'm not thinking straight."

"Not thinking straight about me?" She sounds worried. "Us? Those things you said—"

"I meant." I pull her to me, wrap my arms around her, resting my lips on the damp crown of her curls. "I'm sorry. Sometimes I let my thoughts run away from me. I have a...crazy imagination. It's how I've coped with stuff in the past, but—" *But sometimes reality becomes blurred with fantasy.* I clear my throat. "A friend told me once..." I swallow hard remembering Miriam's face in the school hallway, "that I self-sabotage. I think maybe...maybe she's right. I don't want to wreck this." I move her back so I can look her in the eye. "I don't want to mess this up."

All she does is nod, laces her fingers through mine. "We're two of a kind, Jayden. We belong together."

I don't tell her that her words frighten me.

Don't tell her that maybe she's right.

TWENTY-NINE

SHE KNOWS THE forest as well as I do, or so it seems. We wend our way through the impossible darkness, eventually skirting the area where townsfolk and tourists still throng the forest, whooping with glee from the thrill of the hunt. I don't see my friends, so press on with Alexa until we are far from the boisterous noise, the spectral gleam of flashlights, and finally, almost an hour later, at the mansion's drive. Cautiously, we slip around back to the large tree beneath her window, noting the glow from her father's laboratory window. We pause behind the tree's thick trunk, and she slips into my arms.

"Tonight was magical," she whispers against my lips.

For a moment, I think of Magenta's poultice, the crystal on my bedside table, the impossibility that someone like Alexa could love someone like me. But she does love me. I can feel it. *She wants to stay by my side forever.*

I don't have to be alone.

I wrap my arms around her and hold her close, reliving the sensations from earlier, feeling my body responding to hers yet again.

She shakes her head and pulls away. "Not here, not now. But soon…"

When she pulls away from me, it's like a piece of me goes with her. I watch her scale the tree, admiring the adeptness of her agility, the swiftness of her strength as she scales the rain-soaked limbs, and disappears inside. Surreptitiously, I glance toward the lab then slip through the shadows toward home. The storm has rumbled off to distant horizons, the night scrubbed clean, stars studding the sky above.

Several times along the lonely stretch of road home, I feel as if I'm being watched. Followed. So, I stick to the roads to avoid the unknown of the forest. But tonight, I'm not afraid of what's out there.

Tonight, despite the unsettled feeling in my gut, I feel part of its mystery.

*　*　*

There are lights on in the mobile when I crest the top of the lane near home, the old Ford crookedly parked out front. I hesitate before entering. Inside, Mom is sitting in front of the television on her favorite chair, a cigarette held limply between her fingers. "There you are," she rasps. "I'd wondered if tonight was another one of your nights."

"I've been awake the whole time." I walk past her to the bathroom and shut the door, shaking a little. I stare at my face in the mirror, my lips inflamed from my night of passion. I touch them tremulously with my fingertips, then pull my lower lip down to examine the cuts still lining the inside. I run my tongue over the points of my canine teeth and meet my eyes in the reflection, trying to scrutinize what lies behind them. What secrets. Because instead of self-loathing, I feel something oddly different. A titillating power that spreads through my body to every place that Alexa touched.

I brush my teeth and shower the night off me, regretting any traces of her that I wash away. I'd become more chilled on the walk home, the rain finally soaking through my skin to the core. I stand for an eternity beneath the steam of the shower head, reliving my night with Alexa. Her touch. Her taste. Her eyes... *those ethereal eyes*—

Whatever mysteries formulate her past, it doesn't matter. All I care about now is living up to every promise I made to her tonight. Being the man that my father wasn't. Stitching together a real family that is truly my own. Me. Alexa. Whatever comes from our union.

But what if she's—

I can't think it.

And what if I'm—

"Jayden?" There is a knock at the door.

"One sec." I twist off the faucet and step onto the worn bathmat, snagging a towel. My clothes are too wet to don again, so I wrap the towel tight and open the door to head to my bedroom. Mom's slight figure is framed in the hallway.

"If you weren't wandering, why were you out so late?" Her eyes are slightly glassy. "I heard something about a vampire hunt tonight. You weren't there, were you?"

"It doesn't matter, Mom." I go into my room and rummage around my drawers for some pajama bottoms.

Mom steps into the doorway behind me, her tired eyes skimming over the musculature of my upper body. "You look so much like your father," she murmurs.

I stiffen. She never talks about my father. He's the blank page in my tattered history.

"And the way you act. Both of you...so full of mystery. Such...old souls."

"Mom, I need to get changed."

"Right, right..." she says distantly, and trails down the hall.

I shut the door behind her and drop my towel to pull on my pajamas. The high of the night is wearing away with the presence of my mother, the thoughts of my father. I sit down on the edge of my bed, suddenly weary. I pick up the crystal and palm it. The hall light gleams from beneath my door. Despite myself, I get up and open it, heading down the hall to find Mom returned to her chair in the living room.

"Why are you talking about my father? Why now?"

"Because that Jill Foster is on me about being a better mom."

"What do you mean?"

"I should take you back to see that doctor, Jayden. The one in Seattle."

"I don't need no doc—"

"You're wandering. Maybe not tonight, but you're doing it again, and

I don't want you to end up like your father."

"And how did he end up?"

"Dead."

I can't breathe for a second, the room listing in a dizzying spin. "What?"

"It doesn't matter," she says dismissively. "That was a long time ago."

"You can't just say stuff like that! How did he die?"

"Don't know. He was always going off into the night. I thought maybe he had a lady friend or something, but turns out no. Just demons in his head. Nearly drove him crazy. I didn't know much about his past. Truth is, I didn't know much about him at all, Jayden. It's not like there's some long love story to tell. He was just some guy I met and shacked up with and then you were born. Not long after, he died. There's happily ever after for you."

"What do you mean he went out at night?"

"Just had some stuff haunting him, you know? I don't know if he was awake or asleep like you, but he was out all the time. Finding trouble. Or maybe running from it." She lifts a new cigarette to her lips. A glass of caramel colored liquid sits in a low tumbler next to the ashtray on the side table.

My gut clenches when I look at this diorama of my life. I can't help but picture Alexa nestled in the opulence of their library, my favorite alcove just down the hall where I read *Frankenstein*, felt the loneliness of that godforsaken monster. The abandonment of his creator. The only parent he knew.

"I don't need a doctor, Mom." *I just need to get out of here. Get out of this town, my life. Get out of my head—*

"Whatever you need, Jay. If you want to go back to see him, just say the word. I've...I've got the money for it."

Bile rises in my throat, and I steady myself. *It's not your money, Mom. It's Mrs. Foster's.* And I don't want it. I don't want to be anyone's worry, anyone's pity, anyone's problem. I just want to be the person Alexa sees. A guy with a future big enough to hold her. Big enough to hold us both.

"Goodnight, Mom." I trudge back to my room and shut the door, collapsing onto my bed, hot tears maddeningly welling behind my eyes.

For too long I've felt broken. I think of Alexa, how she too paints her past like a fragment.

And yet...

Two broken pieces make a whole.

I roll over and clutch the crystal her mother gave me, willing whatever magic it contains to protect me from drifting into the night. From drifting away from reality. From drifting away from Alexa. Or from Alexa drifting away from me.

The bathrobe tie knotted on my headboard lies beside my pillow. I stare at it through the glaze of brimming tears, twisting its frayed length between my fingers. The nightstand clock glows 1:42am. I close my eyes and picture Alexa, the storm swirling around her, remember the words we shared, the promises. Tonight, I don't fear sleep. Because it means another night will have passed.

Another night closer to my future with her.

* * *

In my dreams there's a scream. A blood curdling cry. And grief so deep it feels like it's digging out my soul. *No, no, no!* I howl.

You always know when I need you. Always know when I'm in trouble. It's Miriam's voice. *You have a sixth sense, Jayden. Premonition. You know when something bad is about to happen.*

That's all she says, over and over, my dream populated with her voice and snatches of her face in the dark abyss of forest. I get the sensation of running—brambled trees carving my cheeks and chest. I run fast, faster, until suddenly—

I'm awake.

Panting.

Darkness all around

Kneeling in the sludge of rainforest earth.

There's another scream—louder than the last.

It's me. My voice, ripping from my chest like a cannon.
And the overwhelming sense that—
—*I'm too late.*

THIRTY

I RUN, BRANCHES whipping past my face, feet digging into the earth, dirt flying beneath them, until I'm home, dawn cresting the horizon with murky raincloud light. I dash up the front steps of the mobile and shove my way inside. Mom has already left, the front parking space empty, the lingering scent of her cloying in the air. I pace the hall, unsure of what to do. I scrabble into my room, find my phone discarded on the floor and power it on impatiently. For once, I'm grateful for technology, this link to my friends. I need to text Miriam and make sure that she's okay. I can't shake the pitted dread snaking through my belly.

The battery is dead. I tear through my room until I find the limp line of the charging cord and plug it in. My messaging lights up with unanswered calls, unread texts. I see Miriam's name and immediately open it. It's time stamped 10:35pm: Jay, where r u? Did u find Alexa? Please call or txt as soon as you get this. I'm praying for once u have your phone...

I sag with relief. *She's okay. Just a dream.*

Then I open Brody's texts, the first one questioning where I am. Of course. I never told him I wasn't going home with him. Then the next at 11:52pm: where the hell r u?

And the next. 1:15am: PICK UP YOUR PHONE!

The last one, time stamped 3:37am: we can't find Miriam

THIRTY-ONE

I DROP THE phone. It clatters to the floor at my feet. The room starts to spin. My hand catches the wall, as I stagger unsteadily. *No...this isn't happening...*

The rumble of a vehicle pulling in front of the mobile brings me to my senses. Footsteps pound up the front porch and a fist slams against the door. I stagger down the hall and open it.

"Sam...?"

"Get dressed," he instructs.

I stare at my friend. Know why he's here. "Is she okay? Did they find her?"

"No. The Fosters sent me to see if you were here, if maybe she was with you...because you were last seen together."

"Wait...what? No...we were together but then she rejoined the group so I could look for Alexa. Miriam and I separated."

"Separated?" His voice is thick with judgement. "During a vampire hunt, you left her alone in the woods?" His eyes skim my pajama bottoms, the muddied knees, bramble sore chest. "What the hell?"

"I was outside." I turn away from him and stagger down the hall to my room, slamming the door behind me. Breathing hard, I lean against the door then lurch over to my closet and snag some clean clothes.

Sam's back in his truck, waiting, by the time I remerge. I notice Dan standing on his front stoop. "They find another body?"

"No." *Not yet.*

I screw my eyes shut at the thought—*Don't even think it!*

I climb into the truck, and Sam throws it in reverse. We speed out of the trailer park onto the road. I twist my hands in my lap, staring out at the landscape streaming by. "How did you find out?"

"My dad. The Fosters called him."

"You were home? I thought you were..." I can't even think straight to finish my sentence.

His knuckles are tight on the steering wheel. "Yeah, well...I was back."

"Did you even go? On your spiritual quest?" My words are tart on my tongue. *Because I saw you. At Alexa's.* Something stays my tongue. I can't confront him about it. *Not yet.*

His expression flickers slightly, just for a split second. Had I not been watching, I would have missed it. "This isn't about me right now, Jayden, okay? It's about Miriam. The fact that one of our best friends is missing. So, how about you focus on that, got it?"

"Got it," I snipe, a fresh wave of worry washing over me.

Sam's quiet for a minute, the truck radio blaring. He jams his finger on the volume dial, spinning it to silence. "You know, if you weren't so obsessed with your girlfriend, we wouldn't be in this mess right now. You just had to go after Alexa instead of staying with Miriam."

"Hold on, I'm the one obsessed?" I spit. "What about you? And your jealousy?"

"Jealousy?" he retorts. "Why would I be jealous?"

"Because you said you liked Alexa—at the beginning, when I ran into you at the side of the road after the search for Sophie. Remember?"

"Jayden, man..." He shakes his head. "That was a long time ago."

"That was last week!"

"Yeah, well...last week was a long time ago."

"And you warned me to stay the hell away from her, remember?" I close my eyes remembering Sam stepping out from the underbrush, Dr. Johansson's red truck barreling down the street. The way I'd spied

Dr. Johansson later, sobbing in the vacant park lot.

Uneasiness settles into my bones.

"You read that as I was jealous?" Sam wrenches the steering wheel around the corners, pitching my body against the passenger door. "Fuck, man! You have no idea!"

My head is spinning with questions, but there's no time for more conversation as we careen onto the Fosters' street and grind to a halt out front. Chief Hanson's vehicle is sitting in the driveway. He's talking with Mrs. Foster.

Sam draws a steadying breath. "Let's just cool it now, okay? For the Fosters. Mr. Foster's still out looking for her where the hunt happened last night. The chief brought Mrs. Foster home in case Miriam turns up here." Sam leaps out of the truck. He stops, a frown on his face. "You coming?"

I stare out the window at Chief Hanson's profile as he talks to a red-eyed Mrs. Foster. The timeline of last night crowds into my head. Had they noticed she was missing when I was still with Alexa? For some inexplicable reason that brings me relief. That part of the night replaying in vibrant technicolor. *It wasn't me.*

But what about after? When you were wandering?

What if you weren't too late, but were the one who—

"Jayden, come on, man! Brody's ready to go," Sam urges, impatiently. "We're going back up there to look some more."

I glance out the windshield. Chief Hanson is looking over my way, his brow knit, while Mrs. Foster keeps talking, her hands wringing together. Brody barges out of the house and down the lawn, striding purposefully toward the truck.

"What the hell, man?" he shouts ripping open the passenger door of the truck to confront me.

"Brody, chill—" I splutter.

"What the hell did you take off for? I thought she was with you!"

I was with Alexa when Miriam was missing. The words form a mantra in my mind, over and over. *I'm not to blame. It wasn't me. It wasn't Alexa.*

It wasn't us. We're not—

"You going to sit there like a bloody lump or are you going to help find her?" Brody barks.

"Hey, calm down, son, all right?" The Chief says, striding over to the truck to place a firm hand on Brody's shoulder. "What's going on here?"

"If Jayden hadn't left my sister, we wouldn't be here right now!" Brody swipes the back of his hand across his nose, sniffing hard.

"Brody Foster, you are as much to blame as Jayden," Mrs. Foster explodes. "How could you two have even gone on this stupid hunt? And with your sister?"

"I *told* you, *I didn't take her.* She came herself." Brody flinches under his mother's pained glare.

"Brody, I think I should drive," Sam says. "You're in no shape."

"Agreed." Chief Hanson nods. "You three just stick together, all right? Until we get more answers as to what we're dealing with, I don't want you out in the bush on your own, understood?"

I nod, but Brody just wrenches the back door of the truck open and squeezes into the rear bucket seats. Sam jumps into the driver's side and guns the engine.

"Please, boys..." Mrs. Foster pleads. "Bring her home."

"We will, Mrs. Foster," Sam promises, and we reverse in a cloud of exhaust.

*   *   *

Like when Sophie went missing, most of the town is out searching the area. By the light of day, the woods don't look as ominous as last night. Remnants of the vampire hunt litter the ditch with some abandoned beer cans and a scattered stack of hand-hewn stakes carved from fallen branches. Sam finds a spot along the shoulder of the road and swerves to pull over and park.

"There's my dad," Brody says, his breath hitching with emotion. "I'm going to search with him." He jumps out and strides over to where Mr. Foster is talking with some officers and others who have joined the search.

"You can't blame him for not wanting to be around you right now," Sam says.

"They were right there," I say, thinking back to last night. "We could see their flashlights. She was so close to them…" I trail off.

"Why were you looking for Alexa?"

"She saw me with Mir and got the wrong impression. Alexa ran off into the woods. I…I followed her."

"She took off into the woods?" His shoulders stiffen. "You should have let her go."

"What, I'm to protect Miriam but not Alexa? Miriam was near everybody. She should have been able to join them again right away. I thought—"

"Just get out," Sam commands and jumps out of the truck, shutting the door firmly behind him.

"Jayden, Sam…thank you for coming." Mr. Foster approaches, his face pale. He spreads a wrinkled map. "We've already searched here and here." His voice is shaking. "If you want to look out this way," his finger taps north, "…that's where we're trying next."

"Her car…what about her car?" I ask, suddenly remembering.

Mr. Foster looks down the road absently, then back. "It was found. Not where she parked it when she first got here last night, according to Brody. We're trying to determine at what time she would have moved it. The driver side door was left open…" His voice trails off and he swallows hard.

"We're gonna find her, Mr. Foster," Sam assures. He claps a hand on my back. "Come on, Jayden, let's get going."

"Don't stray too far from the other searchers," Mr. Foster warns. "We don't want…" His breath catches, unshed tears magnifying the dark blue of his eyes. "We don't want anyone else to go missing." He places a hand on each of our shoulders and says, "Let's just find her." His voice breaks. "We have to." His hands slide from our shoulders and he turns to rejoin the others, the picture of a broken man.

Sam nudges my elbow, and we head off to follow the road to where it's been reclaimed by wilderness, to trace its beaten path.

The woods stretch out before us, thick with secrets. Sam strides ahead.

"Sam, wait up. Hey!"

He keeps going without responding, twigs snapping back into place behind where he passes. "Miriam!" he calls, joining the echo of other searchers.

Just the sound of her name gives me chills. To think she might be out here. Alone. Scared.

Or worse.

I double over, emotion clawing at my core, the world tilting, warping, as I grapple with what's happened. I want to shout. *Scream!* But all I can do is hold the detonation of grief tight inside.

My shin starts to throb, the ache radiating up my leg. I close my eyes to a flashback of Kam and his friends jumping me, the bat connecting with my shin.

Come on, walk! Don't let the pain slow you down now. You've already walked with it like this. Ran. Done God knows what in the middle of the night when wandering. And with Alexa, I'd—

Heat fills my face. Not just from remnants of passion, but guilt for what I'd been doing while Miriam was alone, separated from everyone else.

Sam turns around, impatiently. "What gives?"

I look up at Sam, glassy eyed. "I need a minute." I need to focus—not let my emotions render me helpless.

"Look," he says, warily taking in my expression. "We're all afraid of what we might find, okay? I can't even think about it. Because what if we find her but she's not ali—"

"Don't say it, okay? I can't go there. Please."

"Just...Jay we gotta keep going. We got to find her."

"I know." I draw in a deep breath, trying to steady the swirl of nausea pocketed in my gut, and push on, hurrying to catch up with him.

The farther we go, the denser the forest becomes, the other searchers' voices fading to silence as we leave them behind despite the warnings to stick close to the group. The hushed rustle of leaves, the spindle thin scrape of pine, spruce, fir, replaces the sound of calling voices.

"Miriam!" Sam's voice is swallowed by the denseness of the woods but echoes through my soul.

Miriam...

We pass a small clearing, colorful meadow flowers pluming between blades of grass. I run my eyes over the glade, looking for any clues that Miriam may have passed through here. The sweet scent of wildflowers rolls in the soft wind, rain clouds deepening in the sky overhead. The gentle stir of grasses sparks a hazy memory of laughter. "This place looks familiar," I say.

Sam pauses, his eyes combing over the thatch of meadow. "This place looks familiar because we passed by it long ago when we were out adventuring."

"*Adventuring*," I echo, catching up to him. "Rex and Brody mentioned something about us being out this way with you when we were younger. Something about some abandoned bunker."

Sam slows. Overhead, rain clouds sift and soften, gliding steadily over the gray sky, casting the trees into deeper shadow, a fine mist penetrating their heavy boughs. "Right. I'd almost forgotten about that. I couldn't find it for you guys. It was lost to the forest." He looks away from me, his face grim, into the labyrinth of woods. "Come on, let's keep going." He turns to plod on and I follow.

Further and further we go, catching a glimpse of a distant river where there is a break in the heavy woods. The clouds change, grow to angry, ashen thunderheads. I slow my pace. "I think...maybe...we've come too far," my voice cracks, taut with emotion. "This is nowhere near where the hunt took place last night. I can't imagine Miriam coming this far— not in the dark. Not on her own."

The sharp scent of cedar wafts heavily into my lungs, terror clutching at my heart, as I realize she likely wasn't alone.

The faint howl of a wolf slips through the forest, a lost and forlorn sound.

Sam scans the underbrush, a distant look in his eye. "The rogue pack," he breathes, a muscle in his jaw flexing.

Unnerved, I glance into the gloom of trees ahead. Behind, branches stir in the gathering storm. "There's not just that pack in the forest. There's a lone wolf too. Out there somewhere. Big as a bear."

Sam's back is to me, his body stiffening. "And you've...seen...this wolf?"

The distant howl fades into the misty ether, the woods falling silent. Sam doesn't move.

"Twice." *Amber eyes steady on me. Mist curling through its fur.* I flinch at the memory. "Once on the way home from First Beach and again..." My voice trails off. Because the second time I'd seen it, Sam had been there. Outside of Alexa's home. Come to think of it...*Sam was there at the first sighting too. On the fringe of beach. Watching. Fading into the forest.* "...when I saw you at Alexa's." A muscle in my face tics as I try to process my thoughts, a fine, cold sweat forming along my upper lip, moistening my armpits. A talon of uncertainty wedges into my sternum, gouging deeper and deeper.

"What do you mean?"

"I saw you, Sam. At Alexa's. There was all that fog..." The words fall away as I draw a breath. "And that wolf..." My throat constricts, my thoughts melding together in a haze of nonsensical thought.

Sam doesn't say a word, his body bristling with tension, his muscles bulky and flexed beneath his waffle shirt and vest, hands bunched into fists.

"Why were you outside her home, Sam? And where have you *really* been this past week?" I swallow hard.

He expels a whistle of air and steps further from me, fallen branches cracking beneath his hiking boots. He stares into the forest, after the fading call of the wolves. "It belongs to them, you know. The forest. It's sacred to them. It's us who are trespassing. Humans." His words are edged, his body a tight vessel of instinct. Somewhere, buried deep in his veins, runs wolf blood. Ancient and deep. I can almost smell it.

"I've wanted to connect with my peoples' traditions more." His fingers flex at his side. "I was gone, Jayden, for that reason. To prepare. But..." His hands ball into fists. "But instead of finding what I was looking for, I discovered something else."

Slowly, he turns to face me, his eyes meeting mine.

All this time I've known him...

...and only now, have I noticed the hint of amber in his eye.

THIRTY-TWO

I FEEL THE swoosh of blood firing through my veins, the throb of pulse at my neck.

He steps toward me. Instinctually, I take a step back, my own hands curling into fists.

So, this is how it is.

Truth stranger than fiction.

My body feels cold, like ice. I wonder at that, for a moment—if I've always been cold and just not noticed. If the throb of my heart is an illusion. A memory haunting my veins. Because I know the story. The story of the cold ones. Of their warm-blooded adversaries.

Sam narrows his eyes at me. "Why are you looking at me that way?"

I close my eyes, my mind caroming from one thought to another, too fast. "The bodies, Sam. They looked like a wolf got to them. Sophie. And that other girl, Lindsay. A wolf...but something with human intelligence." *And the third—* My eyes flicker open.

What about the third girl? Two neat wounds burrowed into her neck—

"What are you getting at?" Sam's fists unfurl in confusion. He meets my gaze, bewilderment interrupting the hardness of his expression. "Dude, what the hell is going on with you? You look possessed."

"You've been away this past week to connect with your traditions, your ancient ancestry. Your people are from wolves."

∞ 296 ∞

"Yeah, but—"

"And this week, three girls died. In the wild. Maybe at the mercy of a wolf..."

"What the...?" He's at a loss for words, his mouth pursing in search of what to say next. "What the hell you trying to say?"

The words pour out of me, untapped. Uncensored. "Maybe you weren't responsible for the third death—" my gut clenches as I say it, "but the first two? Was Alexa who you were after next? Or Miriam—?"

Just like that, he's striding toward me, grabbing me, meaty fists clamping down hard on my shoulders, knuckles boring into the bone of my chest, clenched to strike. "Are you for real, man? Are you *accusing* me?" Rage pours from his pores. "We're out here trying to find our friend, and you actually accuse me of being the one to hurt her?"

"Then where have you been?! This past week—where were you?" Suddenly, cascading down my cheeks, into the iron taste of my mouth— *tears.*

Because what I really mean is: *where the hell have I been this past week?*

Sam rears back, breathing hard, dropping his hands from me, looking at me with disbelief. He studies me, his face ashen. "Jayden...what the hell, man? What's going on?"

"You aren't the only one whose been out roaming these woods." Fear rises inside. I try to grapple with what's left of rational thought, my chest heaving, my mind so sleep deprived it feels like I'm tangled in a nightmare dream. *I* am *in a nightmare dream. Miriam is missing.*

And just like that, I'm afraid. Of him. Of myself—*again.* Of what the hell is happening to me.

To him.

To Miriam.

To my life and what I thought I knew of it.

And we know what raw fear can do.

Turn to rage.

All the fury, all the fear, all the shadows and hurt of a lifetime, culminate inside me into a vortex storm, rising, rising.

I don't know what I am.

But right now—as I catch the amber glint in his dark eyes—I am *sure* of what he is.

"Jayden?"

I charge at him, my shoulder slamming into his chest, forcing him backward.

"What the—?" The words are knocked from him.

We grapple with each other, my training with Dan kicking in as I wheel around to strike him with the blade of my foot, but in one swift motion, he grabs my leg, hurling me off balance. I fall into him, onto him. Together, we roll to the edge of a hill hidden by tall tufts of grass, and plummet over its curved lip, tumbling down to land in a heap at the bottom.

Panting hard, I lie on my back, the wind clubbed from my lungs with the landing.

Sam shoves away from me, yanking thorns from his vest, his face a mask of confusion. "What the hell is wrong with you?!"

The flame of rage has flickered into something colder. A desolate pool of ice. Out of nowhere, I start laughing. Hysterically. The sound manic in the treetops.

Sam glances around, uneasy.

The tears are hot. Salty. They burn a path down my temples into my hairline as I stare up at the cover of trees, the sky murky beyond. A crack of lightning lacerates the deep cloud, veining it with silver.

Sam sinks down beside me. "Jayden...hey...it's okay, man."

I don't look at him. Just stare at the vaporous sky, the laughter tapering to a choked sob, snot pooling in my nose.

"Look...we got to get you back. You're not right. You've been carrying too much." When I don't budge, he slumps down beside me, both of us staring at the culminating storm. "I don't know what you were thinking there—"

"That you were the wolf. And I was the vampire," I rasp.

"Fuck, man. That *Twilight* story has really gotten into your head. *Kam's* gotten into your head. It's hard to blame you, though." He rubs a tired hand across his eyes. "Looking the way you do. But seriously... Come *on*." He runs a hand through his hair and heaves a sigh. "We're just two guys going through stuff. Changing. But this is real life, man. Not some story. You always get your head lost in fantasy, but you can't right now, okay? For Miriam. For *yourself*. You got to hold things together."

"I've never belonged." My mind skips around to flashbacks of my life. Me on the sidelines; Sam, the Fosters, everybody else, moving toward the crowd, some indefinable light. Moving away from me. "At least if I was some*thing* else, everything would finally make sense."

"You have too, belonged," Sam retorts. "We all belonged. Together. You. Me. Brody and Miriam. It's just...things have changed this past year." His eyes grow distant. "Not just with you, but with all of us. Going our different directions, looking to the future...wanting different things for it."

I don't answer, just surrender to the ruptured dam inside.

"I know what you're thinking," he says. "We're all scattering after this year and there will be no one to come home to. Not in the same way." He leans his head back against the steep curve of hill. "I've thought of it too."

But really, he's talking about me. Because he has a home to return to. A father. His people. His land. Something to tether himself to. Miriam and Brody do too.

And I have—

I stare at the cold smog of rain.

—just one thing.

My heart aches, the pain so strong, there's no denying the trueness of my heart. It's realness. It hurts too much to be imagined.

How foolish. To have searched for Alexa's heart, when mine was beating strong enough for both of us. Wanting, needing, so much from her. Needing so much from myself. For myself.

And I can't help but wonder if the one thing I'm holding onto is a figment of my imagination too. Alexa's love. Someone to be with forever.

Had Miriam offered that too, in the end?

No.

My broken self didn't fit into Miriam's perfect world. Not the way it needed to. She knew me too well. Knew how ugly my brokenness could be. She was the shelter to my storm. But I don't want shelter anymore. I want to storm. I want to rage. I want to ride the hurricane winds of my heart to a new life. Love. And I don't want to look back.

The thought of Miriam's face snaps me back to the reality of the current situation, worry and fear biting back to the surface at what might have happened to her. I suck in a shattered gasp of air.

"We'll find, her, okay? Miriam. She'll be okay." Sam's voice belies the worry behind his words. The need. For all of us.

"You know, we Quileutes believe all things have a spirit—that these woods are filled with spirits—and that we each have personal guardians." He stops, his eyes focused on the thick cloud pressing upon the treetops. "I just hope that spiritual protection has been extended to her." He runs his hand delicately over the fronds of a sword fern cushioned beside him. "When you said you saw that wolf—" He hesitates. "You think it was...flesh and blood, or...something else?"

Was it my imagination? Or was it—

Stories. Leaking from pages to my mind. The slippery slope of reality when life is unraveling.

"I don't know, anymore. I don't know what to believe." My mouth is dry. Alexa thought it was a bear. And at her home, the mist had consumed the wolf like a mirage.

Had it even been there at all? Or did I conjure it in my mind?

Sam's staring into middle earth, his eyes distant. "Come on. We have to keep going." He stands and reaches a hand down to help me to my feet.

I don't take it, my mind trapped in a circle of thought. "What I don't understand is, why were you there? At Alexa's? And why did you warn me away from her?"

His tongue darts across his lips and he looks away.

"Look…something's not right about that family."

"But you liked her. Last week—like, *liked* her."

"Her. But not her parents. They're…" He runs a hand down his face and lets out a long breath. "I don't know, man, okay? I don't know what it is. Just that I saw them out in the forest, just the two of them—late— and they just looked like they didn't want to be seen."

"Then why didn't you say anything? With everything that's happened, why not go to the police?"

"Because—I don't know, okay? I didn't want to go saying stuff when I didn't have anything concrete. Dr. Johansson's done a lot for the hospital here, and I know they're both doing breakthrough stuff for medicine, or whatever. I didn't want to open my mouth and cause trouble when I didn't know what it was I was reporting. Like what… Report them for weirdness? Then everyone would think *I* was the one being weird for watching them. There was something off about them, but I couldn't tell what. And I get that some people are talking about Alexa's mom like she's some witch, but I didn't want to get caught up in that, you know? I don't know shit about her, so who am I to say anything about what she practices or believes? I get it. I know what it's like to be looked at just because you come from something different." His body is tense, emotion rippling through the rigid swell of muscle. "But then I saw Alexa…in the same area, not far from here, actually…on her own. She looked like she was looking for something but…" He hesitates. "Something wasn't right. She was…different, somehow. Like it was her, but not her, you know?"

I picture her, her eyes intense behind the curtain of fog, the wisp of nightdress, pale as a wraith, clinging to her body. Her voice soughs through my mind. *Something is happening to me.*

The blood drains from my face. Once again, I'm cold.

So cold.

Her, but not her. "Yeah…" I whisper. "I know."

"I did like her, Jay. When I met her in the summer. But when I saw her again, she treated me like a ghost. Hell, she told you she never even met me. There's something about her, Jayden. Something I can't put my finger on. Look…I just don't want to see you get hurt."

"But you took off that day when Dr. Johansson nearly mowed us down with his truck."

"I didn't take off. You were flipping out so much *you* took off like a bat outta hell before I could even register what had just happened. We both hit the ditch. One minute you're calling my name, and I'm just trying to get my wind back after having it knocked out diving into the bush, then before I can even figure out what the hell just happened, you were on your bike and tearing down the road."

"I'm sorry. I didn't know…"

"Yeah, well. Had you stuck around, I could have told you what I was thinking then."

We're interrupted by the rain as it suddenly intensifies, knifing from the sky in torrents. The air turns platinum as a flash of lightning splits the cloud, thunder exploding.

"Come on, let's get out of here!" Sam reaches down to help haul me up, and this time I grab his hand.

We lurch forward, Sam pulling his vest over his head as I uselessly shield my face from the driving rain with the cover of my hoodie. "Over here," Sam cries over a peal of thunder, pointing to where a jutted overhang sprouts from the hill, vines tumbling over its precipice, "until the worst of it passes!"

We shove aside a trailing web of foliage and huddle, shivering, beneath the makeshift shelter, our clothes already drenched through.

There's movement in the trees beyond, the hint of a shadow. Large. Stealthy. Prowling the tree line beyond the curtain of rain.

Then it's gone.

I rub the rain from my eyes, my heart a staccato thrum. "Sam…Sam…did you see—?"

"Holy shit…" Sam's not looking at me, his hand running along the swirl of ivy. "Look at this!"

But I can't tear my eyes from the blur of forest. "What is it?"

"I think I just found our lost bunker."

THIRTY-THREE

BEHIND THE DROOPING foliage and succession of fringed moss and sprouting fern, his fingers have found a glimmer of steel. He scrabbles against the clinging foliage, chunks of earth falling away to reveal a stretch of solid wall. "Whoa..." he breathes. "Jayden? You looking at this?"

But I can't focus. I glance back toward the labyrinth of forest, searching its hidden places, as another blaze of lightning illuminates the deepest shadows. *Nothing...there's nothing out there...*

Yet a shiver of fear furrows down my spine.

It was just your imagination. There's nothing but trees and brush—

"I'm serious, man—" Sam's voice cuts through my thoughts. "Look..."

"What?"

He gestures toward a cataract of tangled vines.

"I don't see anything."

"Look!" Cautiously, he inches toward the tumble of leaves and hesitates before pushing some of the drooping tendrils aside.

Then I see it. A door. Painted camo green to blend with its surroundings.

Sam edges closer, running his fingers along the door. Tentatively, he twists the handle. "Locked."

"You don't think she's in there, do you?" My voice is a hoarse whisper.

I brush past him and try the handle myself, twisting, shoving my body against the door. I slam the heel of my fist against the steel. "Miriam?!" I shout. "Miriam!" I pace the length of the overhang, wrenching tufts of earth and foliage from where it clings to the steel like a second skin. "There has to be a way in."

"Jayden... Come on, man, take it easy—"

"Miriam? *Miriam!*" I run out into the deluge, examining the slope of hill that hides the bunker, rain washing my face like tears. Through the trees, the distant rush of river water slithers through the shadows.

"Jayden, seriously, man, just slow down, all right? Think! It wouldn't make sense for her to be in there, okay? Look, maybe the military still uses it for something, or maybe...maybe it's been sitting like this for years. Come on, we need to use our heads! Because if Miriam was taken by the same freak that killed the others, she wouldn't be here. She'd be out there!" He gestures toward the expanse of forest. "Left like the other bodies, dumped in the woods." He stops, the thought too hard to process, and fists his hands in his hair.

I stare where the vines have fallen back into place, the door disappearing, swallowed by nature, helplessness filling my soul.

Sam glances at his watch. "Shit, it's already past noon. We've been gone too long and still haven't found anything. They're gonna wonder where we are." He steps out into the rain, scanning back the way we came. "We should head back and check in with the others...see if they've found anything. We'll tell them about this place. But I don't think she's here..." He trails off, hopeless.

"No, you're right. I'm sorry. I just...I can't take this anymore."

"We'll find her, okay?"

"Before it's too late?"

He can offer no words. Neither of us can.

I glance out into the forest. Trees sway beneath the pummel of rain.

My gut clenches, a warning rising in my spine.

I know this feeling.

It's the feeling I get before something happens.

And I'm always too late—

Lightning sparks again before another explosion of thunder crashes overhead, my retinas shimmering with the afterglow.

I swallow hard.

I need to face whatever is out there. Whatever is *in* me. And I don't want Sam to get hurt in the process.

"Sam, why don't you go back and find the others and I'll keep searching out here. That way we're covering all ground."

"Heck, no! I'm not leaving you here. You heard Mr. Foster and the chief. We stick together."

"It's okay...go. Sam, you know I know these woods better than anyone. Like you do. And you know I can take care of myself. You saw what I did to Kam and his friends on the beach."

"I wasn't there—"

"You were. I *saw* you."

He doesn't say anything, just looks away.

"Look, you don't have to explain to me where you've been or why—why you've been pulling back from the group long before you took off this week. It's okay. I've been doing it too. We all got our own stuff going on. We're all...changing—like you said. But trust me when I say this...I need you to go. I need to be here right now. Alone. To figure things out."

"But Miriam—"

"I'm not done looking for her. Trust me. But I need to keep on alone."

He studies my face, takes in my eyes, still glassy with emotion, hurt lingering heart deep. He scrunches his nose and clears his throat. "The weather's shit, man. And if anything happens to you—"

"I'll be okay. I'm not afraid." I want to believe that. Have to.

He palms a fist in his hand, sniffs hard, looks off into the distance then back at me. "I don't like it. Don't like leaving you here."

"You don't have to like it." I pause. "I'd do the same for you. Give you space if you needed it."

He meets my eye, a tacit understanding passing between us, and gives a slight nod. "Don't do anything stupid, all right?"

"Wouldn't dare."

"I guess there's no point asking if you've got your phone."

"Seems I'm not the only one ditching the world lately."

"Yeah. Of all the times." He shakes his head and looks over his shoulder back the way we came. "You'll watch your back, right?"

"Yeah." *I'm all instinct.*

He nods, "A'right then. See you when I see you. Let's find our girl." He steps out into the thrash of rain, climbing the knoll of the hidden bunker.

"Sam?"

"Yeah?"

"You said you've been pulling away to connect with your peoples' traditions...but that you discovered something else out here instead. What was it?"

He stares off into the distance. A long moment passes before he speaks. "Just...that I wasn't embracing who I truly am. My past. My people. That I was carrying resentment still for what my tribe has been through. With...," he gestures his arms wide, "...colonialism. Residential schools. Look what happened to my mom." Sam was just a small boy then. It's not something that's talked about. Her suicide. Her pain so deep it cut into the generation after her. And the one before her. "I didn't even know I was carrying all that. But I was. It came out as anger. Towards my family. My culture—for not fighting harder. Anger towards—" He stops, rubs a hand across his eyes. "I'm sorry—but lately, even you and the Fosters for privileges you don't even know you have." He shakes his head, drawing in a deep breath. "All that hurt was misplaced, man. Because it wasn't your fault. Wasn't my tribe's fault. It was the fault of others. And it shadows everything sometimes. Especially now that I'm older and understand it better. But I don't want to be angry." He paces a few steps, energy building inside him. "I want to be productive, you know? Bridge the gap, even if I don't know how, between my peoples' past and our future. *My* future. Fuck man, I didn't even know I was feeling that way. Just when it was coming to be my time..." He hesitates. "To seek out my own taxilit...I started to see everything differently."

I feel guilt suddenly, remembering what his grandfather said about

Sam pulling away; about him carrying an anger, shadows haunting him. I'd been so caught up in my own shadows I'd not known that maybe he had his own.

"I'm sorry," I say. "I didn't know, Sam."

He shakes his head. "You've had your own troubles, Jay. I know that. We've both had hard stuff in our lives. And you didn't know because you didn't see me as anything other than your friend. Just another kid, same as you, that had stuff in his life. Just different stuff. You didn't see me as different than you. And that's good. Because we're not so different in many ways. Just...two guys trying to figure life out."

"I'm sorry, I should have known—"

"Don't man, okay? It wasn't ignorance, it was respect. You just saw *me*. For me, that was enough. Same as I saw you."

Behind the worry that lines his face for Miriam, there is something else. A newfound peace. A growth that I can't quite understand. Growth I have yet to make. It looks like forgiveness. For all in life we can't control. For a past that isn't our making, though we are shaped by it.

Maybe it's the light, the monochromatic gleam of lightning striating the air, but as he turns away from me the teenage boy I'd known my whole life, he looks more like a man. The clouds overhead move with the wind, morphing, changing, a myriad of animals taking illusory form in the thunderheads as they pass by. Or maybe it's my imagination. But I feel a pang of envy, seeing him standing on the slope of hill, at one with the forest and elements in a way I will never be. Belonging to it. He has his known rites of passage into the years ahead to help him face life's challenges. For him, the shadows in the forest hold wisdom and truth.

Not pieces of himself to fear.

For a moment, I'm ashamed to have thought him a werewolf. That's not who he is. Not who his people are. It's not their legend. Not their past. "I'm sorry...for implying that you were...you know..."

"A werewolf?" He gives a light laugh. "Won't be the first time. You know that."

"Something *is* out there, though, Sam. And it's big."

"Sometimes we see what we want to see in something. Maybe you saw something and colored it with your own fears. Turned it into something it wasn't."

Perception. The other beast. "Maybe."

Something about Sam's expression tells me he's speaking from experience. That he too has made assumptions in his past. That we all have at some point in our lives.

"You know, no matter where we all end up, you aren't alone in the world, Jayden. No matter how alone you feel. You need to remember that." I look at him. *Really* look at him. This friend I've known forever. This friend who I can feel growing away from me. Even now. As I've been growing away from him. But we have our history to knot us together. As complex and messy as it may have been at times with our different, individual struggles, we are wound tightly together.

And that's something.

Thunder erupts, a serrated slash of lightning splintering the sky. Sam turns to press on, leaving me to face the storm. "I gotta go let them know we're okay and find out if they've found anything about Miriam. Just watch your back, Jay. Please."

I watch him go, then turn my eyes upward to stare into the churn of cloud, rain blurring my eyes. Maybe Sam has guardians to watch over him, but I'm not so sure what's watching over me, if anything.

Despite what he says, I do feel alone. Alone to face what's out there.

Alone to face myself.

THIRTY-FOUR

IT'S THERE AGAIN. *That feeling.*

Something bad is about to happen.

And this time I don't want to be too late.

Something passed through the shadows. I saw it. When Sam and I sought shelter under the lip of the bunker. I can't help but feel it's a reckoning of some kind. Come to find me. Because everywhere I look, I see them. All three of them. *The dead girls.* A wisp of blonde hair. Hazel eyes. Pale lips, darkening with death.

It wasn't you. You're not—

But I can't think it. Can't rationalize it away. Because there's no other logical explanation. *If I'm not a vampire, then what am I?* The night wandering. The blood, on my hands, on my lips. The visions of those girls fraying my sanity. And the premonitions Miriam and Mom said I had. As if I could read minds; read the future before it even occurred.

Like a vampire.

My heart skips, stutters, picks up pace. Why do I hear the echo of screams? Feel their pain?

Because you were there.

I stagger toward the thicker part of forest. I think of the guardian powers Sam and those before him have come to the woods to find. *Spirit guardians.* They are here, lingering. Waiting. Spirits to protect the forest and those in it.

Or maybe I'm the one they have to be protected from.

If Sam's not the wolf...then what is? What's out there waiting?

Despite what Sam said, I know what I saw. It wasn't an ordinary wolf that I colored with my own fears. It was something more. Bigger. Darker. Danger flecking its eyes.

It's out here. Watching. Waiting...

For me.

Miriam floods my mind. Her long, blonde hair. Her laugh. The litheness of her body on the lip of a wave. The life. The way she stands up for me, beside me, keeps me strong. Even when I push her away...

If you hurt her...

It's as if a knife wedges into my gut and I can't breathe from the pain of it. I sink to my knees, lifting my hands, like prayer, palms upward, beseeching, to the spit of rain, daring the creature in the woods to exact its revenge on me for what I am, what I've done. *Because if I had anything to do with Miriam—*

"Jayden?"

Trembling, I lower my hands. My face is slick with rain, tears, the drip of shallow snot from my nose. I swallow hard and slowly turn around.

On the mound of hill above the bunker, Alexa stands, backlit by storm, her long, damp curls billowing in the wind. "What are you doing here?" she calls.

Seeing her, my breath catches. My heart swells to its own tide, the pull of her. If there's nothing else to live for, it's her. Even as the desolate monster I am, in her arms, I am something more.

She starts to move toward the knoll of the hill to descend.

"Stop! Don't! Alexa, please...don't come near me."

"Why?" She stops, confused.

You've let Twilight get to you. Kam get to you. You've let everything in the world shape you into something cold and lonely.

"Just...I'm not feeling really sure about myself right now."

That feeling.

Something bad is about to happen.

I scrunch my face, dig my knuckles into my brow.

"Jayden...what's going on?"

"Miriam is missing."

Slowly, she shakes her head, a question in her features, as if not comprehending.

"You must have passed people searching for her. You must have heard—"

"I didn't, Jayden, I'm sorry."

"Then why are you here, Alexa? It's dangerous in these woods right now. Why are you out here?" *With the storm. The murders. With me.*

For a moment, she looks confused, her eyes taking in the slope of hill, the trees, the ancient bloom of forest surrounding the distant river. "I just..." She stops, her brow puckering. "Truth is, I've been coming to this place since we moved here. Before my dad told me to stay out of the woods...though I'd still come. Climb down the tree by my window. Sometimes, lately, though, I find myself here and I'm not even sure how I got here. Even at night, I've come...and I don't know why. But today— I don't know, I just felt like I needed to come, that I need to be here. I—" She looks around the forest, the storm whirling sheaves of gray cloud, uncertainty shaping her brows.

I think of her father wanting to lock her in at night because of the danger in the forest. *Or was the danger in setting her free to roam.*

I draw in a sharp breath, my thoughts running wild.

She gathers her hair in her hand, twists it by her shoulder, worry shadowing the gesture. "I've been drawn to this place. And I don't know why." She turns and looks back from where she came then back to the slope of earth, the tumble of vine. "It's just...I almost feel like I belong here."

"In the forest?"

"No. Here. Right here. On this hill. In this grove. And yet—" Her face crumples a little, then smoothes, her mind wrestling with some unseen emotion. "It scares me." Her voice is a whisper now, lost to the storm.

Slowly, I rise to my feet. "I'm scared too." For her. For me. My eyes roam over her face, taking in the beauty. The strength. The otherworldliness of her eyes. Those blue, blue eyes.

That were once brown.

"Last night...you said you and I...we're alike," I say, slowly moving from the shadow of forest toward her, toward the base of hill. "And I think...I think maybe you're right." I pause, my heart gaining speed. I bite the edge of my lip, feel the curve of teeth. "Because I find myself out here too...at night. But for me, it's different. I don't feel like I belong. I feel like I'm running from something. Like I'm fighting for my life. And I can't help but wonder if maybe—" I stop, unsure of what to say next. "Maybe *I'm* the very thing I'm running from."

"I'm running from something too." She stares into the forest, her eyes strangely bereft. "I don't know what. But I feel like I'm almost out of time."

Something is happening to me.

I close my eyes, hear the whisper of those words. *Her words.*

I look up at her, get lost in the oasis of her eyes when she turns them back to me. "You said that night on the mountainside, that if I was...something else...it wouldn't matter to you."

Her lips lift in a faint smile. "You mean a vampire."

I flush. "Yeah. I know you were just being sympathetic about the stuff with Kam, but...would you think that, really? I mean, if I was some kind of...monster?"

"Would you? If the monster was me?" Her voice is soft, rain falling around her.

Last night comes back to me, the ecstasy of her embrace. The pounding of my heart.

The silence of hers.

I draw in a deep breath, my body starting to shake inside. *I don't want to know.*

But I do.

I need to know.

"My mom says we're leaving." Her hands twist together, a nervous motion. "That we have to go. We have to move again. Soon."

"Where?" I swallow around the lump rising in my throat, the ridge of uncertainty.

"I don't know. But...I don't want to go, Jayden. I want to stay with you—run away with you. Like we talked of last night. Do you think we can do that? Tonight? I'm tired of moving. Tired of trying to find my place in the world."

There's a buzzing in my head.

A warning.

I close my eyes against the bile that rises in my throat. For the nights are coming back to me. The blood. The fear. The echo of screams. Alexa's face. In my dreams. *Were they dreams?*

Wake up, Jayden...

"Are you okay?" Her voice interrupts my thoughts.

"The night of the deaths...were you in the forest? Wandering?" *Like me?*

Her brow tightens. "I don't know. Why does it matter?"

"Because you said sometimes at night...you come here. You come into the forest, and you don't know why. You don't remember."

"Yes, but—"

Blood thrums wildly through my veins. I turn and stride beneath the lip of the bunker, hesitate, then yank at the vines, loosening them from their holds.

"What are you doing?" she calls. Moments later she appears beside me. "What is this?"

My fists clench around a tangle of vines, the camo door swept into view.

"I don't understand..." Her voice trails away.

I stand stiffly, watching her. She approaches the door, her fingers hesitant before trailing them down the steel.

"You know this place?" My voice is tight, my heart splintering inside.

She pulls her hand away, confusion marring her expression.

"You've been here before, haven't you?" I persist.

"I don't know this place, Jayden. I don't—" But a recognition flits across her features.

"Try and remember!" I don't mean to shout. I don't mean to fall apart. But—

Maybe I wasn't the only one there...

When they died...

"Jayden...your face...you're scaring me." Alexa draws back. But there's something in her expression too as her eyes trail the door.

A yearning.

A need.

A hunger.

"She's in there, isn't she?" I whisper.

"Who?"

"Miriam."

"Jayden...I don't know what you're saying..."

I grab hold of her arms. "Listen to me, Alexa. I can see it in your eyes. You know this place. You've been here before. It's okay if you don't remember. I know what that's like. To wake up somewhere and not know how you got there. To not know who you are."

"Stop, Jayden! You're freaking me out."

Thunder punctuates her words, rumbling across the distant sky. I exhale sharply, dropping her arms to grip my forehead in tortured thought. "I'm sorry...I don't mean to scare you." I curse myself, feel the deep welt in my heart that's been there far too long. A welt that is only deeper now with Miriam missing. With Alexa saying she's leaving. Moving away.

Time running out.

I back away from her. I can't look at her. Can't have her look at me.

"Jayden—don't go. You're upset right now. I understand... I know what it's like to get ideas in your head and start thinking things that aren't true. Our imaginations go into overtime so we can cope—try to make sense of things."

I don't say anything but lift my eyes to hers, my body on edge.

"Life is messy. It hurts sometimes. It isn't always fair. I get that. After my accident I thought all kinds of things. Started to believe stuff people were saying, let it get inside my head too. It can make you crazy. You can start to doubt the people you care about. Can start doubting yourself." She takes a step toward me.

When she touches me, I don't pull away. Because even if it hurts, I'm not afraid. Of who she is. Who I am.

What we are together.

"Look, I don't know where Miriam is," she whispers. "I promise."

She moves closer, melds her body against mine. My body instinctively softens against hers in response. Because she feels so right. Everything about her saturates my senses.

Connects.

"Nothing makes sense," I murmur into her hair as she twines her arms around me, "about what's happening. To this town. To me. You."

"Maybe it's not supposed to make sense," she whispers. "I know things are messed up right now, but we have to be here for each other, believe in what we have together—believe love can still exist when everything else in the world seems to be falling apart. Even if it feels impossible right now to be happy when there is so much pain around us. We can't feel guilty for what we are together."

The vanilla scent of her hair mixed with the tempestuous elixir of storm fills my senses. I pull her closer, inhale her sweet essence, because we are the same.

Two souls fumbling through a dark world, looking for love.

"Why don't we just go?" she urges. "We don't have to wait until tonight. We can just leave now."

I wipe the back of my hand across my eyes, blinking back all that I feel. "I want nothing more than to be with you—run away with you. Make you my life. But I have to find Miriam first." I watch her as I say it. Emotions flit through her eyes. I study them, wanting to believe what she's saying about how minds can trick us, make us believe stuff that isn't true about ourselves. Wanting to believe that what has happened in the town and with Miriam is nothing more than a bad dream. Fiction. A story. That none of this is real. Only her. Our feelings. That happy endings can still be true.

Even in a horror.

I can't take it any longer. I have to know. I *need* to know.

I slide her hand up to my chest. "Feel this. Feel my heart. Feel it beating." I press her hand tighter to my chest. "I don't know what I am, but I have this. It's all I have," I choke, "these feelings. But..." I move our hands to her chest. She tries to pull away, but I hold her hands still. She stops resisting. Meets my eye. Says nothing.

Minutes tick by.

A film of tears gather in her eyes.

"You knew..." I whisper. "When I told you I couldn't find your heartbeat, you knew I wouldn't. You said you *feel* it—"

"I *do* feel it!"

"But you *know* it's not there!"

She struggles to pull away, turns away from me, but when I grab her arm again, she doesn't resist.

"Alexa...we're different than everyone. And I don't know what's happened, what we're part of, but all I care about now is saving my friend. Then we'll go. We'll run away. We'll figure out how to be just two people in love. Not two—"

"Freaks?"

My breath catches at the word as she says it.

We stand, staring at each other, a million emotions spiraling between us. A million secrets.

"The rumor the kids said about you when you recovered from your accident, what was it?" My voice is unsteady. "Tell me what they said."

"I don't want to do this, Jayden. I don't want to remember that time of my life."

"What did they say?!"

She flinches at the intensity of my words. "That I came back from the dead." Her voice is quiet. A low river of emotion.

"How?"

A solitary tear lights her eye. Pure. Crystal. "They called me the Miracle Daughter—"

"I'm not talking about what the doctors said! I'm talking about the kids at school—what *they* said! The rumors! *How did they say you came back from the dead?*"

She stares into the depth of forest, the dark center, her lip quivering. "One girl started it all. Her dad worked with mine." Her fingers dig into the chilled flesh of her arms as she pulls free from me and wraps her arms around herself. "And she...she spun a story."

"What story?"

"They called me Frankenstein's bride, all right? A freak..." Her words catch the wind, whirl away. Spiral into the ether.

I stop. It's not what I'm expecting to hear. *That she'd been bitten. Become something else.* That's what I thought she'd say. *Wanted* her to say. That we were the same. Both born of some secret. That we could have forever together.

A happily ever after.

But—

Frankenstein's bride. The bride of a fictional character I felt so connected to, once upon a time. *On the outside looking in.*

I draw in a sharp breath. "I don't understand."

"Look, it doesn't matter, okay? Just kids being mean," she sputters, but she looks away. Her body trembling. "But the worst of it was, I started to believe it. Because when I woke up from my accident...I didn't feel like myself. I mean...I was me...but not me. There's no other way to explain it. And those rumors...they haunted me." Like the illusory animals of the wind and cloud, I see something flash behind her eyes. Hurt. Memories.

Doubt.

"What do *you* think?" I ask, my voice low, husky. "About yourself? About me?"

She turns away, a sadness molding her features.

I reach for her, turn her toward me, gently moving a whorl of long hair from where it clings to her cheek from the rain. "Alexa—?"

"I don't know, okay?" Her blue eyes find mine. Inside them, a tormented fear. "But I didn't hurt anyone, Jayden. Why does it feel like you don't believe me?"

"I do. I'm sorry." I stop, unsure of what to say. Instead, I pull her to me, lean my head down to rest my lips against the curve of her neck, feel her breath, cool, against my own. "It's just there's something about you, Alexa. You're different than anyone else. Who you are…" *What you are.*

We stand like that, bodies together. I inhale the scent of her, our lips against each other's skin. Daring one another to be something else. Daring each other to be like Edward and Bella, maybe. A love, sealed with a kiss. A bite. A lifetime.

In some sick, twisted way…wanting to be like that. Like them.

I nibble on her neck, soften it to a kiss. I feel her exhale against me. A sigh of pleasure. Relief. Longing…

And I wait. Wait to feel the scrape of her teeth against my skin. For her to still my heart into forever. But all she does is return my kiss, flutter-light against the throb of jugular below.

"Jayden," she whispers, "if I could be a vampire with you, I'd be the happiest girl in Forks—in the world. Because it would mean we could stay as we are forever. Together. But…" Slowly she pulls away from me, my lips trailing the length of her neck, her sweet skin, wanting more. Wanting her.

"You know this isn't some story," she says, her hands spread against my chest as if stopping herself. Stopping me. "This is our lives. And trying to hide in a fantasy isn't going to help us. It isn't going to make things better. It isn't going to change the fact that we've let others affect what we think about ourselves. Change us."

The crush of life crowds in. For a moment—just a moment—I thought I had an answer to everything that hasn't made sense in my life. Everything that's hurt. But whatever Alexa and I are or aren't, isn't going to change who I am, where I come from. Or bring Miriam back.

All I can do is hope.

Maybe pray.

I look up to the sky, searching its restless cloud, then out to the forest, beseeching with my heart the guardian spirits that haunt the woods, wanting them to be real. For me. For my life. Needing something to give me strength, some entity to exist for me. To help me.

From the corner of my eye, I see a looming shape. The tuft of fur, glow of amber.

"Don't move," I whisper.

Alexa's eyes widen with worry.

For a heartbeat, I meet its eyes.

This time I don't see danger in them. This time, there is a warning.

"Jayden? What is it?" Alexa turns, her eyes frantically following mine to scan the bush.

But nothing is there. Just branches swaying in the wind, the shower of needles, the spiral of falling leaves.

And I feel it. Like a breath in the wind.

Something is coming.

THIRTY-FIVE

"WE NEED TO go, *now!*" I fold her hand into mine and tug her away from the bunker, the hidden door.

"Jayden, what's going on?"

We stumble through the rain to the shelter of trees and crouch behind the thick boles of bark. "Stay quiet..." I don't know how I know this. I don't know what we're hiding from, but moments later a figure crests the sloped hill of the bunker. Furtive. Wild. The storm blowing the white of his hair.

"Dad?" Alexa breathes.

I cup a hand over her mouth to silence her before she can say more, my senses pure fire.

Dr. Johansson glances around haphazardly then descends to the cascading vines, sweeping them aside, extracting a key.

"I don't understand," Alexa murmurs against my hand, her body straining forward. "Jayden, please, let me go. I need to know why he's here. I need to know what this place is."

He disappears inside, the door slowly heaving closed on heavy hinges. Alexa breaks free from me and sprints to the door, her hand stopping the steel before it clicks shut.

Tense, I watch from my perch in the woods. But she doesn't go inside. She stands frozen with indecision.

Blood beats in my veins. Minutes pass, but he doesn't reappear. Swallowing hard, I run through the rain to where Alexa's standing. The door is open by a hair, the catch not locked in place where her hand has stopped it from closing. We look at each other.

The fact that she's still here, not following her father...

"What do you know, Alexa?" I whisper hoarsely. "Something...anything...about this place. *Think!*"

"I don't know anything, I swear!"

"I saw the look on your face when you saw this door. You must have been here before—been inside this place. You've been coming to this very spot—"

"I don't remember, Jayden, honestly—"

Drawing a deep breath, I put my hand over hers where they hold the door from securing shut. "We'll find out together then?"

Slowly, she nods.

Tentatively, together, we push the door open an inch. Another inch.

The air inside is stale. Low fluorescent lights flicker along the ceiling, glimmering down a long concrete hall that funnels deep into the belly of earth. The faint hum of a generator groans distantly from within. There's no sign of Dr. Johansson.

Alexa gazes down the long hall to the few dusty corridors that branch away from the main passageway. "What is this place?"

"It's an old military bunker. There's several of them around Washington state that have been abandoned. Forgotten."

"I don't understand. My dad was never in the military, so how would he know about this?"

"Maybe he had a reason to find one." *But what would that reason be? What secret did he need to hide?*

I glance at Alexa beside me, rain still glistening on her skin, her damp clothing clinging to her form. My gut twists inside.

I can't help but feel that she's part of that reason.

Stealthily, we slip further inside, the door clicking shut behind us. Alexa reaches back to twist the knob. "It automatically locks from the inside too. It's not opening."

Fear flutters through me at the thought of being stuck here.

Like a trap.

In vain, I try the knob myself as she drifts to the wall to examine a handful of overturned jars scattered upon metal shelving, dust blanketing their surface. Metal piping for electricity or water skirt the ceiling, disappearing down the halls.

"He has a lab for his work," Alexa ruminates, "and an office at the hospital. All the wings of our home...I don't understand why he'd need this. Everything here's so...derelict."

Because he needed a place no one could find.

A place for you, Alexa.

The words come unbidden to my mind. My vulnerability apparent as I stand, my back to the locked door, the corridors down the hall blocked now by Alexa as she moves toward them.

"You coming?" she asks. "Jayden?"

"I need to trust you," I whisper.

"Trust me?" Confusion flutters across her face. "Why wouldn't you?"

"And you need to trust me. We need to know that whatever this place is...and whatever we are—whatever we find in here—we're in this together."

There's a sadness in her eyes as she listens to me. "When will you realize we're just us, Jayden? I spent the last two years trying to figure out what I am, but the answer is, I am who I think I am. Me. Just me. Not what people say. I'm more than this body. More than what's happened to me. So are you. Just believe in that."

Too weak. Too pale. Too poor. Death. Vampire.

Like Dan had said to me, the names I was called had become my identity. Maybe there was more to me, maybe there wasn't. Maybe I was some creature of the night, or maybe the doctor was right—that I was just a guy who had been through a lot and my body was sorting through it the best way it could. Maybe I experienced premonitions, maybe I didn't. Maybe the world got into my head, nightmare-sharp, so that dreams became reality. But in the end, they were nothing more than that.

Dreams. Fiction.

Everything drains from me then, and I'm left tired. Weak. In a different way. My body has grown to become solid but there needs to be more to it than that. I need my mind to be solid too. With belief in myself. "All I want right now is to find Miriam," I say, my voice catching. "And after that..." I bite my lip, wanting more than anything to hit the restart button on life. On my time with Alexa.

But already, she gets me. Already she knows who I am. What I need. Want.

She walks over to me, takes my hand. "After that, we can start our story again. Okay? Where I'm just the new girl in town..."

"And I spot you..." I look at her imploringly. Maybe really see her for the first time. Without the filter of self-doubt. Without wondering who I am. What I am. Without wondering about everything I don't know about her. Because it doesn't matter. Instead, she's just the beautiful girl I fell for at first sight. "...across a crowded room, instead of across your back lawn."

"Yes. No blood on your hands, this time. You just be you, in one of your hoodies." She pushes my damp hood, straightening it. "With that smile of yours. Your brooding gaze."

"And I'll fall for your eyes..." Any color. Brown, blue...*because it's what's inside that matters. Her soul.*

I swallow against the lump in my throat as I raise a hand to the curve of her cheek.

Her smile is tentative, hopeful. "And I'll ask you about Forks, and what there is to do..."

"And I'll take you surfing—"

"I don't surf."

"Then I'll teach you."

"And on my first day at school, you'll help show me around..."

"Tell you who to watch out for..."

"And I'll try and pretend that you don't look like one of the hottest movie stars on the planet." She laughs softly. "I'll notice but I won't tell you, because—"

"Because he's just an actor...a figment of all the girls' imaginations. And I'm—"

"Real. You're real. And I'll fall in love with you for you. And you won't have to be perfect. Because I'm not."

"And I wouldn't want you to be. Otherwise, I'd be too shy to tell you that in the space of a week, you've become the most important person in my life. The thing I live for."

My head is bent close to hers, her lips so close. When she closes the gap between us, my body responds, and I feel—for the first time in a long time—totally and utterly human.

The lights overhead flicker, blink. I can almost imagine them as starlight and we're once again on the mountainside together. Imagine all the horrible things away, to a world where it's just her and me. And this feeling.

I can imagine it, until suddenly—

—everything goes dark.

THIRTY-SIX

"WHAT'S HAPPENING?" ALEXA whispers.

The hum of the generator has faded away, the bunker like a tomb. I fumble along the cold wall, feeling for a switch, body tense as I listen for any sound.

Nothing.

Moments later, the hum of the generator kicks in and the lights stutter on.

"It's okay. The generator just tripped." *I hope.* It's better than believing it was a planned moment of darkness giving eyes to some other beast. I take Alexa's hand and lead her forward. "Come on. We need to search this place—see if we can find any sign that Miriam was here."

"My dad wouldn't hurt anybody; he wouldn't have anything to do with her missing—"

I stop and face her. "Look, I'm not saying he does. All I'm saying is she's missing and something isn't right about this place. I can feel it." *Something bad is about to happen.* My hand tightens around hers, protective. "Besides, don't you want to find out what this place is? You've been coming here. You feel some kind of connection." I stop there. Because thinking any more about it will change everything that just happened between us; will reel me back into thoughts I don't want to have anymore.

She glances around, her eyes straying to the length of corridor. "It's creepy in here."

"Come on... I won't let anything hurt you."

Together, we slip down the concrete and steel corridor, chancing glances into the darkened hallways that branch away from the wavering light of the main passageway. The few rooms we pass look abandoned; old cots, dusty blankets, supply shelves left bare but for cobwebs, motes drifting in the ambient glow from the hall.

Cautiously, we foray deeper into the belly of the earth, the hallway giving way to stairs, and light-foot our way down. Up ahead, the lights seem to grow steadier, brighter, from a hallway that breaks right. The closer we get, the air seems to sift, freshen, as if purified, filtered. Faintly, a sound ebbs down the hall.

I grip Alexa's hand tighter. "Do you hear that? It's voices...singing..." *Like the voices of angels.*

She hesitates. "It's Åberg."

"What?"

"Jan Håkan Åberg. He's a Swedish composer my Dad likes to listen to while working. This song... *I himmelen, I himmelen...* is one of his favorites." She draws in a shaking breath. "It's performed by a choir. And whenever I hear it—" She lets go of my hand and takes a step forward. "It's like a memory of fading away. But..." She turns to face me, a shadow crossing her face. "...also like coming back."

"Maybe he played it when he was with you after your accident? Maybe it's why you feel what you feel when you hear it?"

"Yes...maybe..."

The music is far away, spun down another branch of hall where the corridors are lit with stronger fluorescent tubing. The rooms down this hall look tidy, neat, swept clean—sterile—the shelving stocked with what looks like medical supplies.

"I don't understand why he has this place here, so hidden; why he'd need a lab so far from sight." She pauses by an open doorway where a full life model stands, its internal body colored with highways of fine lines representing nerves from brain to finger and toe, a complex mess of the secrets of humanity. Detailed charts line the walls of the brain, along with a poster gleaming with an iridescent connectome of the neural network. A large computer screen sits silent, screen saver whirling.

"I don't know how your dad or anyone understands all this...the complexity of the human mind and body."

She shakes her head and runs her fingers over papers lining a desk. I walk over to her side, glancing at the names on the letterheads. "What are these places?" *Neuralink, The Brain and Mind Institute, DARPA, The Allen Institute, 2045 Initiative,* just a few from the multitude of names springing from the pages of correspondence and research newsletters lined upon the desk.

"Affiliates or places Dad has worked or been a part of the research," Alexa says in explanation as I pour over the names. "His work has been well recognized. He's travelled a lot, had the chance to work with the best in his field...be the best in his field." She stops, spotting a family photograph of herself with her parents sitting in the sunshine in a beautiful park, sunglasses glinting, smiles broadening their faces. She picks it up. "This was before my accident." A drop of melancholy has entered her voice. "Before everything changed for me. I was happy then."

I come up behind her, place my hands on her shoulders. "You're not happy now?"

Gently, she sets the photograph back in its place and turns to rest her head against my chest. "Of course, I am. I've met you. Just...I felt alone for so long." A wariness passes across her face. "I'd thought the loneliness would last forever. Until you..."

I rest my lips against her forehead as she falls silent. "I'll always be here for you, Alexa," I murmur. "Your parents can move you, but I'll come. I'll follow. Or we'll run away like we talked about." I glance around the room. "But all this..." I gesture to the files, the models, the detailed charts; the years of research consolidated in one place. "I can't imagine your dad wanting to move away with all this down here. All his work. Look, there's more."

Another room holds vials, scalpels, and an assortment of surgical tools, medical equipment, tubing coiled in storage, complicated apparatuses with spectral wires bound away, waiting for use. Alexa examines the larger equipment as I roam to a file cabinet, looking at the model of a brain resting on top. Surreptitiously, I slide the cabinet open, finger the paper inside. I don't recognize the headings of medical institutions and research facilities labelled on the edges and am about to slide the drawer shut when something catches my eye at the back. A slender folder marked, *Alexa*. Hesitating, I slip the file open to find more marked files. On the first one, I see a name: *S Wilkinson*.

"Come on, Jay, we should keep going. I want to find my dad and ask him what all this is."

I don't move.

"Jay?"

My hands are shaking as I open the file. She's there. A photograph of Sophie paperclipped to thin sheets of paper, long blonde hair spooling around her face as she looks distractedly at someone other than the photographer.

I drop the folder back into its slot and take a step back, heart hammering.

"What is it? Jay?"

Trembling, I reach for the folder again, slide out the photograph and its paper attachment. It's a list of medical lab results. Blood type. Results of a urine test. Tissue typing. Antibody screening.

"Who is that?" Alexa comes up beside me. "I feel like I've seen that face before."

"You have." My voice is hoarse. "In a frame on a table at her memorial on the beach."

"What?"

"It's Sophie, Alexa. The first girl who was found dead."

Alexa stares at the file. "It says Forks Community Hospital on the letterhead. Maybe she was a patient of his before...before..." Her voice trails off.

I thrust my hand into the files, shoving them one after the other, skimming the labels, names. *What were the others' names?* Their faces haunt me. Hazel eyes. The darkening line of lips. *What were their names?*

But Alexa pulls another file free from the parted folder. She doesn't say a word as she opens it.

"What is it, Alexa? What do you see?"

Slowly, she passes me the file. There's a photograph, a face, of a girl about our age. Dark skin, curling hair.

"She's someone from the last town we lived in. I remember seeing her face in the local news when she went missing."

"She was found dead?"

"She wasn't found at all..." Her words are barely there. A ghost haunting the cold cube of aseptic room.

There are others. Other files in the drawer. In a shaking voice, I read out the locations and addresses on the hospital letterhead where the lab work was taken.

"All those lab records...those are from towns we lived in," she whispers.

The room feels colder, suddenly. Like there's not enough air. The faint curl of music wafts from far away, filling the room like Zyklon.

Names. Faces. Lab results. And it soon becomes apparent: all the lab results are the same or very close in nature.

I swallow hard. "He was looking for a type."

Alexa crosses the room, arms tightly clenched around her body, to stare out into the hall, her face crumpling.

Then I see it, fallen open, near the back of the small stack—a photograph.

Hazel eyes. Pixie hair.

"Lindsay Sutton," I read, my throat constricting.

The file after it, the next face clipped to the results I barely recognize in all its life, but the name...

The latest victim has been identified as Vanessa Chu. The news reporter from Brody's radio echoes through my head.

"Why would your dad have all these files on these girls who have died if he didn't—if he's not—" I can't say it, my mind tilting in a different direction.

If he's—

—then I'm not—

All this time. Nights lashed with nightmares. Doubting what I am. While all along, someone else was stealing through the night too. Awake.

The distant, wafting choir suddenly seems sinister, tainted. *Like angels of death.*

With trembling hands, I go to place the folders back in the file cabinet. And that's when I see it. Lying at the bottom of the file drawer. A lone file with a clear label.

M Foster.

THIRTY-SEVEN

I STARE AT the image of her face. The blonde hair, laughter sunning her expression. The glint of ocean gray eyes—the assurance in those eyes that the world was hers to be in. The wave of her existence always guiding me. Keeping me afloat.

I detach Miriam's photograph from the lab results, my throat constricting tighter and tighter. "Alexa? Alexa...I—" I turn to face her, knowing what comes next will break her heart into a million silent pieces.

You were right, Alexa. We're just us. You and me. Two hurt humans trying to hide behind fantasy.

It wasn't us who were the monsters. It was—

Your father.

"Alexa?" I don't know what this will do to her. What it will do to us. How the world will shapeshift yet again from the reality we had finally found in each other's love. The future of our story. As I turn to her, ready to hold her, ready to carry her from this godforsaken place, I am faced with nothing but the stark light of an empty room.

"Alexa?" I hiss, palms sweating. I stride to the hallway and glance left and right down the abandoned hallway, Miriam's file slipping from my hands.

There's nothing but that eerie chorus of celestial voices beckoning...

The fluorescent lights waver for a moment, threatening darkness. Numbly, I realize Miriam's photo is still clenched between my fingers, her lab results scattered on the floor by my feet. "Alexa?" I whisper again, a blinding need pressurizing my heart. "Alexa, please—"

She's upset. She's scared. She's in shock. She—a new frisson of fear slivers my spine. *She knows.*

Could it be true? *No. She couldn't.* She was in shock too, wasn't she? When she saw their files?

Or maybe, she doesn't know and these girls—their type—were hunted, harvested for—

Bile rises hot and fierce in my chest.

Organs excised from the bodies of the first two girls.

Two holes punctured in the neck of the third.

Was Dr. Johansson the monster?

Or was he just the one feeding it?

I collapse against the door frame, my legs weak. *Don't do this…don't go there…*

I wrestle with my mind. My imagination. The stark cold reality of the situation.

Staggering slightly, I take a step back to retrace the way we came, then forward, toward the music, unsure of which direction to go. Unsure of what I'll find. Unsure of what to do.

The music grows louder, voices soaring in ethereal tune as I inch along the passageway toward it. I look back, hoping to see Alexa. Hoping she has an answer.

Hoping more than anything that this is just another nightmare and I'm about to wake up.

I hesitate, second guess myself. Because the other girls were found in the woods. Crimes committed under the cloak of night. Not locked away in some secret bunker buried beneath blankets of earth and steel. Bodies left to be found…

I press against the wall, heart hammering, inching my way along. But suddenly I'm lost, for more hallways have appeared, their mysterious corners turning, leading to God knows where. I pause, helpless, sinking to my haunches to think. I dig my teeth into the knuckles of my hand to quell the guttural roar rising inside as I catch Miriam's image staring up at me from the clutch of my hand.

Where are you, Alexa? Tell me what to believe! Tell me I've got it wrong!

There's a sound. Panting. Uncontrolled. Wild. *Me*, I realize. Gasping like a lost animal; a rabid, wounded wolf, emotion coursing poison through my veins, rendering me helpless. Like when Kam would circle me with his gang. The vulnerability. The helplessness. The sheer magnitude of not knowing how to fight back. *But I learned. I learned how to survive.*

Didn't I?

The chorus of music abruptly stops. A new haunting song taking root in the breath that follows.

But in that space in between, I hear another sound. The muffled sound of a scream. A keening wail. A plea.

Miriam!

I lunge forward, hurrying down the hall, following the new trail of music that has swooned into the hallways, volume amplified; the soundtrack of a surgeon about to perform his artistry. Carve his subject into something new: A still life.

I should be stealthy. Move like a bat in the cover of darkness, unseen and unanticipated. But I run, stumble, sprint, following the stifled echo of her cries, biting my tongue not to shout her name, tell her I'm coming, knowing it would be dangerous to announce my presence.

I race down the halls, the past squeezing at my heart. My childhood. Adolescence. As if she were my mother and I her lost son. As if my whole history was hovering beneath some scalpel blade. *I cannot lose you!*

Another scream fills the glass white of the halls. It shatters the air around me. And I run, past the coven of non-descript rooms, to where the air vibrates with her spirit. *She's alive!* I'd know her voice anywhere, raised in joy, in pain, in fear, in hope. I'd grown up with it. All its inflections and tones. All its highs and lows. All its promise.

Ahead, a room glows with bright surgical lights. I stop before it, pressing my hands to the glass of the door's window. Miriam is there, pinned to a gurney, hands and legs bound, a gag worked loose from her parched lips as she stretches them open to cry out again. I wrench the door handle, flinging the door open, snatching up a sharp blade lying on a tray of surgical implements resting by her bedside. "I'm here. It's okay. Miriam, it's okay!" I pull the gag away. "I'll get you out of here!" I begin sawing at the thick bindings.

Her eyes are wild, tears spurting to the surface at the sight of me. "Jayden!" Her voice is ragged, hoarse, her lips cracked and bleeding from the gauze of the gag. "He's coming...we can't...you have to hurry..."

I grapple with the bindings, fruitlessly sawing with the blade, then bend to tear at them with my teeth in desperation to get her free. Because I still don't know—don't know the kind of thing we're dealing with.

Man or beast?

"Come on," I curse, slashing at the bindings, tearing at them with my teeth, all the while careful not to mar the delicate skin welted below it. I feel animal in my desperation, wishing my teeth were fangs—for the first time in my life, *wanting* them to be.

I sense her before I see her. A shadow falling in the solar glow of artificial light.

She stands in the doorway, her face a blank slate. I stop at the sight of her. The gloss of curled hair against the richness of her skin. The blue crystal of those fathomless eyes.

She tentatively edges around the room. Like an animal, tracking the perimeter of its cage. A lost look in her eyes. A forlornness.

She opens her mouth, a whisper escaping from her lips, and I'm reminded of my dream where she and I were alone within the depths of her personal prison, flooded by the fjord. In the dream she'd mouthed, *help me*. But here, in the cold, stark reality of this surreal underground room, her lips instead form the faint words, "I'm sorry..."

"No," I sob, my heart wrenching loose of the tethers she'd anchored within. "Don't do this..." I plead. "Not to Miriam! Not to her! Not to me!" I'm cracked open, a wound spilling free. All the love I'd gathered and balled within, stored in the fragile casing of my heart, hemorrhages from me as I keep prying and gnawing at the bindings clinging to Miriam's body. I tear, until my gums are sore, bleeding. *A vampire who has lost his bite.* The blade slips in my fingers, nicking my hand, but still I fumble to slice and saw away the bondage.

Dr. Johansson appears in the doorway, sterile gloves snapped on his hands, his wild hair trapped in a surgical cap, balanced upon his nose, glasses fitted with protruding loupes. He stops at the sight of me stooped over Miriam.

His surprise gives way to eerie calm. For he knows this is nothing but a tomb. No one to hear the cries. No one to come to the rescue.

"Jayden," he says, his voice thickly accented. His eyes slowly stray to where his daughter half crouches in the corner. They quiver slightly when he sees her. "Alexa..."

"Why?" she chokes. "Why are you doing this?"

It's then that I realize the mistake I've made. She wasn't sorry for her complicity. She was sorry for her father. For being the legacy of a man who moved through the world taking what he wanted with no thought to the consequence. Or no care.

Magenta appears behind Dr. Johansson dressed in scrubs. Her eyes widen when she sees us.

"You won't get away with this!" I sputter at them. "There are others who know where we are." I pray Sam directs the others to the abandoned bunker when I don't show up, pray that help is on its way. "They'll come. They'll find us here."

Alexa makes a move for the door.

"Alexa, no—stop!" Dr. Johansson says, holding up a plaintive hand. "This is all for you."

My heart lurches. *Hunted, harvested—*

As if Miriam was spread upon some dining table.

"No! Don't say it!" She cowers from his words. "Please don't say it's true."

"Alexa, please—"

"Who is she?" she gasps. "In the other room?"

I'm frozen. Watching Alexa slunk against the cold wall, her father's face like that of when I saw him in the woods, contorted in grief, Magenta standing behind, broken resignation in her eyes.

"*Just tell me who she is!*" she screams.

"You *know*, Alexa. You've always known, haven't you?" The doctor's voice is plaintive, tears breaking free from the constraint of his eyes. He pushes the surgical glasses to his forehead, beseeching.

Alexa darts past him. He grabs her arm, tries to prevent her from going. "Alexa, please—don't go—"

But she pushes past him and Magenta into the hallway.

Dr. Johansson turns to face Miriam and me, grief changing him into something else. Not a monster. But a shell. A human shell. "You must make a choice, Jayden," he says, his voice weak. "Miriam or Alexa. For if Miriam lives, Alexa must die."

"What?" I splutter. My hands are still on Miriam's bindings, my heart cleaved in two.

"We are running out of *time!*" Dr. Johansson yells, unexpectedly, his voice reverberating around the room.

Magenta places a hand upon his arm. "Sven…it's time. We must let her go."

"No!" He roars. He lunges forward, grabbing a syringe from a tray, wielding it toward Miriam. "It's my last chance, my last chance to try—" His voice is swallowed by a sob, which he struggles to suppress, his face twisting in broken, primal rage—a rage laced with molten grief.

"I don't understand," I stammer, flinging myself in front of Miriam as he staggers forward.

"One more! Just one more life. It's all I need to buy enough time—"

"Sven, you must stop!" Magenta intervenes. "It's over, don't you see? Alexa knows! There's no question now! How could you ever expect her to live with that knowledge? How could you expect her to choose life like this?"

"She needs the chance!" Sven croaks in response.

"Listen to Magenta," I plead. "She said, let Miriam go!"

"No…" Magenta says quietly, tears silently streaming down her face as she holds Dr. Johansson back while he brokenly heaves himself toward Miriam. "I mean let Alexa go."

The room suddenly seems silent. A prism of understanding. "You mean...let her die?"

Magenta nods silently, her grasp on Dr. Johansson loosening as emotion overwhelms her.

"We just need a little more time. That's it, Magenta! Then we can have her forever. We don't have to lose her—not again!"

Beneath my sweating hands, I feel one of Miriam's wriggle free from her bindings, the sawn edges finally giving way. She struggles to sit upright.

"*No!*" Dr. Johansson yanks himself free from Magenta's grip, lunging across the room, syringe in hand, towards Miriam.

Dan's training fires through my veins in autopilot as I step forward to block Dr. Johansson's arm as it plunges through the air, the sparkling tip of the syringe weeping fluid. "Stop! You can't do this!"

"I can! And I have! It's the only reason Alexa is here! It's the only reason you even have her alive to love," he levels at me, his eyes glittering. "And she can be yours forever...or she can be gone—forever!"

His words carve a crater in my heart at the thought of life without Alexa. The impossible choice of letting her live or die. "I don't understand," I cry. "Why?"

"Because I need her heart," he moans, glancing toward Miriam. "In order for Alexa to live."

Bewildered, I meet his wild eyes.

"You don't understand," he says. "Alexa needs the transplant *now.* It's her last chance. Her organs are failing faster than I can replace them."

"Her...organs?" The room is a whirl of confusion. "Replace them?"

"The organs have been failing faster and faster with each transplant. The last two failed almost right away. And she needed a transfusion...so I took blood from the last one..." he gasps. "Bled the body the fastest way possible, from the jugular. But still...she needs more. More and more and more... and nothing is working anymore. All I need is just a little more time."

"Drained the last one of blood?" *The body was drained of blood.* Details of the murders haunt my mind. *Two holes punctured in the neck.* "And the others?" But already, I know. *The insides taken out. All the organs gone.*

Harvested.

For transplantation.

"The deaths were becoming too frequent," Dr. Johansson bursts out. "I had to move the family too much to escape suspicion. But this place—Forks—with all its obsession with vampires and werewolves was the perfect cover—a place to throw people off the scent with their infatuation of mythology. But it was never meant to be this frequent, the deaths. I never thought I'd have such little time in between." His wrist sags in my grip. "I don't want to do it. Believe me. I don't *want* for them to die. But even more, I don't want *Alexa* to die. It's my daughter, you understand? I'd do anything for her. Anything to keep her with us. Soon it can all stop. Soon it will all be over, and I won't have to do this anymore."

My mouth is dry. "How did you find the matches for her?" I still can't wrap my mind around the vibrant image of Alexa and the transplants Dr. Johansson speaks of. *What incisions? What scars? I've traced the lines and curves of her.* I swallow hard, squeeze my eyes shut against the image of her lying in the storm light, her body next to mine, our souls exposed to one another as we forged our dreams. There was nothing visible. Just the faint scars she'd had since her accident down the center of her chest. One webbed in her hair at the back of her head that she'd told me about. Nowhere else. No fresh ridges. *Where?*

But something becomes blessedly clear. She wasn't some monster in beautiful disguise. Wasn't a vampire. He was speaking of a girl of flesh and blood. A girl whose body was failing her. Yet Alexa stood strong. Vibrant. *Alive.*

"The hospital has records of patients or people who visit emergency or the labs. I collected their information. Scoured the system for matches. I searched for them, you understand? To find what I needed.

Who I needed."

Behind me, Miriam has worked herself loose to push off the table and stagger farther from where Dr. Johansson and I stand locked in place, her body edging to the corner of the room.

"I had to take their lives," Dr. Johansson laments, "to give her life! I wasn't ready yet to let her go. And I hadn't yet finished what I need to save her!" His free hand is reaching for something from the surgical tray beside us, but I'm distracted by his confession. By the flash of blonde in my periphery. But he's seen it too.

He wrenches his arm free, brandishing the syringe and the glistening blade of a scalpel, and hurls himself at Miriam as she darts toward the door. Alexa appears, surging past her mother who reaches for her, and launches herself between her father and Miriam just as he swings the scalpel downward. It collides with Alexa, plunging into the soft belly of her skin.

"No!" I explode, scrabbling toward her.

Sparks spill from the space where the instrument lodges, a burst of pale firework light. Time seems frozen as we stop and stare, stunned. Alexa's hands frame the space around where the scalpel protrudes from her body, her face twisted in horror as the static sparking sputters and falls dark. For a moment there's nothing but silence as she slowly pulls the scalpel out. It pulls away clean. Not even a drop of blood. "No..." she whispers. "Of all the things I thought I might be...not this."

"Alexa—" Magenta moves to her daughter's side.

Alexa shakes her head, bewilderment blanching her expression. "Don't touch me."

Frantically, Miriam slips from the room, her face pale. Her footsteps echo down the empty corridors as she breaks into a run. Dr. Johansson makes no move to follow her, his eyes on his daughter, his shoulders caved forward as if the weight of the world is pressing upon them. "Don't you understand? You needed her to live. You needed all of them," he beseeches.

I find my voice. Caught in the back recesses of my throat. Prickly. Unsure. Disbelieving. "Alexa...what's going on? What's happening?"

But she's not looking at me. "I didn't want to believe it when I heard it," she whispers, her voice guttural. "The rumors of what I was. But then there were...things. Differences. From what I was like before." Her sad eyes look accusingly at her mother. "It's why I can never really cry, isn't it? Why I don't sweat? Why I can run and run...like some...bionic thing..." she chokes, then looks to her father. "Why every cut I've ever had, there's been no blood? It was because I was strong, you'd say. Because the cut wasn't deep enough to bleed. And—"

"Why you have no heartbeat." My voice is small in the room.

Alexa turns to look at me, her eyes filling with the beautiful gloss of tears, forever shining. Never falling. *Why had I never noticed that before?* Her lip quivers, her mouth pulled down in sorrow. "I felt it, though." she whispers. "With you."

My heart explodes inside. Because mine had never felt like it beat either, not really, until it beat for her. It had never known love so strong and consuming.

Before I can formulate words, she turns to her father. "How long does she have, father?" Her lips curl in grief-born anger.

I can't wrap my mind around what she's saying. *Who is she referring to?*

Dr. Johansson raises his eyes to his daughter, sorrow rimming his irises.

"*How long,*" she starts again, "do *I* have?"

"Hours at most," he replies, his voice weak.

Magenta moves to touch Alexa but when rebuffed, turns and exits the room, her shoulders slumped, bereft.

The adam's apple at Dr. Johansson's throat bobs as he swallows. "Alexa, I—"

"Go! Get out of my sight!"

"It's the future, Alexa. One day, you won't be so different. You will be like everyone else. That time is not so far away."

"Alexa...what's he talking about?" I fumble, trying to wrap my brain around what I saw, what's being said. *Sparks. The blade piercing her skin.*

Yet, she didn't crumple. The future...

Of what?

Suddenly, Alexa strides forward to grip my hand and tugs me forward to follow her. I can barely keep up us as we skid down the hallway, pausing outside another room. I stop, peering through the small glass window. Inside, Magenta stands by a computer, despondently punching buttons and analyzing data. Attached to the computer are wires snaking to something lying supine on a bed. A girl. Thin. Withered. Patches of long dark hair curling beneath a mesh cap covered in electrodes. I don't recognize the face, the fine bones damaged, misshapen. But there's something about the flesh of the hand lying lifeless on the bedsheet, the thin arm. *The rich tone of café latte.*

I raise my hand to the cold glass of the door's window. "Who...?" But I don't finish. Don't need to.

I push the door open, feel Alexa's fingers slip from my hand, and walk to the girl's bedside. A complex network of machinery hums beside her, tubes feeding into venal ports in her chest. Another stems from her trachea. A soft whooshing sound softens the room as the machines pump. "Why can't you do your magic?" I demand, angrily, desperately raising my eyes to Magenta. "You heal people! You healed me! Why can't you do something?"

"Because that kind of magic is of fairy tales," she says, her voice filled with sorrow. "What I practice is belief, Jayden. Of the herbs and plants and earth around us. In the spirits that have gone before us. I place my hope in those. But I cannot heal everything. I cannot heal this. Cannot heal my daughter's body." Her eyes move past me to Alexa standing in the doorway. "Even belief cannot answer prayer all the time. Sometimes we have to take a step further. Take matters into our own hands. Let science become the prayer."

Alexa drifts to my side, her face a mask of denial.

"Your brain was all that was left that was viable." Tears are heavy in Magenta's voice. "So, we gave your mind life. Virtual life. So, you could continue living as you deserved. Continue to move. Feel. Enjoy all the senses you were born with. You're our daughter, Alexa, but you are also our prototype. For the work we are doing for the future. So, others may also live on. So, death can become a distant memory, a thing of the past."

Alexa lifts a finger of the lifeless body before her, holds it in her own.

"We needed to keep your organs alive so your brain could survive while we continued our work. The brain can control things with thought using a brain-computer interface. I build prosthetics so people can use parts of their bodies that have failed, my love. And this...for you...was the first successful attempt at telepresence using a full body prosthesis. The technology has been in development for years, but your father has been part of more progressive projects. *We* have been part of them. And with my neuroprosthetic advancements...and his mapping of the brains neural activity and how they communicate...how to translate that neuronal activity into robotic commands..." She trails off.

"And your Hollywood past." Alexa's voice is quiet. "Special Effects...making the unbelievable come to life. Making it real." Her hand reflexively brushes the flesh of her arm, catches the curl of her hair. "With synthetics." She drops her hand and draws in a sharp breath.

"I want you to know that everything you have been through will help others," Magenta says, her voice faltering with emotion. "That every gift you were given by this—"

"Gift? You think this was a gift? Being this?" Alexa cries.

"It *was* a gift! Even you were fooled. You may have suspected something was different, but you were fooled, Alexa. And you got a chance to *live*. Love." Her gaze passes across my face.

"We hoped to place your live brain into your avatar. An avatar that I modelled after your original form before..." Magenta's voice catches. She doesn't need to say anymore. The evidence of the crash's destruction lies before us. "But it's not stable enough to transplant. We risked losing you during the process, so our next step was to attempt—"

"Whole brain emulation," Alexa whispers. "Dad's sci-fi research."

"If we'd had the chance to mind upload your brain, Alexa, transfer your individual consciousness to an artificial brain to sustain your personality, your thoughts, your dreams...you could have become...immortal. Cybernetically. But...maybe it's more than that.

Because we are more than these bodies...there is so much more to us than flesh and bone. Something that haunts us inside. Something that maybe we can...transfer. Transfer the 'I' that dwells within each of us. It is the future of our species. We are so close to a life without death."

"And what of a heaven?" Alexa asks.

"Heaven is but a fantasy, Alexa, for all we know. This earth, these thoughts and feelings...this is all we know for sure. No God has risen to answer my prayers. Only this...us. Finding a way to answer our prayers ourselves. Keep you with us, our loved one. Keep you from experiencing pain, death."

"It's why she would feel weak sometimes, isn't it?" My brain feels as if it will explode as I grapple with her words, try to process this incomprehensible reality. This reality that is more fantasy than anything I had ever imagined.

"Yes," Magenta says. "When her organs are failing, when her body is dying, her mind too begins the process of dying. And her avatar feels that. We have brought her back from the brink so many times... And that injury..." She gestures to where the scalpel had pierced Alexa's skin. "...would have been fatal had you been flesh and blood. Don't you see? There are benefits to this, Alexa. A chance to survive."

My mind is a tangled nexus of thoughts. But suddenly, all I can think about are Alexa's eyes as they pool before me. "Her eyes...I saw a photograph of her before her accident. After her accident...you gave her blue eyes instead of brown."

"For her father. Because he wanted to see himself in her too. The way I could see myself in you, Alexa. Your skin...your hair...you were mine. But this time, it was his technology that birthed you—this new you. I could make the pieces, but he was the one that could bring you to life."

Alexa doesn't seem to be listening any longer. "It's why I felt drawn to this place in the forest, isn't it. Here. Because of her...my body..." Gently, she lowers the lifeless finger back to rest on the cold sheet.

Body and mind not so separate after all.

"We would bring you here sometimes," Magenta says. "So, we could work on your...avatar. Fine tune what we needed to for the interface.

Then we would manipulate your memory so you would forget. I suppose, the mind does not forget everything, though. It senses what is on the outer rim of consciousness. When we would find you wandering the grounds of this place, we'd bring you home, afraid someone would find you here and discover our secret. Afraid you'd remember. But we also enhanced your mind too, Alexa. Gave you the ability to do things you always wanted. The violin…" Her voice trails off when her daughter draws in a sharp breath.

"Don't. Don't tell me how you made me better. More clever or capable. As if who I was before wasn't enough."

"It *was* enough. More than enough." Magenta's voice is pained. "But as our daughter, we wanted to give you everything."

Alexa turns to face me. "Would you have loved this? A…shell? Had you known?" she asks, the iridescence of tears brimming in her eyes. Tears I now know to be the illusion of some cyber circuitry, though I can still hardly believe it.

Don't want to believe it.

"Even when I didn't know what you were—what *I* was—" I feel Magenta's eyes on me. "I loved you anyway. Because what mattered was deeper than the flesh. Was more than what I thought you were." I reach up to touch her face, marveling at the humanness of her skin. How my body had been fooled by its touch.

She leans her cheek into my palm, drawing a ragged intake of breath. "It feels so real. I feel everything." She lifts her eyes to meet mine. "I've felt it all."

Magenta's voice falters as she speaks, belying the magnitude of her impending loss. "We made you as you were, Alexa. Yes, with some enhancements, but it was you. We mimicked the neural circuitry of the body. Each sensation you feel is relayed to your brain so you may interpret as you did before. And each thought you have controls how you move, feel…what you experience. It's *you* inside of there. We molded you…as you were. Human."

But we aren't listening. None of it matters anymore. One thing Magenta said is right. We are more than just these bodies. More than the flesh that cloaks our bones. We are the soul that dwells within. Imperfect as it may be, it is there. Wanting to grow. Wanting to be free. Wanting to love. Be loved.

"Go..." Magenta says, her voice soft. "Enjoy these final hours together. I wish I could have given you your forever."

"Not at the cost of others," Alexa says. "Not if my life was to be sustained by someone else's death. Someone else's murder." She flinches on the word.

"Be at peace, Alexa. It wasn't your doing. And it will happen no more. Go...be together. Enjoy your love while you can." There is lost longing in her voice. A mother who yearns to hold her daughter but realizes she is too late. "Please, understand. I didn't want these crimes. I wanted them to end. But your father was relentless. And you were my daughter too, after all. I would have done anything for you. So, I did. And I must carry the weight of that. But not you. It's not your cross to bear." She rises from where she's sitting, arms hanging empty by her sides as if waiting to be filled by an embrace. "What I do not regret, is these past two years with you. Do not regret extending your life. People say they'd do anything for one more day with a loved one that they've lost. We did just that—did anything. And we got two more years with you for it. That, I do not regret." But in her voice, the double-edged sword is apparent. The cost.

"When your time comes, mother...and when father's time comes too..." Alexa's teeth are clenched as she speaks. "You both will need to extend your own lives to avoid falling into the pits of hell for what you have done. For this attempt at scientific progress."

Magenta bows her head, sorrow making her onyx eyes even darker. "If there is a hell, I shall think it worth it for trying to keep you with me." She raises her head again. "I have regrets, but prolonging your life is not one of them. Nor do I regret trying to find a solution to the greatest pain humanity must inevitably endure. Death. Live long enough and you'll know that pain. I wanted to spare you that pain. Not just of losing your own life too soon—when you still had so much before you—but the pain of ever losing someone you loved. Because that hurts worse than death itself."

A wisp of gray wafts from one of the vents. I notice its thin tendril across the room while Magenta and Alexa stare at each other, a million words still unsaid between them.

Then I smell it. "Smoke..."

As I say it, the wisp curls upward and drifts across the room. Its cloying vapor hangs spectral in the air, like an omen. It catches Magenta's eye. "Oh, Sven...what have you done?" she whispers.

"What is it?" Alexa tilts her head upward to watch the wisp thicken, more leeching from the vent from where it came.

Sadly, Magenta lifts the motionless hand of Alexa's biological form and places it into her own. "Our plan, should this place ever be discovered and our secret risked being found, was to burn it down. How could we explain a body found that forensically is you when you roam the earth as you are? And there are files...things that cannot be discovered." Tears fill her eyes. "We had hoped should that happen, that by then you would be freed entirely from your body's burden, your mind uploaded so you could live on untethered to the biology of your body. We hoped by then, we'd have found your spirit a new home." A solitary tear slides down her cheek.

"Burn it down? You mean—" Alexa takes a step back toward the door, reaches for my hand.

"You're dying anyway, my dear. But go. Run. Find your last bit of freedom outside these walls. There is an emergency exit you can find if you follow this hall all the way to the end. It opens to the river."

Alexa hesitates when her mother makes no move to follow. "What about you?"

Magenta shakes her head. "I'll be sure you feel no pain when the time comes."

In that moment, I see in Alexa the complicated marrow of her emotion as she digests her mother's execrable complicity in the deaths. Digests it alongside the years of motherly love, however imperfect.

"I love you, Alexa," her mother says.

Alexa struggles, her chest rising and falling as sobs swirl deep in her chest. "I loved you too."

Loved. Past tense. The ultimate loss. *To be loved no more.*

I tighten my fingers around Alexa's and gently tug her toward the door. "Alexa...we have to leave. The smoke is worsening."

She turns and we start to run down the hall. She leads the way, the direction Magenta advised us to go to find the emergency exit.

"Stop!" I say suddenly, releasing her hand. "Miriam is still in here somewhere. I have to find her!"

"Jayden, there's only so much time left. For me, it no longer matters, but for you..."

"I can't leave her here. You go—don't let your last bit of time be trapped in here."

"What happiness would I find outside, knowing you were in here risking your life?"

"But—"

"She said she won't let me feel pain. No matter what happens to me, I'll be okay. It's inevitable now, Jayden. As it is for all of us. So, I'm okay. But I need you to be safe. For you to live on. Let me help you find Miriam, so you can leave this place."

I can barely breathe from the thought of life without her. "I won't know how to go on without you."

"But you'll learn."

I pull her to me, lower my forehead to hers. Tears wet my face, travel to touch her cheeks as if the bright blue depths of hers were the ones shedding them. I pull her closer, body to body, my heart beating loud and strong enough for the both of us.

Overhead, smoke swirls velvet thick. Slowly, we break apart and start to run, backtracking through the maze of hallways down the main corridor, passing the room where I dropped Miriam's file, her lab results still scattered on the floor, past the room with the life size model of a human, its miraculous map of scientific artistry charting the neural computation with such intricacy. The mystery of humanity. *How far we have come. Molded from clay to this: molded by the hand of humankind.* I glance sidelong at Alexa beside me. *Making images of ourselves as God molded us after His own image.*

If stories could be believed.

"Miriam!" I call into the web of hallways, smoke filling their flickering lairs. We dash down each one, greeted by dead ends. Most of the rooms we pass are open, empty, nothing but sterile lab equipment and papers— years of research now kindling to a bigger fire.

We backtrack to the main corridor, hurrying down the hall until we reach the stairs where Alexa and I first descended from the upper level of the bunker, the bright rooms of Dr. Johansson's lab giving way once again to the ruins of wartime hiding. The lights are dimmer, the air denser than before as smoke seeps into the stale passageways.

"Miriam!"

We race up the stairs two at a time, to the top passageway, passing the abandoned rooms with their forgotten cots, until we are back in the derelict chamber of the bunker's hillside entrance. Smoke saturates the air. I cough against its particulate poison, my lungs aching. "Miriam!"

I stagger, pulling my hoodie to cover my mouth, my eyes stinging.

Beside me, Alexa stays strong, her cybernetic lungs impervious to the acrid air. She grips my hand and helps me as I stagger forward.

Through the haze I see movement. A person striding through the smoke.

"Miriam?" I gasp.

But it's Dr. Johansson, Miriam in his arms. He's wearing a mask, protecting himself from the press of smoke.

"What are you doing?" Alexa demands, seeing Miriam in his arms.

"It might not be too late," he rasps. "There's still time."

"No!" Alexa rushes at him, pulls Miriam from his arms.

"Alexa, no!" he cries as Miriam tumbles from his arms into Alexa's.

I run forward as she turns my way, Miriam in her arms, and in one heartbreaking moment the truth of it strikes me hard. The two people I've cared for most, standing amid the darkening light. One life saving another. And by me helping save Miriam, I am choosing Alexa's death.

"Don't," Alexa says, her eyes finding mine, reading my expression.

"It's not a choice you have to make. It's not a choice at all."

With that, she steps past me down the hall as the lights flicker, one of the tubes of fluorescents falling dark from the fire.

"How could you?" I holler at Dr. Johansson. I'm wracked by a spasm of coughing. "How could you have done this? Put us through this hell?"

Slowly, he pulls his mask from his face and stands, staring at me, grief flooding his eyes.

"Jayden! Come on!" Alexa cries from the stairwell.

Dr. Johansson tosses the mask to me. I catch it in surprise.

He drops to his knees.

I turn to go but stop. Despite myself, I say, "You can't stay here. You need to get up."

"Go," he says. "Be with her for the end."

"What about your research? Your advancements? The stuff that didn't involve murder."

"It's worth nothing to me if I can't save my own child. All that's left for me is a life of prison. One way or another. A cell, or the personal one of knowing what I did. And what I failed to do, by being unable to keep her alive."

"Jayden!" Alexa's voice has grown desperate.

I take a step back. The smoke has formed a veil around us, Dr. Johansson's form fading in the shroud like a ghost. I take another step back, and another, raising the mask to my face to bolt down the stairs and catch up to Alexa hurrying down the halls. Miriam is unconscious in her arms. I thrust my hoodie up over my face and manage to get the mask over Miriam's as we bolt down the main hallway finding our way back past the lab where Miriam was bound, and the room where Alexa's body remains, Magenta still beside it, one hand holding her daughter's.

At last, we reach the end, a gray door looming in the haze of smoke. I fumble with the handle, unbolting a row of locks and wrench it open. Fresh storm air blasts us with a flurry of blessed rain and wind. We step out onto a long ledge that juts out high above a sparkling reservoir where the river has fattened below.

"We have to jump!" I holler, the crash of thunder pulsating the air. Below, the river rushes onward past the tributary. "There's no other way down!" Any remnants of an escape ladder have long since eroded away.

Alexa looks down to the ripple of rapids below. "I can't...I can't do it, Jayden."

"Alexa, please...there's no other way out. We have to!"

She shakes her head. "I can't. I won't."

And I realize...it's her worst nightmare all over again. Being below the surface, life slipping away. She's already done that once. She won't do it again.

She sets Miriam down, propping her carefully against the bank of stone wall. I pull the mask free from Miriam's face hoping the chilled wind will revive her then stand to face Alexa. We stare at each other, all our dreams blowing in the wind around us, all our plans.

"Don't ever forget me," she says.

"As if I could forget any of this. Forget anything about the time I've had with you."

I stride toward her and cup her face in my hands. The irony of it hits me. The boy that hated technology, the boy that lived in the past with the classic pages of worn books—who refused to join the torrent of his times—was in love with a—

"I'm more than this body," she says, as if reading my mind. "I'm more than what they made me."

"I know that," I weep, kissing her eyelids above the celestial blue.

"If only you'd been right," she breathes, her words catching. "If only we'd been vampires. Flesh and bone. Able to live forever together as humans who still had human hearts. Even if they'd stopped beating."

"I was an idiot," I gasp. "For ever thinking that of us."

"You weren't. I'm grateful for it. For giving me some other kind of fantasy to believe in, even if for a moment. Because the truth...what's happening to our world...to me...I don't want to be part of that future. Part of what makes it happen. A barren world filled with machines..." Her lip quivers.

"Your parents were trying to make you live forever, that's all. In their own warped and misguided way. They just didn't have time, Alexa. No time to do it the right way."

"But who wants to live forever?" she cries. A blast of wind whips her curls across her face. She laughs at the intensity of it. "All humankind does is destroy what it touches. This!" She gestures to the vast tree boughs spread out before us, waving in the wind, the beautiful churn of clouded sky, the plunge of river falls, spray misting the air with silver. "This was created by something bigger than us. Better than us. We cannot forget that. Cannot destroy it. Cannot let the arrogance of our advancements make us forget what we are—products of something bigger. Have we lost so much faith in a greater being that we have to try and become gods ourselves? Because all we're doing is decimating the heaven that is our planet." Maple leaves fan like ethereal flags in the wind as she speaks.

"I don't care about anything but you right now," I whisper. "Nothing else matters."

"But it does matter. I shouldn't be here right now, Jayden. I'm grateful I got to know you, to love you. But I shouldn't be here. You should be loving someone else right now. And you would have—"

"No, no, I wouldn't have—"

"You would have! Don't you see?" She looks down to where Miriam lies. "There are others who love you if you'll let them in. There is always good, it's your responsibility to find it. Find your people and let them in. Don't hide in dreams or fantasy. Believe in your reality. Make your dreams come true."

" *You* still had dreams…"

"And I will continue to dream," she promises. "And love. I'll always love you. I'm not some piece of computer coding to be captured and replicated by human intervention, Jayden. I'm a soul. Belonging to the universe. Belonging with the wind." She spreads her hands wide as the air moves around her.

Further down the mouth of the tunnel behind us, orange flames glow, lapping at the walls.

"Remember how your favorite classic is *Frankenstein*?" she says, gripping my arms.

"It's a story of being on the outside looking in," I confess. "It's why I relate to it."

"No...it's a warning. To all of us. Not to mess with nature. Because when humankind meddles, it comes at a cost."

"But your mom has helped people with mobility, your father with neurological advancements—"

"Yes...but we must be sure not to take it too far. Must not try to become the gods. Must not forget our place in the world. We must honor this earth and take care of it. And take care of all the souls that are trying to find their way in it. *Souls*, Jayden. Not programmed minds."

The scree of an eagle captures our attention as it soars over us, wings spread wide like that of an angel's. The fire behind us burns, rises like a fiery orange sun.

"You have to go now, Jayden. You have to survive. Even when it hurts. It's a rite of passage, you have to believe that. To something more. Something better. Live. For me."

The heat is blistering at our backs, the rain sweet upon our faces. She steps forward to press her lips to mine, eyes open, and we stare into each other one last time. As our lips hold, I see the light in her eyes gradually fading. And I know.

It's time.

She grows weak in my arms and slowly, I gather her and step to the side of the embankment's wall, gently setting her beside Miriam.

"You know I've always loved tragic endings," Alexa says, a sad, wry laugh pulling at her lips. "Doomed love and all that."

"But Juliette was alive still," I echo, remembering our conversation about her favorite piece of literature. "Had Romeo waited, he'd have known her love yet. Known she never really died."

"Nothing really dies," she promises. But her eyes grow dull as she says it.

"Alexa, no—not yet. Alexa? Please!" Agonized, I burrow my face in her neck, run my lips along its contour, hold my teeth to her skin, wishing I had the power to bring her back to me.

But of course, I have no power at all. Not like that. Just the power to love.

With all my heart.

I love you is torn from my lips by the wind. Carried like a spirit to spiral upward.

I choke back a sob and force myself to pull away from her.

Slowly, I turn to Miriam and lift her into my arms. Her eyelids flutter, and she coughs as I raise her up. Smoke billows from the open passageway to funnel into the storm sky, the orange flames growing nearer.

"We have to jump, Mir." *A leap of faith. The belief that everything will be okay. That survival is our human right. Responsibility. Privilege.*

Even when we want to die.

Heart shattered, I force myself to breathe. To step forward. *To hope.* In a tomorrow. One worth continuing toward.

Miriam rests her head against my shoulder as I angle her against me to lessen the impact of the water when we strike its surface. I take one last look at Alexa. Wind blows her dark curls. Her eyes are like jewels amid the rich complexion of her face. Her lips slightly parted.

As if saying goodbye.

I close my eyes and step forward to the lip of the ledge and step off. The wind whistles past and Miriam and I enter the impossible cold of the river below. I grapple with the weight of her, but the frigid water has shocked her into fuller consciousness, and together we kick to the surface, my arm clenched tightly around her, pulling her up against the currents. We break the surface and look up to see nothing but the moving crown of trees, the swirl of cloud, the broken rock of the world, and an explosion of fiery light, like that of a phoenix rising.

THIRTY-EIGHT

A WEEK LATER, I'd hear about it. On the old transistor radio in the mobile. *Esteemed neuroscientist and surgeon, Dr. Sven Johansson, and his biomedical engineer partner in life and business, Magenta Croy, have been implicated in the recent rash of murders in Forks, Washington. The couple are said to have died with their seventeen-year-old daughter in a fiery blaze of an abandoned underground bunker where the doctor is believed to have been conducting unethical research in an illicit laboratory that he refurbished himself on site. Their daughter, Alexa Johansson, was an innocent victim of her parents' scientific quests, allegedly unaware of her parents' actions. Testimony from Forks local, Miriam Foster, who was taken hostage by the doctor, has helped end the terror the town has faced these past two weeks, following her narrow escape from the laboratory with the help of other Forks local, Jayden James. James has yet to speak with the press about his experience, citing a need for privacy at this time.*

Residents are asked to stay away from the bunker as it is an active crime scene and an extreme hazard. Internal structures collapsed during the fire, making it impassable for crews as they continue their efforts to search for any remains that may be found inside.

That was it. No mention of exactly what Dr. Johansson and Magenta were doing in the lab.

What Alexa was.

Maybe Miriam didn't know. Didn't see. Or maybe she had blocked the trauma from her mind.

Or maybe she knew it was a secret best kept. For my sake. I don't know. All I do know is that I haven't spoken to her since that afternoon when I carried her from the river, staggering through the dense forest until we came upon the search party.

Everything else is a blur.

In the few days after, Mom lingered around the mobile, but then the stress led her elsewhere, a bottle tucked in her bag, and life resumed as it was before Alexa.

Just me.

And my thoughts.

There is no room for anything else.

* * *

Sunset stains the sky outside the mobile's window. I am alone, lying on my bed. My eyes are dry. Enough tears already fallen to fill the Bogachiel River.

Enough rage.

I've run the roads Alexa and I roamed by the light of the moon. Revisited the mountain hillside where we first kissed, and the rock at First Beach where we first spoke of our love for books. Our love for stories. Fantasy. Romance.

In the dead of night, I'd lain awake, the purple crystal in my hand, then stole to the abandoned mansion, past the yellow crime tape fluttering in the breeze, to secret away to the library to sit by the empty hearth. I could almost smell the warmth of cinnamon tea, a hint of vanilla. I'd traced a finger along her violin hanging from the wall and the spines of the classics she'd shared with me. Stories that I'd used as an escape. That once seemed so surreal. Yet now I wonder if someday we'll become the story. If one day people will say, *remember the day humans were made of flesh and bone?* If one day our existence will become nothing more than fable to join other fading stories of myth and history and burned-out faith. If people will one day doubt our existence. Our realness. Our past.

I'd retraced my steps up the old logging road, remnants of the vampire hunt and search party still scattered among the foliage like shrapnel. Somehow, I'd found my way to the stony embankment by the rippling pond where we'd shared our dreams of a future together. Made plans. *Love.*

Made believe we had forever.

* * *

A knock at the door draws me from my reverie. I ignore it. Don't want to see anyone. Meals have been left. Cards. Notes. But they don't fill the hollow space beneath my breastbone. I roll over on the bed, my eye catching the bathrobe tie that I'd used to knot to my wrist on the worst of those nights. Thinking I was the one who had caused it all. How little I'd known about myself or believed in myself. *Until she taught me otherwise.*

The knocking persists.

Sighing, I shove myself off the bed and make my way down the hall to open the door. Dan is standing on the stoop. "Get your shoes, I want to show you something."

"Dan, I'm not up to it."

"Just get your shoes." He sidles down the few porch steps to the scant lawn to wait, fishing a cigarette from his pocket.

Sighing, I grab my shoes and hastily lace them, closing the door behind me.

Dan starts walking.

"Where are we going?" I ask.

"Just come." He heads down the lane toward the forest, the sun sitting low behind the trees, painting the cloud a deep rosé.

I trail behind him, my hands jammed into my jeans pockets, following him past the mobile park through the shadow of trees. "Seriously, Dan,

I don't feel like—"

He stops in front of a mouth of rock.

"What? What is this place?" I ask, warily eyeing the granite face until I notice a hollow in the stone above. A flurry of dark wings flit across the deepening sky, emerging from the opening.

"I found the roost." Dan takes a long draw of his cigarette watching the bats streak across the sky.

I don't say anything, watching their tiny bodies flail into the night.

He exhales, the phantom of smoke billowing before him. "Bats symbolize rebirth, you know. The start of a new beginning. As spirit guides, they're said to teach courage to face the dark. That's what I want for you, Jayden. To take courage. Especially now."

I scuff my shoe against a stone, watch the spiral of wings erratic in the air.

"You've been through something terrible, Jayden. Hell, you've been through many tough things. But I'm guessing rescuing that girl ranks near the top. But you lying low this week, it's more than that, isn't it. You lost something."

I look at him, try to figure out what he might know.

He stubs his cigarette against the stone of the rock face. "That girl that died in the fire. Was she the girl you'd been seeing?"

Just when I thought my tears had run dry, I feel their burn behind my eyes.

"Look, don't let this drive you crazy. Don't let anger or upset consume you. Don't let it make you hate the world even more than you maybe already did. Or lose hope in it. Because that gets you nowhere, Jayden. Take it from me. Find a way to turn tragedy into something good. Then make that good your legacy. I know what it's like to lose someone you love. To act out and do stupid things because of it. Things that can ruin you. Destroy everything. Land you in jail." It's a confession. The chapters of Dan's life skimming open then snapping shut. He clears his throat, fishes out another cigarette, his fingers shaking slightly.

"I knew your father, Jayden."

"You—you what? Why didn't you ever tell me?"

"Because it's not a good story." He stares at the opening of the cave, the swirl of bat wings in the dusking sky. "But I knew him, and I promised myself I'd watch over his boy if anything ever happened to him. Kind of to make amends for my own life. The people I lost." His forehead crevasses for a moment with grief then smooths. "His family was from these parts. A grandfather who was Quileute. He wanted to connect with that part of his past. But like all of us, I guess he let his demons get him before he could find what he wanted. Before he could be the man he wanted."

"I have Quileute in me?"

He nods. "Guess so." He pulls a crumpled picture from his pocket and hands it to me. "I brought you this."

I run my eyes over the man in the grainy photo. I don't see myself in him at first. His hair is dark, his stature strong, unlike the wisp of bone I inhabited before I built up the muscle. But his jawline is like mine, the plane of nose. And his eyes. There's something familiar in them. Not quite mine, but something I've seen before. Maybe, in me.

"I was no good for fatherhood myself," Dan says. "But I hope you and me…I hope I can help you find your path. Help you stay on it. Just…keep on, Jayden. Keep finding the light. We're made of both. Darkness and light. We need to choose which we reach for. Which one we seek."

He points toward the bats, now specks in the distant sky. "You know, people think they're blind, bats. But they've just got a different way of seeing things. That's not a bad thing. Seeing things differently." His eyes slide to me. "You're different than a lot of the kids your age, Jay. *You* see things different. And that's a good thing. We live in a time when people are forgetting what's important. They're so caught up in the future, they forget the value that comes from the past. The lessons. But not you, Jay, with your books and your reflections—your refusal to conform or be like everybody else just because it's what's in. Just because you see things differently from everyone else doesn't mean you can't find your place." He gestures again to the bats as they flit across the sky. "See how they not only survive but *thrive?* They've found their place in this world. And you can too."

His lighter flickers to life against the darkness as he lights his cigarette. He draws on it deeply, exhales slowly. "Remember when you thought you were a vampire? All I'm sayin', is if you're going to believe anything about yourself, may as well believe you're something with wings. Someone who can fly. Someone who learns to soar. Then you'll be the one with the best perspective. The one who can see what matters most in life. The one with the skills to survive. No matter what the future holds."

I have a million more questions for him, but he turns and starts to lead us back as the sun slips deeper beyond the horizon, the moon rimming the cloud in its place. "Best we be getting back now," he says, his face falling into shadow but for the twilit glow of his cigarette. "Before the other night creatures start stirring."

* * *

That night, I stare at my father's photograph wondering about who he was, that part of my history. I try to feel a connection, but I feel nothing, for I never knew him. A void sits in his place as it has for years.

And that void is filled with heartache for Alexa.

Eventually, exhaustion burrows me into a deep sleep. Alexa peoples my mind. It's as if she's with me. I can feel her touch, her breath against my skin. Her fingers in my hair as she pulls me down to lie beside her in a meadow of gold. In my dream, I roll over and find she's disappeared. I call her name. When she doesn't respond, I climb to my feet and start running, searching the meadow as it turns to forest, the shimmering stars like lost spirits in the sky.

When I wake up, I'm surrounded by forest, a scream piercing the night.

My own.

I bite my fist to quell the hurt ripping from inside over losing her, choking off my scream with a broken sob. I sink to my haunches, the rough bark of a tree digging into my back.

She's gone. She's really gone.

And I'm still here…wandering the night.

Alone.

But—it's different somehow.

A sensation passes through my body. A ghost of breath.

Something is watching me.

I close my eyes. My heart quieting. When I open them, I see nothing. Only the shadow of night. But there is calm within its shadow. A presence. Life. Secrets that whisper through the branches, through the towering canopy of ancient boughs to catch in the ripple of wind. The only sound, the drip of rain on soft foliage. The scent of autumn air.

And an ending.

A new beginning.

The boggy loam of an earth still growing.

I don't know for sure what happened with those girls that died, if I saw them in my dreams or if I was really there before or after. For I'm not superhuman with my premonitions. Not unique. Because I think sometimes, we all see pieces of the future. Know what's coming. See destruction unfolding and feel paralyzed by it. Don't know how to stop it. But what I've learned—what I hope to have learned—is we can face the dark. Fight back. Save ourselves. Save others. Save the legacy of a world still figuring out its place in the universe. Even if we're lost. Even if we're stumbling through the dark. As long as we keep trying, it doesn't have to be too late.

I've changed. Seen that love exists. For me. That the impossible can be possible. That there is a future out there, still unwritten. That maybe I can shape that story. *Make my own happily ever after.* With the pieces of myself that I have left.

I imagine her then. A spirit haunting the night. With me always.

Alexa.

I stand there for I don't know how long, until a chill starts to seep into my bones. I continue forward, orienting myself, the forest unfolding like an ancient map along the riverbed.

From the corner of my eye, in the thick swath of forest and mist, I think I glimpse a wolf passing through the screen of trees and brush. Big. Gray. Elusive.

I pause, my heart pounding. But then it calms. Instead, I try and listen to the land, its ancient secrets. Ancient spirits. Try and feel that drop in my blood that ties me to this land. To a world that grew from its primal roots, grew from its stories. *When gods were gods of the earth and sky, not the thing we aspired to become.*

I blink and rub the mist from my eyes. When I look again, the wolf is gone. As if never there at all. Yet I feel it.

Guiding me.

Or maybe I've just found my way.

EPILOGUE

GRADUATION DAY. A school year passed. Caps and gowns like vampire capes pepper the field following a ceremony in the Spartan's gym. I stand at the perimeter, watching the tearful hugs of joy and sentiment as students celebrate the closure of this stage of life, preparing for a future of untold adventure and success. The American dream.

"Hey." Brody comes up beside me, his graduation cap in hand. "Congrats, man. The future's finally here. Ours for the taking." His voice is tentative.

This past year I've only been to the Fosters house a handful of times. The secret of Alexa burrowed too deep in my heart—a heart still fractured from her absence. Then there are the secrets laid to rest in the burned-out bunker. I always see them in the shadows beneath Miriam's eyes, so found it hard to sit across a dinner table from her. Hated the way she averted her eyes from mine. The way the trauma rested in her soul like silt.

And I hate the way the first question that comes to my mind whenever I see her isn't, *how are you now?* but, *do you know what she was?*

Brody's voice interrupts my thoughts. "Party at First Beach after prom. You coming?"

"Nah. I'm good." I clutch the scroll of my high school diploma, amazed I managed to pull it together by losing myself in my studies so I wouldn't have to think about anything else.

"Honors, huh? Amazing." Brody gives a small smile, his eyes concerned, evaluating my state of mind. "You should at least come to prom. The dinner and dance. It's the final hurrah. All the girls will be disappointed you don't get to see them in their fancy dresses if you don't come." He falls silent, realizing his mistake in mentioning other girls. As if any could live up to the girl I'd lost.

Girl.

I'd loved her. *Loved* her, loved her. Held her in my arms. Not knowing she was silicone and wire.

Because she was more than that.

Brody tries to change the mood. "Can't believe you actually made it into Harvard, lucky bastard! Full scholarship?"

"Yeah."

"Heard you rocked the sciences on top of your lit stuff. What the hell, man? Becoming a first-class nerd," he jokes.

I'd lost myself in the depths of human biology, the neuronal circuitry that holds us together with information. Tried to dissect our nature. Learn more about the vessel that contains our souls.

See if one could exist without the other.

Across the field, Kam and his group huddle together in a thick cauldron then toss their caps into the air to flutter black against the sky. Kam glances over, sees me watching. His eyes narrow. He'd whispered *vampire* to me once, testing the waters after the dust settled and I'd finally returned to school. With Dr. Johansson and Magenta's guilt laid bare for the town to see, he'd lost his fear of me. *Now that I wasn't a real vampire.* But something in my eyes stopped him from taking it any further than that single word. A distilled anger that emanated from me at losing the one thing I wanted more than anything. The one thing I needed. *Alexa's love.* But it was more than that. He knew that I knew that sometimes monsters are born from other monsters. That they're as vulnerable as the rest of us. It was a secret he kept close to his chest, letting it beat where no one could see. But I saw. I knew.

"Jay, you got to come tonight. Sam is coming to the after party too with some others from La Push. It's going to be big. Oh, hey, did you hear? He's been accepted into Lewis and Clark College in Portland. He's going to study Environmental Law. Pretty awesome, huh? Sam becoming a lawyer. You headed to Harvard to become King of Words and all things literary. Me hitting the world to travel and figure my shit out." He laughs. "Or party, but hey. We tell my parents what they need to hear while I take a year's hiatus, right?"

"And Miriam?" I glance over to where she stands apart from her friends. "She always wanted to go to Stanford."

"Uh...yeah...she got in but..." His voice trails off. "She's not sure what she wants anymore." His face is drawn as he watches her. "Just come tonight. To the beach, at least. It would mean a lot." He raises his hand for what I think will be his customary fist bump, but instead it lights on my shoulder and rests for a second. "Please, come. It's time to turn a new page, bro. All of us." He lets his hand drop and turns to head back to join the throng.

* * *

I stay home while prom whirls through the evening, but come twilight, I put on my shoes to head for First Beach. Seeing Miriam at the edge of her friend group when she used to occupy its center leaves me with a sense of responsibility. It's the least I can do; try and help Miriam find her way again. It's time.

I grab my bike, wheel it down the lane. I sense Dan watching me from his window, catch the glow of his cigarette through the slats of the blinds. But he doesn't come out. The only thing we'd do together anymore is train. He'd put on gear and give me an outlet to put my pain. I didn't ask anything more about his past or my father. I could only deal with the emotion of the present. Besides, I never knew my father and he was gone. *Too little too late.* At least, that's what I told myself. Either way, Dan offered nothing more on the subject, so it was nothing but an ellipsis at the end of a sentence. An old chapter. Another story.

"Jayden?" It's Ms. Cuthbert from the trailer at the entrance of the mobile park. I barely ever speak to her or see her. "Got a piece of your mail in my box by mistake." She hands me an envelope.

"Thanks."

She retreats to her trailer, and I'm left alone standing in the sky's gloaming purple haze. I flip the envelope over. No return address. Just a postmark from Ghana. "Who the—?"

I slit the envelope open. A single sheaf of paper sits inside. I pull it free. Written in the center of its blank page: Nothing really dies.

A chill gusts up my back. *The last words Alexa spoke to me.*

Something small is tucked inside the envelope. I tilt the pouch and tap it into my palm. What looks to be a tiny USB flash drive drops into my hand. I stare at it.

It can't be...

My heart starts to pound. Magenta's voice whispers through my mind. *If we'd had the chance to mind upload your brain, Alexa, transfer your individual consciousness...you would be freed entirely from your body's burden, your mind uploaded so you could live on untethered to the biology of your body...*

Hands shaking, I turn the USB over, staring at it in disbelief. "But how...?" Dr. Johansson's technology hadn't been quite ready yet. *Hadn't it?* They had died in the fire. *I saw the flames.* And if Alexa's body was gone, her biological brain turned to ash...*wasn't her soul with it?*

Or is it hovering? Waiting...

I wet my lips, my bike dropping to the ground and run to Dan's door to use his computer but stop myself before I knock.

It wouldn't be her. Not really. Just files and data manipulated by man to create a simulation. Not the elastic, eternal possibility of a true soul.

Right?

Besides, *how would I even know how to turn her from code to...life?* I think of our bodies, the universe, how the neurons of the brain in Dr. Johansson's charts resembled the cosmic web of our universe's galaxies.

Is it all the same? One big cosmic code that bit-by-bit humanity is hacking? Are our souls tangled in the science of it all?

Is her soul?

I hear Dan on the other side of the door as if he saw me coming, as if waiting, but he doesn't open the door.

I back down his front step, shoving the flash drive deep into my pocket and slowly retrace my steps to my bike and climb on to head to First Beach. For the surf, the wind, the pedals beneath my feet, the pained thump of my heart, are the only things right now that are keeping me grounded.

* * *

When I arrive, the shore is thrumming with the language of life. People still dressed in their finery, hugging, talking, laughing, arms looped around each other as music beats on. I feel it pulse in my bones. *My bones!* Despite myself, I can't help but revel for a moment, at the intricacy of my body. The hidden neurons mapping my reactions inside. The spangle of stars above.

The miracle of it all.

I ditch my bike and tread the sands seeing Sam with Brody clustered in a group raising ruckus to the night air for the ending of this youthful era. For an unknown future.

One full of possibility.

One where we scatter like stars.

I wave at them when they catch sight of me, then scan the crowd for the one person I came to see, finally spotting her in the distance on the same rock where Alexa and I had sat the night of Sophie's memorial. Her blonde hair flutters in the breeze. She's in a prom dress, a jean jacket holding the chill air at bay.

I cross the sand toward her, feeling in the wind another storm brewing across the ocean. Feel its electric current upon my skin. The drive in my pocket burns with the ferocity of a human heart.

I climb up beside Miriam. She offers a sad smile then returns her eyes to the churning surf and shadow of the sea stacks. We don't speak. I just sit beside her until her walls break a little and tears form in her eyes, then I put my arm around her and wait for her to rest her head on my shoulder.

"Mir..." I start, unsure of how to break the silence that's existed between us since the bunker. "I just...I need to know you're okay."

She's silent a long time, the softness of her hair brushing against me in the wind. "Remember when this place was the place of every teenage girl's fantasy? The place of true love. Happily ever after."

"Yeah," I manage.

"I wish we could go back to that time. To when dreams were just dreams. Fantasy just fantasy. And the monsters could be something you closed the book on when the story got too scary."

I don't know what to say. I just hold her, one arm around her shoulders, the spindrift of surf misting us with fairy-light droplets.

"I actually wanted vampires and werewolves to be real," she confesses. "Wanted them to blame for what happened. It's easier than thinking what people can do to one another." She's quiet for a moment. "It was my heart they wanted, Jayden," she whispers. "For her."

I can't breathe. Just thinking of Alexa beside me outside the bunker. Our teeth skimming each other's necks. Daring each other to be something other than what we were. Needing to find a key to forever. I turn my eyes up to the sky, the endless reach of stars spreading like circuits in a cosmic brain. Think of our souls, phantom-light in our bodies, ready to drift away. Find a new home.

Be made new.

"I'd do anything for you, Jayden. You know that. But I couldn't do that. Couldn't let some other girl love you with my heart."

It hurts. To even think about it. "It's over now, Mir." My voice catches. "You're safe. I won't let anything hurt you. Ever."

I hesitate. Because I have to ask. *I have to know.* "I've been wondering...haven't known how to ask..." I swallow hard, feel my pulse stutter with nerves. "When we were in the bunker...in that room...did you see—?"

She pulls away. "I can't talk about it, Jay. I've blocked it out. The details. I don't remember. And I don't want to." She puts her fingers to her forehead, exhaustion making her look older than her seventeen years.

So, there it is. Alexa is my secret. Mine, only. And even if I told, no one would believe me.

"Okay...I understand. I'm sorry. Just please, Mir...don't shut me out again. You're the only family I've got."

Miriam gives a sad smile and leans back against my shoulder. "I'm changed, Jay."

"I know. I'm changed too."

"I guess nobody stays the same, whether bad things happen or not. And now...with us all graduating and going our separate ways..." She stares out to the sea. "No matter what, we just keep...evolving."

Evolving and evolving. Into an unknown future.

We sit in silence, her leaning against me, feeling the wind at our face, the pound of surf against the body of stone, feel the ancient earth teeming with secrets from the time of our beginnings. The beauty of the mystery. The power. And I know. No one can crack the code of the universe. Know what makes a soul a soul. What the future holds. That secret is for the universe and the universe alone to know. The secret of the gods.

And some secrets are meant to be kept.

Despite myself, I hear the echo of Dr. Johansson's voice. *It's the future, Alexa. One day, you won't be so different. You will be like everyone else. That time is not so far away.*

What if he's right?

What if I just...waited?

But try as I might, I can't imagine any hardware holding the soft secrets of Alexa's soul.

The echo of Alexa's voice whispers through my heart.

A gust of wind lifts, brushing against my face with the tenderness of a touch.

And I think I have my answer. Know what to do.

I stand up, reach into my pocket, pull out the flash drive, and walk to the edge of the rock face, the ocean swirling below. *What if there's a copy somewhere? Whoever sent this must have—*

It doesn't matter.

Because there was only one Alexa. One love.

I raise my arm up and throw the flash drive with all my might. Release it. Like ash in the wind.

"What are you doing?" Miriam asks.

Saying goodbye.

*   *   *

Afterwards, when the beach fires are smoldering low and people have flitted away into the night or tucked up for an all-nighter on the beach, I grab my bike and disappear into the dark, following the familiar road back to Forks, pausing at the split in the road that leads to home or to the mansion. It has been a while since I've been there. Not since the crime tape was removed, the contents auctioned off, and a For Sale sign posted on the property's front lawn when it went into foreclosure after no heir appeared. Nobody wanted to buy a home that a serial killer had owned, so it had sat and moldered. Returned to what it once was.

I stand on its front porch. A lone candle leftover from Magenta's collection cowers behind its hurricane holder. The front door is locked, the windows tight, though I can see inside that the floorboards once again look forlorn and mouse-worn. A pang of familiarity hits me. The home I had before Alexa. The broken-down palace of my dreams. The place where I escaped to read. Dream. Hide from the life I didn't want. A place where I could imagine myself into a different life. *A life with love.*

A lump fills my throat as I trace my hands along the faded siding to the backyard, the lab fallen into a state of disrepair, moss sprouting from its roof. I stand on the back patio where I first saw her, moonlight in her hair, rain cloaking her body in its light nightdress. The way she looked at me then. Like maybe I, too, was something from a dream. A fantasy. Something she'd been waiting for.

I open the porch screen, trail my hand along the back door's handle and freeze when the latch gives beneath my fingertips. The door opens. Heart pounding, I let go of the handle, half expecting alarms to jangle, the police to appear, or Dr. Johansson, syringe in hand, ready to stop my intrusion. But nothing happens. Just a veil of cobwebs drifts from the casings to settle on the floor. I slip inside, past the fireplace and remnants of furniture that didn't go with the auction. I creep up the stairs, down the hall, pausing by the library. The room looks bare without its multitude of books, though the portrait of Vlad the Impaler has somehow survived its mount above the fireplace. A lone book sits on a dusty settee that was left behind. I walk over and see it's the first book of the *Twilight* series, no doubt left by some other interloper who found his or her way in to read by the haunted light of the library's dome window. I look at the cover, half expecting to see my image in the face of the vampire character. Instead, there are hands cupping an apple.

Forbidden fruit. *The fruit of knowledge.*

I consider how the world continues to come perilously closer and closer to that cusp of enlightenment or disaster. The napalm of progress. The secrets of an ancient earth burning in its wake. Or waiting to be discovered.

I leave the book and the library, trailing down the darkened hallway to the nook I'd favored over the years to curl up with *Frankenstein* to commiserate with a creature born but not properly loved. A person hobbled together but never made whole.

If only his bride had been completed. Her life sustained.

I slouch onto the window seat and stare out at the strip of driveway below. I can almost hear the echo of Alexa's laughter as we ran down the road toward the hillside, night swarming around us with electric possibility. I touch the glass of the window as she had done when she saw me, imagine her reaching back.

I stare at the line of trees in the forest, feel the presence of their tall limbs like spirits of the night. Feel the weight of the coming storm. Like a premonition. Of the years ahead where I become untethered to the past.

Harvard.

Life.

A future filled with things I cannot predict.

But also, a future that I help shape, create. With strength. Values. Hope. Honoring the past. So, I can face whatever is yet to come.

I'm ready.

Am finding my wings.

I close my eyes, burrowing deeper into my hoodie to stay warm, and picture her face. Her beautiful blue eyes. Like an ocean tide, pulling me back. Back to the beginning. One last time.

I open my notebook, place a pen to paper. Because memories are stories. And stories take on a life of their own. Find alternate endings. A million different versions. A way to live on.

Thunder rumbles, a smatter of rain scatters across the window's glass. When my hand grows tired of writing, I slowly drift off to sleep, my imagination roaming wild with visions of Alexa and me on the hillside, the pond's rocky shore beneath a tempestuous night sky. Visions of what life was and what it could have been. What it can be yet.

If you believe in fairy tales.

And I do.

* * *

In my dream I'm running. Maybe I really am running and just not yet fully awake. But I feel her with me. In the shadow of forest. The mountainous peaks and valleys. The endless expanse of glittering starlit sky. *She's here.* Wind stirs upon my skin, soft as a fingertip.

In the distance, there's a howl. Ancient and deep. But together, we keep going. Forward. Forward.

Toward the breaking of a new dawn.

AUTHOR'S NOTE

To my dear readers, thank you for all your support! Without you there would be no audience for Jayden, Alexa, and all the characters in SOMETHING ABOUT ALEXA to gain fictional life, so I thank you for sharing their journey with me.

An author's success is dependent on your loyal readership, so I invite you to please leave a review to help others find my writing and join our community. Please sign-up for my mailing list to be the first to know about upcoming releases or events, for this novel is just the beginning. Above all, I wish you all the very best in life and the perseverance to make every one of your own dreams come true.

newsletter@quillandchrome.media
www.leannehockley.com

♪ @Leanne_Hockley

▶ https://www.youtube.com/@leannehockley

◉ @quillandchromemedia

𝕏 @Leanne_Hockley

∞ https://www.facebook.com/leanne.hockley.1

ACKNOWLEDGEMENTS

My deepest thanks and gratitude to my parents for your unending love and support, and for fostering an interest in the wonderful world of fiction since my early childhood. I have always counted my lucky stars that fate placed me in the hands of such phenomenal parents!

To Quill and Chrome Media, thank you for giving SOMETHING ABOUT ALEXA a place to call home. You are and will be the place where dreams come true.

Larissa, Megan, Heather, and Candice, your friendship has been foundational in my life, and I am eternally grateful for your unending support in listening to ideas and in reading early manuscripts. You have been such a great cheerleading team!

To my grade five and six teacher, Mr. Barman—you always read my writing out loud in class and were one of the first people to tell me I'd publish a book one day. You have no idea how those words planted a seed that would take deep root into belief that my dreams could become reality.

Jamie, Peyton, and Zachary...everything I do, I do for you. Your patience and help in realizing this published goal means the world. Fantasy doesn't hold a candle to the reality of the love I have for you. You are my life.

And finally, it would be remiss of me not to thank Stephanie Meyer for the creation of her beautifully imagined saga. Despite some of the memes and controversy that came with it, her story sparked an unprecedented love for its characters, and a following that inspired many to read, write, and most importantly, dream. After all, what's life without a little imagination.

Something

is

Coming...

2024 - 2025

Manufactured by Amazon.ca
Bolton, ON